Julie

Catherine Marshall's Nineteenth Bestseller:

"IRRESISTIBLE!"

Kirkus

"Fans of Catherine Marshall's best-selling novel *CHRISTY* won't be disappointed by *JULIE*!"

The New York Times Book Review

"A FINE STORY!"

Miami Herald

"A WONDERFUL LOOK at what a young girl thinks and how she reacts to situations all young women experience as they move into womanhood . . . Every woman will enjoy reading JULIE."

The Charlotte News

"MAGNIFICENT . . . In many ways Catherine Marshall's own story . . . the passion for causes, the quest for faith and courageous spirit in Julie were also in Catherine Marshall LeSourd."

The Listener

CATHERINE MARSHALL'S other bestsellers include CHRISTY, BEYOND OURSELVES, THE HELPER, A MAN CALLED PETER, SOMETHING MORE, and TO LIVE AGAIN, all available from Avon Books.

Avon Books are available at special quantity discounts for bulk purchases for sales promotions, premiums, fund raising or educational use. Special books, or book excerpts, can also be created to fit specific needs.

For details write or telephone the office of the Director of Special Markets, Avon Books, Dept. FP, 1790 Broadway, New York, New York 10019, 212-399-1357. *IN CANADA:* Director of Special Sales, Avon Books of Canada, Suite 210, 2061 McCowan Rd., Scarborough, Ontario M1S 3Y6, 416-293-9404.

Julie

CATHERINE MARSHALL

AVON
PUBLISHERS OF BARD, CAMELOT, DISCUS AND FLARE BOOKS

Books Used in Researching Julie

David McCullough, *The Johnstown Flood*, Simon & Schuster, New York, 1968 (a Touchstone Book). Books used for facts on Frank Higgins (Francis Edmund Higgins, 1865-1915), the prototype for Big John Hammond in *Julie*: Norman Duncan, *Higgins, A Man's Christian*, Harper & Brothers, New York, 1909 (BX9225.H5D8); Thomas Davis Whittles, *Frank Higgins, Trailblazer*, Interchurch Press, New York, 1920 (BX9225.H5W5); *The Parish of the Pines:* The Story of Frank Higgins, the Lumberjacks' Sky Pilot, Revell Westwood, N.J., 1912; Frank A. Reed, *Lumberjack Sky Pilot* (BV4470.R42)
Lumbering Songs from the Northern Woods.
George William Huntley, Jr., *Sinnamahone: Story of Great Trees and Powerful Men*, 1945 (F157.S49H78)
Irving Bernstein, *A History of the American Worker: 1933-41: Turbulent Years* (HD8072.B38)

Books on Johnstown: Connelly and Jenks, *Official History of the Johnstown Flood*, 1899; McLaurin, *The Story of Johnstown*, 1890; Johnson, *History of the Johnstown Flood*, 1889

Books on Printing: Thomas D. Clark, *The Southern Country Editor*, Bobbs-Merrill, Indianapolis/New York, 1948 (PN4893.C5); James Clifford Safley, *Country Newspaper and Its Operation*, D. Appleton & Company, New York, 1930 (PN4888.C7S3); Phil C. Bing, *The Country Weekly: A Manual*, D. Appleton & Company, New York, 1917 (PN4888.C7B5)

AVON BOOKS
A division of
The Hearst Corporation
1790 Broadway
New York, New York 10019

Copyright © 1984 by Calen, Inc., Lincoln, VA 220
Published by arrangement with McGraw-Hill Book Company
Library of Congress Catalog Card Number: 84-4448
ISBN: 0-380-69891-9

The McGraw-Hill edition contains the following Library of Congress
Cataloging in Publication Data:

Marshall, Catherine, 1914-1983
Julie.
I. Title.
PS3563.A7212J8 1984   813'.54   84-4448

First Avon Printing, August 1985

*To
the Wood-Marshall-LeSourd family
for thirty-four years of forbearance
and understanding and support*

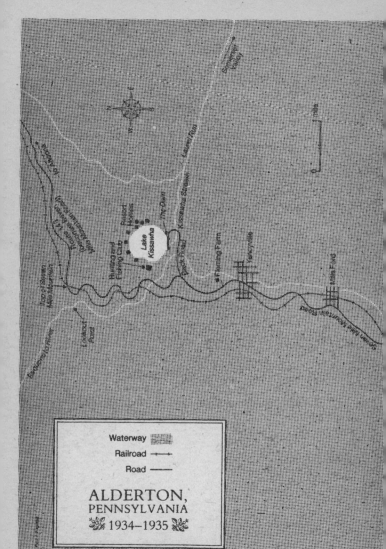

ALDERTON,
PENNSYLVANIA
🌿 1934–1935 🌿

Waterway
Railroad
Road

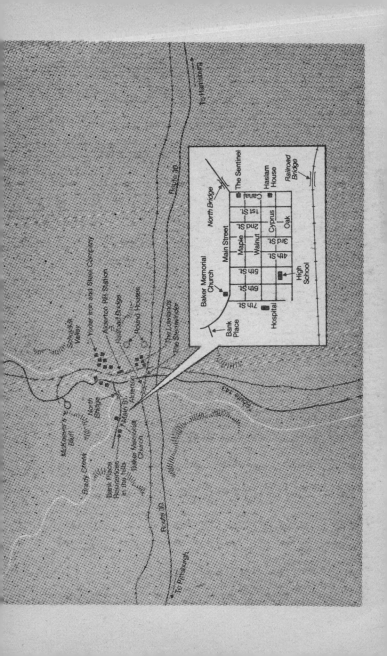

With Gratitude

I wish to express my appreciation to Ed Kuhn, longtime editor and friend, for his wise counsel until his death in December 1979; to Randall Elisha Greene for his creative guidance as my editor over several years; and especially to Elizabeth Sherrill, who has been my friend and editorial consultant extraordinaire since the early 1960s.

I want to thank the following people for valuable research help: Richard Schubert, former president of the Bethlehem Steel Corporation, and Gary Graham for making it possible for me to go through their Johnstown plant; Governor Edward T. Breathitt, vice president, Southern Railway, for making his private railway car available; Alton Carns and other staff members of the *Loudoun County Times-Mirror* in Leesburg, Virginia, for anecdotes concerning weekly newspapers; Jane Price Sharp of the *Pocahontas County Times,* Marlinton, West Virginia, for information and suggestions; Lewis A. Pryor, Arcata, California, for material on printing presses; P. L. Gwynn-Jones of the College of Arms, London, for research on the Wilkinson family crest; Olive James, Chief, Loan Division, the Library of Congress, for her gracious help; Mrs. John Hershberger of the Johnstown Flood Museum; Louis McCready of the *Johnstown Tribune Democrat;* Bob Sefick of the *Johnstown Tribune;* and Miss M. J. ("Lyn") Kreitzburg of the University of Pittsburgh at Johnstown for all their helpful suggestions; and Margaret Shannon, my indefatigable research specialist, who always knows where and how to find anything and everything.

I am grateful to my brother Bob for supplying the humorous account of the wine train mishap, an episode he took part in as a boy, and to my mother (the Christy of my first novel), whose steady guidance has been rocklike and whose confidence in me unflagging.

I have been richly blessed by the following people for their expert secretarial and typing help during this project: Jean Brown, Ann Glegg, Belle Hill, Linda Johnson, Karen Shaw, Alice Watkins . . . and especially Jeanne Sevigny, my longtime personal secretary and close friend, whose broad knowledge and background made her invaluable in all stages of this project.

Finally to my husband Len, with whom I have worked so closely and effectively since our marriage in 1959 that the writer-editor relationship has become an integral part of our lives. I am especially thankful for that prodding, insistent quality of his mind that has so often sparked my own thinking. Our mental "jousting" proved especially fruitful in the writing of this book.

The Characters

Julie Paige Wallace, eighteen-year-old high school senior and parttime reporter at *The Sentinel*

Kenneth Timothy Wallace, father of Julie and editor and publisher of *The Sentinel*

Louise Wallace, wife of Kenneth and mother of Julie

Timothy "Tim" Wallace, the Wallaces' eleven-year-old son

Anne-Marie Wallace, their nine-year-old daughter

Randolph Munro Wilkinson, assistant manager of the Hunting and Fishing Club

Emily Cruley, typesetter, assistant editor at *The Sentinel*

Dean Fleming, retired railroad machinist and repairer of equipment at *The Sentinel*

Hazel Fleming, sister of Dean

John Hammond, pastor friend of Dean Fleming

Margo Palmer, high school classmate of Julie

Sam Palmer, father of Margo and owner of the Stem-winder, a roadhouse

Graham Gillin, high school athlete

Troy Gillin, his younger brother

Spencer MeLoy, pastor of Baker Memorial Church

Thomas McKeever, Sr., board chairman of Yoder Steel and head of the Hunting and Fishing Club

Thomas McKeever, Jr., son of above and president of Yoder Steel

Bryan McKeever, son of above and high school class-mate of Julie

Munro Farnsworth, Pittsburgh businessman, board member of Yoder Steel and the Hunting and Fishing Club

Cynthia Wilkinson Farnsworth, his wife

Cyrus Stearns, executive of the Pennsylvania Railroad

Neal Brinton, "puddler's helper" at Yoder Steel

Cade Brinton, brother of Neal and union organizer at Yoder Steel

James Sanduski, watchman at the Hunting and Fishing Club

The Vincent Pileys, across-the-street neighbors of the Wallace family

Jean Piley, their daughter

Donald Whipkey, chairman of Baker Memorial Church Council

Florence Whipkey, his wife

Ted Gillin, Sam Gaither, Salvatore Mazzini, Floyd Townsend, Wade and Stover Alcorn, Barry Simms, Sheldon Wissinger, Janet McIntyre, George Cummings, Alderton business people and town personalities

Foreword

Julie is Catherine Marshall's nineteenth and final book, and her second novel. It is a companion piece to *Christy*, her first novel, published in 1967.

Both *Christy* and *Julie* give readers a fascinating look at unforgettable segments of American life and history. *Christy* portrays life among the mountain people of eastern Tennessee in 1912. *Julie* depicts the depression years of 1934–35 in a flood-prone town in western Pennsylvania. Both books took a long time to write: *Christy*, nine years; *Julie*, seven. Both works are based on Catherine's family life: Christy Huddleston was nineteen-year-old Leonora Haseltine Whitaker, Catherine's mother. Julie Wallace, the central character in *Julie*, is in part drawn from Catherine's own memories of her life in Keyser, West Virginia, as an eighteen-year-old.

Research on *Julie* began in 1977 as Catherine became fascinated by both the Johnstown Flood of 1889 and the inner workings and mechanics of operating a small weekly newspaper. She also took a refresher course in the events of the depression years of the thirties. Soon the research spilled over into dam construction, the early union movement in America, steel making, private railroad cars. Poems written by Catherine as a teenager found their place.

I married Catherine in 1959 after she had been working on *Christy* less than a year. She was a courageous woman to become, at forty-four, a mother to my three young children, ages three, six and ten. *Christy* was put aside for a time as we established a new home together.

Soon it also became clear that as an editorial team, Catherine, the writer, and I, the editor, struck a good balance. We began spending countless hours together talking through characters and plotting the action and suspense of *Christy*. This close relationship continued through Catherine's nonfiction books: *Beyond Our Selves, Adventures in Prayer, Something More, The Helper, Meeting God at Every Turn,* and a book we bylined together, *My Personal Prayer Diary.*

When Catherine spent forty-two days critically ill in the hospital during the summer of 1982, working on the manuscript of *Julie* was a form of therapy for me at this very difficult time. Even during visiting hours we sometimes found ourselves talking about the book's characters. So often—perhaps too often—did our absorption in the editorial process spill over into family life, vacation periods, travel, even illness.

By January 1983 Catherine seemingly had recovered from her lung collapse of the summer before. She and I began the new year by spending several days on *Julie* with our longtime editor, associate and close friend, Elizabeth Sherrill. Months of revision work were still needed.

Catherine was in the hospital for tests when she passed away suddenly of heart failure on March 18, 1983.

What a tremendous loss to her family, as well as to a book audience of millions! Her writing career had spanned thirty-four years, including eighteen books that sold somewhere over sixteen million copies.

In many ways *Julie* is Catherine's own story, because the passion for causes, the quest for faith and the courageous spirit in Julie Wallace were also in Catherine.

I know. I lived with these qualities for twenty-three years. Though the void she leaves in my life can never be filled, I am sustained by memories- of our adventures in faith, of our tumultuously creative family life and of our fulfilling editorial partnership.

Leonard LeSourd
January, 1984

Lookout Point

As I stood on Lookout Point and viewed Alderton seven miles below, I wondered what changes I would find. Fifty years had altered the town very little. The population was now about forty thousand, with the growth centered in residential areas built on higher ground, but downtown Alderton was much as it had been when the Wallace family first arrived in September 1934. A few more stores, several new shopping centers, two more theaters. Yoder Steel still dominated the town's economy.

Lake Kissawha glistened a short distance away in the bright sunlight. Boats with multicolored sails covered the water, just as they had that fateful summer of 1935. I noted that a few more cottages dotted the surrounding shores than at my last visit. The rebuilt dam was not visible from Lookout Point.

A mile or so below the lake, on the twisting road leading down the mountainside toward Alderton, I spotted the Fleming cabin. What would I discover there? Would the ax still be above the fireplace—a sign that The Preparers were continuing their work? For so many years I had yearned to write about this group. Permission had finally been granted three years ago when it was agreed that I should tell the whole tragic story of Alderton 1935. I had done that, and sent copies of the manuscript ahead to my family. Only one small piece was missing. This visit now would complete the story and end the book.

Each of my trips to that cabin had been a turning point for me. What would it be this time? With growing anticipation, I walked back to my car. I started the engine but still did not pull out onto the road. So many years, so many memories. I recalled the night a group of us had celebrated our high school graduation on this very spot, dancing on the asphalt to the music of a Chicago station on Bryan McKeever's car radio.

And before that, the very first time I stood here on Lookout Point. That was in September 1934, when my family and I stopped for a glimpse of the town that was to be our new home. The sky was fresh-washed that afternoon, the storm clouds lifting. How soon those clouds were to return, and with what devastation, none of us in the fall of 1934 could have dreamed . . .

1

Our 1928 Willys-Knight had been climbing for at least ten miles, one hairpin turn after another, under a threatening sky. Though it was early September, the temperature was close to ninety degrees. There was a stillness in the air and a steady buildup of dark, lowering cloud banks to the east.

"Kenneth, the car's overheated!" Mother's voice was anxious.

"I'm aware of it," Father replied. Rivulets of perspiration were streaming down the back of his neck.

"Shouldn't we stop and let the radiator cool off?"

"I will, Louise, as soon as I can find a place to pull over."

There had been increasing irritation between my parents ever since Mother, custodian of the map, had suggested some sixty miles back that the most direct road to Alderton was west on Route 30. Dad did not agree and had chosen Route 143, which approached Alderton from the northeast. A mistake. Route 143 was poorly paved and endlessly curving.

We were all on edge this late summer day of 1934. Four consecutive days on the road, seven-hundred-odd miles, four blowouts, five people jostled all the way from Timmeton, Alabama, to western Pennsylvania. Mother had driven most of those miles because I had yet to obtain my driver's license and my father was still having those attacks of malaria.

3

For most of the trip I had been shut up in the back seat with the animal energy of Tim, eleven, and Anne-Marie, nine. Every waking moment my younger brother and sister had wriggled and fidgeted, poked one another, and me, and chattered incessantly. I felt bruised and battered, my clothes a mess.

In an effort to ease the tension, Mother began giving us a running commentary on what we would see on Dad's alternative route to Alderton. "We'll be going down Seven Mile Mountain now. The map shows a little village not too far ahead. Yancyville, it's called. Oh, and here's something interesting," she added. "A lake." She held the map to get a closer look. "It's called Lake Kissawha. Indian name, I suppose."

As she spoke, dark clouds suddenly blanketed the landscape. Then the sky emptied. There were no separate raindrops; rather it seemed as if giant hands had overturned cloud-buckets. Lightning and thunderclaps followed—eerie, terrifying. And at that moment white steam began to rise from the car radiator.

Anne-Marie started to cry softly. Hunched over the wheel, Dad searched through the downpour for a place to pull off. There was a bump; we skidded off the road and began sliding to the right. Frantically Dad twisted the wheel, fighting the slide. No use. We ended up with the two rear wheels in a water-filled ditch.

As Dad turned off the ignition, his hands were shaking.

"Now let's all stay calm," Mother said crisply. "Nobody's hurt. We'll be all right."

After about five minutes the deluge stopped and the sky lightened. Gratefully we rolled down the windows; the closed car had been like a steam-oven. Dad started the engine but the back wheels only spun crazily, churning mud. Gunning the motor merely sank the heavy old Willys deeper into the ditch.

Then we heard a heart-stopping sound—a roaring, crashing noise from the steep slope just above us. Startled, we looked up to our right and saw a river of water pouring down the side of the mountain. It crashed onto and over the car, water gushing through the open windows, soaking us. Then it surged across the road, tore off a route marker, and churned down the asphalt surface for fifty feet before plunging over the side of the mountain to our left, sweeping along rocks and small trees in its path.

We sat silently in the car, paralyzed by our narrow escape. Then dazedly, almost like a film in slow motion, my parents began mopping up the water in the front seat. Suddenly Dad's body slumped forward against the steering wheel. I could see a vein throbbing in his neck.

In a panic I clambered over Tim and opened the car door. "I'll go for help," I said, catching Mother's distressed eyes.

High school tennis had strengthened my legs. I ran back along the road we had traveled, avoiding the debris and the worst puddles. My eyes were searching the downhill side of the road, now to my right, for the building I thought I had glimpsed through the trees.

Yes, there it was, some kind of rustic lodge or inn near the shore of the lake. The side road I turned into was steep, slippery underfoot. As I ran, I spied in the distance the figure of a man in a green sports shirt emerging from the building.

At that instant my foot caught in a fallen branch. Down I went, sprawled on all fours—mud all over the front of my skirt, spattered on my blouse and face.

"I say, what a nasty tumble—"

The man was now standing over me, hand outstretched. He was younger than I had thought.

"My family needs help," I stammered, spurning his hand and scrambling to my feet. I pointed toward the road. "Up there."

"Was there an accident?"

"Yes, our car slid into the ditch. I think my father's hurt."

"Should I call an ambulance?"

"I don't know."

"Let's have a look." He set off at a rapid pace, with me trotting to keep up, trying to get my tangled hair out of my eyes and wiping furiously at the mud.

"Beastly day for motoring. Tell me what happened," he tossed over his shoulder at me.

A clipped English accent, reddish-blond hair. He seems nice, I thought. "We were driving up from Alabama. My father's Kenneth Wallace, the new publisher of *The Alderton Sentinel.*"

At the main road I pointed the way toward our disabled car. After rounding several curves we saw it. My father was still in the driver's seat, but I rejoiced to see that he was sitting upright.

The young man bounded forward. "I'm Randolph Wilkinson. Are you injured, sir? How can I help?"

Insisting that he was all right, my father climbed slowly out of the Willys. By now Mother too was out on the road to greet us, with Tim and Anne-Marie tumbling after.

"Julie!" Mother cried. "What happened to you?"

To my relief the two men became absorbed in examining the car as I explained my fall to Mother while wringing out my sopping skirt. *What a way to meet a stranger . . . fall on my face in the mud practically at his feet.*

Brushing aside Mother's protests, my father climbed back in behind the steering wheel, turned on the ignition, and began a gentle rocking motion—forward, back, forward. As the rocking pattern stepped up, the Englishman didn't hesitate to step into the water behind the car, flex his muscular arms, and at the right moment give a mighty shove. The heavy old Willys lurched forward from the ditch onto the road.

"By Jove, we *did* it!" Our rescuer shot one hand into the air while Tim and Anne-Marie whooped in triumph.

Dad set the hand brake and climbed from the car. "How can we thank you!"

"No need to." Mr. Wilkinson was looking at me again. "But I insist that you come back to the Inn for a cleanup. Can't go on as you are."

"Thanks so much," Dad replied. "But I think we're all right now."

"Kenneth, please," Mother urged. "Let's accept the young man's offer."

"And Dad, don't forget the radiator," Tim put in.

My father grimaced. "I'd forgotten. Our water boiled over, Mr. Wilkinson."

This time the Englishman climbed behind the wheel. He drove several hundred yards down the mountain to what he called the back entrance to the Inn. We wound through a woodland, then crossed over the top of a tall dam. To our right was an immense lake; below, on our left, water from the spillway formed a gurgling stream.

After we pulled up in front of a large building, the Englishman showed Mother, Anne-Marie and me to a powder room off the front entrance hall. One glance at myself in the mirror made me shudder: my wavy light brown hair was hanging in stringy ropes; mud spots on my face gave the effect of chicken pox. I stared down at my filthy saddle shoes, my rumpled skirt and blouse, and groaned. I looked more like a lumpy twelve-year-old than almost eighteen. After cleaning up as best I could, I fled outside.

Lake Kissawha was larger than I had first thought. When we drove in, the far banks had been lost in mist. Now they were just visible, perhaps half a mile away. As I strolled down to the shore, I noticed that the steep face of the dam was a wild aggregation of loose rocks and boulders, with saplings and scrub pines growing out of the crevices.

Odd way to construct a dam, I mused. Then I turned and walked back to our car.

When our family reassembled by the Willys, the handsome Englishman was there to see us off. As I started to climb into the back seat he took my hand and held it for a moment. "I'm glad we met, Julie," he said.

Startled, I looked up into his hazel eyes. They were warm, sparked by a mischievous twinkle. Then, very slowly, he winked!

My eyes must have shown my confusion. I reddened, murmured something unintelligible and stepped into the back seat, aware that my legs were strangely weak.

Mr. Wilkinson then strongly urged us to go back a mile or so, where he said we would find a scenic spot called Lookout Point, which had a breathtaking view of Alderton and the whole valley. Though road-weary and eager to end our long journey, we decided that a good first look at our new home town would be well worth retracing our route.

A few minutes later, with Mother now at the wheel, we pulled into an asphalt parking area and climbed out of the car again. The dark angry clouds were now vanishing to the east. Through breaks in the overcast we could see the narrow Schuylkill Valley spread out below, surrounded by the towering Alleghenies, with Alderton on the valley floor.

I stood there fighting disappointment. Before leaving the flatness of Timmeton I had tried to visualize what it would be like living in the mountains. All afternoon we had been driving through glorious scenery, misty-blue peaks soaring over undulating ridges, each horseshoe bend opening a new and breathtaking vista. I could scarcely wait to see Alderton.

But spread below us now was something very different. Alderton looked pinched, hemmed in by the mountains. In many places the hills were denuded, the slopes pocked with slag heaps. The peace I had sensed in these mountain heights was gone. A dissident note had entered in—as if men and nature were antagonists.

We stood there in a tightly huddled family group, our eyes sweeping the landscape below us. For a moment no one said anything. I was feeling let down, betrayed, but dared not voice it.

Still, there was beauty mixed in with the ugliness. Just below us in the twilight Lake Kissawha was like a multi-colored mirror. A sparkling stream, like a glistening strand of pearls, wound down Seven Mile Mountain to Alderton. Consulting the map, Mother reported that this was the Sequanoto River, that it was joined by Brady Creek just north of Alderton, and that the combined streams flowed through the center of town.

Father, pale and drawn, pointed out the two bridges spanning the river, including the railroad bridge built at the turn of the century. On his previous visit here, local citizens had described it as an architectural monstrosity because of its ponderous concrete arches. As our eyes searched the town, tongues of flame would leap from tall brick smokestacks, then die again. A thick sooty haze hovered above the scene.

"That's the Yoder Iron and Steel Works," Dad said, indicating the smokestacks. "Employs over twelve hundred men. Headed by Tom McKeever, a tough old man who runs this town, I'm told."

"Including *The Sentinel?*" Mother asked.

My father shrugged. "I don't think he'll pay much attention to us." He pointed again. "There's the Trantler Wireworks, a Yoder subsidiary. Makes barbed wire and such. Those and the Pennsylvania Railroad yards are the town's chief industries. See the yards on the east side of Railroad Bridge—apparently a major east-west transfer point." From where we stood we could see two round-houses surrounded by glittering skeins of tracks.

"Just like a model train set!" Tim breathed excitedly.

"Sure looks that way from here, son."

Dad then indicated the residential areas, mostly tucked into the hills, and a section of drab gray houses east of town. "Workers' houses," Dad explained. "They're called the Lowlands." The name fit; they were certainly the ugliest part of this industrial center of over twenty thousand people. Alderton was a stark contrast to quiet Timmeton, where our family had lived for almost nine years.

With sudden nostalgia my mind drifted back to those last days of our uprooting . . . packing boxes, crates and steamer trunks to be sent by rail, the last visits to my favorite places, the final good-byes.

Mary Beth. Sandra Lee. Merv, the boy down the street who was so sure I was to marry him someday. How could I start in, my last year of high school, to make all new friends?

There had been pain in leaving the setting, too: the huge century-old oak trees that arched over Macon Street like the green-vaulted roof of a cathedral. There are precious things that you can't pack and take with you, like the all-pervasive fragrance of the honeysuckle. Would there be honeysuckle in the North? I would miss the drapery of purple wisteria that all but smothered the old woodshed in our back yard.

I looked at my parents as they stared silently at the town below us. My father's tall frame was stooped, neck muscles still twitching, eyes clouded, hands clenched tightly together. In contrast were Mother's firm, patrician features, her determined manner. How did they handle a change like this? I had no clue and could not bring myself to ask. I had always had trouble talking about whatever meant most to me. Shyness? The fear of something important to me being belittled or made fun of? I didn't know—only that I had always kept my joys and doubts locked inside myself.

Like my fears now for my father. Could Kenneth Timothy Wallace, prematurely gray at forty-one, who had known nothing but the Christian ministry, really turn overnight into a newspaper publisher?

Certainly the decision to buy *The Alderton Sentinel* had not been made lightly. I had always known that journalism was Dad's second love, had sometimes suspected it was his first. Dad remembered with sentimental delight his two years of college newspaper work; he had written continually for church publications and local newspapers ever since. The *Timmeton Times* had printed his weekly column, built around the relevance for today of a selected verse of Scripture.

Then there had been all that trouble at my father's church, followed by his illness. Apparently he had contracted malaria during a summer preaching mission in rural Louisiana. It became so bad that he had to be hospitalized for almost a month. Soon after that, the letter had arrived from Paul Proctor, one of Father's college friends, who owned a weekly newspaper in western Pennsylvania. Would Ken like to buy it?

For weeks my parents discussed the offer, both openly and behind closed doors. It came out that we had the necessary money in a savings fund—which had providentially survived the recent bank closings—a $15,000 inheritance from the estate of Mother's Aunt Stella. The money had initially been set aside to provide a college education for myself, Tim and Anne-Marie.

All of us agreed that Dad should take a week's trip to Alderton to go over the facilities. If it seemed right, he should look for a place to live. When he returned, the decision had been made. My father felt he "had a call" to publish and edit *The Sentinel*.

But questions had kept rising in me and would not be put down. How could someone who loved people as much as my father did leave the ministry? What had gone wrong at his church? Had Dad lost his faith? Why had God let so many bad things happen to such a good man? This depression year of 1934 seemed a poor time to start a new business venture. Inside me churned the suspicion that even in the best of times, my father's skills were not really attuned to the business world.

One thing was certain: the Wallace family was being plunged into unknown adventure in this unappealing town, Alderton.

2

I AWOKE the following Saturday morning in my still-strange bedroom in our new home to the sound of rain drumming on the roof. No matter. For over two years now I had enjoyed waking up early when there was no school, so that I could write down my thoughts.

Something about the hour of dawn intrigued me, drew me. In Timmeton it had been the quietness—silence so intense as to be almost palpable. Here in Alderton, the early morning calm was shattered by the distant clanging and screeching of engine whistles in the railroad yards.

My Timmeton classmates, all of whom slept late on Saturday, had made fun of my early morning rendezvous. This taught me that a person who is different can also be rejected. After considering this fact carefully, I decided that I liked being different and would accept the cost.

Five days in Alderton found me dazed by a kaleidoscope of first impressions—the ancient high school . . . new faces . . . the steep streets . . . the grime and soot on everything . . . the changeable weather. I turned on the bedside lamp and reached into the drawer of my nightstand for the lined notebook I had dignified with the name *Journal*. Propped up in bed, a robe around my shoulders, I wrote at the top of a fresh page: *Alderton, Penna. Saturday, September 15, 1934.* My pen went speeding across the page as I described the three-story white frame house Dad had rented for us on a short dead-end street called Bank Place, west of Alderton's business center. The house towered over a street so narrow there was barely room for two cars to pass. I wondered why the builder had decided on a ten-foot, postage-stamp-size front yard, leaving an outlandishly long hundred-foot lot at the back. In Timmeton, broad front lawns had been the rule. Perhaps northerners expected snow and wanted to be close to the street.

The long back yard, however, did provide plenty of space for vegetable and flower gardens. There was also an old wooden garage sandwiched between a cherry tree on one side and a walnut tree on the other. The back of the lot ended in a gradual dropoff of stone ledges, leading to a narrow street below. Tim, Anne-Marie and I had christened this area The Rocks. From there stretched a panoramic view all the way down the valley.

Next I tried to describe the disorder inside our house. Paul Proctor had arranged for the unloading of the moving van that delivered our furniture two days before we arrived; he had seen to it that our beds were set up and the basic furniture uncrated and positioned. Yet most of our things were still in barrels and boxes.

I got on paper the picture of our tall, willowy mother with her head almost buried in a barrel of china—brown hair disheveled, bits of excelsior clinging to it, beads of perspiration on her lined forehead, in her eyes a constant look of worry.

We were all scared about Dad. The long trip and the cloudburst episode seemed to have completely unnerved him. Not until our third day in Alderton did he make it to the *Sentinel* office.

I turned to a fresh page, a fresh subject: putting out a newspaper. Would I have a chance to make my oldest dream come true—to write something other people would read? Something that might change the world . . . no reason to think small! The world certainly needed to be changed. The man they called Il Duce in Italy and that new leader in Germany, Adolf Hitler, believed force was the way to do it. Could the League of Nations find no better way?

Finally I struggled to put down something about our near-disastrous entrance into Alderton last Sunday and that truly awkward meeting with Randolph Wilkinson when I tumbled into the mud almost at his feet.

Was that the most embarrassing moment of my life to date? Surely it was! More so than the night I lost my place while playing piano accompaniment for Tibbe's solo—and before the whole school assembly. Or the evening of my first double date when, like a two-year-old, I knocked over the whole glass of chocolate soda into Smithy Jordan's lap.

Randolph Wilkinson excites me . . . not so much his good looks as that British charm . . . I love the clarity of his speech . . . And that good-bye wink . . . There's something magnetic in this man that I felt through my whole body, I wish I could have impressed him . . .

I climbed out of bed, removed my bathrobe and pajamas and looked at myself in the oval mirror over my dresser. The glass reflected large eyes—blue, almost violet—and an upturned nose, near-shoulder-length wavy light brown hair, fair complexion. But too little color in my face. I turned sideways and grimaced. Some nice curves—and some unnecessary ones. Why had I allowed an extra ten pounds to creep up on me? As a defense? Against what? *I am going to lose weight,* I resolved.

The delicious aroma of our customary Saturday breakfast—buckwheat pancakes with maple syrup and sausage—was wafting upstairs. "Some things do not change," I thought. "Mother will see to that." But I had taken too long writing; I should have been down there helping her.

The kitchen was large, with a big pantry on one side and on the other, narrow back stairs leading to the second floor. An icebox sat on a screened-in back porch.

"'Morning, Julie,'' Mother greeted me. "What held you up? You're almost too late to help.''

Tim bounded in, with Anne-Marie, fourteen months younger, trailing him closely as usual. Tim had a cowlick on the crown of his blond head and a pug nose liberally sprinkled with freckles. Anne-Marie, a tomboy with cropped straight hair, was dressed in coveralls for Saturday. Father stood waiting for us; he was dressed in his dark blue serge suit, the one he had worn every Sunday during his last year in the Timmeton church. It was his good suit; the two others were threadbare.

After blessing our food, he turned to me. "So, Julie, are you ready for your first trip to the office?''

Mother frowned. "Kenneth, I could use Julie here today. There's no way I can do all the unpacking myself.''

"I know, Louise.'' Dad seemed to be struggling for composure. "But to keep food on the table, I've got to get *The Sentinel* going. And Julie can help.''

"Can I help too?'' Tim piped up. "Will you pay us?''

"Me too, Dad?'' Anne-Marie enthused.

Deliberately, my father took a sip of coffee. There was still a tremor in his hands, I noticed. "With our financial situation,'' he rejoined quietly, "we may *all* have to pitch in. And without pay.''

Mother said nothing more.

The decision of what to wear to the office was not very hard for me. With money so scarce, I made do with a wardrobe of three skirts and five blouses in mixable colors, a blue taffeta dress for Sundays, a rose-colored silk one for parties, several sweaters, and an old playsuit for dirty work around the house. Everyone wore saddle shoes to school—mine were brown and white. One pair of good shoes, assorted hats, gloves, belts and underwear completed the wardrobe. I needed more winter clothes, especially a coat, but could get by with my blue leather jacket.

* * *

It was a downhill trek to the drab-gray business section. Since Dad was still a bit trembly, we walked the sixteen blocks to the *Sentinel* office slowly, stopping to look into store windows. I'd never lived in a town this large and was shocked at the untidiness: the sidewalks and gutters littered with bubble gum and candy wrappers, squashed Dixie cups, popsicle sticks, torn bits of old newspapers. At the Five and Ten Cent Store loud hillbilly music was pouring forth from a scratchy phonograph, penetrating the street in gasps as the doors swung to and fro. Against the building sat a beggar with both legs off at the hips, balancing himself on a platform on wheels and selling pencils.

Between the stores, dark entrances led up narrow metal-edged stairs to offices on the upper floors: *Dentist, Chiropractor, Insurance, Attorney-at-Law.* All surfaces were encrusted with the accumulation of years of soot. About seven feet up from the sidewalk there was a brown line on all the buildings—the high water mark of the 1932 flood, Dad informed me.

Unsteady on his feet Dad might be, but still he missed no opportunity to introduce himself and me to the people we passed. "You are Sam Gaither, are you not? I am Kenneth Wallace, new publisher of *The Sentinel* . . . my daughter Julie." Warmed by my father's manner, the owner of Gaither's Clothing Store asked us to drop by some time.

Dad gave an equally hearty greeting to some chambermaids going to work at Haslam House, Alderton's main hotel. They giggled as we shook hands.

We stopped to talk a minute with Mr. Ted Gillin as he opened Gillin Auto Supply.

Then there was stout Mr. Salvatore Mazzini, who owned the shoe repair shop. Mr. Mazzini's response was a hearty handshake that made the corners of his handlebar mustache twitch. *What a way my father has with people,* I thought. *In no time at all he'll know everyone in town.*

As we turned the corner from Main Street onto Canal,

I asked him, "Dad, you haven't told me what I'm to do at *The Sentinel.*"

"I haven't told you because I don't know. This is all so new to me."

My father was already immersed in his own crash course on newspapering. He had been flinging around terms like "learning the case," "justifying a line," "loading the chases," "logotypes" and "printer's devils." It was another language, all right! For instance, how to guess that "accumulating boiler plate" had nothing whatsoever to do with furnaces or even pieces of metal? He had explained at dinner one night that this meant acquiring a supply of fill-in material to be used whenever news items ran short.

A few more strides and there it was: *The Alderton Sentinel* painted in curving gold letters on the plate glass window. The *Sentinel* office occupied the first floor of the three-story corner building on Canal Street and Maple. The second floor was an Eastern Star recreation hall, used mostly at night. The third floor was a storage area.

As Dad pushed open the door to the office, a mixture of unfamiliar smells greeted me. Later I sorted them out as new paper, printer's ink, machinery oil, hot metal and dust. We walked into a large room, forty feet wide and ninety feet long, with walls that begged for a fresh coat of paint. To the right of the door sat a scrawny woman well past middle age, at what looked to be a large kitchen table heaped high with papers. When my father had bought the almost-defunct *Sentinel,* he had also inherited the elderly Miss Cruley, whom he described to us as "riveted to the floor of that place as firmly as the old Babcock press."

"Miss Cruley, my daughter Julie," Dad said cheerily.

"Very pleased to meet you." Upon my father's entrance she had popped to her feet. The words coming out of her tiny mouth were as clipped as a bird's pecking. In fact, Emily Cruley was birdlike in every way, with her nervous, quick movements, her pipestem arms and legs. A dark green apron filled with pockets covered a cotton print dress, while a matching green visor sat firmly on top of her close-cropped gray hair.

"There is something I wish to speak to you about, Mr. Wallace," she chirped.

"Yes, Emily?"

"You've simply got to hire another person. I've never handled all the machine work. Never! Mr. Proctor always had Jake do that."

"I understand how you feel, Emily." Dad's voice revealed the strain he was under. "But I have to remind you that Mr. Proctor did not make a go of the paper financially. It was all but bankrupt."

"I know nothing of that. I was not privy to Mr. Proctor's bookkeeping."

"The point is," Dad persisted, "we must keep costs down. Jake has been offered an excellent new job in Boston, and I simply cannot afford to replace him." Dad paused and took a deep breath, his face twitching slightly. "He's assured me that you can handle the linotype."

Impatience fluttered through every line of her narrow body. "Of course I can. Composing is no harder than typing. But did you ever see a machine that didn't get out of whack every few days? When the linotype got 'squirts' or a roller had to be welded, Jake always knew what to do." Miss Cruley's bony forefinger was pointing to the big ungainly machine at the back of the office. "That old Babcock needs a mechanic to handle it."

Dad's shoulders sagged. "I promise I won't expect you to be a mechanic. Jake has already taught me a lot about that press. Please don't worry. I'll master it before he leaves."

He moved away from her and motioned me to follow him to the rear of the building. Dad's private working space was a thinly partitioned room, about six by ten, in the rear right corner. He pushed open the door and smiled wanly at me. "Enter the Publisher's office." I closed the door and sat down in a wooden cane-bottomed chair, while my father sank into the swivel seat in front of a long flat wooden desk. A bare spot had been scuffed into the linoleum-covered floor beneath the swivel chair, with grime caught in the edges of the torn linoleum.

As a publisher's office it wasn't much. Paul Proctor had left on the walls some old campaign pictures of political candidates, a couple of Alderton flood scenes, a few colorful theatrical posters and a faded picture of a billowing American flag cut from some magazine.

I felt a sudden pang of fear for my father as he faced this new adventure. Could he do it? I studied his thin, lined, still handsome face, brown eyes dulled by anxiety, hair turning from brown to gray. He had always had a lively sense of humor and a ready smile that revealed white, even teeth. Lately the smiles were uncertain and infrequent.

"Actually," he murmured, more to himself than to me, "Emily's right. I *am* going to have to find some help, at least for press days—Wednesday and Thursday."

"What day is the paper delivered?"

"Friday. It's hand-delivered locally. Mailed to subscribers in the surrounding communities."

I wondered if now was the moment I had been waiting for. Ever since Dad had purchased *The Sentinel*, I had seen it as my opportunity to become a journalist. If only my father would realize that I was no longer his little girl but a young adult with a brain and at least a degree of talent. But even as I was deciding how to put my question, Dad pre-empted me.

"Julie, you've always gotten A's in your English courses—would you be willing to give me some afternoon time for proofreading?"

Hastily I reduced my lofty thoughts. "What's involved?"

"Proof sheets are 'pulled,' as they say in this trade, by Monday afternoon. It means reading them carefully to catch any printing errors, misspellings, or mistakes of the

sort that would embarrass anyone. Actually, it's a big responsibility.''

I wondered if Dad was trying to make proofreading
sound more important than it was. "I'll be glad to try,"
I told him cautiously. "I'm not so hot at spelling, though."

There was a tap on the flimsy door and Miss Cruley
stuck her head in. "Someone to see you, Mr. Wallace. A
Mr. Dean Fleming."

As I relinquished the cane-bottomed chair, an older
man appeared in the doorway. He had a sunburned bald
head, a leathery face, and wore a plaid shirt and corduroy
pants above thick-soled worker's shoes. As he moved toward Dad, I noticed that he dragged one leg behind him.

"Came by," I heard Mr. Fleming inquire, "to see if
you'd print some handbills for my union, the International Machinists."

"Happy to. Do you have the copy with you?"

"Right here." He pulled a folded paper out of his
breast pocket.

As the two men sat down together at my father's desk,
Miss Cruley took me on a tour of the outer office. The
Babcock press took up the rear left corner of the room,
close to the back door, which led out to an alley. Next to
the Babcock was the cutter, then came a platen press for
small job work. A long make-ready table was positioned
in the middle of the room, cases of type on the opposite
wall. There was a sink under the staircase leading to the
second story, where, she primly explained, separate
men's and women's toilets were located. I wondered
where I would do my proofreading.

The men emerged from my father's office. Dad
nodded toward me: "My daughter Julie, Mr. Fleming.
She will be helping us with the newspaper."

Mr. Fleming gripped my hand in his work-roughened
one. The most striking feature of this homely man, I
thought, was his penetrating eyes. When he had gone, I
noticed a strange look on my father's face as he stared after the departing visitor.

That night at dinner, Dad seemed more relaxed than usual. "It's been a good day," he luxuriated, pushing his chair back from the table. "Louise, a man named Dean Fleming came by the office. Union man. Wanted a print order, some handbills. Guess what he said to me just before he left?"

"I can't imagine," Mother answered.

"Made me an offer of his time for two hours a day, five days a week, as maintenance man for our printing equipment. Insisted he would take no payment for this."

"Why would he do that?"

"He said"—here Dad groped for words—"he said that he had an 'inner guide' who told him to come to me because I needed help."

"Did you take him up on his offer?"

"He didn't leave me much choice."

"But is he any good?" asked our always-practical mother.

"I can't tell yet. He seems to know quite a lot about machinery. He told me he worked thirty-five years as a machinist for the Pennsylvania Railroad. Hurt his leg in a train wreck and retired a few years ago. A widower. Has a farmhouse in Yancyville, where he lives with his sister, who's nearly blind. She keeps house for him."

My father paused a moment, then chuckled self-consciously. "He knows that I left the ministry. Gave me a little pep talk about holding on to my faith."

A machinist who was both a union man and a preacher —what a strange combination. I didn't think I was going to like this Mr. Fleming if he was going to use his volunteer status to force his philosophy of life on us.

3

THE room we were already calling "the study" was still in disarray as we gathered that Sunday evening for a family conference. Cartons of books piled against two walls were awaiting the floor-to-ceiling bookshelves Dad intended to build.

As I looked across the room at my father, I yearned to go over and hug him. But I held back. Was it shyness again? I didn't honestly think so. I no longer felt free to give him that kind of spontaneous affection in front of Mother, though I wasn't sure why. The difficult times of the past few years had somehow lessened the flow of affection in our family.

Though they had tried to hold their discussions in private, I had overheard some of the sharp and critical words erupting between Mom and Dad when the opportunity came to buy *The Sentinel*. "Are you sure, Ken, that this isn't just an escape from a difficult situation in your church?" I'd once heard her ask. Leaving Timmeton had been harder on her than on any of the rest of us. Now she reached for her mending basket and selected a darning needle as though it were a dueling weapon. I chose the old Morris chair in the corner, glad that it had not been left behind when we moved. For years it had been my favorite study chair, with its wide arms for books and papers.

I smiled at how easily my father gravitated to the chair in front of his golden oak rolltop desk. To me he already looked like an editor. "I don't want you to think this is a crisis session," he began, "but as I learn more about the real situation at *The Sentinel*, I see what a big job lies ahead."

Mom picked that up instantly. "New problems, Ken?"

"Not new, really. We're short on cash. The depression hurts everybody."

"How bad has Alderton been hit?"

"Business here is in poor shape, Louise. A number have folded recently. The *Alderton Daily News* was one. Leaves us as the only paper in town."

"Why did that one fail, Dad?" I inquired.

"Newspapers have never done well in Alderton for some reason. Proctor said people read the Pittsburgh dailies for general news. Local stores have been slow to advertise. In fact, most merchants in town are carrying so many people on credit now, they're barely making it. This town couldn't keep going one week without credit."

Dad sighed, then in a cheerier voice addressed Tim and Anne-Marie. "You children need to understand something about your father. People in Timmeton used to call me 'Reverend Wallace' or 'Pastor.' They won't be doing that in Alderton. I have a new job now as an editor and publisher."

"But aren't you still a preacher?" queried Anne-Marie.

"Once an ordained clergyman, I suppose you always are. But I'll need all my time and energy now to make a success of the newspaper."

My earlier impressions of Dad at his desk focused into words. "Why don't we call you 'The Editor'? That's better than 'Reverend.' "

Dad smiled. "Call me whatever you want. But now to family finances. There's no way," he began, a sudden tremor in his voice, "that we can make it unless the five of us accept the fact that we all are now in the newspaper business.''

"Me too?" Tim sounded surprised.

"You too, son. And Anne-Marie. I'll tell you how in a minute. But first, some facts and figures." Dad consulted a sheet of paper in his hand. "You may remember that Paul Proctor first asked $15,000 for the paper. We finally got it for $12,000. So that left us a cushion of only $3,000 from the education fund to get the paper going and to live on this year.

"Moving all our stuff up here from Timmeton cost us $250," he continued. "Our trip north in the Willys ran us a bit over $100." Dad had budgeted the five-day trip for exactly $100, figuring $3 a day per person for food and lodging, $5 a day for gas, oil and other car expenses. Staying in tourist homes for a dollar a night per room, including breakfast, had certainly been the economical way to travel.

"Our house rent is $22 per month," Dad went on, "plus utilities—gas, lights, the phone. Coal has gone up to $4 a ton."

As Dad ticked off items, I tore a sheet out of a notebook and began jotting down the figures. "The rent for the *Sentinel* building is another $38 per month. I have to pay Miss Cruley $20 a week. What would you say about food, Louise? And clothes this year?"

"I'm doing my best to hold food down to $10 a week," Mom answered. "Clothes? Let me think. As a businessman you really ought to have a second presentable suit. A two-trouser one will be $12. This winter Julie will have to have a new coat. That's, uh, about $15. Oh, maybe $100 for clothes for the year. That is, if I do a lot of sewing."

I winced. Mother was a passable seamstress, but there were limitations. Homemade dresses were all right for little girls, but not for me now, at almost eighteen.

"These are estimates, of course." Dad was referring again to the paper in his hand. "Not counting anything for recreation or medical or dental bills, or major repairs to the car, it adds up to almost $3,000. And remember, the Willys is over six years old. Got to expect trouble."

I was staring at the figures I had put down. "Dad, you're forgetting about me and college next year too."

My father gave me a tight smile. "No, I haven't forgotten about your college. There may be a little delay, that's all."

Suddenly college seemed a long way off.

"Ken," Mother protested, "your calculations appear far too high to me."

"I don't think so. Trouble is, we lived in another world. We're used to having our home and utilities paid for by the church. Office and secretarial expenses too. Emily Cruley's salary, for instance, accounts for $1,040. And she's doing so many jobs, I should raise her a dollar or two a week."

The room was silent for a moment.

"But Dad," I finally asked, "Won't the paper make any money?"

"I hope so," came the uncertain reply. "The purpose of business is to make money, Julie. But *The Sentinel* was not a money-maker when we bought it. There's a lot of building up to do."

Mother's darning that sock with such big stitches, I thought, *that Tim will never wear it.* Suddenly I ached for her. Mother had been so proud to have Aunt Stella's inheritance set aside for our college educations. Now it was gone, down a hole with seemingly no bottom to it.

Dad's deep voice resumed. "According to Paul Proctor, we need $6,000 a year just to print the paper that goes out to our 4,340 subscribers. I'm hoping that by cutting corners we can do it for $5,000. But to pay family and business expenses, we need a whopping $12,000 income each year from the paper."

"How many people in the entire area?" Mother asked.

"Counting villages, about 25,000," came the reply. "So *The Sentinel* reaches barely a fifth of them. Lots of room for growth. Anyway, with 4,340 subscribers and *The Sentinel* priced at 3¢ a copy or $1.50 a year, that's $6,150. But believe me, we won't collect it all.''

"But as the paper gets better, surely more people will *want* it,'' I said hopefully.

"That's our goal.'' Dad grinned. "I'm told that folks love to see their names in print. So the more thoroughly we cover the local news, the better we'll do.''

There would also be some income from "job printing,'' Dad explained, such items as handbills, theater tickets, stationery, wedding invitations—all manner of things. "But according to Paul Proctor, we can't count on much there,'' he said. "I hope he's wrong.''

Then Dad launched into his plea to the family. "You can see that Emily's salary is a big drain. We really *can't* afford to hire anyone else. Yet there's no way Emily and I can handle everything.'' He located another piece of paper on his desk. "I have here a list of the jobs that have to get done somehow each week.'' He read them aloud:

News gathered
Stories written and typed
Advertising copy collected
Makeup, layout and headings set
Linotype work
Proofs read and checked
Printing (the Babcock can handle 2,000
  impressions an hour)
Prepare papers for mailing and hand delivery
Subscription list kept up to date
Billing and bookkeeping
Maintenance

"On top of all that,'' Dad went on relentlessly, "there is the matter of taking orders for job printing, handling the job press and delivering the finished product. Plus sweeping out the office, emptying wastebaskets, general cleanup.''

"Dad, you make it sound impossible," I gasped.

"Don't mean to," he replied, "but you must understand what we're facing."

Father reached for another sheet. "Here are some tentative assignments. I'll write an editorial each week, handle most of the stories and collect the advertising. Emily Cruley will be responsible for the short items, prepare advertising copy, set the heads for all stories, operate the linotype machine and handle subscriptions. Dean Fleming will service the equipment and help Miss Cruley run the presses.

"Louise—" Dad looked intently at her. "Could you give a few hours occasionally in the afternoon to help Emily process new subscriptions and supervise Tim and Anne-Marie getting the papers ready for mailing each week?"

Mother's face was expressionless. "That will take some juggling. Remember, there's no help here to do housework except Julie. I'll try, Ken." Her voice trailed off.

"Good. Now, Tim . . . Anne-Marie. You'll be chief postal clerks. All papers have to be folded, address labels attached, taken to the post office. That's one job. The second is to hand-deliver about two hundred fifty papers to downtown Alderton. The third, take out the office trash each day and sweep up. If you kids do a good job, we'll talk turkey on the allowance.

"Now, Julie. Will you handle proofreading?"

"Sure, Dad. But there's something else." *Surely the right moment has finally come.* "I'd like to help write stories too."

My father looked thoughtful. "Well, now, Julie, that can happen. But most journalists go through an apprentice period."

"Meaning what, Dad?"

"Meaning research at the library, finding short filler

items, chores around the office. Matter of fact," he went on thoughtfully, "I could let you do legwork for some of my editorials."

"Dad, that's super! Which reminds me," I rushed on, "I've made this friend at school named Margo. We were thinking of driving up to Lake Kissawha some Saturday. I was wondering—how about my writing an article about that place?"

My father looked doubtful. "Let me think about it."

As that hot September turned into a chill October, Alderton's economic plight worsened. The Pennsylvania Railroad announced plans to close down one of its two roundhouses. Yoder Iron and Steel began laying off men. Since most of these workingmen lived from payday to payday and were already in debt to the local merchants, the whole town suffered. The sluggish stream of local ads slowed to a trickle.

The situation throughout the entire nation had become critical. A year and a half before, on March 4, 1933, every bank in the United States had locked its doors. This was more traumatic than the 1929 stock market crash had ever been. In '29 only investors in stocks and bonds had been directly affected; the bank closings had imperiled the checking and savings accounts of every American. There was no deposit insurance. Fear had stalked the streets of every city, town and hamlet.

That same morning, with remarkable timing, the thirty-second American president had been sworn in— polio-crippled Franklin Delano Roosevelt. His inaugural address exuded confidence: "This nation asks for action and action now."

Action had followed with a speed that dazzled everybody. An emergency banking bill passed in record time. Four days later the banks had reopened, though most people received only fifty cents for each dollar they had deposited. In the hundred days that followed, Congress had passed a series of emergency measures that only now were beginning to be felt in towns like Alderton. Five hundred million dollars—an astronomical sum for the day—had been funneled into programs collectively known as the New Deal.

As a result some industrial production picked up. With Federal Deposit Insurance, people had begun to trust the banks again. Thousands were getting temporary work through the new NRA agencies. Even so, an economic malaise still hung over most of America, especially in places like Alderton.

In history class one day we talked about how this depression was the first tarnishing of the American Dream, the first nationwide disappointment. As awful as the War Between the States had been, many of the western states and territories had escaped its full impact; nobody was escaping the effects of the depression.

After Dad's talk to us, it came home sharply to me that many people would consider newspapers a nonessential luxury item.

On a Friday evening in early October, the Vincent Pileys, who lived just across the street on Bank Place, unexpectedly came to call. We had learned that Mr. Piley was the comptroller of the Pennsylvania Railroad and was also reputed to be the town expert on stocks and bonds. The Pileys were said to have a beautiful daughter, Jean, who was a senior at some eastern college.

The Piley wealth had already made a deep impression on me that afternoon when Mother, in a frenzy of pie-making, had sent me across the street to borrow a cup of lard. There was a baby grand piano in their music room, glass-fronted bookshelves in the library, lovely antiques and so many carpets—no bare floors anywhere.

Tonight, as Dad helped Mrs. Piley off with her coat, I gaped at her dress. It was a stunning blue silk; a gold brooch, set with small sapphires, sparkled at the neckline. Mr. Piley was half a head shorter than his wife but made up for this deficiency with an officious manner. I noticed a large diamond ring on the little finger of his left hand.

As I followed them into our parlor I was painfully aware of its sparse furnishings: a worn Axminster rug, several large rockers, a revolving bookcase in a corner, a tall standing lamp with fringe on the shade, gas logs in a fake fireplace, and an ancient upright player piano. On the wall above this hung a picture from Greek mythology—Diana with flowing garments running before a chariot.

As if Diana were not bad enough, there was the love seat with the broken spring. Why my parents had carted that all the way from Timmeton, I couldn't imagine. I watched the inevitable sequence as Mr. Piley sat down on it: first there was the complaining twang of the loose spring; next his involuntary lurch forward as the offending spring jabbed his backside; finally his increasing discomfiture as the angle of the seat slid him irrevocably toward the floor. Hopefully *The Sentinel* would make enough money so that the love seat could be replaced.

I had my homework papers spread out on the arms of the Morris chair in the adjoining study and was only half attending to Mr. Piley's bleak predictions for Alderton's economic future when the name Randolph Wilkinson brought me to full attention. "Very bright young man," Mr. Piley was saying.

"He was certainly helpful to us when we had car trouble a few weeks back," Mother agreed.

"Jean finds him utterly charming," Mrs. Piley enthused. "He always remembers her favorite blend of tea when he comes back from England."

I slipped from my chair and headed swiftly for the back stairs, unwilling to hear more.

Late that night, on the way to my bedroom after washing my hair, I heard voices from my parents' bedroom.

"The bank turned down my request for a loan, Louise. Seems I have no credit rating—and no way I can see of getting one."

"What about your brother?"

"He's as strapped as I am."

"Then what can we do, Ken?"

There was a long silence. I stood there, frozen, not wanting to hear any more yet unable to walk away.

"I'm sorry I got us all into this." Dad's voice was almost a sob. "It was a stupid mistake to come here, to take this big house, to pretend I could be a big-time publisher. You married a failure, Louise."

"I won't accept that, Ken. You have to keep trying. And I'll see that we keep eating even if I have to make soup from the bark of our trees."

Quietly I crept back to my room, turned out the light and climbed into bed. Sleep was a long time coming.

4

On Saturday, October 6, I awoke with a deep heaviness in my spirit. The idea of Dad's being a failure terrified me. Was there something I could do? Quit school, perhaps, and work full-time in the office?

Even as the idea came, I knew Father would reject it. Well, at least I could get up and help Mother with breakfast. After overhearing their conversation last night, I could better understand why she had so resisted our move to Alderton.

As I dressed, my thoughts shifted to the day ahead. My new friend, Margo Palmer, had the use of her father's car on most Saturdays, and today we were to take a trip to Lake Kissawha. Why was I so eager to go there? *Be honest with yourself, Julie. You're dying to see Randolph Wilkinson again.*

Mr. Wilkinson was years older than I, probably in his mid- or late twenties. For all I knew he might have a fiancée back in England or be planning to marry this Jean Piley, with her special blend of tea. Nonetheless, I had thought about him constantly since our arrival in Alderton a month ago.

For breakfast there was dry cereal instead of buckwheat cakes. When Tim protested, Father cut him off sharply. The Editor was dressed as usual in his blue serge suit, much-laundered white shirt, conservative tie. As we walked to the office in the crisp October air, I detected no lessening of his warmth to all passers-by we met on the sidewalk.

On Canal Street he turned to me. "What exactly do you and your new friend—is it Margie?—plan to do today?"

"Her name's Margo, Margo Palmer. You and Mom would like her."

"I'm sure we would. You're driving to Lake Kissawha in her car? Just the two of you?"

"Not her car, Dad. It's her father's car."

"What does her father do?"

"He runs a restaurant."

"Is it a roadhouse?"

"It's a respectable place," I said defensively. Yet the minute the words were out of my mouth, I realized that I did not really know much about it, only that it was called the Stemwinder and that it did have a bar.

"I've never been there, Dad," I admitted. "Anyway, that's not where we're going. Mr. Wilkinson said we could come back and visit the Club sometime. Remember?"

"Julie, Lake Kissawha is a private lake and the Club is closed for the season. I think you may be reading more into a few kind words than you should. In any case you shouldn't drive there without checking first with Mr. Wilkinson. He may have gone back to England."

Deep down I knew Dad was right, but I quailed at the thought of telephoning the Englishman. What if he did not remember me? What if out of my discomfiture, I stumbled and sputtered like a witless schoolgirl?

Involuntarily my fists clenched. It was time to get out of my fantasy world and begin living as an adult in the real world. "I'll telephone Mr. Wilkinson now," I told my father.

I put the call through from Dad's office after carefully shutting the door. *No need for Miss Cruley to hear this.* When a woman's voice answered, I asked to speak to Mr. Wilkinson.

"May I tell him who's calling?"

"Julie Wallace."

"Is this a business matter?"

My stomach was churning. "No, not exactly. I need to ask him a question."

"Perhaps I can help you," the voice purred.

I gripped the telephone firmly. "No, I'm afraid you can't. I need to speak to Mr. Wilkinson personally."

Silence. Then, "One moment, please."

That deep, pleasant voice with the clipped accent came on. "This is Randolph Wilkinson."

"Mr. Wilkinson, this is Julie Wallace. You were so kind to our family four weeks ago when our car got stuck in the ditch. I don't know whether you remember or not."

"I recall the incident well. And you too, Julie. What can I do for you?"

"A friend of mine—a girl—and I would like to drive up to the lake today and, well, just walk around some. Would that be all right? You were kind enough to invite us to come back sometime."

"So I did." Was there a momentary hesitation? "I see no reason," he was saying slowly, "why it wouldn't be all right for the two of you to come today. Please look me up first so that I can meet your friend."

As I hung up the receiver, I noticed that my hands were damp. But I was astonished at how my spirits had picked up.

Just before noon Margo pulled up at the *Sentinel* office in a black Ford sedan with *The Stemwinder* painted in oversized gold letters on the door. Emily Cruley stared at it through the window, frowning disapproval written all over her thin, heart-shaped face. *I bet she tells Dad I'm riding around in a roadhouse car.*

Forget it, I told myself. *This is a day for fun and adventure.* I settled comfortably into the seat beside Margo, thinking how much I enjoyed being with her. She was an attractive girl, taller than I, with a blunt honesty that I found appealing. Her hair was black and straight. With her dark eyes and high cheekbones, I wondered if she might have Indian blood in her ancestry.

As we were heading out of town, I asked her with assumed casualness, "Anything you can tell me about the Englishman who manages the Club?" Margo had worked at Lake Kissawha as a substitute waitress this past summer.

"You must mean Randolph Wilkinson. He's assistant manager. Mr. Clayton, the manager, died last year. They haven't replaced him."

"I see. Mr. Wilkinson was sure in charge when we had car trouble near here a few weeks back." I described for Margo our arrival in Alderton.

"I think he got the job because he's the nephew of Munro Farnsworth, a big shot at the Club and also at Yoder Steel."

"Is he, uh, married, or engaged—or anything?"

"Not as far as I know. The girls all fall for him, but he plays the field. Around here Jean Piley seems to be number one."

As we drove up Seven Mile Mountain Road, Margo explained that membership in the Club was limited to just one hundred families. Some had built their own cottages; the rest stayed at the Inn. The yearly membership fee was $2500.

I was appalled. "Why, $2500 is more money than a lot of families have to live on for a whole year."

"The depression hasn't touched these Club people," Margo assured me. She swung onto the shady dirt road that led into the Club grounds. "You should see the production they make of a two-week vacation. Mountains of baggage, wardrobe trunks full of clothes. The Club has three limousines that shuttle back and forth to meet the trains."

When Margo drove into the parking lot, memories of our family mishap came surging back. *This time I'll at least look decent, not like a muddy clown.* I took my vanity out of my bag and peeked in the mirror. Then I smoothed out my skirt and blouse, chosen carefully to make me look older.

We tried to open the door to the Inn and found it locked. There was no bell. My knock was muffled by the heavy thickness of the wood.

When no one answered, Margo and I began walking toward the lake. A slight breeze had stirred the water; the span of blue ripples extended from the shoreline out to— and then I saw the boat.

It was a small white skiff with one occupant, a rower. The boat was cutting through the water at surprising speed, rhythmically propelled by someone very skilled in the art. Fascinated, I strained to identify the person whose powerful arms were directing the skiff to the near shore.

Randolph Wilkinson! Surely he once had been an oarsman at one of those English universities. We watched in admiration as he finished with a burst of speed that almost catapulted the boat up onto the sandy beach. In an instant he had leaped from the skiff, pulled it farther out of the water and started to lope in our direction. When he saw us, he waved.

I studied him as he approached. He wore a white sleeveless crew-neck shirt, navy sweat pants and sneakers. About five foot nine. Lithe, rippling arm muscles. There was a jaunty gait to his walk and a twinkle in his eyes as he stopped in front of us. "Miss Wallace," he intoned, taking my hand. "This is a happier occasion and a sunnier day."

Despite myself, I blushed. When I introduced him to Margo, a look of recognition crossed his face. "Haven't I seen you here before?"

"Yes, I worked several times as a waitress last summer."

"Ah, I thought so." Randolph Wilkinson looked at his watch. "If you girls will give me fifteen minutes to change, I'll take you on a quick tour."

In less time than that he was back, having showered and slipped into slacks and a sports shirt.

First he ushered us through the Inn, a wooden frame structure, three stories high, with forty-seven bedrooms, now closed for the season. There was a series of lounges, each with a huge open fireplace and a name—the Assembly Hall, the Great Parlor, the Ladies' Parlor, the Pool Room, the Smoking Room and so on.

In the Great Parlor Mr. Wilkinson pointed out the wide overhead beams, the walk-in fireplace of rough-hewn stone, the large animal trophies. "The members want a rustic flavor," he commented. "The wealthier they are, the more bally pleasure they get out of pretending that they're roughing it." He threw open a large door. "This is the Anglers' Room."

I blinked in astonishment. Blues and blue greens had been used to give the effect of undulating water. Mounted fish and fishing rods hung on the walls and collections of elaborate flies, carefully labeled, occupied huge walnut plaques.

"This room may seem bizarre," our host said, sounding a little defensive, "but some of our members are fishing-mad. They spend hours in here discussing the right flies to use, what weight rod—that sort of thing."

My eyes swept over the flowing colors. "I feel a bit seasick," slid off my tongue.

"You say you like books, Julie." Margo pointed to a wall of glass-fronted bookcases.

Sidestepping some big leather lounge chairs, I moved over for a closer look. All the books were about fishing.

The Englishman saw my surprise. "Oh, angling's a science. Quite! Look over here." He led Margo and me to a freestanding glass case inside which a number of books lay open. "Rare first editions," he told us. He pointed to one. "That is a 1653 copy of Isaak Walton's *The Compleat Angler,* and that one's an 1836 edition of Alfred Ronald's *The Fly-Fisher's Entomology.* There's W. C. Stewart's *Practical Angler,* 1857, considered quite a classic. Here's a complete card file on fishing books.''

"Do you live here?" I asked Mr. Wilkinson as he led us outside, eager to get the conversation onto more personal ground.

He grinned engagingly. "Yes, while I'm in America. Right now I'm its only night resident. A small staff comes during the day. I leave for England in two weeks.''

"You come to America every year just to do this work?"

"I'm here at the Club about seven months of the year, then possibly a fortnight with my auntie and uncle—the Munro Farnsworths, y'know—in Pittsburgh.'' Something about the way the Englishman said this name implied that I should be impressed.

The three of us stood on the porch and I looked across the lake. The breeze was stronger now, kicking up whitecaps across the water. "The lake is lovely," I commented, "and so big. I still find it hard to believe it's artificial.''

"Oh, it's artificial, all right. Dive deep and you may bash your head on tree stumps. It's a five-mile walking tour all the way around.''

He led us down the porch steps and along a narrow boardwalk to point out the cottages scattered through the woods. The first had mustard-yellow shutters and a sign over the front steps that read *Sunflower*. Margo caught my eye and guffawed. "Each house is named after a different flower,'' she explained. "Where would you rather live? In a *Pansy* or a *Delphinium?*''

Mr. Wilkinson chuckled. "Sounds a trifle coy, doesn't it?''

As he led us back toward the Inn, our host was less talkative. "All this wealth bothers you, doesn't it, Miss Wallace?''

I took a deep breath, not aware that my inner feelings had come through so strongly. "Yes, it does. There are so many people right here in Alderton who don't have enough to eat." I told him about the long lines in front of the NRA soup kitchen.

The Englishman did not reply. Determined not to be a gushing schoolgirl, was I instead coming off as disagreeable? The whole day was turning out so strangely. Mr. Wilkinson was probably eager to get rid of us.

He remained urbane and gracious, however, as we continued the tour. He told us that the original dam on the lake had been finished in 1854. Eight years later a big section of it had collapsed, fortunately at a time when the lake was only half full, so there'd been little flooding. The Pennsylvania Railroad had purchased the property in 1881, reinforced the dam, dug a channel to divert the overflow into a different stream, and built the original Inn as a resort area for its executives.

Then in 1926, the lake, the dam and some six hundred surrounding acres were sold to fifteen wealthy Pennsylvania industrialists, headed by Thomas McKeever, Sr. The Hunting and Fishing Club had had its official opening in the summer of 1927.

The Englishman led us down an almost perpendicular path beside a spillway to the base of the dam, where little rivulets of seepage flowed into the creek bed.

"If the dam broke once," I asked, "how can you be sure it's safe now?"

"It's inspected twice a month." He looked at his watch. "Now, is there anything else I can show you young ladies?"

A trace of formality had crept in. The tour was over. But at least, I thought, we were now young ladies, not girls. As the three of us scrambled back up the steep incline to the parking lot, I felt irked at myself. Mr. Wilkinson had been warm and friendly; I had been testy. What could I say to retrieve the situation?

I drew a deep breath. "Mr. Wilkinson, you've been so kind to us. I'm sorry if I seemed—well, difficult. It's just that I have strong convictions about certain things and they seem to spill out."

He gave me a searching look. "Don't ever apologize for having strong convictions, Miss Wallace. We could use more of that here."

He turned to Margo. "I hope events conspire to bring you here to work again next summer."

He paused, reflecting. "It's too splendid a day just to motor back to town. Feel free to roam the grounds."

"We'd like that," I told him. "May we find a spot to spread out our picnic lunch?"

The Englishman looked surprised. "Oh, indeed so! Quite. I'll try to inform James, the groundsman"—the clipped accent took on a teasing note—"that you're legitimate guests."

It was almost two o'clock and Margo and I were famished. Taking the picnic basket and a blanket out of the car, we headed back toward the dam. We skidded again down the hillside to the base of the immense structure and began walking along the creek formed by water discharged from the spillways on either side of the dam. On ahead the stream curved to the left in a channel that had obviously been widened and deepened by earth-moving machinery. For a hundred yards or so, the right-hand ridge of this man-made streambed was reinforced by a high concrete retaining wall.

It was Margo who spotted the enchanting nook in a nearby wooded area. The gold and brown autumn foliage formed a canopy overhead, and the ground was covered with moss and bracken. "It's like a little woodland room," I enthused.

I spread out the blanket while Margo unwrapped the sandwiches and poured root beer into collapsible tin cups. I took deep gulps of the crisp fall air. Perhaps here I could find some of the peace and joy that had eluded me all day.

Margo was staring at me, a quizzical expression on her face. "You don't care much for this place, do you, Julie?"

"I thought I would. I've looked forward for weeks to

coming. But there's something about the atmosphere
that's depressing.''

"What about Randolph Wilkinson?''

"I like him. He's very nice.''

"You didn't show it.''

I munched on my sandwich moodily, wondering why
suddenly I had become so outspoken. ''I guess I don't
like the way wealthy people fling money around on silly
things.''

"He's used to that. He comes from a wealthy family.''

"What about your family, Margo?'' I knew my friend
led a lonely life at home. ''Your mother—when did she
die?''

"Almost a year and a half ago. The end of my sophomore year.''

"What happened, Margo?''

"She was going to have a baby, but she had a miscar-
riage. And then she died. A traveling blood clot, they
said.''

As I cut an apple in two and gave Margo half, I tried to
visualize what it would be like to have one's mother there
one day and gone—forever—the next. Despite the recent
tensions, my parents had always been so—*there*.

"You have no brothers or sisters?''

"I did have a brother. He died when I was five. Now
there's just my father and me. We come and go. Dad
gives me too much freedom, but he doesn't have much
choice. We live separate lives.''

Our lunch finished, Margo lit a cigarette, then lay back
on the bracken-covered ground. As I stretched out beside
her, I wondered why in the short time we had been in
Alderton I felt so attracted to Margo. One reason had to
be her frankness about her own weaknesses and blunders.
This drew me because my inclination was to protect myself and guard against the intensity of my feelings. Little
chance that other people would understand the deep
passion I could feel over this idea or that cause.

Margo's voice brought me back. ''You should wear

more makeup, Julie. A little eyebrow pencil would set off those lovely eyes of yours.''

"I never thought about it.'' I didn't tell her that my parents had held out against even the palest shade of lipstick until recently, and were strongly against smoking. Nor did I say anything about my resolve to lose weight. I would just do it, not talk about it.

We lay there for a few minutes until we both suddenly realized we were shivering. All at once the woodland cranny had a gloomy, foreboding feel. The bracken-covered undergrowth, which had seemed so inviting, now appeared to be littered with dying things intertwined with the snakelike roots of mountain grapevine.

"Margo, let's get out of here.''

We snatched up the picnic things and retraced our steps up the rechanneled stream. At the base of the dam I looked up at the towering embankment, which was all but covered with saplings, shrubs, small pines. With the sun under a cloud, the dam suddenly took on a new shape—it was like the back of a dark, hairy, headless beast. I stared, shivered, closed my eyes. We began climbing quickly up the path beside the spillway.

"Hey, you down there!''

We jumped at the sound of the gruff masculine voice. A heavy-set man in stained corduroy pants and a dark shirt stood rocking unsteadily on the roadway above us, holding a hunting rifle over one arm.

"Didn't ya see the No Trespassing signs? This is private property.''

"Mr. Wilkinson invited us here,'' I told him.

"Don't believe ya. Nobody told me nothing.''

"Then go ask Mr. Wilkinson.''

"I'll ask nobody nothing. I'm the watchman here and my orders are to keep off all trespassers. And that means you. Now git—*and don't never come back.*''

Frightened now, we struggled, panting, up to the level of the lake. As we headed toward the parking lot, frustration over the whole day welled up inside me. Rashly, I turned and shouted at the watchman. "You're drunk!"

He raised his gun and fired. A branch splintered off a tree to our right.

"Let's get out of here—fast," Margo gasped as we reached the parking lot.

Quickly we jumped into the car, the engine roared to life, and we zoomed up the dirt road onto Route 143.

5

On Sunday the Wallace cash situation was so desperate that Father called another family meeting to explain a new, stringent family budget: for the time being, no use of the Willys, no purchases of anything but basic food supplies.

When I arrived at *The Sentinel* after school Monday, I could hear Dad's voice and Miss Cruley's through the thin partition of the Editor's sanctum. Proofs for the week's paper were spread out on what I grandly called my desk. This was a rickety wooden table against the side wall outside the Editor's office. With it was a bent metal chair, which Dean Fleming had scrounged, along with the table, from the third-floor storage area. The prize feature of the table for me was that it had a drawer, too small for my schoolbooks but large enough to hold paper and writing tools.

I was halfway down the first sheet when I realized that the conversation behind the closed door concerned me.

". . . never works," Miss Cruley's voice piped, "hiring members of one's family. Nepotism can spoil any business."

Struggling not to listen, I consulted my list of proofreader's marks. Soon I would have them memorized.

"Nepotism is far too grand a word, Emily." The Editor's voice sounded tired. *"The Sentinel* is not Yoder Steel."

"Same principle. No difference between a small busi-

44

ness and a large one. Everybody means well at the beginning. But then the boss starts making concessions because it's his daughter or his brother or his cousin or his
wife. Never works, I tell you."

"In theory," I heard Father reply, "I couldn't agree
more. What I still haven't communicated to you is that I
have no choice here: there simply isn't any money to hire
outside help."

Here an idea apparently struck Dad. "Emily, you
don't think I'm *paying* the members of my family to
work here, do you?"

"How would I know? That was not discussed."

"Well, I'm not. We make it together as a family or we
fail."

There was a short silence. "Well," Miss Cruley concluded, "I'm sorry for you. Sorry for the paper."

My father's voice lifted. "I do have some good news
for you, Emily. Since I'm asking you to take on more responsibility, I'm raising your salary one dollar a week
beginning next paycheck."

Another silence. Then, "I'm obliged to you for that.
It's hard to make ends meet nowadays. You'll get your
money's worth."

"I'm sure I will," Father responded. "I'm counting
heavily on your experience and know-how. Just give us a
chance, Emily."

A scraping of chairs and then Miss Cruley emerged
and crossed to her desk with the merest nod at me. For an
hour the three of us worked in silence, each at his own
desk. I could hear every squeak of my father's chair
through the flimsy wall, the rattle of his papers, even the
scratch of his pen. I had a sudden longing to confide in
him about my Saturday experience at the Hunting and
Fishing Club. As far back as I could remember, Dad's
masculine strength and the assurance of his loving concern about anything that troubled me had represented my
whole security. His illness had changed that, shown me a

man filled with doubts and unsteady emotions. What a devastating disease malaria was . . .

Impulsively I rose, tapped on the door and opened it. "Dad, may I interrupt for just a minute?"

"Sure, Julie. My thoughts aren't coming too well anyhow." He took off his reading glasses and placed them on his desk.

"It's about last Saturday. Something I haven't told you—"

Dad swiveled his chair around and leaned back. "Sit down, Julie. What's on your mind?"

"After Mr. Wilkinson showed us the grounds, Margo and I had a picnic lunch in the woods down below the dam. Dad, did you ever have a feeling inside that something's wrong and you're not sure what? Sort of like a warning?"

"Yes-s, once in a while."

"Well, it was like that when we were at the dam."

"Be more specific, Julie."

"It's just—not like I think a dam should look. All those things growing out of it."

"It's an earthen dam, Julie. Wherever you've got earth, plants are going to grow."

"I suppose I thought all dams were made of stone blocks or concrete—something solid like that."

"Mercy, no! Matter of fact, the earthen dam is the classic kind. It's only in the past fifty years that masonry and concrete have begun to replace them. My Uncle Whit taught me a lot about dams. He was an engineer, you know, the uncle I worked for, summers, as a teenager."

"What I don't understand is how just piled-up dirt can hold back such a lot of water."

The Editor swiveled the chair and leaned forward. "Earthen dams can be surprisingly strong, especially when reinforced with puddle or masonry or—"

"What's puddle?"

The Editor threw back his head and laughed. "Julie,

you've got the tenacity of a bulldog. Puddle's a gravel and clay mixture."

"Okay," I admitted. "I know nothing about dams except that this one gives me a funny feeling."

Dad pulled his watch out of his vest pocket, looked at it and rose to his feet. "Your imagination is running wild again, Julie, but at least you've gotten me interested in the Kissawha construction. When I can afford to run the Willys again, I'll drive up and take another look. Now I've got to go to Exley's Drug Store and see Mike Dugan about an ad."

"One more thing before you go, Dad. I can quit school and work here full-time if you need me."

My father's eyes suddenly filled with tears. He shook his head firmly, patted me on the shoulder and hurried out the door.

For another hour I concentrated on my proofreading. I had just started on the advertisements when I heard the front door open. Looking up, I was stunned to see Randolph Wilkinson.

Hastening to straighten up my pile of proofs, my hand knocked over the inkwell. *Clumsy oaf,* I chided myself as I reached for old newsprint to sop up the spilled ink. Mr. Wilkinson exchanged a few words with Miss Cruley, then headed for my work table. The proofs were ink-spotted and my hands were a mess.

He paused in front of me, his hazel eyes pleasant, his reddish blond hair windblown. Then he stuck out his hand. "Hallo, Julie."

My pulse was racing and I felt ridiculous. "Mr. Wilkinson, I can't shake hands with you. Mine is covered with ink."

A smile crossed his face. "Proves you're a real newspaper reporter."

I sighed. "I wish it did. What it really proves is that I'm a clumsy proofreader."

His eyes studied me. "And an honest proofreader too."

Again I felt the warmth creeping up my cheeks. Why couldn't I be relaxed, witty, composed? "My father will be back shortly," I told him, trying to steer the conversation into other channels.

"It isn't your father I came to see, Julie. Did you and your friend enjoy your stroll around the Club last Saturday?"

How much should I tell him? "We had a very nice picnic, thank you."

The Englishman's penetrating gaze held mine. "Was everything really all right?"

"Nearly everything. Your groundsman wasn't glad to see us."

"What did he do?"

"Oh—asked us to leave."

"I'm so sorry. James can be churlish. I rang him up when I got back to the Inn to tell him we had guests on the grounds, but his phone didn't answer. Julie, did James *do* anything, other than ask you and Miss Palmer to leave?"

I felt trapped. No matter how nasty the watchman had been, I hesitated to get him in trouble. But I wasn't going to lie about it. "I think he had been drinking. He fired his gun. Off into the woods. Just wanted to scare us, I think."

"I thought so! I could have sworn I heard a shot. James isn't good for anything when he's been tippling. Which is most of the time. He's got to be sacked."

"Please, Mr. Wilkinson, not because of us."

"Yes, Julie. Because of you and the other incidents that are bound to follow if we keep him."

His manner grew formal. "On behalf of the Club, I offer my apologies, Miss Wallace. Please tell Miss Palmer too. I hope this hasn't spoilt the place for you both." He paused. "I'm leaving for England, as you know, but I'll return the middle of March. I hope you'll come back and see us in the spring."

"Thank you," I managed to murmur.

With a sigh, I wondered if I would ever learn to be poised with a man like Randolph Wilkinson.

Or even Graham Gillin.

I had been startled in school earlier that week when Graham stopped me in the hall and asked if I would like to go to the movies with him this coming Saturday.

"Well, I guess so, Graham. I mean, thank you—yes."

He seemed amused at my confusion and I was furious with myself. Why did I have to act so dumb? Graham Gillin was fullback on the high school football team; he was big, strong and good-looking, with blond crew-cut hair, popular with both girls and boys.

At seven-thirty Saturday night he picked me up in his bright green Dodge roadster. Inwardly I rejoiced that I had lost five pounds since coming to Alderton.

The Palace Theater was a hangout for high school students on weekend nights. It had a balcony where the older kids flocked because smoking was allowed there and couples could neck a little, if they weren't too obvious.

The movie was *It Happened One Night* with Clark Gable and Claudette Colbert. Graham had led me to the top of the balcony. No sooner were we seated than he placed an arm over the back of my seat. When the picture began, I forgot everything else. Clark Gable became Randolph Wilkinson. There was no physical resemblance, but the same sophistication, the same charm—things I'd never before encountered off the screen. I of course became Claudette Colbert. Never had I so lost myself in a movie, especially the scene on the bus when the cold, haughty Colbert awakes after a nap to find herself snuggled in the arms of Clark Gable. When the movie was over, I found that I had moved close to Graham Gillin and was clutching his hand.

I drew back, mortified. *How had I let myself go this way?* Graham, however, was grinning from ear to ear.

Outside the theater he asked if I'd like to go to the Stem-winder for a beer.

I shook my head too emphatically and we settled on a soft drink at Exley's Drug Store. As we sat opposite each other in the booth, I was still too embarrassed to look him in the eye. Our conversation was stiff.

"Let's go for a drive," he suggested when we were back in his roadster.

As he headed up Seven Mile Mountain, I was still upset over my performance in the theater. *What must he think of me? What does he expect of me now out here in the night? Why didn't I insist that he take me home?*

Graham drove up the twisting road past the Hunting and Fishing Club to Lookout Point, from which our family had first viewed Alderton. There were already a half dozen cars parked there, couples in each car. I was getting panicky. "Please, Graham, let's go home."

He stared at me a moment. "I don't like this spot either."

He drove back down the winding mountain road. We'd gone perhaps four miles when he suddenly turned to the right onto a dirt road. He drove a few hundred yards, then pulled to the side, stopped the engine and snapped off the lights.

"Know where we are, Julie? Just ahead is McKeever's Bluff. That's where he brings his special railroad car."

Graham moved close beside me. "Let's pretend we're back in the theater," he said brightly. He put his arm around me. I pulled away.

"What's the matter, Julie? You give me one signal in the movie, another one now. Is my breath bad?"

"No."

"Do I have B.O.?"

"No."

"Then what is it?"

"I don't know."

"Let's start all over again."

As he reached for me, I groped for the door handle and

the door sprang open. I stepped out and began walking back toward the main road. Graham started the car, turned around, drew abreast of me.

"It's a long walk, Julie."

I kept going.

"Get in the car. I promise not to get within two feet of you."

I did and he kept his promise.

It was a miserable experience. Obviously, where men were concerned, I had everything to learn.

6

As Miss Cruley had predicted, the ancient Babcock printing press, vintage 1903, needed careful repairing almost every week. Dean Fleming kept the intricate contraption going, and also regularly adjusted and cleaned the old hand-operated Ludlow press used for job printing. He oiled the cutter, which trimmed the edges of newsprint, made minor repairs to the typewriters, started the coal furnace in the basement when the building supervisor dawdled.

When Mr. Fleming first volunteered to help, the Editor could not have guessed that so much work would be needed. But his unpaid assistant never faltered in his commitment; in fact, he worked more than the promised hours when necessary, so that Dad was soon talking about his maintenance man almost reverently. As friendship grew between the two men, they had long talks in the Editor's office.

One day in early December I overheard the Editor querying Mr. Fleming about local churches. "We've tried several," Dad said, "haven't found one we like. What church do you attend, Dean?"

"My sister and I like our little Yancyville Community Church. Probably too far away for you. Have you tried Baker Memorial?"

"Louise and I went there once. They have no pastor."

"Oh, but they do now. A young man, full of fire. I think you'll like him."

As a result of this conversation, Dad decreed that the whole family was to go to Baker Memorial the following Sunday. I was annoyed to have to cancel plans for a drive with Margo. As we walked the six blocks to church, I found myself resenting Dean Fleming's growing influence on our family.

Baker Memorial was on the corner of Main Street and Elm. We passed it every time we walked to downtown Alderton. The original stucco walls of the church must have been white, but years of Alderton's soft-coal grime had turned them a leprous gray. The leprous look came from huge bubbles or blisters in the stucco. Clearly, they had proved too great a temptation for generations of boys walking past: every bubble within reach of a rock or stick had been punched into an open sore where dirt could gather.

Inside, however, the uncertain December sun filtering through the stained glass windows laid patterns of soft color across the mahogany pews. And if the attractive interior was a surprise, the young preacher, Spencer Meloy, was even more so. He was tall, well over six feet, I guessed, had dark hair, dark-rimmed glasses, a lantern jaw, and a ready smile that transformed a rather angular face. A man in his twenties seemed too young to be the pastor of a prestigious church like Baker Memorial.

The Pileys, who attended Baker, had given Dad additional information about him. Spencer Meloy was the son of Judge Carleton Meloy of Philadelphia, a well-known lawyer and judge of the circuit court. The young pastor had come to Alderton in early November, leaving a small, 150-member church in a Philadelphia suburb. Meloy's name had been given to the Pulpit Committee by Thomas McKeever, Sr., president of Yoder Steel and the most influential member of the church. (Was there anything in town this man didn't run?) McKeever's long friendship with Judge Meloy seemed to be the deciding factor—plus the youthful pastor's vigorous, enthusiastic preaching style and, Dad suspected, the low salary he was willing to take.

"Vincent Piley says that Meloy's sermons have been controversial," my father reported. "And apparently he's raised some eyebrows by inviting workingmen and Negroes to church. I gather that the church officers selected him because he is so personable and, they thought, young enough to be malleable. Now they're not so sure."

The pleasant voice from the pulpit was reading Scripture:

He hath anointed me to preach the gospel to the poor; he hath sent me to heal the brokenhearted . . . to preach deliverance to the captives.

Soon the pastor was into his sermon, describing village life in Jesus' day. Why, I wondered, did I have such trouble keeping my mind on sermons? I could get excited about the plot of a story, or racial injustice, or even about a concept like the League of Nations, yet never experience that same kind of involvement with preaching, not even my own father's, back in Timmeton.

Then I noticed something. This new preacher may have invited workers and Negroes to attend services, but I could not find one person who fitted these categories. The congregation seemed to be made up entirely of middle- or upper-class white people. *Just like Timmeton.* Unbidden, unwanted, a host of memories crowded out the softly colored sanctuary in Pennsylvania, brought back those painful last years in Alabama . . .

It had begun with Mother searching for someone to make some curtains and help with household mending. I had first seen Mattie Howard when she appeared at our house one day to measure our front windows. The tall, dignified black woman was not only an expert seamstress but also a teacher in her Ebenezer Baptist Church's Sunday School.

A few months after she came to sew for us, Dad had somehow paved the way for Mattie and two women from other Negro churches in our area to attend a national Christian Education meeting in Indianapolis. All three had come back to Timmeton with enthusiastic plans to improve their Sunday School curricula. They invited Mother, who taught a women's Bible class at Dad's church, to meet with their teachers once a week as they launched their new programs.

Mother agreed. Since the Negro churches were small and scattered, she suggested the basement room of our own church for this weekly meeting. My father needed the permission of his Board of Elders for this use of church property.

Dad reported to us that at first the opposition seemed mild and good-humored: chivalrous objection to how much of Mother's time the teacher-training course would take; the practical necessity of keeping church heating and lighting expenses down by limiting evening meetings.

Then one of Timmeton's outstanding lawyers and a close friend of my father's had risen to his feet and, according to Dad, said something like this: "Now, Ken, we all realize how open-hearted you are to people. But you're a Virginian. What you must understand is that the ratio of coloreds to whites here in Alabama is at least four to one. That's always handed us special problems. After the Great War, Negro soldiers came back from overseas restless and ready to cause big trouble. We've had to be on guard. A thing like this will boomerang every time. You're a good man, Ken, and I want to protect you and your family. I vote a flat No against letting down the bars this way."

My father had obviously been nettled. "Do you mean to tell me that intelligent men like you would make a decision like this on the basis of *fear?* What are you afraid of? An uprising sparked by Mattie Howard?

"Look here, I love you guys. You're my friends. But gentlemen, *you're missing the point.* Jesus Christ gave us clear instructions: 'Feed My sheep . . . feed My lambs.' All Mattie Howard has asked for is a little feeding. Isn't that the business of this church—any church?"

Silence. Two or three of the men present, I gathered, had looked decidedly uncomfortable. But as my father studied the faces of the others, he saw only a sudden and inexplicable hardness of heart in men whose basic nature was generous and loving. He told us later that his faith in the ability of the Christian church to change men's hearts began to drain away at that point.

In the days that followed, although my parents tried to hold their conversations away from us children, I knew they were upset. Mother then suggested that she go to Mattie's own Ebenezer Church to conduct the weekly teacher's training class. Surely no one could object to that.

Wrong again. One of the elders got wind of it, talked with the other men on the Church Session, then came to see my father at his church office one afternoon. The elder had been polite but firm. The wife of their pastor could not teach a class in any Negro church. If she did so, she would end up being the most gossiped-about woman in Timmeton; the officers of the church would then be helpless to protect her good name and reputation.

"Are you going to let them do that to us?" Mother asked, as angry as I had ever seen her.

In the end Father had capitulated to his elders because, as he pointed out, under church law he had no choice. But looking back, I wondered if this hadn't been the beginning of the series of things that went so very, very wrong for Dad. A few months later came that teaching mission in Louisiana, the attack of malaria, the hospitalization . . .

* * *

Belatedly I reined in my runaway thoughts. Spencer Meloy was about to close his sermon. And he seemed to be looking directly at me:

> So this morning let's take a good look at the way our church is going, be ruthlessly honest with ourselves. *Are* we preaching the gospel to the poor? Really ministering to the brokenhearted among us? What about the captives of all kinds—captives of alcohol, of disease, of racial prejudice?
>
> Where would Jesus be in our town? I'll tell you where. He would accept invitations to dinner at the wealthiest homes—without hesitation, gladly. But most of the time He'd be down in the Lowlands, yes, even in and out of the bars, seeing what burdens He could lift from the bruised shoulders of men.

Mr. Meloy lowered his voice.

> My friends, you and I together in this church are making a new start. Let's have the courage to forget traditional barriers that divide "them" from "us." We have to be willing to forge new paths if we would follow the Master.

Something stirred in me. No pastor would have preached this kind of sermon in Timmeton. For the first time, I felt a rush of affection for my new home town.

On the way out of church, Mr. and Mrs. Piley joined us and introduced us to some of the members. Among them was a florid-faced man in his mid-sixties, balding except for a white fringe around his head. His thickening figure carried, with unaffected grace, a suit of the finest woolen fabric I had ever seen.

"Good morning, Mr. McKeever," Mr. Piley greeted him deferentially. "How is your family today, sir?"

"My son and his wife are in Pittsburgh for the weekend. I'm here with my grandson."

Bryan McKeever and I had already nodded to each other. He was in my math and English classes, a boy who had a history of trouble in various private schools: poor grades, unexcused absences, drinking. Small for his age, Bryan was the only boy who had asked me for a date (which I had declined) in the months that followed my humiliating evening with Graham Gillin. The word had spread through school, Margo told me, that I was not very friendly.

"Mr. McKeever," Mr. Piley went on, "I'd like you to meet Kenneth Wallace, new owner of *The Sentinel.*"

The two men shook hands, stepping to one side so that the line could move on. I found myself fascinated with McKeever's face. The skin was rutted, dotted with small brown blotches, the gray eyes penetrating, stormy. I learned later that he had been a widower for the past four years.

"You're a man of courage, Mr. Wallace. Newspapers haven't done very well in Alderton."

"Why is that, Mr. McKeever?"

"Because they've been run by idiots." His eyes bored so fiercely into my father's that Dad stepped back. "I hope you can learn from their failures."

"I hope so too."

"By the way"—those intense eyes never seemed to blink—"Yoder might have a printing order for you. Get in touch with my son. We're preparing a new booklet for our employees."

My father was in high spirits as we walked home. "I like this church and I like Spencer Meloy. And a Yoder Steel print job! What a windfall!"

If the company was laying off men and slowing production, I found myself wondering, why a booklet? That wasn't going to put food on workers' tables.

But Dad was so elated that I kept my thoughts to myself.

7

I⊤ was doubtful that *The Sentinel* would survive the winter. Over five hundred people had dropped their subscriptions since Dad took over. He continued sending the paper to hundreds more who didn't pay their bills. Somehow we got through December, including a very lean Christmas. Dad ran out of money in January and again the bank refused to give him a loan.

One mid-January morning the Editor told us at breakfast that this week's would be the final edition. No one said a word.

In school that day I didn't hear a thing that went on in any of my classes. That afternoon I opened the door to *The Sentinel,* dreading the I-told-you-so lecture I expected from Emily Cruley. But the green-visored head was bent to a paper-cluttered desk.

The Editor was in his office, a dazed look on his face. "Dean Fleming came here this morning with a check for five hundred dollars."

I stared at my father, speechless.

"He said it should get us through the winter."

"A loan?" I asked numbly.

"Don't know. Dean just handed me the check and left."

When my father began to sob, I did too.

Disaster had been averted for the Wallace family at the very last moment, but not for others throughout the nation. Thousands of businesses closed that bleak winter of 1934–35. The recovery program was getting some people back to work in the big cities, but in smaller places like Alderton, the economic malaise hung on.

My father had contacted Tom McKeever, Jr., by phone the day after the conversation with his father at Baker Memorial. The younger McKeever was encouraging and told the Editor that Yoder would soon be in touch about an order. Weeks passed, however, and nothing happened.

Since Dean's money had been earmarked to save *The Sentinel,* Dad decreed that none of it could be diverted to family needs. Meat disappeared totally from the table; soup and crackers, macaroni and spaghetti became our standard fare. My own worst moment came one Saturday when Mother had an abscessed tooth—dental visits were out of the question—and we were without cash for the week's groceries. I had to ask for credit at the A & P. The store manager sighed wearily at my request, then gave me a form that required my father's signature before the groceries would be released.

Our plight was doubly frustrating because, it seemed to me, we'd come so close to succeeding, those first months in Alderton. The Editor had worked days, nights and weekends, to learn everything he could about Alderton. He had run a series of articles on community services: snow removal, hospital care, how to use the library, flood protection. His editorials called for a job information center, more public parking facilities, a town beautification program. Since ads were few, there was plenty of room in the four-page *Sentinel* for local color items and service features.

To establish a personal relationship with his subscribers, Dad had been calling on a certain number each week, often receiving compliments on how "lively" the paper had become.

As for me, my own private fantasy had taken flight. I loved my after-school work on *The Sentinel,* but my long-range dreams went far beyond writing for a weekly newspaper. Only in my most secret thoughts could I admit the full scope of it: I wanted to be an author, a real author like Emily Brontë or Louisa May Alcott or Ellen Glasgow or Mary Roberts Rinehart. That I was a high school girl in a town stuck away in the mountains of western Pennsylvania did not matter. I would become the best proofreader and researcher I could possibly be—and hold on to my dream.

Sometimes I wondered how and when this dream had started. For as far back as I could remember, the sound of words, the reading of stories, even the handling of books had not been merely a delight—it had been irresistible enchantment.

A scene from Timmeton often rose in my mind. I was a very little girl, standing on a kitchen chair and reciting Robert Louis Stevenson's verses to our cook, Josephine. I could still remember my ecstatic, almost sensuous pleasure in the music of rhythms tripping from my tongue . . .

> *Dark brown is the river,*
> *Golden is the sand,*
> *It flows along forever*
> *With trees on either hand . . .*

Some years later a particular book had brought my dream into focus. Not a great book, just a girl's romance: *Emily of New Moon*. Emily, the heroine of the story, yearned to be a writer too. And her feelings and thoughts about this had flowed onto the pages of the book with such emotion that instinctively I knew: Emily's creator, Lucy Mand Montgomery, had been writing about herself.

Sharing Emily's thoughts and hopes had crystallized my own, spurred me into keeping my early-morning journal and trying to capture on paper events and impressions, sights and sounds. It was fun to hear a snatch of conversation in the grocery store and to wonder how the words would look on paper. All speech had certain cadences and rhythms.

But it had seemed a colossal step from my secret journal to breaking into print—until the move to Alderton. Through *The Sentinel,* I believed, a door was opening before me. Just a crack, but I intended to be ready. The article about the Hunting and Fishing Club was to be my entrée. If I had a few such pieces written and, at just the right moment, slipped them to the Editor, maybe, just maybe . . .

I had also typed up two poems I had composed. Unsure of their merit, I had deliberately left off my name when I deposited them with a pile of other work on the Editor's desk. To be doing something tangible—even anonymously—about my ambition had felt so good.

But now, in spite of all our effort, Emily Cruley's loyalty and Mr. Fleming's generosity, *The Sentinel* was still in trouble. Subscriptions dropped month after month.

One morning in early February my father did not get out of bed. "Another malaria attack," Mother told us at breakfast. When I looked in on him, he tried to smile at me, but his eyes misted up. Filled with fear, I went to the *Sentinel* office that day instead of going to school. Between Miss Cruley, Dean Fleming and myself, we somehow got the paper out that week. And the next. And somehow Mother found food to put on the table.

It tore my heart to see my father lying there day after day so weak and haggard. Hardest for me to take were the tears. They came at unexpected moments and over the smallest setbacks. The doctor gave him quinine pills, the standard medication for malaria, but the Editor's illness seemed unaffected. When I mentioned this to Mother, she looked sharply at me for a moment, then stated that Dad had a combination of malaria and flu.

Each evening I went to Father's bedroom with my notebook to write down instructions for the next day's work at *The Sentinel.* I gathered data for articles through phone conversations or in short interviews after school. I typed up the items, read them to him (he rarely had changes) and presented them to Miss Cruley as from the Editor himself. She never questioned the procedure. For the whole month of February we ran *The Sentinel* this way.

More and more Dean Fleming would come by the house. He would limp upstairs and sit by my father's bedside for hours. Neither Mother nor I could figure out what they found to talk about at such length.

On the Third of March we had our first springlike day. In the mail that morning was another cause for celebration: orders for two quarter-page ads, one from Wagner Lumber and another from Mason's Hardware—both totally unexpected. When I called Dad, he sobbed over the phone. That night he dressed and took his place at the dinner table for the first time in almost four weeks.

Two more ads came in the following week: Rosemont Funeral Home and Gaither's Clothing Store. I wondered—had *The Sentinel* under its new ownership passed through some kind of testing period and been found trustworthy? The slide in subscriptions had also stopped. Later that week the Editor returned to work.

Equally inexplicable was the fact that I seemed to be more acceptable to my high school peers. My seriousness about school work and a straight-A average had initially drawn such labels as ''bookworm'' and ''snob.'' After our fiasco of a date, Graham had ignored me for weeks, and this had somehow communicated a stay-away message to the other boys. My reticence and perhaps a bit of stubbornness kept me from attempting to correct this image.

Margo had tried to help me. ''The kids just feel that you're stuck up, Julie.''

''If only they could see inside and know how unsure I am about everything.''

''But you *are* very pretty, Julie, and you look so confident, and you know so much. There's a lot of jealousy too.''

Now, one by one, my classmates were warming up to me. Was it sympathy for my father's illness and the fact that I had to stay out of school a lot to help at *The Sentinel?* Did my new slimness make a difference? Twelve pounds had come off since last fall. The stringency of Mother's food budget sure had helped.

Whatever the reason, Bryan McKeever asked me for a date a second time and I accepted. We went bowling, which I enjoyed; he drank two beers, but there was no wrestling match in his car. Dates with others followed, even a couple of decorous goodnight kisses. I realized I should feel excited as well as flattered by all this, but in pouring out my feelings in the pages of my journal, I discovered to my surprise that nothing gave me as much of an emotional high now as listening to Spencer Meloy exhort his congregation each Sunday.

This amazed me. I hadn't thought anyone could stir me the way Randolph Wilkinson had. I was continually learning things about myself. One Saturday morning, I made these observations in my journal:

What is there in me that makes me want to reach for the unreachable? Here are two older men who live in completely different worlds. What an enormous ego I must have to think I can get their attention. Is this a kind of haughtiness? Do I feel, deep down, that I'm better than other people?

I had other friends now, yet Margo was still the one closest to me. Sometimes when I finished early at *The Sentinel,* I'd walk over Railroad Bridge to the Stemwinder and help her set up tables while we chatted.

The Stemwinder was a sprawling two-story tavern-restaurant, painted barn red. Over the door was one of those colonial-looking taproom signs with Old English lettering, swinging from a wrought iron hanger. *Sam Palmer, Proprietor* was printed at the bottom.

The restaurant section was generally deserted in the late afternoon, giving Margo and me plenty of chance to talk and occasionally even to escape upstairs to her room in the living quarters on the second floor. The adjoining barroom, though, was jammed at this time of day, mostly with workmen in soot-blackened overalls coming off the day shift at Yoder. Margo's father, a small dapper man with a neatly trimmed mustache and dark eyebrows, presided behind a long bar with rows of polished glasses and bottles of wine and liquor glittering in the big mirror behind him. He was very insistent that neither of us set foot in the bar area while what he called "the regulars" were there.

That was fine with me. My second time there, I'd caught a glimpse of a face in the bar mirror, clearly visible from the dining room, that almost made my heart stop beating. *James, the watchman at Lake Kissawha.* The one who had fired at Margo and me that day in October when we visited the Club. A solitary figure hunched over his drink at the far end of the bar, he appeared to be listening rather than taking part in the boisterous conversations around him. I slipped to the rear of the room, out of sight of the mirror, but when I whispered to Margo who was there, she only shrugged. He'd been coming to the Stemwinder for months, she said, and had never seemed to recognize her. "He was too drunk that day to remember," she concluded.

During this same visit I met Cade and Neal Brinton, brothers who worked at Yoder. They stopped at the Stemwinder often after work and took their drinks in the dining room because, Margo admitted a bit self-consciously, "Neal likes to kid around with me." Neal was craggy-faced, broad-shouldered, a giant of a man. Cade, the older, was shorter, bearded, argumentative.

While waiting in the vestibule to say good-bye to

Margo, I overheard an explosive bit of dialogue between the two brothers.

"Can't understand, Neal, why you listen to their garbage."

"How do ya know it's garbage?"

"Because anything Yoder Steel offers is garbage. I wouldn't trust 'em as far as I can spit."

"Cade, you haven't even s-s-seen their plan."

"No need to. I know McKeever."

"S-s-so, what's *your* plan?"

"Set up a *real* union. Make demands that mean somethin' for a change. If the McKeevers don't give, then strike. If every worker walks out, they'd hafta concede to us."

"S-sounds good, Cade, except that if they shut the furnaces down, we'll have a lot of families s-starvin' in Alderton."

A string of obscenities poured from the one called Cade.

"Cade, workers are not going t' get everything we want right off. Sure, conditions s-stink at Yoder. But if Tom McKeever is offering a plan that'll give us more benefits, let's look at it."

More epithets from Cade. "You make me sick to my stomach, Neal. And you my own blood brother. Don't you understand yet? This rotten ERP's no better'n a yellow dog contract."

Margo appeared and I left the Stemwinder with Cade's angry words ringing in my ears. I didn't like this man, but I sensed he was expressing the feelings of many Yoder steelworkers.

8

WHEN I arrived at the office late one afternoon in early April, a set of freshly pulled proofs was on my work table. The Editor, I was informed, was out calling on merchants.

The front door opened and closed, and a well-remembered voice began talking to Miss Cruley. My head shot up.

Randolph Wilkinson! He had returned from England.

Trying to stifle the fluttering in my stomach, I forced my eyes back to the proofs. But everything in me was straining to hear the conversation. The Englishman was asking for prices on the printing of menus, and Miss Cruley was very formal, saying, "You'll need to get this information from Mr. Wallace."

Why couldn't the woman be more friendly?

If only Randolph would look up and see me! But he did not. He nodded politely to Miss Cruley, said "Cheerio," and walked out.

I was crushed.

Later in the week, still smarting over Randolph Wilkinson's indifference, I was standing at the make-ready table inserting correction slugs in ad copy when I felt a tap on my shoulder. I turned to see the smiling eyes of our pastor, the Reverend Spencer Meloy.

"Julie, do you have a few moments to talk?"

Quickly I looked at Miss Cruley. She was deep in conversation with one of the paper's local correspondents.

"Would you like to sit down here at my work table or go into my father's office?" I asked. "Dad's gone home."

Reverend Meloy nodded toward the office and insisted that I take the comfortable chair behind the desk. He was looking at me in such an open and friendly way that I was momentarily tongue-tied.

"I'm sorry we don't have a more comfortable place to talk, Reverend Meloy," I said lamely, annoyed that my face was getting warm.

"This will do fine, Julie. And please don't call me Reverend. That's for older and more learned pastors. As I get to know my people, I want them to use my first name."

He paused, his restless eyes taking in everything about the small office before they settled back on me. "I have no purpose in coming here other than to get to know you," he said calmly. "I'm especially interested in young people and I'm hoping that our church will soon be teeming with them."

"I have a friend, Margo Palmer, who might come." Then, after a short pause to reflect, "Her father runs the Stemwinder."

"Please do invite her, Julie. Tell her we're a church that cares about all the people in our community."

"My father felt that way too about his church in Timmeton," I said impulsively. "Very few people in his congregation went along with him."

Meloy's eyes searched mine. "I know a little about that, Julie, and I'm sorry. I wish it could have been different for him."

"Is it different in Alderton, Mr. Meloy?" I asked. "I mean, are people here more accepting somehow of colored people, foreign people, poor people?"

Meloy did not answer immediately. "I don't know for sure the answer to that question, Julie," he said at last. "But I intend to find out."

The last words were so charged that I looked at the

pastor in astonishment and was struck again by his almost boyish manner. It was reflected in the casual sports jacket and slacks he wore, and the two-tone suede shoes. This pastor of one of the more affluent churches in Alderton was startlingly honest and, yes, uncertain about himself. More than that, he was reaching out to me for something. What was it? Acceptance? Support? Friendship? Possibly all three.

"Julie, just because your family had one bad experience, don't write all churches off."

"I'm sure we wouldn't do that," I said, too quickly. "I guess it's hard for me to believe the McKeevers and Pileys and others like them are very eager to sit next to workers from the Lowlands."

"Our church is open to everyone, Julie. You've heard me say that from the pulpit." He paused. "Did you know that it was largely through the McKeevers that I was called to this church?"

"Yes—and that surprised me."

"My father is a close friend of the McKeevers. But few people in the church really know me, including the McKeevers," he went on. "I'm the son of a famous judge, acquainted with the right people . . . therefore my credentials seem faultless. The truth is, Julie, I've never gotten along too well with 'the right people.' I don't think I even like them. I don't believe what they believe; I don't share their goals; in fact, I'm opposed to most of the things they stand for. That would put me in an awkward, yes, impossible spot—except for one thing. I believe God has me here for a purpose. So I intend to hang around until I find out what it is."

Getting such an inside look at this impulsive man numbed and confused me for a moment. Perhaps he sensed that. "Julie, I tell you these things because for some reason I felt we were kindred spirits the first time you came to our church. It was something I saw in your face when I was preaching. Being a pastor is a lonely life, especially when you're a bachelor. I seek friends. Will you be one to me?''

I was so moved by his plea that I impulsively reached out my hand to touch his. "Of course I will."

Quickly I tried to draw it away, but he wouldn't let me. Instead he took it in his. "This handshake seals it." He smiled. "And, please, call me Spencer."

As he walked out of the office, he turned around and smiled at me again. "I'll expect to hear from you, Julie, if you have any ideas for helping people here in Alderton."

The rain began that afternoon. *Something foreboding about this downpour,* I thought as I stood at our front window that evening, staring at the wet blur of the corner street light on Bank Place. Almost four hours of it: a steady tattoo on roofs and pavements, rain splattering off windowpanes, running in twin rivulets down the gutters of our street. With a violent thunderstorm the fury was soon spent, but this was different. There was something ominous in the settled-in, unremitting quality of this rain.

My thoughts turned back to Spencer Meloy and to his astonishing statements. He was so young to be preaching to people like the McKeevers. I wondered what would happen if the elders and trustees of the church knew of Meloy's deepest convictions.

"Tim? Anne-Marie?" I spun around to see my father entering the study, quickly followed by my brother and sister. "I have a surprise for you two." There was a twinkle in Dad's brown eyes. "Several weeks ago, Dean Fleming's collie, Queenie, had a litter of five whelps. He has one for you. That is, if you'd like it—"

"Oh, yes!" Anne-Marie exulted.

"Dad, what's a 'whelp'?" from Tim.

"That's a puppy who's still living on his mother's milk. Mr. Fleming says that all the puppies are weaned now. I'll drive you up there Friday afternoon, provided you have *all* the papers delivered and in the mail."

* * *

By Friday we still had not seen the sun. Six to seven inches of rain had fallen and the muddy, swollen waters of both Brady Creek and the Sequanoto River were beginning to overflow their banks. In the trough amid the mountains where Alderton nestled, there had been intermittent letups in the soaking rain, but the radio verified that it was still coming down steadily in the higher mountains all around us.

With all the papers delivered and mailed by late afternoon on Friday, Dad got out the Willys for the drive to Yancyville, the first time we had used the car this year. I decided to go along because Dean Fleming had been a mystery man to me ever since he had first appeared at the *Sentinel* office. I was curious to see him in his home situation.

Mother had agreed to the puppy with one reservation—that he be regarded by all of us as a yard dog, not a house dog. That meant a dog house. With some suggestions and a little help from Dad, Tim and Anne-Marie had already started building a fearful and wonderful "mansion" for the puppy.

Yancyville was a hamlet of several hundred people, boasting one grocery store, one general store, a small community church and two gasoline pumps. Mr. Fleming's farm was a quarter of a mile beyond the village.

As we drove into the yard, we saw a white frame house, three stories high, with dormer windows on the top floor. A wide front porch was overshadowed by towering oaks and maples, their bare limbs showing the first buds of spring green.

Mr. Fleming came limping from the porch through the rain with an umbrella to greet us, then guided us one at a time across the soggy grass toward a woman who was standing in the doorway.

"My sister, Hazel," he introduced her.

As I took her groping hand, I remembered Mr. Fleming's description of his sister's blindness. Her visual

world was one of muted light and dim shadows. She was
a tall, spare woman, wearing a cotton calico dress with a
full skirt almost to her ankles. Thin, graying hair was
pulled straight back into a bun; thick glasses sat astride a
rather large nose.

It was soon apparent that Miss Hazel had memorized
the shape of every piece of furniture in the farmhouse,
along with the width, depth and height of every room,
doorway and closet. Later in the kitchen I marveled at
how surely she moved about. She and Dean were a physically handicapped sister-brother team who served each
other well.

Dean Fleming rumpled Tim's already disheveled hair
as he led him and Anne-Marie into the house. "Queenie's
on the back porch."

We followed them down a wide center hall, through a
spacious kitchen to a screened verandah. Queenie was lying there on an old quilt; somersaulting all around her
were five balls of fur. The mother was a beautiful dog,
mostly butterscotch, with the snow-white ruff and white
breast of a collie.

"She's still protective of her babies," Mr. Fleming
warned. "So look, don't touch yet."

We left the children on the porch and joined Miss Hazel in the kitchen, where she was pulling out of the oven a
batch of molasses oatmeal cookies. From the conversation that ensued, I gathered that Dean Fleming's unmarried sister had come to keep house for her brother after
the death of his wife five years before. The old farmhouse, surrounded by its twenty acres, had been home
most of Dean Fleming's married life. The two children
who had been reared there were now married, living in
other states, with children of their own.

Before his retirement from the Pennsylvania Railroad,
Mr. Fleming told us, he had been forced to rise each
morning at four-thirty in order to get to work on time
from the farm. In his eyes this was a small price to pay
for the embrace of the fields around him, the stands of

timber, the tumbling stream that originated high in the mountains.

"Dean, are you a native Pennsylvanian?" Dad asked him.

"That I am. Born in Port Allegheny." Our host went on to say that his father had been killed in a logging accident when Dean was eleven. At fourteen he had dropped out of school to apprentice himself to a machinist, though he'd kept up his education on his own, reading everything he could lay his hands on. By eighteen he was head maintenance man on a logging train. After marriage and two babies in three years, Dean went to work for the Pennsylvania Railroad.

He was interrupted by a call from Anne-Marie. Soon I was alone in the kitchen, staring out the window at a small log cabin on higher ground at the edge of a small grove of trees. The rain had started again and was pouring off the roof of the cabin in a small stream. Then I noticed a glistening object fastened to the side of the wide stone chimney. My eyes strained to see what it was.

"The cabin interests you, Julie?"

I jumped. The question came from Dean Fleming, who had returned.

"Yes, it does, Mr. Fleming. That shining object on the chimney. What is it?"

"An ax. Not a real one. I cut it out of aluminum."

"An ax! It looks more like a cross."

Dean Fleming chuckled. "John Hammond followed the cross, but he also carried an ax."

"John Hammond?"

"You must have heard me talk about Big John—quote some of his favorite sayings?"

"Yes-s." I didn't want to admit how easily I tuned out conversations that tended to get "religious."

"Big John is a legend northeast of here in logging country."

Something in his voice made me turn around to stare at Dean Fleming. He was still gazing at the cabin with a

warm, tender look on his homely face. I was about to ask
what Big John had to do with the cabin when Dean suddenly changed the subject. "I'm curious about you,
Julie. Not many people who come here notice the
cabin—scarcely anyone the symbol on the chimney."

"The rain made it shimmer. It's almost luminous."

Dean's eyes were studying me. "You have a way with
words. What kind of writing do you want to do?"

"Articles for Dad's paper, to start."

"What do you want to write about?"

I paused, suddenly uncertain about how much to share.
Dean's eyes were reassuring.

"When I know more, I'd like to write about deeper
things."

Dean Fleming did not answer immediately. He looked
away from me to fasten his eyes again on the log cabin.
"Someday you may want to write about that cabin.
There's a story there that should be told by someone
who's meant to write about deeper things."

9

WHEN I awakened Saturday morning, my father was already up and dressed. He hurriedly ate a bowl of cereal and despite Mother's protests, strode off in the rain for *The Sentinel*. I stayed home to help with the housecleaning.

Dean Fleming had predicted the night before that if the rain did not stop, the water would reach flood level in downtown Alderton sometime Saturday afternoon. "I'll have some men at *The Sentinel* in the morning," he had promised as we were leaving his farm.

"For what, exactly?" Dad had asked tensely.

"To move stuff upstairs. That office is in a bad spot."

Now the Editor had really shown alarm, the vein throbbing in his neck. "How'll we move the Babcock press or the cutter or . . ."

"Hold it, Ken!" Dean's voice had been soothing. "You don't move heavy machinery. You grease it like they do at Yoder Steel. No need for concern yet. The rain may stop."

But it had not. By noon we were getting flood bulletins. At three came an alert from Station KDKA, Pittsburgh:

Important announcement for all residents of Alderton and surrounding areas! This is a General Flood Warning. Waters of the Sequanoto River and Brady Creek are now rising three inches an hour; they have reached flood crest and are overflowing their banks. Stay tuned to this station for bulletins.

Mother could scarcely pull herself from the radio to prepare supper, she was so worried about Dad. Tim and Anne-Marie even left their new puppy, a taffy-colored male they had named Boy, to listen to the reports. We tried phoning *The Sentinel;* the line was dead. When the Editor still had not come home by seven o'clock, I asked Mother to let me take some sandwiches and a thermos bottle of coffee down to the office. She shook her head.

"How can those men do heavy work on empty stomachs?" I pleaded. "I'll wear my boots. If I can't get through, I'll turn around and come back."

Mother finally gave in and we set to work making sandwiches. At last I set out in yellow slicker, matching hat, and knee-high boots. On each arm I carried a hamper as waterproofed as we could make them. Mom's parting admonition rang in my ears—I was to take no chances. If downtown Alderton looked dangerously flooded, I was to turn back. Not defined: what constituted "dangerous."

When I turned the corner from Bank Place into Main, the frothy, muddy water racing down the street was already licking at the top of the curbstones. As I walked past Baker Memorial toward the business section, the interiors of homes were easily visible through their lighted windows. It was like viewing a series of stage sets on which intimate dramas were being enacted. Families were feverishly taking up carpeting; women were standing on ladders or chairs to lift down draperies or curtains, children were emptying the lower shelves of bookcases, piling papers and bric-a-brac on tables. In one home a group of men were straining to lift a piano onto chairs. In another, residents were passing tray after tray of glass jars through a cellar door.

By now I was sloshing through water lapping up over the sidewalk. Ahead, in front of the first block of stores, the sidewalks and the street were indistinguishable—just one lake of muddy water. Six inches deep? A foot? Well, I would soon know.

Under a street light almost at the bottom of the hill, I stopped, staring, not sure I could believe my eyes. The corner house had a fenced-in yard, and along the top railing of the fence scurried several large, ugly rats. I shivered and waited until they were well out of sight before going on.

I shoved down the thought that if Mother could see this whole scene it would easily qualify as "dangerous," for the water in places was already gushing over the top of my boots. But Dad and the others needed that food and coffee. I had to go on. A few steps more and there was a new problem . . . my boots were so full of water that I could scarcely lift my feet.

Suddenly the street lights went out!

I nearly panicked as I stood in the inky blackness, feeling the clammy water slosh into my boots, unable to move for fear of falling. To my great relief, faint glows began to appear in the stores—kerosene lanterns, flashlights, even candles.

I walked slowly on, passing Exley's Drug Store, the A & P and B. J. Scott's. Many employees were working against time to clear all lower shelves of stock.

At the corner of Main and Canal, I heard laughter coming from Gillin Auto Supply. I knew that laugh: Graham Gillin, son of the owner, Ted Gillin. Graham had been cool to me for months. I hoped he would be friendly now; I had great need for human contact and a moment of rest. Cautiously, I waded towards the front door.

Graham stared at me as I splashed in. "Julie Wallace! What are you doing here?"

"Taking some food to *The Sentinel*," I gasped.

Graham rushed forward to grab the baskets and place them on a high shelf as I now stood in only ankle-deep water. I noticed that Graham, his father, and two other men, all barefooted with pants legs rolled up, were lifting new tires and other automotive products to metal shelving built high off the floor.

Graham was looking at my boots. "Easy to see you've never been through this before," he teased. "Bare feet or hip-high fishermen's boots—nothing else is any good at all."

Before I knew what was happening, Graham had hoisted me onto the counter. What relief when he tugged the boots off and laughingly emptied out what seemed like a gallon of water from each one.

I gave myself five minutes of rest, then put my boots back on. In all probability, Graham told me, they were going to have to work most of the night to save the new tires in their paper wrappings from water damage.

As I pushed open the door of the *Sentinel* office and the men spied the baskets of refreshments, an avalanche of loud cheers, whistles and bear hugs greeted me. Apparently Dean Fleming's volunteers had already worked long hours without nourishment. They had not stopped to eat because the water had been rising so rapidly; it was already seeping onto the *Sentinel* floor.

Dad looked unutterably weary. He was surprised to see me—amazed that Mother would let me come. Dean and the three rugged-looking men with him were in shirtsleeves and wearing old work pants held up by suspenders, "galluses" as they called them. With their faces streaked with grease, dirt, and black ink smudges, and only the whites of their eyes showing in the dim candlelight, they looked like actors in a minstrel show.

As I poured coffee into tin cups and handed out the sandwiches, I got a quick overview of what they had been doing. My father was boxing away subscription lists, accounts, editorial files, copy and layouts for the next issues. These would go to the second floor.

The other men had been moving to the second floor all typewriters, furniture, the small Ludlow job press, and valuable type racks and trays with our growing assortment of fonts. How did Dean Fleming round up such efficient volunteer workers, I wondered.

When I had first walked in with the sandwiches and coffee, the men had just finished greasing the lower parts of the Babcock press and the cutter. I was told that they did not dare apply grease to the rollers and the folder machinery or these parts might never operate smoothly again.

As the men took big bites of their sandwiches and gulped coffee from their cups, they were trying to decide how to move the two unwieldy containers of paper used by the flatbed Babcock press. This was Dad's sole supply for printing *The Sentinel* over the next month or so, all he had been able to afford. The problem was, each container weighed over 700 pounds.

"How'd you get them in here, Ken?" one man asked.

"I hate to tell you. They backed the truck close to the rear door. Four men on the truck made a roadbed of old tires set up side by side, from the truck through the back door. They slid the paper off the truck, onto the tires, and into the building."

"*Jehoshaphat!* That don't help us none. Don't have no truck tires. No way the five of us can haul the paper up those steps."

"Gillin Auto Supply may have truck tires," I volunteered. "If not, I just saw four people there who might help."

Deam Fleming nodded. "Tires or not, we sure need more manpower to get these big containers up to that landing—"

Automatically, all eyes went to the flat area some sixteen steps up.

The food and hot coffee had miraculously restored strength and morale. One man dashed out in the direction of Gillin's and was soon back with Graham and his father, ready to lend a hand at *The Sentinel* in return for reciprocal help at their store. They brought along two steel upright hand carriers to hoist the containers up one step at a time. With the new equipment and the heft of so many men, the paper was soon safely deposited on the landing and covered with a tarpaulin.

That done, my father issued an ultimatum to me. "And now, you, Julie Wallace—time to go home."

I started to protest, but the firm look on Dad's face told me it was no use.

"He's right, Julie," Dean confirmed. "You took a chance coming down here. From here on, this is strictly man's work."

With that remark, I saw Graham Gillin grin and stick out his chest. *Botheration!* I thought. *Males have such egos.*

"Let me go with you," Graham offered.

"Thanks, Graham." Dad smiled at him. "There's a rowboat anchored outside. You may need it now."

"Hey, that's a great idea. C'mon, Julie, let's go rowin'."

Outside, the glow from flashlights and candles flickered eerily over the rising water. Graham waded through knee-deep muck to untie the rowboat and held it for me as I climbed in. Then he took one oar, moved to the rear of the boat, and propelled us forward with short, twisting strokes. "Sculling," he called it.

As we glided down Main Street, past the darkened stores, I felt a new warmth toward him. "This must be like riding a gondola in the canals of Venice," I ventured.

"You prefer this to a drive up Seven Mile Mountain, right, Julie?"

"I don't like to think about that night, Graham. I felt like such a fool."

"You made me feel like the fool."

"I'm sorry for that. Can we forget it and be friends?"

"Sure, Julie." In the semidarkness, he had stopped sculling and was staring at me. "But let's define friendship." He grimaced. "Do you want us to be platonic, like pals?"

"Well, sort of. That is, at first. I mean until—"

He grunted and sculled me to a spot where I could walk the rest of the way to Bank Place.

Hours later Dean Fleming and my father arrived home, exhausted. Mother and I served both men steaming mugs of hot chicken broth; then she gave Dean a pair of Dad's pajamas.

Soon after dawn of that short night, I heard someone moving around in the upstairs hall. Mother, looking bleary-eyed and worried, had an empty hot water bottle in each hand.

"Your father tossed all night," she whispered. "Now he's having a chill." She held out the hot water bottles. "Fill these as fast as you can, please."

The words stabbed me. My father was still under par, physically and emotionally. Not to mention his worry about *The Sentinel*.

Hot water bottles filled, I took them to Dad. His face was flushed and his forehead hot beneath my hand. The malaria was back.

"Louise," he blurted out, his voice quavery, "I've been lying here thinking—I don't have enough insurance to cover the presses and all. If everything down there's lost—" His hands, picking at the covers, were shaking as nervously as I'd ever seen them.

"All is not going to be lost, Kenneth." Mother's voice was firm. "Come on now, where's your faith? Dean Fleming and his men are watching out for our interests. Relax and try to sleep some more."

The National Guard had cordoned off most of Alderton's business area, declaring it off limits to anyone except the police and designated officials. Thus not even Dean Fleming could get back to the *Sentinel* office to check on the damage. We could but live in a state of hopeful suspense.

In the next few days I learned more about what Alder-

ton people called a "little flood." To me there seemed
nothing little about it. Power gone. Telephone service
out. Telegraph lines washed away. By Sunday morning
the water on Main Street had crested at almost eight feet.
Uprooted trees, broken telephone poles, branches and
floating planks propelled by the swirling water had
rammed through store windows and even the sides of
buildings.

From high ground I could see stalled vehicles, abandoned by their drivers. In some places cars and trucks
were nearly submerged. So far, because of proper warnings, there had been no deaths, but five people were missing. Three small bridges had been swept away and a
section of the road washed out between Yancyville and
Alderton. The Pennsylvania Railroad reported miles of
track gone, as well as extensive damage to their roundhouse and yards. For several days our town was virtually
cut off from the outside world except by radio communication. Stern warnings about natural gas breaks were circulated by radio. The KDKA bulletins also announced
the rationing of water. All drinking water should be
boiled. Typhoid shots were recommended as soon as se-
rum was available.

What grocery staples people could get to, or that water
had not ruined, were quickly sold out. Crucial drug supplies like insulin and digitalis were dangerously short.

On Sunday, Fox Movietone News flew adventure-
some cameramen to a nearby airport where they rented a
car and drove to Alderton. From the steepest hill overlooking our town, they filmed the devastation to show the
rest of the nation.

The more than six hundred people who had been
driven from their homes by the rising water (seven
houses had actually been destroyed) were allowed to
camp in the Town Hall and high school gymnasium,
where rows of cots had been set up. Spencer Meloy also
opened up Baker Memorial's Christian Education Building to these refugees. The second floor was designated

the sleeping-mat area, the first floor a canteen to dispense food and hot coffee.

Since Spencer was in desperate need of volunteers to staff what he called his "Caring Place," he asked me if I would help him round up some of the town's teenagers. With no telephone service, how could we reach them? The answer was by word of mouth and through amateur radio hams.

Margo was one of the first to sign up as a volunteer in the church canteen. A dozen others followed. Soon we were peeling and cutting up bushels of potatoes and other vegetables for soup, making mounds of sandwiches, and above all, keeping two huge urns of coffee filled and steaming hot.

It was a revelation to me that the heart-center of the canteen was not the food but those coffee urns—an eye-opener because I had not yet acquired any fondness for coffee. Day after day, Margo and I would watch the weary workers—their clothes wet and malodorous from the foul-smelling mud, their faces gray and lined with fatigue—stumble in and push through the crowd to those coffee urns. Once steaming cups were in their hands smiles would return, then become laughter as the talk grew animated.

The other revelation was the enthusiasm of Spencer Meloy. He seemed to be everywhere at once, meeting needs with minimal equipment and his all-volunteer staff. Both Margo and I found ourselves drawn to his side whenever we could arrange it. Or somehow he would appear beside us. Margo admitted that she had never encountered a man like Spencer to whom she could attribute no selfish ulterior motivation.

One night I was refilling the coffee urn in the canteen when a familiar face appeared at my side. "You're Julie Wallace, right?"

"Yes."

"Met you at the S-Stemwinder recently. I'm Neal Brinton."

"I remember you."

From then on Neal appeared regularly at the canteen following his emergency duties at the steel plant. Though being with Margo was his main interest, the towering, craggy-faced steelworker was a conscientious helper. One night during a quiet interlude, he told us how troubled he was about his brother Cade—three years older than he, married, with two children.

"A bright one," he told us. "Good with words. Not s-slow, like me."

I guessed that Neal was referring to his slight speech impediment, an inclination to stutter over the sound "s."

"Cade can talk the hind legs off a donkey," he went on. "Right now he's getting the men stirred up against ERP—you know, the company's Employee Representation Plan. Could lose his job there any day."

"Because the plant is laying off men?" I asked.

"Not that." Neal took a quick look around him. "At Yoder they fire those who complain about company policy."

"But, Neal, an Employee Representation Plan would seem a fine idea. Why is your brother so opposed to it?"

"Cade considers ERP a dummy front, management's last-ditch s-stand to prevent collective bargaining."

"Can Cade prove that?"

Again Neal was cautious. "Cade has s-s-some points on his s-side. It would take a while to tell you."

As Neal talked on, I liked him more and more. For such a big man, he seemed gentle, considerate, fair-minded.

"Cade and I can get along if there's distance between us," Neal told us. "Trouble is, now we're gonna be thrown together."

"How do you mean, Neal?" Margo asked.

"Cade's house was wrecked so bad in the flood that he and his family had to move in with us." Neal went on to explain that after their parents' death, the Brinton home had been willed to him. He had already rented out half of it to a married couple. Now with Cade, his wife and two children, there would be seven people under one roof.

As Neal turned away to pour water into one of the coffee makers, Margo and I looked after him sympathetically. Between the depression and the flood, most of Alderton faced disruption.

By late Sunday the water was slowly beginning to recede, leaving behind a chaotic mess. Monday morning Dad, moving shakily, got out of bed for a few hours. We heard that the National Guard would allow merchants back into downtown Alderton on Tuesday morning; schools would not reopen until the following week.

Tuesday dawned with leaden gray skies, rather like our spirits. When the Editor insisted on going down to the *Sentinel* office, Mother and I urged him to drive the Willys. I went with him when Mother decided that she, Tim, and Anne-Marie should stay at home.

The car made it for twelve blocks; we had to walk the final four through oozing, slimy, stinking mud, the consistency of chocolate pudding. All around us was a meld of decaying animal bodies, rotting food, sewer gas, and small fires spewing up fumes from burning wood, rubber, metal, cloth. The stench made us gag.

We passed one house whose front wall had been sheared off, leaving the first and second floors open to the elements, like a dollhouse with no front. A few other buildings had been moved off their foundations and stood askew. In one house the staircase had washed out, so that the family had to use a ladder to get to the second floor.

On Main Street state guardsmen patrolled with 12-gauge shotguns over their shoulders. At Gaither's Clothing Store, a naked mannequin lay seductively on the edge of the wrecked display window, one of her arms dangling over the window frame, the other thrown over her head, as if in mute appeal.

Our suspense grew as we walked on. Suppose the

presses and all the equipment were ruined? What would we do then? Only one block more and we would know.

As we rounded the corner from Main Street, Dad exclaimed, "At least the building's still there!"

A minute later we were standing in the doorway. One look told us that the Babcock press and the cutter were in place. The water had risen almost to the top of the twelfth step, just four steps short of the rolls of paper on the landing. Dad turned and hugged me, then muttered softly, "We're still in business, thank God!"

10

Early the next morning I was in my room, writing in my journal, when Mother tapped softly on the door, then opened it a crack. "Your father wants to talk to you," she told me.

"How is he?"

"Weak." Mother smiled wanly. Then she went downstairs to prepare breakfast.

I found Dad lying propped up in bed, awash in papers. His face was puffy, his eyes dull.

"Julie, the doctor insists that I should go back to bed for several days. Thinks I'll overdo it if I get involved with the cleanup at *The Sentinel.*"

"That makes sense to me."

"Maybe so. But there's so much to be done." He sighed. "I'll stay here two days, no longer."

"Any way I can help?"

"Yes, Julie, there is. The paper should come out with a post-flood issue as soon as possible. We'll need lots of local facts and human interest details. Since school won't resume for at least a week, I'd like you to try being our special reporter. Dig in and get the total story." He looked me full in the face, his eyes studying me. "Can you do it?"

Excitement rose in me. "I'd like to try. What about pictures?"

"I'll make arrangements to use wire service photos.

88

Plus whatever good pictures local photographers come up with.''

With a sense of anticipation, I dressed and gulped down breakfast. Then, snatching up a handy canvas tote bag to hold pencils, note pads, and my own small camera, I headed for downtown Alderton.

On Monday CBS newscaster H. V. Kaltenborn had reported that the governor of Pennsylvania had declared martial law in Alderton and sent in additional units of the National Guard to protect against looting, that the American Red Cross was flying in food and setting up first aid stations, and that six persons had died in the flood, four with heart attacks and two from drowning.

For two days now reporters and cameramen from big-city papers had been descending upon Alderton. With Fox Movietone News shooting the more dramatic scenes, I knew that people in theaters all over the country would soon be familiar with our town.

Everywhere I looked there was debris: roofs ripped off houses; pieces of buildings looking like giant matchsticks; blocks of concrete from torn-up sidewalks and streets; all kinds of household goods—tables, stoves, chairs, refrigerators, pots and pans, broken crockery, shoes, children's toys.

The assortment of articles on the floor of Wagner Lumber Company's warehouse seemed typical: a lawn mower, a davenport, a dead cat, a telephone pole, two trees, several cars, a child's doll, and tons of vile-smelling mud.

The lower floors of Municipal Hospital were an unbelievable mess. The water had completely flooded the storage rooms where records had been kept. I wondered why they had not been moved to an upper floor along with the stocks of drugs and medical supplies. I took a picture of the walls of files coated with mud. The oozing brown mass still clung to the ceiling in globs. Could the records ever be dried out and made readable again? No one knew.

Our high school suffered only minor damage, but two of the three elementary schools had flooded basements and heating systems out of commission or ruined. As a result, a two-week spring recess was declared for the entire Alderton school system.

In my roamings I discovered an ever-present element of the bizarre. Such as: when the Lutheran pastor took several men with him to assess damage to the church, they were astonished to find the floor of the sanctuary covered with sprouted oats, already two to three inches tall. The oats must have floated in from the feed store down the street.

And the unexpected plague of earthworms. Evicted from their natural habitat, masses of them went crawling, wriggling, and squirming inside homes and stores to the shrieks of housewives and the discomfiture of everybody. How could there be that many earthworms!

While Yoder Steel buildings were on higher ground and did not to have to close, the Trentler Wireworks' offices were three to four feet deep in the worm-infested mud.

Word came from Harrisburg, the state capital, that three hundred Works Progress Administration men were being trucked in to help with the cleanup. They were to bring steam shovels, cranes, heavy trucks, and the equipment to pump out basements and to dredge the silt from rivers and creeks. The cleanup was expected to take a month.

For the more detailed work, shovels were prized. In fact, next to food, water, and crucial medical supplies, the most urgent necessity was for shovels and more shovels. An SOS went out to Harrisburg.

Mud a foot deep, two feet deep, in places waist high. Mud trampled and churned up and swirled and stirred and waded through and mixed again, sticking gluelike to everything it touched, the foulness acrid to the throat, stinging the eyes, churning the stomach . . . guardsmen poking their billy clubs into that mud as they probed for the bodies of animals—or even people.

Down at *The Sentinel,* day after day, members of our family took turns shoveling. I was seeing mud in my sleep—heavy, sticky mud blackened by the coal and liquefied coal dust from a thousand basements—pursuing me like a gigantic octopus.

The soggy pile of shoveled-out debris in the street outside the newspaper office grew—six feet high, eight feet. Everywhere the WPA men were working feverishly. Bulldozers were creating small mountains of the gluey mass for dump trucks to haul away. Watching these operations, I wondered if there could be any topsoil left on the steep hills encircling our town.

While filling a notebook with facts, I became aware of something: most people in Alderton possessed an inner core of courage about getting on with life. They refused to give up, no matter how tough the hardships. That inner strength stirred me, moved me. I wanted that kind of stouthearted spunk for myself.

By Friday, the mud in the *Sentinel*'s basement had been pumped out. Then came the next job—hosing down the floor and walls; when that was done—sweeping out and mopping and scrubbing. Still there was no way to get all the sediment out of the cracks.

As I wandered in and out of homes, stores, public buildings, it seemed to me that everything had a dingy look. Despite the use of strong disinfectants, the smell of mud, like a bad memory, would linger for many months.

When Dad returned to the office after his forced two days of recuperation, he made a list of the small items of equipment which had to be replaced in order to resume publishing. With a pained look, he showed me the total—a minimum of four hundred dollars' worth. Our savings were exhausted, and income to the paper had virtually stopped. At this point, almost no one was paying

his bills. How I ached to be able to do something to ease
our financial crisis!

I expected my eighteenth birthday that Friday to slide
by without notice. But Mother baked a cake, and we celebrated at dinner that night although we were so tired we
could scarcely keep awake. In my journal I logged this
comment:

> On the day that I was officially a grown woman, I
> felt anything but feminine; rather, befouled from the
> sweat of hard physical labor and the stinking mud. I
> wanted nothing so much as to sleep for a week.

Yet early the next morning, I was back in downtown
Alderton, adding to my pages of notes about the flood. I
was just coming out of the town hall when I saw a familiar figure striding toward me—Randolph Wilkinson. He
was wearing a natty blue windbreaker. Would he remember me?

As I slowed my pace, watching him approach, he saw
me, smiled, stuck out his hand. "Well, Julie Wallace.
How are you keeping?"

"Not very clean," I answered, amused by his phrasing.

"I heard your father was ill," he said softly.

"Yes, But he's back at work now." That my voice
sounded breathless made me furious with myself.

"Capital! When will you publish again?"

"Next week. I'm out covering the flood for the pa
per."

"The local reporter. Well, now." There was an intangible change in his appraisal of me.
"I'm not surprised, though. You've the look of a re-
porter."

"What kind of look is that?"

He laughed. "Questioning . . . tenacious."

I was suddenly emboldened. "Mr. Wilkinson, may I
have a short interview with you—right now?" I tried to

make it seem casual. "About damage to the Club and dam, things like that?"

"There's really nothing to report, Julie," he replied slowly, the geniality slightly diminished. "We had no flooding at the Club and the dam, of course, was not threatened."

"I guess it's the dam that interests me most," I said, with a persistence that surprised me. "I don't know much about earthen dams."

"They've been around for a long time," he said. "The inspector, Roger Benshoff, is the one to interview on that subject."

"How can I get to see him?"

"You might ring up the Club office on Monday, Julie, and I'll see what we can do."

The interview was over before it had really begun.

Later that same day I was back in the office, compiling my notes, when I saw Miss Cruley leading a man in a brown leather jacket and knee-high boots to the Editor's office—Tom McKeever, Jr. He was taller than his father, his smile readier. I had seen him several times in the foyer of Baker Memorial Church.

He nodded to me as he passed by. "You are—?"

"Julie Wallace, sir."

"Of *course*, Julie Wallace. Yes, yes."

The man was certainly more congenial than his father. I warmed to him despite an inner tendency to dislike the entire McKeever family.

"Happened to be downtown, Ken," Mr. McKeever said heartily. "Thought I'd drop in to see how you fared. Looks like you're back in business."

"We were fortunate, Tom. The paper could have been wiped out. It wasn't. I'm hoping to get the presses rolling next week."

"Any reason you can't?"

"I need to replace some damaged equipment, and we're short of capital."

"Try the bank on Monday. Alderton's getting disaster relief from the government. Let me know if you have any problems."

"That's great to know, Tom." All the heartiness was back in my father's voice.

"We all need to help each other any way we can," Tom continued. "That's why I'm here. Yoder Steel is concerned about all of you." He paused. "By the way, Ken, how soon would your press be able to print that special booklet for Yoder?"

"Most anytime, Tom. The job press wasn't damaged at all."

"Good! We're working on the copy. I'll be back in touch soon. Good to have seen you, Ken. You too, Julie."

The entire visit had lasted less than five minutes, but what a lift it had given to the Editor!

Young McKeever's friendly excursion to town that day stirred much comment. He had even walked through the Lowlands, inspecting damage and reassuring the people that Yoder would move quickly to clean up and repair damaged homes.

Dean Fleming, along with others in town, questioned McKeever's motives; he commented wryly that neither father nor son had ever before made such a gesture.

My father was more generous. Later I heard him say, half musingly, to Mother, "Do you suppose that the son does not see eye-to-eye with the father's tough policies? There's a lot to like in young McKeever."

When the bank opened on Monday, my father was there to apply for a disaster loan. He returned an hour later, looking happier than I'd seen him in months. "It went through," he beamed.

Later, when the Editor had gone on an errand, I slipped into his office to call Randolph Wilkinson. I wondered, would he remember his promise to get me an interview with Mr. Benshoff, the dam inspector?

Randolph came on the line almost immediately. "Hullo. Yes, Julie, I spoke with Mr. Benshoff. He inquired of me about the purpose of your interview.''

"It's just that I think people need to know more about earthen dams . . . how safe they are . . . things like that.''

"I . . . see. Well, as of yesterday, Mr. Benshoff buzzed off to some city or other. He'll be here again in a few days. Why don't I request that he ring you up himself?''

"I'd like that.''

There was a short silence. "Julie, I need to be honest with you about something. The chaps who run this Club have made it clear that they aren't the least interested in publicity.''

"But that doesn't seem fair, Mr. Wilkinson. The Club owns and operates a large dam and lake. This is of interest to everyone in the area. People have a right to be informed, and that's the job of a newspaper.''

"Yes, quite. I understand that, Julie. It's just that I can't promise you much cooperation from anyone here.''

I swallowed hard in an effort to keep my voice steady and calm, "Well, thanks for doing whatever you can.''

By Wednesday, the post-flood issue was written and set in type. My fifteen pages of copy had been chopped by the Editor into four different reports and in some places rewritten. There was no byline. I kept my disappointment to myself, aware that Miss Cruley strongly resisted my growing role on the paper. She accepted me as a proofreader, errand girl, and researcher, but not as a feature writer.

On Thursday Dean Fleming made the final adjustment of the press and then called us all together for the big moment. The sheets were in place. The special issue of *The Sentinel* would be eight pages, double our usual size. An extra three thousand copies would be printed.

Dean turned the switch. As the big press clomped down on the newsprint, he let out a cheer.

Miss Cruley clapped softly, a smile tugging at her mouth.

There was a big lump in my throat as I stifled back a sob.

The Editor stood there unmoving, tears in his eyes.

11

Spencer Meloy's study served as both office and meeting room. Its drabness was lightened only by some bookshelves, a bedraggled philodendron plant and a faded red scatter rug. Material things apparently were not very important to the gangling young pastor.

Even on such short notice, six of us high school students had gotten there for this Saturday morning "flood meeting" called by Meloy.

Margo was there. She had a crush on Spencer and, in her honest way, admitted it. Graham surprised me by coming. He had not been that active with the canteen. Neal Brinton was also there, his interest in Margo stronger than ever. The big surprise was that Meloy had prevailed upon Alderton's mayor to send one representative, a burgessman Also on hand was Mrs. Janet McIntyre, president of the Ladies Association.

Spencer arranged us in a circle and opened the meeting with a true story about a twelve-year-old girl. Carrying a baby and dragging two toddlers behind her, she had knocked timidly on a neighbor's door at three in the morning that Sunday the flood struck. The children—drenched, hungry and crying—had pleaded to be taken in. Neither their father nor their mother had returned home that evening.

"We're still searching for the missing parents," Mr. Meloy reported as we sat there, silent and numbed by the story. I noticed that when the pastor got emotional, his

97

dark-rimmed glasses tended to slide slowly down his nose.

"But I thought all the missing had been accounted for," Margo ventured.

Spencer shook his head. "Unfortunately, there's no way those statistics can be final in the Lowlands, where people come and go all the time. Am I right, Neal?"

"I'm afraid you are, Pastor," was Neal's reply. "It's hard to believe that parents would abandon their children like this, but they do."

"This is just one of the many human dramas taking place every day in the Lowlands," Spencer Meloy continued. "These problems are not just due to the flood. They've been there a long time, like an open sore on the body of our town."

"I do not quite see," Mrs. McIntyre said impatiently, "where our discussion is going."

"Then let's get to the point," the pastor continued. "Whose responsibility is the plight of these needy Lowlands families? The church's? But Baker Memorial is just one of a dozen churches in town. The town's? But the town is already rocking under the totatlity of its economic and flood problems. The state of Pennsylvania's? The federal government's? Yoder Steel's?"

"Has anyone approached the elder McKeever about all this?" I asked.

The burgessman and Mrs. McIntyre looked at me sharply, as if they thought my question brash.

Spencer seemed amused. "No-o, Julie, not that I know of. You believe in going to the top, I see."

"Why not? That way, we could at least find out what Yoder Steel's willing to do."

There was silence. None of the adults seemed willing to pick up my idea. Then the burgessman spoke up. "I think we should appeal for more assistance from government agencies, like the WPA." He then divulged that a local campaign was already underway for citizens to write letters to President Roosevelt in Washington—not only asking for more flood relief but also requesting federal funds to make Alderton "floodproof" for the future.

"Even if Washington comes through with major repair help," Spencer Meloy protested, "that will be weeks, probably months away. There are *human beings* in the Lowlands who need help now."

The final consensus of the group was that yes, Baker Memorial should do something in the Lowlands, and calling on families there had to be the first step.

"We'll go two by two," Mr. Meloy stated, "and always in daylight. Say that we're from the church and want to help out."

"But what can we *do* for them?" Margo questioned. "I mean, the people there could think that all we're trying to do is get them to go to church."

The pastor was thoughtful. "Remember, Margo, some of those families were fed by our church canteen. So mention of that can be your entree. Find out what their needs are. Friendliness is the key."

The pastor then passed out a list of Lowlands families for us to visit. Margo and I quickly decided that we would work together as one of the teams. Mrs. McIntyre and the burgessman asked to be excused from making calls. Neal Brinton suggested that he serve as an advisor.

Margo and I chose a Tuesday afternoon for our venture into the Lowlands. There were three teams in action. Neal Brinton drew rough maps to help the six of us find the families on our lists.

Margo was tense when we met after school on Tuesday. As we walked over Railroad Bridge, she explained, "It's not the Lowlands families I'm afraid of. After all, I'm a part of this area myself. But there's one street I avoid. It's listed as Washmer Street, but everybody calls it Saloon Street. Just one bar after another. And drunks everywhere. We have to go along that street to get to the first family on our list."

When we turned onto Washmer Street, I was struck by the drabness of the drinking joints. Peering in as we walked by, I saw that each had a long bar without even a mirror behind it; there was only a row of bar stools, a few crude tables, rickety chairs, and a bare floor. On windows were scrawled words in foreign languages: *Sot . . . Bier . . . Pivo.*

"It's almost empty now," Margo said, "but when each shift ends at Yoder, most of the men are so thirsty and exhausted they head straight for here. Those few with cars are usually the ones who come to the Stemwinder."

The conversation broke off when we suddenly came to a chasm in the street where rushing waters had carved out the pavement in a jagged line—underpaving, foundation and all. We stared into a hole nearly ten feet deep. Beyond was the section of Alderton hardest hit of all. A series of flimsy shacks had been sheared off their foundations. Several had broken up completely. Household articles still lay in the debris—an old ice chest, a smashed stove, bent pots and pans, ripped mattresses, broken furniture, parts torn off cars and trucks. Everything was coated with that awful blanket of mud. Since it was now over two weeks after the flood, we wondered why no cleanup crews had yet appeared.

Carefully we detoured around the crevasse. Because many street signs were down, it took us half an hour to locate the first name on our list: the Balazes. Their home was the third in a row of six houses, all attached. The front steps had been washed away, glass in one window was gone, and some soggy mattresses were propped up against the porch wall to dry. Otherwise this house seemed to be intact. I noticed a large bow of soiled white cloth hanging from the front door of the adjoining house.

At our knock a pink-cheeked, stocky young woman timidly opened the door.

"We're from Baker Memorial Church," I began. "I think you and your husband came to the canteen there—"

A look of fear leapt into her face. "They said the food was for free."

"Oh, yes. It was free," I answered hurriedly. "We just came to see if there's any way we can help you."

Astonishment now crossed the face in the doorway.

"Vaht you say? You vant halp us . . . but . . . Is doity here . . ."

In the midst of her fluster, however, half in embarrassment, half with pleasure, she motioned us to enter.

One glance told us that the front room was their living room, dining room and bedroom, with a small kitchen in the back. There were no bathrooms in these houses, only privies out back. Electricity had come to this section of town, but still no sewer lines.

In the front room, two iron bedsteads were ranged against the wall, but the mattresses and bedding had obviously been ruined. An old round oak table stood in the center, a bare light bulb dangling over it. On one windowsill was a tin can in which a single red geranium struggled for life.

We sat around the table, each of us wrestling with the language barrier.

"My name Sonja. Come to America to marry vith my Karesi."

We learned that Sonja's husband was a breaker at Yoder, earning $32.24 a month. Of this, $14 a month was due Yoder for rent. The only way they could afford this was to bring in another couple, along with two unmarried workers, who all shared the cost.

Sonja said she was from Czechoslovakia—and nineteen years old. I was startled. Just a year older than I! She looked thirty!

Even with Sonja's broken English, she managed to convey something of her story: "My country very bootiful. So clean. Lots flowers. Big farm in country, near Hiboka, nice l'eel town. Ve vork plenty hard by fields. Lots of hops for make *pivo*—vaht you say?—beer. Ve like *Svatek*—how you say?—holiday. Eat good—hams, big, pink, juicy, from own pigs. And geese and beeg barrels beer. Lots music, alvays singing.

"We love our country, but lots trouble. Bad men come take away men for service in army. Czechs vant free. Karesi and I afraid—so all right, ve come to America to be free."

As I listened, watching Sonja's expressive gestures and the emotions written on her face, troubling thoughts were whirling through my mind. This idealistic young couple had come to America for the good life. How disappointed they must be! What could the church do but provide a few material things? Yet through Sonja's fragmented sentences it was easy to glimpse needs that went deeper than that. Finally it came out that her concern was not for herself and her husband, but for the couple next door: they had lost an eight-month-old baby girl.

"Oh!" I exclaimed, "is that what the white bow on their door stands for?"

"Ya!" Sonja described how the young mother and infant had been visiting a neighbor. The house had broken up, plunging the women into the surging water, the mother frantically hanging on to her baby girl. But debris in the rampaging water had smashed into the young woman, who must have momentarily passed out. When she came to, her baby was gone. The little body had yet to be recovered.

"Her name Janey," Sonja told us. "But she not home now. She cry, then cry some more, can't bear to be home."

Since it was obvious that the Balazes must be having to sleep on the floor and decidedly doubtful that those mattresses leaning on the porch would ever be usable again, we wrote down opposite their name "mattresses and bedding." One glance into the kitchen told us there was little food in the house, so groceries were also needed.

Our search for the next name on our list, the Griswolds, led us up a flight of rickety wooden stairs to a second-floor apartment. Two men slunk away when they saw us coming but left the apartment door open. Inside I caught a glimpse of broken windowpanes stuffed with papers and rags. A baby with only a shirt on—no diaper—was lying on a pile of rags on the floor. Sores covered the lower part of his body.

An old woman, who had only a thin covering of sallow skin stretched over the gaunt bones, was lying on one of the four beds in the room. An absurdly young mother, wearing red ankle socks, picked up the baby from the floor and began nursing him.

The young mother smiled at us. No, the Griswolds didn't live there. No, she had never heard of them.

In the small, dark room the air was stale, the smells vile. The one attempt at decoration was a garish cross on the wall with the contorted figure of Jesus writhing on it.

Margo and I fled the scene. At home that night, I could only pick at my food as the memories of that afternoon clogged my mind and deadened my spirit. When Mother pressed for details, sudden emotion welled up inside me and to my embarrassment tears suddenly spilled out of my eyes.

It took two more trips to the Lowlands for Margo and me to visit all five families on our list. When the group gathered again in Pastor Meloy's study to give our reports, everyone had horror stories to share along with heart-rending scenes. It came out that the Lowlands people had been surprisingly vocal about their needs. A long list of items was compiled and plans were made to supply as many as possible.

A lively discussion took place as to a summary of what we had learned. First, about the housing. It seemed that originally Yoder had built some three hundred tenement houses out of cheap pine boards with no insulation. Most were one story with four rooms; some two stories with six rooms. All were set on concrete slabs. For economy, each block had eight or ten houses joined together, with few windows for ventilation.

There were no trees and little shrubbery around the houses. The few growing things were black and withered from lack of care and the polluted air. Piles of trash and garbage were everywhere.

"I realize that what you saw in the Lowlands seems shocking and unfair," Spencer Meloy said thoughtfully. "You need to understand, however, that company towns like this are everywhere. Some industries could not operate without them. And many immigrant couples would otherwise be homeless. The Lowlands is not the worst—nor the best."

"What bothered me was that apparently not a single house was occupied by just one family," I noted.

"That's true. Yoder keeps its rents so high the families are forced to double up. Some couples run a boarding-house for bachelor workers."

Others pointed out that the men worked in shifts, some starting at six in the morning just as the all-night turn ended. As soon as one man got up to go to work, a sweaty, grimy man just returning from his shift would often fall into the same bed.

Mr. Meloy then explained something few of us had known. In steel making, the night and day shifts were a necessity: once a furnace was fired up, it had to run continuously. If ever allowed to cool, then its fire-brick lining almost always had to be renewed, an incredibly costly business. This was one reason for management's all-out opposition to strikes, which would shut down the furnaces.

"But maybe strikes would result in better living conditions for these people," I suggested.

"More likely, the loss of wages would cause even more suffering and hardship for them," was the pastor's retort.

"Doesn't Yoder do any *good* things for its workers?" one student asked.

Spencer Meloy then told us about Yoder's own volunteer fire department and baseball team, and the company-built hall with an auditorium on the first floor and a library on the second where night classes were held for the workers in various subjects like metallurgy, mining, engineering, and mechanical drawing.

There was also a three-story company store employing fifty-five people. Fresh produce and even meat for the store came from company-owned farms. Yoder had a shoe factory and a woolen mill, as well as a gristmill for cereals and flour products.

The main reason that steel families shopped at the company store, he explained, was that they could always get credit there. A worker had only to speak to his mill boss, who then "arranged" the credit with the store manager.

"But with prices so high, families are always in debt to the company," Margo exclaimed. "Three of the mothers made a special point of this."

Spencer Meloy summed it up: "We're dealing here with a system of paternalism—thoughtful in some ways, ruthless in others. I suggest that our church, especially you young people, be solely concerned with helping the people down there right now. Are you with me?"

We were—enthusiastically.

In the days that followed, I saw a progression of tortured faces from the Lowlands. Such hopelessness in their eyes as they looked out at the dirty, stinking deadness that permeated everything!

For some reason, I could not let the subject of these people drop at our dinner table. "Dad, I'm sure Baker Memorial can't do very much for the Lowlands. Pastor Meloy is trying, but he has to face all those Yoder executives on his Board of Trustees. Is there some way we could help through *The Sentinel?*"

"Like what?" The Editor's eyes were lifeless.

"Why couldn't *The Sentinel* suggest some sort of town project? Planting trees and flowers there as a start. Some fresh paint would sure help."

"But how could *The Sentinel* campaign for improving land owned by Yoder Steel? We'd need company support."

"Maybe the McKeevers and others wouldn't object if they didn't have to pay for it."

Dad just shook his head.

"Well then, if you think we can't take on Yoder Steel, maybe we could at least suggest the name 'Lowlands' be changed."

"To what?"

"Well, how about River View?"

"Julie, changing a name won't change negative thinking or bad conditions. But keep at it. Your group is on the right track."

A grin spread slowly across his face and a flicker of enthusiasm lighted his eyes. "By jiminy, we do own the only newspaper in town. There must be some way we can use it to do some good there."

12

THANKS to Dean Fleming's skill with machinery, *The Sentinel* missed only one issue. In fact I was surprised at how quickly Alderton businesses reopened despite flood damage to almost all the downtown buildings.

As I walked down Main Street the following Friday, however, I could see that many broken store windows were still boarded up. Main Street itself was not yet open to traffic since the pavement was cracked, broken or heaved up in many places. The look and feel of gloom pervaded the town.

But not at Exley's Drug Store. Excited people were streaming out the front door and hurrying toward the river. Some were running

"What's happened?" I asked one man.

"Freight train jumped the track just a few minutes ago. Other side of Railroad Bridge."

It must be a big wreck, I figured, with so many sprinting to the scene. Quickly I rushed to *The Sentinel* to pick up my camera and notebook. Then I joined the streams of people all going in the same direction.

But there was something puzzling: many were carrying containers. A boy had an empty milk bottle, a girl had a fishbowl. A man in a red plaid shirt was carrying a thermos jug.

We crossed Railroad Bridge, then Route 143, and saw the train dead ahead with the engine facing us, freight cars strung out behind. From where I approached, it did not look like a wreck at all: the engine was on the tracks, as were a string of dirty red and yellow freight cars that stretched out of sight around the curve behind. Finally we saw the problem: the last three tank cars and the caboose were lying on their sides. It was like a gigantic reproduction of Tim's electric train jumping the track after a too-fast run.

The center of attention seemed to be the last tanker; there was a small split in a metal seam near its top. From the rupture red fluid was spurting, fountainlike. A man in dungarees rushed forward and used his cupped hands to get a deep drink. "Hey, folks," he shouted, "good California wine!"

"Ain't nobody here gonna plug *that* hole," came one voice.

Loud applause.

Three men emerged triumphantly from the caboose waving tin coffee cups. Each in turn thrust his cup under the red fountain, took a nip, then, in the growing conviviality, passed the cup to someone else. But bigger receptacles were now arriving from every side.

Then I saw them. But it couldn't be! Tim and Anne-Marie with the largest container of all—Mother's galvanized washtub balanced precariously on Tim's wagon.

"What are you doing here?" I shouted, grabbing Tim by the shoulder.

"Let go, Julie! We wanta get a little wine before it's all gone." He wrenched himself free.

"But—a *washtub!*" I exclaimed, following him. "What would you *do* with a washtub of wine?"

"Lots of things. We'll figure that out later."

Crazy kids! They had never seen wine in our home, with Mother and Dad both being teetotalers. Nor had my father even used wine for communion services—only grape juice. Tim and Anne-Marie were heading for trouble. And yet I didn't try to stop them. Something of the carnival spirit was getting to me too.

Nearby, I was astonished to see Sam Gaither, the

clothing store owner, with Floyd Townsend, the barber, happily passing a milk bottle of the wine back and forth between them.

The ground beside the railroad tracks had already been six inches deep in mud before the tanker had tipped over. Now hundreds of scrambling feet were churning mud and wine together into a slippery, sticky morass. Soon it was sloshing over peoples' shoe tops, splashing onto pants legs and dresses.

"Get in line, everyone." Gilio Mazzini, son of the local shoe repairman, was tugging and pulling along—of all people—the crippled Barry Sims on his platform on wheels. Barry was hugging a square lard can with the look of one going to a party.

As people poured in, a jubilant holiday mood soon prevailed. No one seemed to mind standing in the glutinous ooze of wine and mud, nor inching forward in the line. As the townspeople sipped wine and filled their containers, I figured that the downtown area must now be empty.

No shoes would be sold today. Wade Stover and his brother Alcorn were lurching back and forth, holding each other up and offering a strident, off-key rendition of "I've Been Workin' on the Railroad."

Salvatore Mazzini, member of shoes, immediately ahead of Bryan McKeever in line, was in a jolly state of euphoria. He saw me and bowed from the waist. "*Buon giorno, signorina,*" followed by a flood of sonorous Italian words ending with *festa*.

"Good afternoon, Mr. Mazzini. Yes, it *is* a real festival—"

He shouted to a friend. "*Ce la farai, amico. Non te la prendere.*" Then his laugh boomed out. His big stomach shook. His handlebar mustache jerked and bounced as if it were about to jump rope.

When it was Mr. Mazzini's turn in line, he peeled off his jacket, spread his feet wide, and thrust his wide-open mouth into the red stream. The wine flowed down his

throat smoothly, as if he had not bothered to swallow.
The crowd cheered.

How the mood of our town had changed! An hour ago
Alderton had been gloomy, gray . . . the town more than
half wrecked by the flood . . . merchants with customers
who had no way of paying their bills . . . a procession of
able-bodied men with families to feed but unable to find
jobs . . . eyes on the ground, glazed by all the mud,
murky skies, no stars to see . . . nothing on the horizon.
Then suddenly a party, with no invitation required.
Something to laugh about, to be carefree and gay about,
like children. Drink from the biggest punch bowl in the
world, folks, joke with neighbors you haven't spoken to
in months.

For a few minutes I backed off, watching and making a
few notes on my pad. Carefully I took several pictures.
No out-of-town photographers were covering this episode!

Then I saw that Tim and Anne-Marie's turn had come.
When the stream of wine struck the bottom of Mother's
tin tub, it sounded like someone squirting a hose into a
metal drum. With the tub filled within four inches of the
brim, Tim tried to pull the wagon from underneath the
fountain. It would not budge. Anne-Marie strained to
help by pushing from behind. Still no movement.

"Get that thing goin'," someone shouted.

Embarrassed, I moved forward, leaned down and
added my strength to Anne-Marie's. With that the washtub rocked sideways, spilling wine on my shoes and
socks and splattering my dress. I had almost slipped to
my knees when I felt a viselike grip on my arm.

"Let me do it."

It was Randolph Wilkinson. "I'm always around
when you're in trouble, Julie," he chortled. With ease
his muscular arms lifted the wagon onto higher ground so
that Tim could pull it away.

"It's all rather silly, isn't it?" I stammered, aware that

once again, the man I dreamed of as a prince was seeing me as soiled as a scullery maid.

The journey back was agony as we tried to keep the tub from tilting and spilling the wine or from sliding off the wagon. When we turned into Bank Place, our rambunctious puppy, Boy, came streaking to meet us, barking joyously and leaping up to lick us in glad welcome. The moment of truth was approaching. What would we say to Mom and Dad? How could they use a tub full of wine?

As we stopped in front of the house, the Editor, who had been ill and in bed most of the day, walked slowly out the front door. From his vantage point we must have presented a strange tableau. "Where on God's green earth have you children been?" he asked.

"To the big train wreck, Dad," I answered.

But Dad was staring at the wagon. "What—have—you—got—in—that—tub?"

Anne-Marie piped up, "Dad, it's good red wine."

"It's *what?*"

I took over, talking staccato-fast. "A tank car full of California wine on its way to a bottling company in New Jersey overturned just beyond Railroad Bridge. Wine spurted out. The whole town was there with pitchers and bottles and cups, quite a scene. I think it's a front-page story—"

"Hold it, Julie. We'll talk about the story later. Meanwhile, we now have a tub full of wine!"

Tim mumbled, "It's only half full now."

"Where did you get the tub?" Dad asked sternly.

"From our basement—it's Mom's washtub." Tim's voice was low.

Thrusting Anne-Marie aside, Dad stuck one fingertip into our prized booty, then his finger to the tip of his tongue. "M-mmm, that's wine, all right."

My father turned back to us. "Exactly what will you do with it?"

Silence.

Finally Anne-Marie suggested almost inaudibly, "Sell it to the Episcopalians for communion wine?"

Dad choked and swallowed hard. He turned sideways, pulled out his handkerchief and coughed into it. "For the sacrament of holy communion, eh? How thoughtful! Well, let's go tell your mother about this great find of yours."

As we appraoched the house, Mother appeared at the door. Dad prepared the way. "Louise, the children have had quite an adventure with an overturned wine car . . ."

Mother's face was a study. I waited for an explosion, knowing how she felt about alcoholic beverages. Silent communication seemed to pass between our parents. When she opened her mouth, only one strangled sentence came forth, "You can't bring that dirty stuff in here."

"But, Mother, wine kills germs," Tim protested.

"Nonsense!"

"We could strain it, Mom," Tim persisted.

Mother withered him with one look.

"You could cook with it, Mom," I put in. "Gourmet recipes, stuff like that." Even in my ears it sounded a mite limp.

Our father took over at that point. "Let's get the tub to the basement for now."

While Mother looked on with disbelief, Dad helped us carry the tub down the stairs and into the cellar. After he found some empty half-gallon jars for us, we filled them and poured the rest of the wine down the basement drain.

Throughout dinner, Mother said little. A certain grim quality in her silence made all too obvious the strong feelings she was choking back. Later I overheard her talking to Dad in the kitchen.

"Kenneth, how can you allow that stuff in the house? What would your parents think?"

"What my parents would think has nothing to do with it."

"And you a clergyman!"

"Have you forgotten, Louise, that Jesus drank wine?" Then, warming to his subject, "Do you realize how much water He turned into wine at the wedding feast in Cana? Those jugs held twenty to thirty gallons."

Mom ignored this burgeoning sermon. "Kenneth, the basement smells like a winery. What got into you, encouraging our children to bottle that stuff?"

"Louise, dear, I couldn't throw it out now. Not after what they went through to get it here. Relax! We'll dispose of it later. I'm simply not going to squelch that kind of initiative."

I worked hard on the story, trying to bring to life how a train accident and a ruptured wine car had lifted the spirits of our townspeople. The Editor patted me on the shoulder after he read it. The article appeared in the next issue. On the front page. With my first byline.

13

THE long, dismal Pennsylvania winter, followed by the disheartening flood, had made everyone yearn for spring.

Then in late April, all at once it happened. The earth was renewed! On the steep mountainsides towering over Alderton wild crabapple, rhododendron, and laurel burst into bloom. All over town forsythia bushes were masses of yellow exclamation points. The cherry tree in our back yard was a drift of pale pink. Beyond were the locusts, fragrant with clustered white blossoms, a haven for the honeybees.

On a Sunday afternoon, with my back against the trunk of a locust tree, my journal on my lap, I let myself be flooded with a wild assortment of yearnings and dreams of the future.

Life was also changing for me in a number of ways. After my eighteenth birthday, I had obtained my driver's license. Mother and Dad relaxed their restrictions on my use of cosmetics. Experimenting, I was astonished at how a little lipstick and eye makeup seemed to improve my social life.

Or was part of this a change in my attitude? For I was learning to make small talk with the boys—even to laugh at some of their jokes, instead of just looking at them with embarrassed disapproval. I didn't understand how and why these changes were taking place in me; perhaps it all came from my desire to be less of a loner.

But dating boys my age, I was discovering, still did not

fulfill my inner dream of real romance. Try as I might to focus on the boys in my high school crowd, my thoughts always turned back to Randolph Wilkinson.

Why? At twenty-five he was so much older, and from another country and culture, already a man of experience. His family was wealthy. His speech reminded me of Leslie Howard, the charming British actor. All of this made me more than a little self-conscious around the Englishman, not to mention my tendency to tumble in the mud at his feet or spill ink all over myself as I did that afternoon when he came into the *Sentinel* office. Or fall on my knees before him in a puddle of wine. These memories stung me like nettles.

Yet dream on I did. Plus spending hours of research at the local library where I sought out everything I could find about the Wilkinson family home near the village of Wolsingham, County Durham. The facts I uncovered filled pages of my notebook. What really sent my imagination soaring was discovering a full-color reproduction of the Wilkinson family's coat of arms and crest, with these explanatory sentences underneath it:

The Wilkinson name is very old, one of the 25 verified names attached to the Magna Carta (1215). The original coat of arms belonging to this family is of very ancient date. The crest is of more modern origin, and was granted September 18, 1615.

"Of more modern origin . . . 1615!" *How can we consider anything in the United States of America old?* I wondered ruefully.

What puzzled me was the strange symbolism—two unicorns at the top of the crest, then a larger unicorn rising from the crown. What did they stand for?

And then the family motto: *Nec rege, nec populo, sed utrioque.* With the help of the vocabulary in my second-year Latin book, I was able to translate it: *Neither for king, nor for people, but for both.* But what did that mean? There had to be a story behind it.

Questions were stacking up in my mind to ask him. *Silly,* I scolded myself. *Randolph Wilkinson is a man of the world who can take his pick of all available females. Why would he be seriously interested in the likes of you? Cut out your silly daydreaming, Julie.*

For some reason the Kissawha dam also kept intruding into my thoughts. Twice I had dreamed that it spurted water on me as I walked carefully by the lake. Meanwhile, the call from Mr. Benshoff, the dam inspector, had not come. The Englishman had warned me that the Club people wanted no publicity. Probably this included the inspector. Should I call Mr. Wilkinson again about it? No, I decided, that would only annoy him.

My father continued to worry us. Just when he seemed better, his body would start shaking and he would go to bed. Yet the loan from the bank had certainly eased our financial pressures. We were beginning to see meat now and again on our dinner table.

Dean Fleming and the Editor continued to find time to get together, including most of one Saturday. Dad returned so weary that night that we assumed that he and Dean had spent the day working around the Fleming farm.

Thinking about Father, I turned to my journal:

I have been wondering all over again why Dad decided to leave the ministry. Surely there was more to it than the unfortunate Mattie Howard episode. Something damaged his faith and helped to bring on these attacks of malaria.

My pen lifted. How I longed to see inside my father's heart, especially since I had become active at Baker Memorial Church. Spencer Meloy had so challenged my thinking that I felt a need to know more about what I believed and why. Understanding about Dad would help me with that.

Over the months the first excitement of my proofreader job at *The Sentinel* had worn off. Most Alderton news items were not interesting, and proofreading advertisements was ho-hum monotonous. There was an increasing number of advertisements too, through Dad's persuasive efforts with local merchants—hardware, food specials, furniture items, Exley's one-cent sales.

Late one afternoon, after Miss Cruley had left, the proofs spread out on the table before me were duller than usual—a ladies' tea at the Methodist church, advertisements for shirts and Kelvinator refrigerators, a sale of ladies' dresses. Determinedly I plunged in. Then I heard the front door open, and there was Randolph Wilkinson. He gave me a cheery greeting as he walked by and into Dad's office.

Concentrate on the proofs, silly!

I could clearly hear the Editor's booming pulpit voice and then the English one. Decisions about paper stock, typeface, and quantity did not take long. Then Randolph was standing near me.

"Did you and your family drink all that red wine?" There was amusement in his voice.

"Good heavens, no. My parents are teetotalers. Dad finally let us bottle some of it in the basement."

"I see. There's a trick to bottling wine. Better check it out with an expert."

"Thanks, Mr. Wilkinson. We'll look into that." I wondered if he had noticed my byline on the wine-car story.

He turned to leave. "Well, good-bye for now, Julie."

He was at the door when impulsively I called to him. "Mr. Wilkinson, what do the three unicorns in your family crest stand for?"

The young Englishman spun around and stared at me for a moment. "How did you know about *that?*"

"I looked it up in the library."

"You found our family crest in the Alderton library?" He began walking slowly back to my work table.

"Yes, in a book about the history of British families dating back to the eighth century. Yours was in it. And the family motto in Latin—how does it go?—*Neither for king, nor for people, but for both*. What's the story behind that?" I did not tell him that the Alderton library had borrowed this book for me from Pittsburgh's Mellon Library.

The astonishment and interest on the Englishman's face threatened to wreck any composure I had left. "But why? I'm a bit thick. I say, was this some sort of class assignment?"

I steadied my voice in an effort to sound coolly casual. "No-o, nothing like that. I was just curious—nothing more."

"Well, Julie, you've asked two questions that will take some time to answer."

He picked up a chair from across the room, set it down opposite my desk and smiled at me. "Let's begin by striking a more informal note here. We English tend to be, well, stuffy about our names, I've been told. The people I know well here in America call me Rand."

"I'd like that, Rand."

"Good. Now about the family motto. I had an ancestor, Lawrance Wilkinson, who was a lieutenant in the King's army during our Civil War back in 1640. Lawrance so hated the thought of fighting his own countrymen that he came up with the phrase, 'Neither for king, nor for people, but for both.' "

"What happened to him?"

Rand leaned back in the chair, crossed his legs and related how Lawrance's side, the Royalists, had been soundly trounced by the Scottish armies led by Oliver Cromwell. It seemed that Harperley House and its surrounding estates, in the Wilkinson family since 1603, had then been confiscated—"sequestered," as they put it.

"But, Rand, wait a minute. You said last fall that your family, the English Wilkinsons, still live in Harperley House. Is this the same house? And when did you get it back?"

Rand laughed. "You don't miss much, do you? We *still* live in the original Harperley House— what we called a manor house. It was returned to our family by the government years after the Civil War was over."

Now a faraway look came into Rand's blue eyes. "I get homesick every time I think of the view from the terrace of Harperley—the rolling green pasturage, with the misty-blue Pennine hills on the horizon. As a boy, I played on the stairs of the great hall under the skylight. We children slid down the curved balustrades, with the portraits of our ancestors frowning upon us."

Suddenly Rand shook his head as if coming out of a reverie and jumped up to leave.

"But, Rand, wait a minute. You still haven't told me what the three unicorns in your family crest stand for."

He looked at his watch. "I'll have to do that another time." And with a "Cheerio," he strode out the door.

I sat there working on my smudged proofs in a daze, a girl in a grimy mill town dreaming of a manor house called Harperley. Rand's parting words at least held the possibility of "another time."

That Friday the Editor had a copy of the week's *Sentinel* with him when he returned from the office for dinner. About seven o'clock, as Mother and I were clearing off the table after dinner, the telephone rang. Dad answered it.

"That's a bad mistake, Sam," we heard him say. "I'm really sorry. I know it's embarrassing for you. We'll certainly forget about payment for that ad."

My father hung up the phone, picked up *The Sentinel* where he had flung it down, and turned to the back page.

He groaned, "What a beaut!"

"What's wrong, dear?" Mother was quickly at his side, the rest of us close behind her.

Color had crept up to the roots of my father's curly brown hair. *"The Sentinel* has made the most mortifying mistake of the year."

"Where?" we chorused.

"On the back page. The Gaither shirt ad. Sam just called about it."

All of us crowded around the newspaper, which was spread flat on his desk. Tim tittered.

Special Clearance Sale!
(as long as they last)

MEN'S SHITS

98¢ each—3 for $2.69

THE BUY YOU CAN'T
AFFORD TO MISS

Gaither Apparel Store

36 Main Street

Then the truth hit me. The mistake was mine. As proofreader I had not spotted the "r" missing from "shirts." If only a hole would open up in the floor to swallow me!

"Dad, it's all my fault," I confessed limply. "I read the proofs for this ad and just didn't catch the mistake." I was close to tears. And I could not justify it by explaining that Rand had interrupted me at the very moment I was going over that particular advertisement.

The phone rang again. Dad listened a minute and I saw

his face tighten. "No one is blaming you, Emily. Julie has already admitted it was her mistake."

Another long silence on his end. When he spoke at last, his voice had an edge to it. "Anybody with any intelligence at all will know that there was nothing deliberate here, Emily, just a plain oversight. No, we will not change our procedures because of one mistake in proofreading. Emily, I'll see you at the office tomorrow. We'll make an immediate adjustment on Mr. Gaither's bill." With that, Dad hung up.

"Dad, I'm really sorry." Now my eyes were spilling over with tears.

He put his arm around me. "Look, daughter, don't take it so hard. People will either think it very funny or else be sanctimoniously incensed about it."

Dad patted me again and settled down to the work on his desk.

My father had been correct about people's reactions. I dreaded going to school on Monday, but to my amazement it was the big joke of the day. I pretended ignorance at first, but by the afternoon, I had admitted my gaffe and found myself in a near-heroine role.

However, when I entered the *Sentinel* office after school, I had to face a fiery-eyed Miss Cruley.

"I've been in newspaper work for thirty years," she flung in my face, "and this is the worst mistake I've ever seen."

"I'm sorry, Miss Cruley," I answered, determined not to be intimidated.

"Being sorry changes nothing at all," she snapped. "People are blaming *me.*"

"Then tell them that I did it. Or do you want me to wear a sign around my neck reading 'I'm the guilty one'?"

"That's being insufferably impertinent. You Wallace kids are all too young to be involved in this business. I tried to warn your father. *The Sentinel* could go under, you know, with this kind of irresponsibility."

Sudden anger rose in me. "Has anyone called to cancel their ads or subscriptions?"

"Not yet. But just you wait. People won't put up with that kind of vulgarity."

"Not vulgarity, Miss Cruley. An innocent mistake. You made it, setting type. I missed it, reading proof."

"Hrumph!" She glared at me and stomped over to her desk.

A thought hit me—*I really should go down to the store and apologize to Mr. Gaither himself.* Without another word to Miss Cruley, I turned and left the office.

I stopped in front of Gaither's Apparel Store, stomach churning. Slowly I pushed open the swinging doors and walked inside. Suddenly I saw Mr. Gaither coming directly toward me. His arms were outstretched. He was beaming. Quickly he silenced my apology.

"Julie, would you believe it? Today's the best day this store ever had! Every last shirt on sale is gone. Sold out!"

Mr. Gaither insisted on paying for the advertisement. He also came back two weeks later and asked the Editor to run the same advertisement, misprint and all, upside down. Dad talked him out of it.

14

I PUT off to the last minute my choice of a term paper subject for my economics class. It had to be on some aspect of the free enterprise system and would constitute half the semester grade. When the Editor announced one day at breakfast that he had a date later that week to see the younger Tom McKeever at the steel plant, I had an idea: why not choose as my subject the process of steel making? Real-life research would certainly make a more interesting paper than using the encyclopedia.

Perhaps, just perhaps, I could persuade Dad to let me go with him, and maybe Mr. McKeever would allow someone to show me around the plant. I might even get a story out of it for *The Sentinel*. A lot of perhapses and maybes, for sure.

When I presented my idea to the Editor after school that afternoon, he promised to query Mr. McKeever. A few hours later he reported back, "You're in luck, Julie. McKeever said he would pick a—let me think—ah, yes, a *puddler's helper* to show you around. Advised wearing old clothes."

The Yoder Iron and Steel Company occupied considerable acreage north of town on the other side of the Sequanoto River. No sooner had Dad and I driven across North Bridge than we found ourselves amid the cacophony of noise we had heard day and night in muted form at Bank Place: clanging metal, grinding machinery, detonations and sirens jarring our eardrums.

High, heavy wire fencing encircled the grounds. A sign at the entrance read STOP FOR CLEARANCE. From a pillbox guardhouse a very old man stepped forward and directed us to the office. As we drove on into the yard, my first impression was of a sprawling maze of long iron sheds, narrow but tall, the whole area crisscrossed by a network of railroad tracks along which moved small open coal cars.

Dad parked outside the office and we walked into a tiny reception room furnished with only a few straight chairs. The bare floor was gritty underneath my feet. *My gosh,* I thought in surprise, *and I considered the* Sentinel *office plain and bare!*

A receptionist asked us to be seated. Soon young Mr. McKeever came striding into the room. He was wearing a natty tweed suit.

"Tom, I hope it isn't an imposition bringing Julie."

"Not a bit of it." His friendly eyes looked me over searchingly, noting with approval that I was wearing serviceable garb and rubber-soled shoes.

As we followed the erect figure down the hall, Mr. McKeever said over his shoulder, "I've asked Neal Brinton to show you around. I understand you know him from our church canteen. He's one of our best puddler's helpers. A young 'buckwheat' with ambition."

"Neal—that's great!" I enthused.

Young McKeever's office was more comfortably furnished: a large walnut conference table surrounded by armchairs dominated the large rugless room. A desk piled high with papers and file folders took up one corner. In another corner was a black metal safe with *Yoder Iron Company* in old-fashioned gold lettering on the front.

Mr. McKeever picked up one of the three phones on his desk. "Jim! McKeever here. Tell Neal to hustle on over." He banged down the receiver.

Once again he studied me. "Young lady, I hope you

have a good memory. You're about to see a lot in a short time."

"I brought a notebook."

He shook his head. "Doubt if you'll be able to take notes."

"That's all right. Outside research can fill in holes."

"I see." He lit a cigarette. "You'll find steel making a beautiful spectacle. Are you interested in the Bessemer process or just the open hearth method we use today?"

"I scarcely know. My paper's not supposed to be too long."

"Well, a lot of steel history has been made right here in this plant. Thomas Yoder, my grandfather, started this company in 1852. At first the plant mostly turned out— well, give a guess."

"Shovels? Picks?"

"Big iron kettles for the New Orleans sugar cane market."

A familiar figure appeared in the doorway.

"Ah, Neal, there you are—think you know both these people."

Neal grinned at us. "S-sure do. How long a tour, s-sir?"

"Oh, say, thirty minutes."

Outside Neal and I strode along briskly, our feet crunching a surface that was two to three inches deep in dust mixed with gravel and cinders. I noticed that Neal was carrying a white hard hat and several pairs of goggles. He saw my questioning look.

"When we get inside you're to put on the s-safety hat and plain goggles," he told me. "For protection. Later you'll need blue goggles to s-see molten flames of 3,000 degrees Fahrenheit. The naked eyes can't s-see heat that white. We'll begin with s-shed Number Two."

"How many sheds are there?"

"Twenty-one."

As Neal talked, I noticed that despite his slight speech impediment, he had a good command of English.

"Neal, what's the glittery stuff there on the ground? Almost looks like sparkly snow."

"Particles of graphite. No way to keep them from flaking."

Suddenly, off to our right there was a screeching noise so dreadful that I cried out.

Neal laughed. "They're cold s-saws biting into s-steel."

"How do you stand it?"

"You get used to it." He paused before an open door. "It'll be too noisy in there for talking. Any other questions?"

"Yes. Mr. McKeever called you a 'buckwheat.' Explain, please."

The craggy-faced giant smiled. "Just means I'm plain American, that's all. Plant started off with the S-Scots, Welsh, Irish, S-Swedes, a few Russians. Back in 1910 only about a fourth of all s-steelworkers were Americans. Last few years we've gotten mostly Germans, S-Slovaks, Italians and Poles."

"One more question. Mr. McKeever said something about the Bessemer process and open hearth. What's the difference?"

Neal's brow furrowed. "Before Bessemer they made just iron. But during the Civil War iron tracks would get brittle in real cold weather and break. Trains derailed. So they discovered that if you cook iron ore together with coke and limestone to a temperature of about 3,000 degrees, then force a great blast of air into it—well, you get s-steel. That's the Bessemer process."

I looked at him, uncomprehending.

"You have to understand chemistry. The lucky guys who get ahead in s-steel are those who dig in on chemistry and metallurgy." There was a note of wistfulness in his voice. "Perhaps the simplest way to explain the difference is that the Bessemer converters will accept only high-quality pig iron," he continued. "Open hearth furnaces, however, will take all kinds of scrap metal in them. That's why they're preferred today.''

After I put on the hard hat, we walked into a long shed where the atmosphere was so murky—swirling cinders, smoke, hissing steam and sulphur-smelling fumes—that the far wall was barely visible. Once inside, I understood why the building had looked so tall from the outside. The blackened walls of the brick furnaces were considerably higher than a two-story building. The toiling, sweating men seemed like pygmies in contrast to the cyclopean size of everything around them. Close to the roof of the shed were heavy steel girders forming narrow walkways like catwalks. At places along the catwalks were small platforms with safety railings. Neal saw me looking upward.

"Galleries," he shouted.

Here and there I saw salt tablet dispensing machines and continuously running water fountains for the sweating men.

Some of the steelworkers were stripped to the waist, the upper part of their bodies glistening with sweat, but those nearest the furnaces were wearing heavy woven safety clothing and goggles over their eyes. Several stared at me. Their looks were not friendly.

Neal suddenly gripped my arm and I sprang back as a car on railroad tracks bore down on us like an enraged bull. As the machine ground to a halt in front of the furnace nearby, a man Neal later called the boss-melter opened the furnace door and out belched flames—red and orange and white. Fascinated, I watched him as he pushed levers to move a gigantic metal arm forward, thus deftly dumping his entire load into the furnace. As the door slammed shut, the flames in the furnace roared up so loudly I would have thought kerosene had been poured on them.

When the empty car moved away, Neal put his mouth to my ear. "That machine was loading limestone into the furnace. I think Furnace-Fifty-Nine is ripe for tapping. Follow me. But s-stick close.''

He need not have worried. How could the anteroom of hell be more dramatic than this! Now I understood what Mr. McKeever had meant about my seeing more than I could take in. So far I had not been able to write a word in my notebook.

The noise of the furnaces was suddenly punctuated by a shrill siren. I jumped. ''Where's the emergency?'' I shouted.

Neal laughed at me and roared into my ear, ''That's just the *telephone*, Julie.''

I looked at him in astonishment. Apparently everything in connection with steel making had to be grossly exaggerated—titan in size, ear-splitting noises, fiercely high temperatures, loads measured in hundreds of tons. What, I wondered, would it do to a man having to live every working day with such extremes?

Neal beckoned me to follow as he led the way to the rear of Furnace 59. A man in a protective suit was probing around in the furnace with a long steel rod. All at once a burst of flame shot out and the man jumped back out of the way. With our faces burning, Neal and I retreated too.

His mouth close to my ear, my guide answered my question before I could ask it. ''That's called 'ramming the taphole.' '' Neal handed me one of the goggles. ''Better put the blue ones on here.''

Next we saw a crane sliding a huge ladle full of molten pig iron along an overhead track toward the open furnace door. When the contents of the ladle entered the furnace, it sounded like a cannon going off, flames leaping almost to the roof.

With the cobalt-blue goggles on, there were incredible colors in the liquid steel: indigo, sapphire, violet, mauve, magenta. The swirling ripples and waves, encircling, made it seem like looking into the eye of a cyclone.

One of the helpers near us was wearing a strange device over his face. Despairing of making Neal hear me, I pointed to him.

Neal cupped his hand around his mouth and raised his voice. "That's Hans. He's an optical pyrometer. By looking at the s-steel through those things, he can tell the temperature to the degree."

Hans signaled with his arm, and the ladle moved under the furnace spout where it received a gush of molten steel throwing off red-white sparks. When the ladle was filled, it eased away, with Hans alongside it.

"He's testing it now," came the voice in my ear.

Following another signal from Hans, several men came forward carrying what looked to be giant spoons: each hurled something into the molten mixture.

"They're adding dolomite," he shouted.

I yelled back at him, "Looks like a giant pot of soup."

He grinned. "That's what they call it—'s-soup.' A potful of two hundred fifty tons."

Like cooks tasting a stew, the men kept thrusting elongated "soup spoons" into the heart of this molten brew. When a sample was poured into a testing mold, then plunged into a container of water, it would solidify enough to be dumped out of the mold and smashed to pieces with a sledgehammer.

I glanced over at Neal with questioning eyes.

"The grain of the break tells them the carbon content of that heat," he answered. "They're ready to tap now." He steered me to a nearby iron ladder which we climbed to a small platform (Neal called it a "pulpit"). There we had a perfect view of the drama below.

The crane on the track overhead moved over the ladle, and two big hooks closed over the ladle handle and effortlessly picked up the 250 tons of "soup." Then the crane carried the bucket, like a dog carrying a basket in his teeth, to an empty mold. The ladle tilted, and liquid steel poured into the mold with a shower of sparks, as though a hundred thousand sparklers had been simultaneously lit.

"That's called 'pouring a heat,' " Neal explained. "When it hardens, it's called an 'ingot.' Each one weighs five tons. Time for us to head back now."

As soon as we were outside the building, away from the noise and heat, I posed the question that troubled me most. "Neal, why did some of the men keep looking at me so strangely?"

He shrugged. "Workers are s-superstitious about women coming into the plant. Think it brings bad luck—an accident or something."

"How awful!"

"Don't let it get you."

As we walked back to the office one overwhelming concern took root in my mind. How could the men stand the heat, the noise and the danger hour after hour, day after day? No wonder they staggered to the nearest bar after work. I voiced this to Neal.

He did not answer for a moment. "They get used to it," he finally answered.

"But—it's inhuman!"

He suddenly stopped and turned and looked at me, a glint of anger in his eyes. "That's why we'll have a union here someday."

As we entered the administration building, slatey low-hanging clouds were beginning to spit rain. But my thoughts were not on the weather. I was wondering how Neal Brinton would come to terms with his circumstances. My mind played back to me his comment about the lucky guys who could go on to study chemistry and metallurgy. Where was this ambitious young "buckwheat" headed?

Mr. McKeever greeted us affably. "Learn anything, Julie?"

"More than I can remember. Your puddler's helper was a super tour guide." I shot Neal a grateful look.

"Steel is a world of its own," was McKeever's reply. "It's been *my* world all my life. When I was a little boy, Grandfather Yoder would take me by the hand and trot

me down to the plant to see and learn. Wily old Quaker.''
He chuckled. ''He wanted to make sure that the love of
steel would be part of my blood and bone and marrow, as
it was my father's.'' For an instant there was a softened,
faraway look in his eyes. Then he was all business again
as he dismissed Neal and wound up his conversation with
my father.

''Remember my slogan, Ken,'' he said in parting.
''It's easier for all of us if we work together.''

At dinner that night my visit to the mill dominated the
conversation until dessert. Then Mother asked Dad how
his meeting with McKeever had turned out.

''All right. I have the order for the ERP booklet.''

Mother stared at my father. ''Ken, you don't seem
very enthusiastic. Are there conditions?''

''No . . . Well, in a way.'' Dad looked uncomfortable.

''What's wrong?''

Dad saw that Tim and Anne-Marie had finished dessert, so he excused them from the table to get started on
homework. He looked at me doubtfully. For a moment I
thought I would be asked to leave too. Then he shrugged.

''I see no problem with the booklet itself. After all,
I'm just filling a print order. Certainly it's not the printer's role to censor the content of what he prints. And let's
face it, the money will be a godsend,'' he added, taking
his napkin and folding it neatly beside his plate. ''But after McKeever and I had gone over all the copy, he threw
something else into the pot.''

''What was that?''

''He talked about the Yoder ads they want to run in the
paper. Said he and his father want to build up more respect for the company in Alderton—'institutional advertisements,' they're called.''

''Anything wrong with that?''

''No. Many big companies are doing it. And I've the

clear impression, Louise, that the younger McKeever is constantly trying to stretch his father's thinking."

"Then what's troubling you, dear?"

The Editor looked pained. "It's not easy to describe because it's so subtle. Tom's a master at positive talk about our cooperating toward the same community goals. He hopes that *The Sentinel* will take a noncritical, positive approach to life in Alderton. I had the feeling that Tom was holding all of that in one hand and the many Yoder advertisements in the other."

"If he's putting pressure on you, Dad," I said with heat, "why not turn down the ads? *The Sentinel* can live without them."

Dad looked unhappy. Then he turned to me, his face cloudy. "Julie, not a word about this to anyone. You understand?"

"Of course," I said. Then came a sinking sensation as I sensed the agony of choices my father might have to face in the months ahead.

So far, every conflict had driven him to his bed.

15

AFTER I had concluded that Roger Benshoff did not intend to see me, the dam inspector telephoned one Friday morning. Miss Cruley took the message: Come for a short interview in the Club offices at four p.m.

The Editor made the old Willys available and I was at the Hunting and Fishing Club promptly at four, wondering if Randolph Wilkinson would be in on the interview. To my disappointment, Rand was not there. An officious secretary led me into one of the offices. "This is Julie Wallace of *The Alderton Sentinel*," she announced.

Roger Benshoff, a heavyset man with iron-gray hair, was seated at a small desk, a look of impatience on his face. He nodded curtly and waved me to a chair. "We need to do this quickly," he said. "I have to leave in fifteen minutes."

I sat there for a moment, feeling unwanted and ill-at-ease. "May I ask, Mr. Benshoff, why seeing me is so distasteful?"

He looked up at me, startled. "Not distasteful," he said quickly. "Just a waste of my time."

"*The Alderton Sentinel* has a wide readership," I said, in a huge overstatement. "The dam is of interest to these people."

"Why?"

"Because the danger of floods is always on their minds."

"The dam is perfectly safe."

"I'm glad to hear it. Would you give me some facts supporting this statement?"

He stared at me for such a long time that I wondered if he was going to refuse to answer. Then, with a shrug, he pulled out a paper and handed it to me. "Here's the schedule of my inspections," he said. "They will confirm the fact that it is inspected regularly." He stood up and reached for his coat.

Quickly I looked over the schedule as Mr. Benshoff stuffed some papers into a briefcase and placed the coat over his arm.

"Mr. Benshoff, this lists your inspection visits to the dam, but gives no details about your recommendations for repairs. The recent flood, for example. What damage did it do?"

"None."

"But there are small leaks—"

"Those are not leaks but normal spillage," he said sternly. "You will give wrong information if you report those as leaks." He suddenly thrust a hand toward me. "I'm already late for my appointment, Miss Wallace. Any further information about the dam should be obtained from Mr. Thomas McKeever, Sr." He shook my hand and departed.

Curtly dismissed, I walked outside to the Willys, wondering why Club officials were so touchy about the dam. If it was "perfectly safe," why weren't they more open about it?

Though facts were few, I did a story on the dam and placed it on the Editor's desk, explaining in an attached note how little information I had obtained from Mr. Benshoff. He read it through quickly.

"Good job, considering what you had to work with," he said. "But some things are missing. I think I'll go and see young Wilkinson myself. What am I to call him now?"

"R-a-n-d."

"Rand it is. Maybe he'll give us some more information."

Early Sunday morning I was in the kitchen helping Mother get breakfast. Dad was still upstairs dressing.

"Julie, your father came home so exhausted last night he could barely undress himself. That's why he's so slow this morning."

"Did he say where he'd been?"

"Out somewhere with Dean Fleming. A tub bath helped some, but his hands were blistered like he'd been digging with a shovel."

"That's probably right."

"Why would he spend a day doing that?"

"For the same reason Dean and his men came twice to the *Sentinel* to help us in an emergency. And all for free."

"So Kenneth is returning the favor."

"I guess so, Mother. These men, now including Dad, seem to go about quietly helping people in situations of need."

"It all seems a bit strange," Mother said just as Tim and Anne-Marie bounded into the kitchen.

It took the Editor a week to make a date with Rand, and then he returned from the interview without comment. I decided the story was dead. Perhaps my father did not want to take any chance of upsetting the business deals he was working out with young Mr. McKeever.

I was mistaken.

The following Wednesday afternoon when I arrived at *The Sentinel*, I found a fresh set of proofs on my desk. Attached was a terse note from Miss Cruley: "Have corrections to me by 4:30 today."

The Editor had completely reworked my story on the dam. Quickly I read through it:

ALDERTON'S THRIVING SUMMER COLONY

Only eight miles above Alderton, set in the grandeur of the Alleghenies, is one of Pennsylvania's beauty spots. Lake Kissawha, said to be the largest man-made lake in the United States, has become the focal point of a thriving summer colony.

I read on about the early history of the dam, the creation of the lake in 1854 by the state out of an area of forest and farmland, its collapse in 1862 due to erosion at the core, and its purchase in 1880 by the Pennsylvania Railroad, which repaired the dam and built the hotel in 1882 to serve as a resort area for its officers and executive personnel. The lake was then named Kissawha.

The railroad had also widened and redirected the bed of the stream below the dam so that all spillage from the lake would no longer flow into the Sequanoto River, but would be diverted into a new waterway which, several hundred yards to the southeast, joined another stream called Laurel Run. The waters of this stream wound down the mountain into Somerset Valley.

The Editor then went on to detail how, in 1926, the dam and hotel property were sold to fifteen Philadelphia and Pittsburgh men who renovated it and named it the Hunting and Fishing Club. My interest picked up at the next paragraph.

In 1927 repairs were made on the dam under the supervision of Mr. Roger Benshoff, a native of Alderton, who served as foreman and superintendent of the work. Mr. Benshoff holds the position of railroad contractor in the Pennsylvania Railroad. He has also been hired to inspect the dam at regular intervals.

The original dam had been seventy feet high. The height of the rebuilt dam was lowered three to five feet with dishing (an engineering term for central sag) at the crest. The spillways, cut into solid rock at both ends of the dam, were left as originally constructed.

According to Mr. Randolph Wilkinson, Club Assistant Manager, the lake covers 450 acres and upon occasion, especially during spring rains, fed by numerous mountain streams emptying into the lake, it can be as deep as seventy feet. The equivalent of 500 million tons of water is backed up behind the dam.

At this point, the Editor had crossed out several sentences about local flooding conditions. I guessed why. No need to relate the dam to the floods that had so often beset Yancyville, Mills Ford and Alderton.

But mere facts and figures can in no way do justice to the beauty of Lake Kissawha, surrounded as it is by rugged mountain scenery. The Hunting and Fishing Club has shown us the benefits of careful planning in conservation. For instance, Lake Kissawha has been lavishly stocked with bass, pike and trout to the obvious delight of the Club's anglers. The spillways have been covered with iron gratings to keep the fish from escaping downstream.

That should please Rand, I thought.

On the other hand, have we in the Alderton area been so preoccupied with making a living and with industrial growth as to be oblivious or indifferent to the marring of our environment? The fact is that few areas of this nation were blessed with as many natural resources or as much beauty as the Pennsylvania Alleghenies. Yet man, in his eager questing for wealth, has seldom been wise in his handling of these resources.

These last paragraphs were turning an article into an editorial. I did not know whether this was considered proper newspaper procedure, but I liked it.

I urge you to check this out for yourself. Drive up into the mountains some weekend soon and feast your eyes on the scenery. Upon your descent back into the valley and the town, you may find the contrast a shocker.

You may ask, as others have, must the open sores of strip mining on the hills around Alderton be left that way? What about the denuding of all the hills, with no effort at reforestation? Is there a feasible solution to deal with the slag heaps and the air pollution? The genius of American industry has handled many seemingly insurmountable problems. Can we not handle these also?

These questions and many more we citizens of Alderton need to consider for the good of the community as a whole.

The Editor

Emotion choked me as I finished proofing the copy. Considering the power the McKeevers had over us, my father was showing a surprising new courage in printing this editorial.

When I arrived at the office after school the next day, Dean Fleming was making some repairs on the press. It had broken down for the second straight week and delivery of *The Sentinel* would be late if he could not fix it.

Unflappable as always, Dean soon had the press running again. But he was shaking his bald head as he limped into the Editor's office. "Don't know how long we can keep fixing it, Ken. The roller had jumped out of the frame, got wedged, and cracked part of the frame."

As long as Dean sticks with us, that press will make it, I thought to myself.

In fact, our family was seeing so much of Dean Fleming now that he seemed like someone we had always known. His walking into the *Sentinel* office that first day and voluntarily offering Dad the gift of ten hours each week had been an extraordinary commitment. Again the question haunted me, why would he be so generous? We'd been strangers to him at the time.

Though he often unsettled me, I admired his way of slipping unobtrusively into the office to get on with whatever needed doing. With Dean available to repair breaks or loose bearings or to hang a new shaft line or to adjust the take-up on the main bearings when they had been shimmied, some of Miss Cruley's fluttery nervousness was beginning to subside.

After Margo met Dean at the *Sentinel* one day, she told me a story about him that she had heard from one of the gossipy patrons of the Stemwinder. Two years before, a small private airplane had developed engine trouble and been forced down in a grassy field on the outskirts of Alderton. There was no airplane mechanic in our area. Then somebody thought of Dean Fleming and sent for him. Though Dean had never before seen an airplane engine, within three hours he had the plane flying again.

Dean had won the hearts of Tim and Anne-Marie with the gift of Boy, who had become a member of our family. His loan of money to Dad had probably saved the paper. Mother had quite warmed to both Dean and Hazel. Which left me in the rear, struggling with some mixed emotions.

Was I jealous of Dean's close relationship with my father? I had to admit I resented the many hours that Dad was with him and those other men. If they were playing golf or tennis or even hiking, I could have better understood it. I agreed with Mother: the secretive nature of what they did was a bit strange.

Yet I liked going to the Fleming farm. It had a comfortable atmosphere with its old furniture and rugs of turkey reds, indigo blues and mustard yellows. The mellow mood was also evident in the ancient copper, brass and pewter, as well as old china, glass and antiques. But the farm passed another test too: liveliness.

The kitchen was continually in use, with Miss Hazel always baking, canning or preserving. A spacious red barn contained four horses and two Guernsey cows. Milling about outside were pigs, dogs, chickens, geese and even some rabbits.

The animal that most completely won Anne-Marie's heart was the oldest and most decrepit of all—the horse called "Shorty." He was a moth-eaten brown, sway-backed, with his ribs showing. A split hoof, along with rheumatism, limited Shorty to a slow walk around the pasture. No wonder! Multiplying Shorty's years by four made him 105! He was so bony that no saddle could be used on him. Therefore the only way Anne-Marie could ride him was to clamber on the board fence and climb onto him bareback.

My little sister loved and petted the old horse, fed him sugar lumps, crooned to him while currying and stroking him. "Julie," she said once, "his big brown eyes make me want to cry, especially when he turns his head and looks at me."

The rest of us knew that Dean had been on the verge of getting rid of Shorty; now the old horse would be prince of the pasture until he dropped.

On one subject Dean and I did strike a note of mutuality: trees. As a tiny girl I had wept rebellious tears when a huge two-hundred-year-old oak in our front yard in Timmeton had to be cut down. In my eyes, the men were killing a living thing as they hacked at the proud old tree.

Dean Fleming's love affair with trees dated back to his youth. He told us he saw trees as the crown and glory of nature's handiwork. Shade and beauty, fuel too, timber for houses and a thousand other benefits. They controlled the purity of the air above and the water in the ground; they were the earth's greatest single controller of the climate.

In most sections of Pennsylvania birches were scattered through the forests, their white trunks contrasting with the deep emerald evergreens. "Grace notes of the woods," Dean called them. But on his farm, he had taken such good care of the birches that they could no longer be called "grace notes"—more like a melody all their own.

Late that Friday afternoon, the Editor and I locked up the office and climbed into the old Willys. Mother was going with Anne-Marie to a church supper for the junior Sunday School classes; Tim left with Graham Gillin and his younger brother, Troy, to attend a sports dinner. When Dean heard that Dad and I were free, he invited us out to the farm for dinner.

When we were gathered about the picnic table outside, the subject of Dad's editorial on the dam came up. "Dean, do you think it will rile certain people?" the Editor asked.

"Nobody in Alderton expects anything controversial from a weekly newspaper," Dean answered slowly. "So my guess is, most people will read it with mild interest, figuring you're saying what the McKeevers want said."

"Only mild interest?"

"The Club and the dam are remote to most people in Alderton, Ken. But," he continued, "something you said about how *ugly* we've made the Alderton area may arouse a few people."

"Who, for instance?"

"The McKeevers. Railroad officials. Businessmen."

"I hope they'll do something constructive, not just get mad."

Dean smiled. "Stick a needle into someone and he'll yell 'Ouch!' I'm glad you did that story. It could lead to something good."

After dinner, Miss Hazel and I were clearing the table when Dean Fleming rose from his chair. "Would you mind if I took Ken and Julie over to the cabin for a while?"

She shook her head. "Cleanup's no problem with a picnic."

As the three of us walked toward the cabin, I was feeling conscience-stricken. Was it selfish of me to prefer talking with the two men rather than staying to help Miss Hazel?

As Dean opened the cabin door, my anticipation shunted aside all other thoughts. We were standing in a rustic pine-paneled room with huge ceiling beams from which were hanging old-fashioned kerosene lanterns. At the far end was a pot-bellied wood-burning heating stove. Along both walls were built-in bunk beds in two tiers. Wooden benches filled the remaining space on the side walls.

Adjacent to where we stood was a fieldstone fireplace and in the space before it, several Adirondack-type chairs around a large wooden-slatted beer keg upturned to form a table. A deep blue cloth with a white cross appliqued on it had been thrown over the keg.

But what really caught my attention hung over the fireplace mantel—a double-edged woodsman's ax, or what Dean called a double-bitted ax, the real thing as compared to the decorative aluminum ax on the outside chimney. Standing on the hearth and tilting my head, I could barely make out an inscription burned into the wood of the handle: *And now also the ax is laid unto the root of the trees . . . Matthew 3:10.*

"There must be a story behind that ax," I blurted out.

Though I knew Dean had heard me, he did not respond immediately. He struck a match and soon a log fire was blazing on the hearth. Then he stood up and faced my father and me. "The ax, Julie? That was a special gift from Big John Hammond. It's a symbol of a covenant relationship between the two uf us."

After we found comfortable positions in front of the fire, my eyes kept returning to the ax. How could simple firelight reflect so many colors in the polished steel?

I hoped that the mystery about Dean and Big John Hammond was about to be revealed.

16

Dean Fleming sat for a long moment, staring silently into the dancing flames.

"John Hammond was an extraordinary man, Julie," he began. "Most people spend ninety percent of their time thinking about themselves, ten percent about others. With Big John it was just the opposite. He was the most selfless man I ever knew."

Dean got up to rearrange the logs with a poker, then settled back in his chair, repositioning his bad leg. "I first met him in a saloon in a timber camp outside a town called Cameron, east of here. I was in my early twenties, married, with two small children: worked as a machinist on a log train. My problem was booze.

Dean then went on to describe how greed for lumber during the last part of the century nearly destroyed the vast forest land of hemlock, white pine, spruce and poplar in central Pennsylvania. Roads were cut, crude camps for lumberjacks erected. Each camp contained bunkhouses, a dining room and adjoining cookshed, an office, a "store" for necessities like tobacco and patent medicines, barns for the horses and a blacksmith shop.

Soon the faces of small Pennsylvania villages were altered beyond recognition. What had been quiet, unspoiled communities became lusty, boisterous frontier towns, always dominated by the saloons.

Dean described how a motley collection of brewers, bartenders, and saloon "touts" would meet all arriving

143

logging trains and genially lure newcomers to the nearest bars. Awaiting were the professional gamblers, pickpockets, short-change artists and brothel keepers, all with their hands out to strip from the lumberjacks their "stake"—the wages earned back in the "tall timber." Towns were irresistible to the lumberjacks since there was neither recreation nor relief from isolation back in the deep woods.

Most of the boisterous, thirsty men couldn't wait to pull out their rolls of bills and slap the money on the counter. For those slow in loosening up with their cash, there were often knockout drops in their drinks. In one night a man could lose all he had earned in six months and be tossed into the Snake-Room.

"I'll never forget the first time I ever saw a Snake-Room," Dean reflected. "Julie, it won't hurt you to hear this. It was about two in the morning when I entered this upstairs room. There was no ventilation; the foul air was a combination of unwashed bodies, stale tobacco, overpowering whiskey breaths, and the stench of vomit; plus head and chest colds in all stages.

"On a filthy floor, men were lying like huge rag dolls, sprawled one atop another. Some were sobbing, others groaning, talking to themselves, snoring, cursing, singing in cracked voices. Several men were hallucinating, clawing at spiders in the air or fighting mad dogs or snakes.

"The Snake-Room was necessary for every saloon, since usually it was too cold to throw drunks outside. Men sometimes smothered to death under the weight of the bodies. If a man died back there, who cared? Local undertakers did a booming business."

By that time, Dean explained, he would be away from home on hard drinking sprees for three to five days. "I would come back from each fling penitent but broke, like most of the lumberjacks—everything blown in the bars. Each time I would promise my wife, Betty, that I would stop. Then would come the temptation of just one drink and off I would go again.''

Dean sighed heavily. "I could see Betty's love for me dying by inches. By then her father hated me. He was having to help us financially and that 'most always tears a relationship.''

Our host got up to poke the fire again. "One night I strolled into Willie's Place, which was the newest and largest saloon in the village. A lumberjack had just staggered in ahead of me and was shouting to everyone in sight, 'Come on you road-monkeys and river-pigs, it's all on me. Turn on the spigot. This here'll cover it.' And he slapped a fat roll of bills on the bar.

"I watched the bartender reach for the money. Suddenly another hand shot out and picked up the bills. 'I'll be your banker until morning, Frank,' the stranger said firmly to the drunken man. 'You've had enough booze for one evening.'

"The bartender was furious. 'Give me that money, Big John,' he shouted, 'or I'll knock your head off.' Then he picked up a wooden club and leapt over the counter.

"The stranger called Big John had already pocketed the roll of bills. He was not a big man, really, well under six feet, strong but not overly muscular; he had a round face, which was ruddy from outdoor life, and reddish, disheveled hair. Looked like a woodsman. And he obviously knew the bartender. 'This is my business, Denny,' he said, 'I'm takin' Frank out of here. He's too drunk to handle his money right now.'

"The bartender named Denny sprang forward, aiming a blow at the stranger with his weapon. The stranger ducked and a fist shot forward, making a crunching connection with Denny's face: it was followed by a battering-ram blow to his stomach. The bartender fell, glassy-eyed, to the sawdust-covered floor. The stranger then turned to the drunken lumberjack. 'Let's go, Frank.'

"But Frank had slithered to the floor in a stupor. As if

the big lumberjack had been a child, his rescuer picked him up in his arms, tossed the limp body over his shoulder, and made for the door.

"What astonished me about this scene was not so much the stranger's unexpected raw strength and quiet courage, but the way the spectators, with ill-concealed glee, had been rooting for him. It didn't make sense. Free drinks had been jerked from under their noses, so to speak, and to a man they were a thirsty lot.

"I asked a lumberjack standing beside me who the guy was who had flattened the bartender.

"The jack stared at me in surprise. 'That's Big John Hammond. You don't know *him?*'

"I shook my head. 'Why is he called Big John? He's not so big.'

" 'It ain't his size.' The jack looked at me in disgust. 'He acts big. Talks big too. He's a preacher—'

" 'A preacher! I'm not believin' you.' For the rest of the evening I sat with three lumberjacks over drinks at a corner table and we talked about John Hammond. They told me that for some years now, Big John had been moving from one logging camp to another in Pennsylvania, New York, and West Virginia, bringing the Word, as he liked to say, to isolated men. Not even blizzards or below-zero weather could stop Big John."

Dean ministered again to the fire as I sat there silently, fascinated by the raw masculinity of the story, both attracted to and repelled by it.

"In the beginning, no one understood Hammond," Dean continued. "He had trouble even getting inside logging camps. But soon, even the bosses had to admit that Big John's visits helped the men, raised morale, enabled them to turn out better work."

Dean went on to describe how at each camp, Hammond would first bring to the jacks stacks of secondhand magazines to help supply the camp's almost nonexistent reading material. He would pray with the victims of accidents—frequently himself getting an injured man to the nearest hospital. Not until he was accepted did Big John begin holding evening services in the bunkhouses.

At first the lumberjacks had been as suspicious of Hammond's motives as the camp bosses were. "What's in it for you?" they had put it to Big John. "You sure ain't preachin' for nothin'. That jest ain't human nature."

"You're right about that, boys," he had replied. "That's not the human nature any of us is born with. But there's a different kind of nature waiting for us, much better, let me tell you. You there—" He pointed to one of the oldest jacks in the circle questioning him. "I've been watching you. You're a fine top-loader. How long have you been at this business?"

"Since I was a boy. Forty-seven winters."

"So how much do you have to show for forty-seven years of such hard work?"

Ruefully, the gray-haired man had turned his pockets inside out. "Nothin' but this." In the palm of his hand was an old jackknife.

"The leeches and bloodsuckers always cleaned you out." There was sadness in Hammond's voice. "What kind of life is *that*, men? So now you have the answer to why I'm here. There's some mighty good news for you. Not a one of you needs to end up like that."

Then, in the simplest terms, he told them about a Carpenter who traveled hot days and cold nights, across wild rocky terrain, through desert winds and dust, to help people caught in thickets of illness and pain, or of poverty, or of hatred, or discouragement and disillusionment, or booze. "He cares enough to find you and rescue you today, wherever you are, whatever you've done," he stressed.

Big John, knowing well that no mere words would break down the skepticism about his motives, followed through with the kind of action that won the admiration and love of even the roughest lumberjacks. One summer Hammond lived an itinerant life—with a group of loggers, hitching rides on freight trains, wielding a pick for a while in the West Virginia coal mines, joining migratory pickers harvesting peas in Imperial Valley, California, ending up that fall as a deckhand on a boat plying the Columbia River.

After he had traveled by boxcar with these refugees from logging camps, slept with them in cheap lodging houses, camped with them in the fields, shared their panhandling and meal scraps, Hammond not only understood these rough men, he was as tough as any of them. He learned to use his fists. He could wield an ax. If a crew was shorthanded, he worked side by side with the men at no pay.

Meanwhile, Dean's drinking problem had worsened. Neither high resolves nor will power could pull him out of his morass. One bitterly cold January night, he had sought the warmth of a bar before returning home. One drink was all he needed, Dean told himself. . . . He was coming down with a cold. Must be grippe, because he was aching all over. A hot toddy would help him shake this off.

When he came to, he was lying in bed in a strange room and a ruddy-faced man was sitting beside him. A look around told Dean nothing. Underneath the blankets piled atop him, he still had on his long underwear.

"Where am I?" he muttered.

The man reached out a calloused hand and gently touched Dean's forehead. "Take it easy. You've had a tough pull. I'm John Hammond and I know who you are because I've been through your pockets for identification."

Then Dean remembered. All those stories the three lumberjacks had told him that one evening about Big John. But how had he ended up here in this room with him?

The ruddy man beside him sensed his question. "I found you in the Snake-Room three nights ago and trundled you here in a wheelbarrow. You've been mighty sick. Now try and lie still. I'll get you some hot broth.''

With Dean propped up against one of his arms, Hammond patiently fed him the broth, one spoonful at a time.

Dean whispered hoarsely between swallows, "My wife?''

"Found out about your wife when I went through your pockets. Sent her a message to let her know you're in my care.''

With each sip of the steaming broth, the sick man began to feel stronger. Over and over during the days that followed, the question went through Dean Fleming's mind: *Why would Big John be doing all this for me?* The two had never even met before.

As he began to recover, the old thirst for "just that one drink" gnawed at his vitals. Finally Dean appealed to Big John. "Just one little drink would sure get me on my feet quicker.''

Hammond shook his head. Then it came out that Dean's rescuer had more in mind than curing his grippe. Big John intended to see Dean through a drying-up period, cold turkey. The boardinghouse room had been stripped of all clothing except what Big John himself had on his back and the longjohns Dean wore in bed. Not even a desperate man was likely to walk into the winter cold in his underwear. If he attempted such an escape, Big John told Dean, he would strip him naked.

Dean tried every argument. Nothing budged his rescuer. Crazed with thirst one day, Dean threw himself at Hammond. Big John handled him as if he were a small child.

At different times Dean hated his captor, marveled at him, puzzled about him, then hurled obscenities at that round, ruddy face. None of it affected Big John. He was compassionate about the battle being waged, but like tempered steel in his determination to see it through.

Unable to bend Hammond, Dean began to ask him

questions. Why was he out in the boondocks doing what he was doing?

Hammond admitted that in the beginning, he had dreamed of having an important city pulpit. Then, while pastoring a small church in Johnstown, his wife had died in childbirth. Angry at God, Hammond had left the church and become a roustabout in and about logging camps. One morning after a wild drinking bout, he awoke in a strange boarding house to find a Bible on the table by his bed. He had not read it in weeks, but something made him pick it up. He turned to a passage in the book of John about another man named John, who roamed the countryside, eating locusts and wild honey.

Fuzzy-minded as he was, Hammond couldn't shake off the coincidences. His name was John too; he was wandering about the country, eating anything he could find. Suddenly he knew that this was the Lord giving him another chance. He was being called to a new mission—in the logging camps. Like John the Baptist, he would prepare the hearts of the people he met for the coming of a Saviour.

By the time the worst of the drying-out period was over, a bond between Dean Fleming and John Hammond had been forged. Here was a man, Dean recognized, who had found a source of power he had never known existed. Gradually his hunger for this power overcame his thirst for liquor. As Big John's helper and pupil, Dean witnessed scenes he could never forget. . . . Such as that night when Hammond was holding an evening service in the bunkhouse of a logging camp. Outside, the snow-drifts were waist-high. Inside, there was only the dim light from a few hanging lanterns, the air pungent from unwashed bodies and tobacco smoke. The only ventilation was one trap door in the roof.

A keg turned on its end with a horse blanket thrown over it served as Hammond's pulpit. The "pews" were the floor or bunks—dozens of stockinged feet swinging over the edge of the top bunks.

The jacks began by singing lustily some old Gospel hymns, beginning with "What a Friend We Have in Jesus."

Big John was just into his sermon when, at the other end of the bunkhouse, a logger began singing drunkenly. The noise made talking or listening impossible.

Three times Hammond stopped and appealed to the man. Each time the raucous singing would start anew. Entertained by the battle of wit and will, the lumberjacks waited to see how Big John would handle this one.

After the fourth interruption, the disruptor aimed a punch at Hammond. Big John ducked, grabbed the man, hoisted him above his head, carried him outside and, as the jacks cheered, tossed him headfirst into a snowdrift.

"The message that night," Dean continued, "was the same Hammond used over and over. He would read them this Scripture from Matthew:

And now also the ax is laid upon the root of the trees: every tree therefore which bringeth not forth good fruit is hewn down and cast into the fire.

"Using terms the men understood, Big John would lay before them their need for God, letting them know that the road to Him was not smooth and easy; that first they had to repent of their sins. Otherwise God would cut them down like bad fruit and cast them into the fire. Hammond was John the Baptist, returned after nineteen hundred years, thundering his message, preparing the men for the second coming of the Saviour, exhorting, demanding—a spellbinder in the boondocks."

Dean paused a moment to reflect. "I was with Big John constantly during his last years. Lacking strength to continue his missions to logging camps, he began to train some of us to carry on the work in the bigger world. I've been at it now for fourteen years."

* * *

The story was over, the fire had gone out, but before leaving the cabin, I moved toward the fireplace to take a closer look at the ax handle. There was something that had escaped me before—two words in very small letters underneath the verse: *The Preparers*.

Outside, the mauve twilight had turned into night. Fireflies now twinkled on the grounds. As we walked back toward the farmhouse, many questions flooded my mind.

"There's still one missing piece to this story about John Hammond," I ventured. "That ax over the fireplace. Why did Big John give it to you, Dean? It must have some significance between the two of you."

"Yes, Julie, it does."

That was all he would say.

On the way home, my father and I were silent, lost in our thoughts. Contentedly, I leaned my head against his shoulder. Suddenly I was aware of something. A barely perceptible change had occurred in my father over the past few weeks, sometimes appearing in his conversation, in his smile, in the way he walked. The sag was gone from his shoulders.

17

THE spring weather was now so beautiful that every weekend I headed for the woods near the Fleming farm to search for plants for my wildflower garden. Dean Fleming had encouraged me, pointing out such unusual spring flowers as columbines, false lily-of-the-valley and silver-fuzzed fiddlehead ferns. He taught me secrets gleaned from his years in the woods, such as how the aromatic broad-leaved sarsaparilla plant could usually be found near clumps of cedars; or about the tiny wildflower goldenthread, whose name came from its delicate root of purest gold color.

Questions I asked Dean about John Hammond were answered fully. When I probed into his "covenant relationship" with my father, he was closed-mouthed except to say, "The basis of such a friendship is the way John Hammond cared for me when I was in trouble." As for The Preparers, he merely said we might talk about them later.

Meanwhile, my work load at *The Sentinel* was increasing. The proofreading had remained heavy, in fact, taking even more time since I was determined not to make any more serious mistakes. There were more short news stories to do, plus the major article on my visit to the steel mill which I had hoped would be considered as a feature story in the newspaper, as well as being my school term paper. Research on steel making covered one end of my table. I kept my papers hidden from Miss Cruley as best I could.

After seven months, Miss Cruley's reception of me at the office continued to range from cool to icy. She still disapproved of my doing the proofreading, never letting me forget the Gaither ad. She sniffed every time the Editor referred to me as a ''reporter.'' She looked at my piles of research books with sharp suspicion. Only reluctantly did she take time off to instruct me on how to use the linotype machine.

Since Emily Cruley was Alderton born and reared, Dad had turned over to her the task of preparing for publication all material sent in by the paper's local correspondents. In rural districts and small towns, he had discovered, readers wanted to know which child had won the local essay contest or which farmer brought in the first of the apple or watermelon crops, or who had just announced their engagement to be married. Of less interest to them was a tornado in Kansas or Eleanor Roosevelt's latest social action project.

A quality of unquenchable enthusiasm in these correspondents was one of their best assets. Next came the self-discipline needed to get copy in every week and on time. Far down in importance was the quality of writing. Their pay was a free subscription to *The Sentinel*, complimentary tickets to certain civic events, and a supply of personal stationery. There were other compensations: the fun of being a writer, the feeling of importance in reporting local news and having a byline.

Paul Proctor had given my father one essential tip: folks like to see their names in print. It was also a good idea, he had advised, to publish letters from readers. Such items were often clipped out and pasted in scrapbooks or in family Bibles, or even framed.

Some local correspondents were flavorsome characters. Carrie Price Harrison, for example, was a local history buff who collected genealogies and was fascinated with inscriptions on old tombstones. Once she wrote about "a colonial gentleman of quality"—indeed, none other than John Custis, Martha Washington's father-in-law—who decreed in his will that he should be buried standing straight up because, having never bowed his head to anyone in life, he was not about to do so in death.

On another occasion, she triumphantly brought in line drawings which showed twin mausoleums built by a wealthy couple on their land; the tombs were fifty yards apart. The inscription on the wife's was standard; that on the husband's tomb, most revealing:

> Never together in life,
> never together in death.

One week's contribution was about someone not yet dead—one B. C. Barnhouse. The initials in Barnhouse's name fascinated Mrs. Harrison because Barnhouse was 113 years old.

Yet another correspondent was always coming up with marvelous "guaranteed" home remedies and herb cures. For arthritis he recommended "three cups of milk per day, with five drops of turpentine in each cup." He tried it for three months, he wrote, and the pain in his joints ceased. Probably, I thought, from an intense desire to be rid of such a gaggingly noxious drink.

Then there was Matilda McWorth, age seventy-nine, who had a love affair with Victorian gentility and was certain that modern manners "were leading our nation to ruin." Her advice:

> When a gentleman takes a lady's arm, he should not grab her at the elbow. That is passé. A man of culture bends his arm at the elbow while his hand rests on his hip. Thus, a niche is formed for the lady's fingers to slip into it, affording all the support she needs.

Or another week . . .

Clumsiness in kissing is inexcusable. It is not necessary to walk on a girl's feet or smash her corsage or take a viselike grip on her dress. Nor should kisses be fired broadside at an eye, an ear or her neck. Try to remember, men, that the aims of male and female are identical. Keep cool, pull the lady gently toward your manly form, and let nature do her work.

Collating all this news, advice, and never-ending stream of prose was a big job—also a touchy one, because the feelings of so many people were involved. I knew that the Editor was uneasy about leaving all this to Miss Cruley, but he had no alternative.

Miss Cruley took this responsibility very seriously. Her telephone calls to check on reporters soon became imperious: they were to do their writing by Sunday and get their copy to the *Sentinel* office by Monday. "Copy brought in here on Tuesday is simply too late," her piping voice would shrill into the telephone.

The Editor's article on the Hunting and Fishing Club produced little reaction from readers. Two letters applauded the Editor for his concern about the environment issue. Only one, postmarked Yancyville, indicated concern about the dam. I think Dad felt let down because of the seeming disinterest.

The Yoder booklet was printed the following Tuesday. It was dull and wordy, yet reasonable enough. Only one sentence bothered me: "The management of Yoder Steel reserves the right to discontinue this employee program on one month's notice."

Before delivering the booklets to Yoder, the Editor announced to us that he planned to drive the Willys to Pittsburgh on Wednesday. There was a college roommate to see, plus some business to attend to. He would be gone overnight.

"This week's *Sentinel* is pretty well set up," he told me. "I think you and Emily can put it to bed."

The following afternoon, since the Editor was away, I was reading proofs more carefully than ever. I caught the typo that Mrs. J. J. Rogel from New *Pork* City had arrived in town to visit relatives.

Next, I noticed some strange phrasing in this item sent in by the social correspondent:

Mary Slifko, Alderton's chief telephone operator, underwent surgery on Friday last week at Municipal Hospital. This very popular young lady's man friends wish her a speedy recovery.

That "man friends" leapt out at me. Surely Miss Cruley had inadvertently left off the "y" when setting this copy.

Proof in hand, I went to Miss Cruley, who was poring over the *Sentinel* subscription records, which she kept in a closely guarded black leather case. "Would you please look at this, Miss Cruley? I believe there may be a mistake here." I slid the galley in front of her.

The thin face flushed "You're a fine one to talk about mistakes, my girl! Where? Where is it?"

I pointed. "Shouldn't that be *many friends?*"

"Hmm. Well, yes," she agreed coolly. "I think you're right."

She seemed to be struggling with herself. Then she must have decided to play a new role with me. "You are showing a little improvement, Julie. If you continue to be this careful, perhaps you can yet be of some use to your father."

Oh, well, I thought as I went back to the proofs, *even condescension is better than disdain.*

Ten minutes or so later, I saw something so startling that I almost shouted. There, set in type, was one of my poems that I had handed over to the Editor months ago. It had been placed in a column by itself under the heading "Poetry Corner."

Spring Growing Pains
I wonder if these tiny blades of grass,
Bowing to all the winds that pass
Have growing pains.

I wonder if this newborn beauty here
Almost too much to bear this year
Hurts them too.

I sat there, stunned, trying to think. How could this have happened? I remembered that I had purposely not typed my name anywhere on the sheets; also, that after reading the poems and commenting on them briefly, my father had thrust them into a desk drawer. Had he arranged this before leaving for Pittsburgh? I doubted it. Somehow, "Poetry Corner" did not sound like my father. Emily Cruley, then? Curiosity got the better of me, but I knew that I should be cautious.

Once again, I carried the proof to her. "Excuse me, Miss Cruley," I asked delicately, "this is a new feature, isn't it—having poetry?"

"Yes, it is," she rapped out. There was just a trace of defensiveness in her voice.

Should I tell her the poem's mine? I do believe she thinks she's pulled a coup. If I confess, that could spoil everything for her.

Miss Cruley's eyes were on the poem. "It does read well, doesn't it? I thought a Poetry Corner would add, well, a bit of class to the paper."

"A good idea," I agreed. "So glad you thought of it."

She was beaming as I went back to my work.

Thursday afternoon, Dad returned from Pittsburgh. Once home, his first move after greeting us was to look over the current issue of *The Sentinel.* All agog to get his reaction to the Poetry Corner, I stood there watching as he scanned the paper.

Then he saw it. Spreading the page out flat, he bent

over to take a closer look, then wheeled to face me. "Julie, what did you do?"

"Honest, cross my heart, I had nothing to do with it. The first time I saw it was in proofs."

He burst out laughing. "Did you tell Emily it was yours?"

"Of course not. She might have destroyed the whole press run."

"So, Emily needed more filler and came up with your poetry—unsigned."

"Did you put it in the filler file?"

"Must have. Probably when everything was re-sorted after the flood."

"Only thing is, she'll want to print more—at least one each issue. She's proud as anything of her Poetry Corner idea."

"Actually, Julie, I think you're too shy about your poetry. Oh, I know it feels more 'private' to you than prose. But I thought some of your poems quite good. I just wasn't sure poetry belonged in a weekly newspaper. So then I turned my back and Emily decides for me." He was still chuckling when Mother called us to dinner.

After dinner, as Mother and I were washing the dishes, she voiced a question that I knew had been on her mind for weeks. "Spencer Meloy has phoned here three times for you, Julie. Are you working with him on some kind of church project?"

"He's trying to develop a young adult group. Thinks I can help, I guess."

"He has also been to see you at *The Sentinel.*" Mother smiled. "Are you sure there isn't more to it than a church project?"

I sighed. "Spencer is young, single and looking for friendship."

"You call him Spencer?"

"He asked me to."

"I see."

"Now, Mother, don't make a case out of this. He hasn't asked me for a date. But I like to talk with him and, well, I find him rather amazing for a preacher. He's so young and yet so dynamic."

Mother still had that questioning look in her eyes. "Spencer's sermons are not at all what you would expect from a pastor chosen by the McKeevers."

"I don't think he believes in much of what the McKeevers do."

"What does he believe?"

"For one thing, that the Church should be doing something for poor people."

"I have no objections to your seeing Spencer Meloy," Mother said finally. "But he's years older than you."

"He's ten years older. Somehow it doesn't seem important. He's not only interesting, he's fun to be with."

"Fun."

"Mother, is it somehow wrong for a preacher to be fun? He laughs a lot. He has a sense of humor. He says the unexpected."

"I see. Well, he's a mature man. You're still in high school."

"But only for a few more weeks," I said wearily.

I was in my room studying later that night when I looked up to see my father in the doorway. "I need answers to a couple of questions, daughter," he said.

"I'm ready."

"After your sidewalk interview with Wilkinson—the one right after the flood—you reported back that there had been no damage to the dam."

"That's what he said."

"Well, when I was at the Club to see Rand several weeks later, there was repair work going on at the dam—truckloads of fill and what appeared to be the insertion of metal supports."

"I guess Rand was wrong," I said, a little protectively.

"Or the damage might have appeared later. Another question. When you saw Mr. Benshoff, did you think to ask him if there was a recent engineering report on the dam?"

"Gosh, Dad. No."

"Well, I didn't think of it either, until I talked to Rand. At the end of my interview with him, I asked if there was such a report. He said he didn't know of any."

"Old Man McKeever would be the one to ask about that," I volunteered.

"Yes, I guess so. Which I'm not about to do." The Editor seemed alert, almost tense, for so late at night after his long day. "I discovered some things today in Pittsburgh that will interest you, Julie," he continued. "The college roommate I went to see is a man named Cyrus Stearns. He's an executive in the advertising department of the Pennsylvania Railroad."

"Then he should know Roger Benshoff," I shot back.

"My thought too." Dad continued. "When I telephoned Cyrus earlier in the week, I asked him if he knew Benshoff. He didn't, which isn't surprising since railroad personnel are spread all over Pittsburgh. Then I told him about the sale of Lake Kissawha to the Club nine years ago and the questions we had about the safety of the dam. I asked Cyrus if he felt there could have been an engineer's report done at the time of the sale. He said he would make inquiries and asked me to see him when I came to Pittsburgh."

"So, what did you learn?" I interrupted, now fully excited.

"Stearns had a friend in the records division, so he put in a routine request to see if there was an engineer's report done on the dam before its sale. His friend checked the file and found through the sales contract that an engineer's report had been done and should have been attached. But the report was not in the file."

"Stolen?" I gasped.

"Possibly. Or misfiled. Or lost. Once the transaction

was completed, the railroad would no longer be concerned."

"If the dam broke and destroyed railroad property, they would be concerned," I said.

My father smiled at me. "There's nothing more we can do about it now. I suggest we focus our attention on other matters."

In a way I agreed, since our interest in the dam had not exactly strengthened our relationship with Randolph Wilkinson. Yet my mind would not drop the intriguing phrase: *missing dam report.*

18

MORE and more the big old *Sentinel* office was beginning to feel like a second home to our family. Tim and Anne-Marie were in and out often, emptying wastebaskets, sweeping the floor and preparing papers for delivery. Wherever they went, our collie, Boy, trailed after. Boy was at the office so often that Dad was already calling him the paper's mascot.

The only problem was that every time the cutter was used, as its wicked guillotine like blade would descend, shaking the building and rattling the windows, Boy would dart frantically about, howling and barking as if the place were being invaded. This ever-repeated performance irritated Emily Cruley no end. "Dumb dog!" she would mutter between clenched teeth. "Never learns. Shouldn't be allowed in here a'tall."

While Miss Cruley still objected to so much family participation, the Editor's warm acceptance of her Poetry Corner had made her a trifle more mellow. With great curiosity, I waited to see what she would do the second week. On Tuesday, I found out. At the bottom of the column she had inserted:

Our new feature, Poetry Corner, has been received with enthusiastic response. Undoubtedly there is unknown and unsung talent hidden in our town. Your original contributions are solicited.

My father winced when he saw this, though he let it pass. He knew that some terrible verse could be submitted, and in a small town, how would the Editor reject contributions without causing hurt feelings?

Miss Cruley printed another of my poems in the second Poetry Corner, one I had written about my beloved locust trees on the hill behind our house. Miss Cruley used this one before I could rescue it from Dad's desk drawer to improve the last line.

> *The Locusts*
> *Tall and gnarled, gaunt they stand*
>   *Upon a windswept hill,*
> *Majestically, with arms outstretched*
>   *Dignified and still.*
>
> *Others seek, but do not know*
>   *My trees upon the hill—*
> *Torn by wind and bruised by storm,*
>   *And yet unconquered still.*
>
> *You ask me why I love them so?*
>   *I really do not know—*
> *Except that they're a part of me,*
>   *A part I dare not show.*

Actually, the "enthusiastic response" of the *Sentinel*'s readers had impressed Miss Cruley more than me—a total of one verbal comment and a single letter. But my reward was not so much reader reaction as just the thrill of seeing in print something I had written.

Meanwhile, our old Babcock press was giving more and more trouble. Dean Fleming, who had previously known nothing about printing presses, was having to spend so much time repairing the Babcock that he was rapidly becoming an expert.

Ordinarily Dean would be the last one to give up on any piece of machinery. But it was he who finally persuaded Dad that the laborious Babcock was a relic and could expire any day.

Soon after that, Dad heard of a good secondhand Goss press being offered for sale in Langley, Pennsylvania; the bargain price was $3,000. The elderly owner of its weekly newspaper, *The Langley News*, had finally been forced to sell out because of a long-overdue mortgage. Dean offered to check out the press.

He came back with a favorable report. "It's covered with dirt and grease," Dean admitted. "Hasn't been taken care of right. But *The Langley News* has had such a small circulation that the Goss has gotten almost no wear and tear. I'd say the signal is 'Go.' "

There remained the matter of money and here the Editor was very resistant. "Dean, we're hardly making it now. You saved us with a loan back in January. Then the government bailed us out after the flood. I don't see how I can take on a bank loan now, even if I could get it."

Dean then pointed out what a big step forward for *The Sentinel* buying the Goss would be. The Babcock had to be hand-fed and could print only four pages at a time, after which the operator had to "back it up"—flip the paper to print the other side. Even this was accomplished only by operating the clutch, starting and stopping the press with the left foot.

In contrast, the more modern Goss was automatic and could print eight sheets at a time, or a total of 3,500 an hour.

"I know all that," the adamant Editor protested, "but I can't put myself and my family under more financial burden."

"I've got real respect for that wish, Ken. But on the other hand—"

At this juncture, two factors made my father decide to take the plunge. A second order for the Yoder booklet came in, bringing the total payment to $2,700. This was followed by a spurt of advertising activity by local merchants. The Editor paid $1,500 in cash and the First National Bank then agreed to accept my father's note for the balance of $1,500 at 3½ percent interest.

The deal was made and the Goss press was ours. Now came the problem of transporting it. The way Dean handled that was an education in itself. He borrowed a bigger truck for Saturday, rented a block and tackle, then enlisted the services of three "volunteers" who would drive his own smaller truck to Langley. On the day of the big move, the Editor and Dean agreed to let me go along with them in the borrowed truck.

The *Langley News* office turned out to be a converted pool hall, so old, musty and rundown that I was surprised it contained any usable pieces of machinery.

First the press was washed down with gasoline. Then Dean started it up and watched it run for a while before he pulled a piece of chalk out of his pocket and began numbering the parts—on the larger pieces adding arrows and hieroglyphic messages to himself. Only then did he begin loosening bolts and taking the press apart. When the huge piece of machinery was dismantled and moved, I was amazed to see a big hole in the floor underneath it.

Once the two trucks were parked in the alley behind the *Sentinel* office, a problem arose that not even Dean Fleming had anticipated: the main parts were too large to go through any door.

"Let's rest a moment while we figure this out," Dean suggested. When I took cold drinks to the men who were seated on top of the Goss press in the back of the truck, their heads were bowed. Praying?

I drew back, somewhat embarrassed. One man opened his eyes, saw me and winked. "We need all the help we can get," he said.

A few minutes later I saw Dean measuring the frame of the large display window in front of the *Sentinel* office. "That's the solution," he said jubilantly. "We can get the press through here."

Soon he and one of his helpers had removed the glass pane. Then the truck was backed up to the new opening at the front of the building and the cumbersome parts were lifted out onto heavy skids on the floor inside. By the time the window had been replaced, it was dark and time to call it a day. Dean insisted that he would be back at eight o'clock the next morning.

"But tomorrow's Sunday," Dad protested.

"I know," was Dean's prompt response, "but there's no way you'll get the paper out next week unless you and I work tomorrow. Today was the easy part."

Easy? The weary faces of his three helpers denied that anything had been easy.

"We've got almost a day's work before we begin reassembling the press," Dean continued. "The Goss has to have a crawl hole beneath it for repairs and maintenance. That means sawing out a five-foot-square hole of the floor and riveting in a metal frame. Even that's just the beginning."

Dean found another volunteer for Sunday and the three men worked straight through the day. When I got to *The Sentinel* after church, the crawl hole had been sawed out and the frame was under construction. Dean explained that the press's ink fountains had to be filled from underneath in a process pro000mon called loading the chassis." After the Goss was reassembled and in place, he would build steps leading down into the pit. Next, pipes would have to be run from underneath the press to the coal furnace in the basement to keep warm certain metal parts of the Goss. This would prevent the ink fountains from congealing in cold weather and would guard against static electricity.

"Some country editors still use kerosene lamps underneath the ink fountains to keep them fluid," Dean told us. "But that's makeshift. I want to do better than that by you."

By Sunday afternoon it was obvious that the Editor knew Dean's volunteers quite well. He was familiar with their jobs and spoke to them about their wives and children. There was real camaraderie here.

But why were they so closed-mouthed to the rest of us? Why so much anonymity? Still so many unanswered questions.

By early Monday afternoon, Dean was reassembling the press. As I watched him at work, studying his chalk-mark arrows and messages to himself, it was obvious that he was enjoying the challenge, like putting together a gigantic jigsaw puzzle. He would hum or whistle or burst out in snatches of boisterous ballads, or laugh when he succeeded in puzzling out an especially tricky part.

While Dean's hands were busy, he and my father fell into quiet, serious conversation. I was at my desk, working on my steel mill paper. I think they forgot I was there.

"Dean," I heard the Editor say, "I've a question for you."

"Shoot."

"Say you're the pastor of a church and the chairman of your trustees began an affair with your church secretary. How would you handle it?"

Down in the hole in the floor, Dean paused in his work to look up at his friend. "I've never been a pastor, but it seems to me that the Bible answers the question directly and common-sense-like. If a member of your church strays, you go to him in love, point out what he's doing wrong, let him know that God will forgive him, and ask that he give it up."

"Yes, but suppose you do that only to have the trustee hotly deny he's done anything wrong. Yet you know he's lying."

"How do you know?"

"Because all this happened in my church. The secretary came and told me the whole story, submitting her resignation. Said the weight of guilt was crushing her, that the trustee had a wife and three children."

There was the clang of a heavy tool flung down on metal. Dean maneuvered his crippled leg so that he could vault out of the pit and sit on the edge of the sawed-off flooring, where he could look into Dad's eyes.

I stared at the Editor, my mind awhirl. A missing piece of our life in Timmeton was being put into place.

"So the square-off between you and the trustee failed," Dean continued. "The next thing is to take one or more trusted Christian brothers with you to face the man. If his heart is still haughty and hard and he won't receive any correction, then it's up to the pastor and his officers to remove the man from his position until he confesses and gets right with God."

"But, Dean, the trustee happened to be a very powerful man in a small town. The others wouldn't go along with those Biblical directives because they were afraid of financial retaliation."

Dean nodded. "Then the pastor hasn't much choice, has he? He can't compromise his faith, else God would withdraw His blessing from the ministry. So he should resign."

There was silence for a moment. From where I was sitting I could see my father's clearly chiseled features in profile as he looked Dean full in the face. "Eventually I did resign."

"Then, Ken, you did the right thing."

"But this was months later. And I resigned from the whole Church and left the ministry. I see now that I should have used this episode as the reason for leaving. With the exception of one dear old retired hardware merchant, the trustees said I should just forget it. Their viewpoint was that it was all solved anyway by the secretary's resignation."

"The secretary's resignation did nothing to change what was inside that trustee's heart," Dean observed mildly. "And he was still an officer of Christ's Church."

"This trustee remained unchanged. He came to see me in my church office. Threatened me. Said that if I ever again raised any question about his morality, he would personally see to it that I'd be booted out of my pastorate.''

"How long after that did you leave Timmeton?''

"About eleven months.''

"What happened during that time?''

"Not much, really. Everything went on just as though nothing had happened. Except that something had gone out of the church and out of me. I felt I had been weak and was a failure. I went into depression, then became ill. You know the rest.''

"Your father won't be here for dinner,'' Mother announced when I arrived home. "He just called. He's out with Dean tonight. I wonder what they're doing this time.''

"Probably working on the new press,'' I replied.

Later, the two of us were alone in the family room. I had finished some schoolwork and had started to my room when, for some reason, I turned to look at Mother. I really looked at her for the first time in months. Her face was more lined, she was thinner. Suddenly I wanted to tell her how much I admired her strength and patience with Dad—and with all of us. The words stuck in my throat. Instead, I knelt by her chair and kissed her on the cheek.

A sob rumbled in her throat and she threw her arms around my neck. "Oh, Julie . . .'' The words she wanted to say wouldn't come out either. We stared at each other with tear-filled eyes for a moment, then I kissed her again and went to my room.

When I tried to go to sleep that night, I kept seeing that vulnerable look in my mother's eyes. The strong one, I had always called her. Was it human nature for us to withhold affection from the strong ones?

19

LATE that Wednesday afternoon I was at my desk when my father burst from his cubicle office, a glint of excitement in his brown eyes. He headed for Dean Fleming, who was still tinkering with the newly installed Goss press.

"Dean, what do you know about McKeever's private railroad car?"

Dean straightened up from his work. He twisted his torso from side to side and massaged his lower back. "Called the *Vulcania*. Pretty fancy. The Old Man uses it mostly to go from Alderton to Pittsburgh and back. Parks it on a bluff overlooking the town."

"That tells me something."

"What?"

"I just received an invitation to lunch tomorrow aboard the *Vulcania*. More like a command."

Dean frowned. "Any way to get out of it?"

"Why should I?"

"Because the Old Man will badger you. He's a bully."

The Editor shrugged. "I think I can handle him now."

"Don't be too sure. I'd feel better if you'd cancel out."

I could see that my father had no intention of declining the invitation. Meeting McKeever in the *Vulcania* intrigued him. Besides, Dad a throbbing curiosity about trains and railroading. Mother teased him about filling the entire bottom drawer of his desk at home with an assortment of railroad timetables. Before Tim was really old enough, Dad had given him an elaborate electric train and had kept adding to the layout ever since.

With that kind of obsessive fascination with trains, I knew that our family would get a full report on every detail of the *Vulcania*. Could be, I thought, that the McKeevers had hit upon the surest way to impress Dad and then put pressure on him.

We did get that description of the car. But it was weeks, even months, before I learned the whole story of what had happened at that lunch in the *Vulcania*.

McKeever's Bluff was a natural ledge, reached by a side road, one fourth of the way up Seven Mile Mountain. Dean said that Yoder money was used to construct a spur from the Pennsylvania Railroad tracks, which ran from Altoona through Yancyville, Alderton, and on to Pittsburgh. The ledge was widened to accommodate the *Vulcania*, plus a parking lot for automobiles. Yoder also installed the telephone and power units there to connect with *Vulcania* equipment.

The project had taken years of work, no one seemed to know how much money, and caused much comment from local people, mostly negative. Some said it was unsafe, others muttered that it was McKeever's way of exercising his physical dominance over Alderton; board members at Yoder were supposedly upset over the cost to the company of a ridiculously expensive and inefficient office.

The Editor had driven the Willys up Seven Mile Mountain to the ledge as directed. There he was treated to a breathtaking view of the entire Alderton area. The small parking lot—large enough for only six cars—was bounded by a metal fence to protect the unwary from a fall of several hundred feet.

The *Vulcania*, painted green and burgundy red on the outside, was longer than he had expected. The back end

was an open observation area, its railing of ornately de-
signed brass, with a scalloped striped awning overhead.
The word *Vulcania* was painted in big gold letters on the
side of the car; beneath this was a mural of fire, with a
raised arm and an anvil depicting the Roman god Vulcan.

A uniformed footman was waiting by portable steps
beside the car. The uniform—navy with brass buttons,
the Vulcan emblem in gold over the breast pocket, red
and white stripes down each side of the pants legs—
seemed to the Editor ridiculously elaborate.

"Right in here, sir."

Young Tom McKeever met Dad with a hearty handshake. "Welcome to the *Vulcania*. Best restaurant in
town, we can guarantee it."

My father was amazed at the spaciousness of the interior: large arched picture windows with leaded art-glass
lunettes at the top set off by brocaded gold-colored draperies; a raised dome ceiling; wall-to-wall crimson and
gold carpeting; overstuffed chairs.

Behind a large ornate corner desk at the other end of
the car, the older McKeever rose ponderously to his feet.
His eyes were a deep-set blue under shaggy eyebrows.
His massive head seemed still larger because of a wealth
of bristly white hair around his ears.

"Good to see you again, Mr. Wallace." He made a
little welcoming gesture with his right hand and sat down
again.

McKeever's desk not only was oversized and heavily
carved, but to my father's surprise, it was raised up on a
small platform. As the Editor and Tom sank into comfortable overstuffed armchairs, they had to look up to
Thomas Yoder McKeever, Sr.

A white-coated waiter was now hovering about, the
right side of his face badly scarred and drawn to one side,
most of the hair on that side gone, little of his ear left, and
his right eye covered by a gold patch. Dad tried not to
stare, but a second surreptitious look revealed that the
waiter was still a young man.

"A glass of white wine before lunch?" young Tom suggested.

My father hesitated for an instant. "Fine."

"It's a Niersteiner 1923," the deep voice behind the desk volunteered.

While the steward was gone, preparing drinks in the galley, the younger McKeever answered my father's unspoken question. "Karel is a Slovak, was a first-helper in the plant. Most unfortunate accident three years ago. A crane arm with a ladle of molten steel gave way. Exploded as it hit the floor."

The Old Man cleared his throat. "These things happen. You can see we've made everything right for Karel."

As Dad and Tom lifted delicate wine glasses off the silver tray offered by Karel, my father noted that the Old Man had ordered whiskey and water. The atmosphere was noticeably strained as they drank. In the presence of his father, Tom seemed tense; there was a decided edginess in both of them.

To cover an awkward silence, the Editor asked, "Who built the *Vulcania?* Pullman or Wagoner?"

"Ah, you know something about railroad cars," the older man commented approvingly. "Only two real builders of fine cars in the country. We chose Pullman. Solid steel throughout, Standard Pullman." He took a long sip of his drink. "If you're willing to pay for it, you can trust Pullman's woodworking too—bring their cabinetmakers over from Germany."

"Handsome," Dad agreed, his eyes taking in the walnut paneling between the wide windows, the tasteful gold lining around the domed ceiling, the beveled-edge French mirrors giving the feel of space. A small oval conference table to one side of the car was covered in crimson baize. There were built-in pull-down map racks and an ornate Seth Thomas wall clock.

"The *Vulcania* actually saves us a lot of fuss and bother," Tom said, a little defensively. "No working out of schedules, no waiting for trains. Always a place for top-level conferences handy. It's well used by our high officials here and in Pittsburgh.''

Through an open doorway to the rear, the Editor caught a glimpse of what must be the master stateroom. In it was an oversized bed covered with a cream damask spread.

As soon as the Old Man finished his whiskey and water, the waiter promptly appeared to replace it with another. Impressed by Dad's knowledge of railroad cars, the elderly industrialist reminisced about what were popularly known as the "private varnishes" of other eras: Jay Gould's *St. Louis* with a baggage car carrying a cow whose milk was required for the multimillionaire's dyspepsia . . . concert pianist Jan Paderewski's *General Stanley*, which was equipped with a Steinway, two certified French chefs, and a skilled French waiter . . . the romantic *Virginia City* owned by Charles Clegg and Lucius Beebe, which carried not only a Chinese chef but a 185-pound St. Bernard, Mr. T-Bone Towser . . . and Henry M. Flagler's two private cars, Florida East Coast's *No. 90* and the *Rambler* for the St. John's and Indian River Railroad. Both sported white mahogany paneling, gold plated plumbing fixtures, gold table services, English butlers, and concealed wall safes.

"Luncheon is served," McKeever's butler announced.

The men rose and at last the elder McKeever stepped from behind his desk.

Forward of the car was the chef's galley and dining area. The table was set with white linen, heavy sterling silver flatware, and a bouquet of fresh flowers. Overhead the domed roof had been elaborately painted in Italian Renaissance style: dancing figures carried cornucopias spilling over with the earth's bounty.

The moment they were seated, the butler set before them a first course of Italian prosciutto and melon. He filled the wine glasses with French burgundy.

"Putting out a newspaper is a big responsibility, Mr. Wallace, and expensive."

When his guest merely nodded, the elder McKeever continued, "We need a newspaper that reflects the beauty of this area and the opportunities open to all who are willing to take advantage of them. Tom and I have a vision of how a newspaper like *The Sentinel* can really be built up. We can be of help to you."

"I'm so new to newspaper work," my father replied, "that I'm grateful for any and all help. What do you have in mind?"

"Our public relations man has come up with some rough drawings for advertisements," Tom interjected. "After lunch we'll spread them out on the conference table for you to see."

"These ads show Yoder's contribution to the community," his father added. "Name me another company that provides a better library, gymnasium, or health clinic for its people."

"The other side is," Dad countered mildly, "Yoder Iron and Steel wouldn't have gotten very far without the skilled hands and ready hearts of hundreds of workers."

"They're paid," the Old Man snapped. "Paid well. Strange, how greed takes over in the lower echelons of society. Most workingmen think only of the dollars they get in the weekly pay envelope. Can't see beyond that."

Tom spoke up, rather too quickly, "But before we get to the ads, there's some ground we need to clear."

Suddenly the atmosphere was charged.

"That editorial you ran, Mr. Wallace," the deep voice of the Old Man boomed out as he cut into a piece of veal smothered in velvety sauce. "Can't say I like that. Mighty poor timing for a newcomer to town. Some implications printed there were bad judgment. Not a grain of justification."

"What implications, Mr. McKeever?"

"You imply that Roger Benshoff isn't qualified to inspect the dam just because he's head of the Pennsylvania

Railroad's freight department. Roger knows plenty about dams, all he needs to know. That's not reporting, just negative propaganda. Doesn't help anybody.''

My father felt his face redden. Before he could reply, Tom tempered in a milder voice, "Look at it this way, Ken. What do you want your editorials in *The Sentinel* to accomplish? My father and I would like to know what your editorial policy is to be. Are you going to try to be constructive, encourage people, build up community confidence? Or are you out looking for phony crusades to scare people to death?''

"Come on now, Tom," the Editor protested as moisture gathered on his forehead. "I want no part of phony crusades. Of course I'm for building up community confidence.''

Tom cleared his throat, his gray eyes accusing yet also troubled. "Then what was your thought, Ken," he questioned, "in going to Pittsburgh to seek out more information on the dam? I just don't see how that could possibly be any concern of yours.''

So my visit with Cy Stearns got back to the McKeevers, Dad had thought. *I wonder if they know what I uncovered about the missing engineer's report*

"Let's try to understand one another," the Editor replied, fighting to keep his voice even. "I was concerned by the fact that the recent flood did some damage to the dam—"

"Very little damage," the Old Man contradicted vehemently. "Of no consequence. Happens every spring.''

"Some people are nervous about the dam," my father continued, "so if the dam's safe, then they need to be reassured. What better way than through the only newspaper in Alderton? But if the dam is not safe, then that needs to be corrected. So gentlemen, I went to Pittsburgh to seek information. What can possibly be wrong with that?''

"What's *wrong,*" the Old Man lashed out, "is that you went far out of your way to get what you call facts.

Why didn't you go directly to Tom here and ask *him* questions? With all the money that Yoder Steel has invested in this valley, if there were anything dangerous about the dam, can you seriously think we wouldn't be concerned?''

"That's logical," Dad admitted. "Indeed, irrefutable. Nevertheless—" and here my father admitted that he began to fall apart "—I felt a responsibility to our readers to inform them about the dam's safety."

"The dam is perfectly safe." The Old Man slammed his open palm on the table. His wine glass jumped off it and crashed on the floor; a red stain was left on the linen cloth.

Karel rushed in, knelt to sweep up the bits of glass and to mop the table.

The Old Man's thoughts scarcely missed a beat. "Mr. Wallace, you can take my word for the safety of the dam. And if you aren't willing to accept my word on this, then there's no way we can do business together."

A silence hung in the dining car as the steward retreated, carrying the broken glass and his mop-up cloths toward the galley. The Editor unsuccessfully fought down a surge of fear. He decided not to mention the missing inspection report. He knew his next words could well determine his future in Alderton. "I want to serve the people of this community," he said, miserably conscious of his trembling voice, "and I would like to do business with you. I am *not* an irresponsible journalist. If you say the dam is safe, I believe that you mean it sincerely. Certainly, I accept your sincerity."

The McKeevers visibly relaxed.

"I knew you had the good of the community at heart," Tom said approvingly, "just as we do."

The older McKeever took out a cigar and nipped its end with a silver pocket knife. "These are tough times, young man. To survive, we must all learn to cooperate."

Smoke drifted into the Editor's eyes and nose. He coughed, moved uncomfortably in his chair. Tom broke the heavy silence with a suggestion that they retire to the parlor area and look at the proposed ads.

The three men arose from the luncheon table and moved back to the oval conference table, where Tom pulled a manila folder from his briefcase and extracted from it a sheaf of papers. For the next half-hour, Tom and the Editor pored over the layouts while the Old Man sat back, smoked his cigar, and watched through narrowed eyes.

20

I FINISHED my paper on the steel mill late on a Tuesday night. There were two versions. The longer, more detailed one was my economics term paper. The shorter was for *The Sentinel*—I hoped.

At breakfast Wednesday, before Tim and Anne-Marie appeared, I slipped the short version to the Editor. "It's my article on Yoder. Please read it and see if it's right for *The Sentinel.*"

Watching the typed sheets being placed carefully in my father's briefcase, I felt a surge of pride in my accomplishment. It had turned into a much bigger project than I had expected, taking many hours of research and some extra interviews with people in the Lowlands. While the term paper was replete with statistics and footnotes, it seemed to me I'd managed to get human interest and even strong emotion into *The Sentinel* article.

The more facts I had uncovered, the more sympathy I felt for working-class families. Newspapers, meanwhile, were full of labor unrest. Most members of Congress also had strong empathy for labor and were about to enact legislation to make management bargain more fairly.

I struggled to understand the extremes of wealth and poverty in our country. In the writing, words had seemed to pour out of me with a power I hadn't known I had. I could scarcely wait for my father's reaction. There was even the possibility that if my article were to appear in

The Sentinel, it could soften the hearts of leaders so that they would change their policies.

All day at school I kept envisioning the Editor reading my paper and feeling the impact of it. I could even see new respect in the eyes of Miss Cruley as she set the story up in type.

After school I almost ran to the *Sentinel* office. At his desk the Editor was looking at proofs of this week's paper, his brow furrowed in thought.

"Hi, Dad."

"Julie!" He seemed surprised to see me. "School out already?"

"Yes. I hurried down here as fast as I could."

"Oh? You have proofreading to do?"

"No, I finished that yesterday."

"Well, why don't you go home then and see if your mother needs some help there." He swiveled his chair back to his desk.

"My article. Did you read it?"

"Oh, that. Yes, I did. Very well written, daughter. A fine job. No question but that you'll get an A on it."

Feelings of frustration poured through me. "Dad, don't you remember—what I gave you was not my term paper but a special article to consider for *The Sentinel,*"

Slowly my father turned around to face me and took off his reading glasses. His brown eyes were kind, gentle, serious. Suddenly I knew what he was about to say and I had a little-girl urge to put my fingers in my ears and run out of the office.

"I'm sorry, but it isn't right for *The Sentinel.*"

"Why, Dad? Why not?"

"It makes a strong, emotional case for the working people, but management comes off as a bunch of tyrants."

"Well, they are."

"Not all of them, dear. An article like this has to have balance. You don't tell the other side—the creative genius of some industrialists. A few of *them* began as workers too. Their courage in staking everything on a vision, a dream . . . their resourcefulness in building America into the most economically powerful nation in the world. Those are *facts*, Julie. Facts.''

Fighting back tears, I stared at my father. Sensing my distress, he patted my hand. ''You'll write some great stories for *The Sentinel*. Don't let one disappointment get you down.''

This time, the little-girl urge did take over. As calmly as I could, I walked out of the office, then fled up Main Street to home and The Rocks. There, with my back against the big locust tree, I sat crying, trying to assimilate my disappointment over the article and, yes, my disillusionment in my father.

I got home from school the next afternoon to find the dining room table set for company and Mother bustling around the kitchen.

''What's going on?''

''Something that will please you. Randolph Wilkinson is coming to dinner.''

I looked at her in astonishment. ''How did *that* happen?''

''Randolph called for an appointment with your father. Ken suggested he come to dinner and Randolph seemed pleased with that.''

I took a deep breath to calm the excitement rising inside me. If only I had not been too sleepy and too upset to wash my hair last night. *What dress should I wear? The blue taffeta, I guess.*

Mother broke into my thoughts. ''Julie, would you peel and quarter these apples for me? And I do need a centerpiece. How about scouting the yard for flowers?''

When Rand walked through the front door, dressed in a natty blue sports coat and tie, I was annoyed at my quickening heartbeat. *Calm it, Julie. You're still like a sister to him. Don't betray your feelings.*

His smile was as warm as ever when he took my hand, yet I sensed that for some reason this poised Englishman was a little tense with us. During dinner the Editor asked Rand about his years at Oxford.

"Education at English universities," he replied, "is almost a process of osmosis. I was quite on my own. The only requirement was that I sleep the necessary number of nights in my room."

"No required attendance at lectures?" I asked, amazed.

"No. What happens, though, is that both in and out of classes there is a stimulating exchange of ideas. You live with history every day, aware that men like John Locke or Sir Christopher Wren or William Gladstone or the poet Wordsworth might have slept in your room. The end result is that you learn to reason and think—which, to me, is the main purpose of education anyway."

The subject of education dominated most of our dinner conversation. Rand also described some of his experiences in a racing shell when he rowed for Oxford. Afterward, while Dad helped Tim and Anne-Marie with their homework, Mother smilingly drew me aside, whispering that she would wash the dishes. So I took Rand on a tour of our spacious back yard. The June days were longer now and the view of the sunset from The Rocks was breathtaking.

For several moments we drank in the enchanting evening sights and sounds. Then Rand turned to me. Once again, his eyes had that roguish look in them. "Julie, I seem to remember that you and I have some unfinished business."

"Yes. Sort of peculiar business—unicorns. Why are there three on your family crest?"

"I hadn't forgotten. It's just that a number of things have happened at the Club recently. That's why I want to talk to your father."

"Did my father's editorial cause you problems?"

He smiled at me. "That disconcerting directness again. Yes, I got a mite of chewing out for giving the interview to Ken."

"Old Man McKeever?"

"The one."

"He uses his wealth to push people around."

"He's my employer. I got myself in this muddle by not getting his permission to have the interview."

Rand was silent for a moment, then he looked at me sharply. "Why do you so resent wealthy people, Julie?"

I was caught off guard. "I—didn't—realize it showed so much."

"It shows. Sometimes you make me feel that I must defend all these people around me—even my relatives— when I'm not even certain that I want to."

Tears were close to the surface. Desperately I fought to hold them back. "This is the second time in two days I've had my knuckles rapped for being antagonistic to the rich," I said quietly. "I wrote an article for *The Sentinel* about my visit to the Yoder Steel plant. My father liked it, but told me yesterday he couldn't use it because it was too one-sided. All for workers, against management."

"Was he right?" Rand's eyes held mine.

I sighed. "Yes, he was right." *But,* I realized, *I haven't been able to admit it until this very moment.*

Two tears trickled down my cheeks and I turned away. Rand patted me gently on the shoulder, and as we turned back to the house, he stooped down to pick something from between the rock ledges. "Julie, I'm not believing this. It just can't be—"

Astonishment written on his face, he was holding one of the delicate-stemmed wild bluebells.

"Beautiful, aren't they? But why are you so surprised?"

"Because this is *real* Scottish harebell. It's indigenous to northern England. How amazing to find it here! Makes me positively homesick." The delight of a small boy was on his face.

Lovingly, he held the harebell between two fingers, slowly twisting the stem as he looked down at it. "I plucked you out of the rock crevice . . ." His voice was low and soft. "Reminds me of:

Flower in the crannied wall,
I pluck you out of the crannies,
I hold you here, root and all, in my hand.
Little flower—but if I could understand
What you are, root and all, and all in all,
I should know what God and man is.

"England in the spring is so beautiful," he continued, "so carpeted with wildflowers."

"I'm surprised you know so much about flowers. I didn't think men cared about such things."

"I grew up with them. Don't forget I'm a country lad. We children were quite certain that fairies and elves lived amongst the flowers in the beech wood." Rand suddenly shook himself. "I've kept you standing here talking and it's gotten dark on us. We're keeping your father waiting."

His warm hand held mine firmly as we walked back to the house. Once on the lighted back porch, Rand groaned. "I can't believe it. Here I've talked on and on and still haven't answered your question about the unicorns."

For days the Editor sidestepped any probing questions about his talk with Rand. The following Monday afternoon, Emily and Dean were out of the office and I was going over the subscription lists when Dad approached me. He was smiling.

"Still upset with me for turning down your article?"

The feeling of rejection was less now and I could smile back at him. "Just you wait. I'll get it published in *The New York Times*. Then you'll be sorry."

"A good piece of writing. I wish the people in the Lowlands could read it. But it did lack balance."

"Rand helped me see that you were right."

"How did that happen?"

I hesitated. All at once, I felt shy about revealing an

experience I had been savoring for days. "It's just that he told me I was too hard on the rich."

"Hmmm." The Editor's face was reflective. Then he pulled up a chair beside me. "Perhaps you should know something of what we talked about that night."

He paused again, suddenly in the father role, his brown eyes full of love. "You like Rand a lot, don't you?"

I was startled. "Does it show?"

"Some."

"I'm afraid he thinks of me as he would a younger sister."

Dad chuckled as if he did not quite accept that. "Maybe so. But you're turning into a beautiful young lady, Julie." Then he shifted in his chair and once again became the Editor as he summarized his discussion with Rand.

It seemed that the elder McKeever had not only rebuked Rand for granting the interview, but had angrily confronted the Club staff and the Board of Directors about rumors being spread in connection with the dam's safety.

"The inspections will attest to its safety," he had snapped. Then he promised the Board that repair work to the dam would be done as it was needed. The Board meeting had closed with a unanimous endorsement of management policy regarding the dam.

My father had then asked Rand if he knew of any engineer's report on the dam other than the ones filed by Benshoff. Rand had stated that he knew of none.

"I told him that there had been an engineer's report made on the dam prior to its sale to the Club," Dad continued, "but that it had disappeared from the files of the Pennsylvania Railroad. Rand said he knew nothing about that either, and I believed him. Then I said I'd very much like to reassure people about the dam in *The Sentinel* if I were given a report by a qualified engineer (not Benshoff) which revealed that the dam was safe."

"Where does that leave us?" I asked.

"Probably nowhere. I think it's a dead issue unless the report turns up."

21

After Spencer Meloy had worked out an arrangement with the Editor to have his weekly church bulletin printed at *The Sentinel*, he brought us handwritten copy every Thursday afternoon. On Friday he would return to pick up two hundred freshly printed bulletins for the Sunday service. After the first run, Dad turned the project over to me.

I was surprised at how readily Spencer accepted my hesitant suggestions for small word changes and layout revisions. As we talked of his goals for the church, he would probe me constantly for my ideas. I loved it.

In turn, he read my paper on Yoder Steel and praised it lavishly. When I gave him the Editor's reasoning for not using it, he sighed. "I understand his position, and I guess he had no choice, considering Yoder's influence here in Alderton. Yet businessmen need to hear these words, Julie," he said, rattling the pages of my article. "If they don't change, the labor situation will explode in their faces."

I felt so encouraged by Spencer's reaction that I actually did mail my article to *The New York Times* with a short letter explaining—a bit extravagantly—that I was a staff writer for *The Alderton Sentinel*, whose editor had decided that my piece was too controversial to use, given our local situation. I was being naive, I knew, to believe that the *Times* would even read it.

* * *

Late one afternoon in mid-May, Spencer Meloy entered the *Sentinel* office, smiled a greeting to Miss Cruley, and headed directly for my desk.

"Julie, I think we've found it!"

Startled, I stared at him while he grabbed a nearby chair and positioned himself directly across from me. That was the instant I knew: *Spencer Meloy's interest in me went beyond that of a spiritual mentor who is attracted to one of his charges.* I'd known he liked me from the beginning, but until this moment, I had not thought it went any deeper. I felt a tremor, an inner excitement. "Found what?" I heard myself saying, as I brought my racing thoughts under control and met the piercing intensity of his dark brown eyes.

"A place for the Community Center. Remember?"

"Oh, sure." Spencer had spoken often of the need for some building in the Lowlands where the people there could gather for talk, recreation and small meetings. One possibility was the flood-damaged house which Cade Brinton and his family had vacated.

"I think I've found a way to persuade the McKeevers to let us have the Brinton house." Meloy paused a moment to stare at me so directly that I let my eyes drop. "It involves you. Tom McKeever, Jr., is coming to my office Wednesday afternoon at four," he went on. "Trustee matter. Can you be in the church between four and five? I want you to tell McKeever why the young people in our church want to renovate this old house."

"Why would he pay any attention to me?" My resistance was rising at the thought of being cross-examined by a McKeever. I had seen the effect of this on Dad.

"He'll listen to you because you're the same age as his son, Bryan. And Bryan might become involved with our project. Does that surprise you? Well, he surprises me at times. For example, did you know he was a nature lover?"

I shook my head and started to tell Spencer how critical Bryan was about the Church, but stopped. Bryan's problems with his parents, with school, and with his drinking were so well known—why should I go into them? I drew a deep breath, realizing I could not let Spencer down.

On Wednesday afternoon I arrived at the church a little before four o'clock and told Spencer Meloy I would be in the Social Hall. Tom McKeever, Jr., appeared shortly thereafter and the two men closeted themselves in Spencer's office. I had brought proofs to read, but I was so nervous that it was hard to concentrate. Shortly after five, the pastor asked me to join them.

McKeever looked harried and uncomfortable, though he was gracious as I shook his hand and took a seat.

"Julie, I've filled Mr. McKeever in briefly on our ideas about a modest Community Center in the Lowlands. I think he needs to hear more about it from one of the young people in the church."

McKeever listened restlessly as I described our visits to the mothers and children in the Lowlands and the needs we found there.

"I know all about that," he interrupted. "What I don't understand is why the teenagers in our church should be so interested in, well, things that are of no concern to them."

"But, Mr. McKeever, these things *are* of concern to us. When people we know don't have the right clothing or enough to eat, it bothers us a lot."

"Our country is in a serious depression, Julie, and many people don't have the clothing or food they need. I sometimes wonder why there are so many tears shed over the poor worker and so little interest in businessmen like your father, who struggle so hard to survive and whose success means jobs and income for working people."

Spencer then intervened. "Mr. McKeever, one reason for this Community Center is to ease the overcrowding in so many homes there."

Tom McKeever frowned. "No way to change that."

"But given the *fact* of the crowding," Spencer persisted, as his glasses slid a bit down his nose, "if there were a place where women could bring their babies and toddlers, where they could read or sew or cook or attend child care classes—perhaps even have some Bible study—it would relieve some of the pressures on your steelworkers.''

"Sounds nebulous," McKeever interrupted. "Who's going to do the teaching? And who's going to pay?''

"If we find a place, the WPA will find the teachers and hire them.''

McKeever shook his head vigorously. "Don't you see the danger of all this? It's the beginning of government control. Whenever central government grabs power—with whatever emergency excuse—no matter how they bait the hook with gifts or handouts, every citizen loses part of his liberty. What's more"—he leaned forward and jabbed the air with his forefinger—"in the long run, handouts do nothing except weaken a man's character.''

Spencer Meloy opened his mouth to reply, then shut it again.

For a moment the silence in the room was so intense that we heard the ticking of Spencer's small brass desk clock.

I was determined not to be shut out of the discussion. "The money part doesn't concern me or the other high school students involved, like your son, Bryan. These people in the Lowlands are hurting and we want to go down there and help them.''

At the mention of his son's name, the hardness left McKeever's eyes and his resistance suddenly vanished. "I'm surprised Bryan is interested," he said quietly. Then he turned to Spencer. "Perhaps we can work out something with the house.''

The first work party for the Community Center project in the Lowlands was set for Saturday, June 15. Because Cade's water-wrecked house was a mass of debris, shattered floorboards, broken fixtures and ruined furniture,

Spencer asked Neal Brinton to help round up the needed skilled labor.

Margo Palmer and I had made a list of students who might help, then divided up the names between us for telephoning or contacting in person. Everyone was to wear old work clothes and bring his own lunch. Beverages would be supplied by the church.

Margo and I tried to approach everybody with the idea that this kind of work could be fun. On the whole, we got a good response. Working for us was the fact that even on weekends, Alderton offered scanty recreational inducements. That particular Saturday movie at the Picture Palace was to be *Jimmy the Gent* with James Cagney and Bette Davis, a picture most of us had already seen.

Early that week, following my English class, I drew a deep breath and walked up to Bryan McKeever and asked him if he would like to come to the work party.

"Don't think I can make it," he said, staring at me.

"Then forget it, Bryan. I heard from Mr. Meloy that you might be interested, but I guess he was wrong." His blandness riled me.

Later he stopped me in the hallway. "I'll make a deal with you, Julie. You go to the graduation dance with me on the twenty-second and I'll go to that church thing in the Lowlands this Saturday."

Nonplussed, I hesitated. I had already refused two invitations to this dance, reluctant to be a part of what I heard would be an all-night drinking party. Yet it was important to have Bryan at the work party. "Okay, Bryan. You have yourself a deal."

At nine on Saturday morning sixteen of us, including Bryan McKeever, showed up at Cade Brinton's water-damaged house in old work clothes. The Brinton residence was at the end of a row of six; it had obviously taken the brunt of the devastation. The outside corner both upstairs and down had been sheared off, leaving these rooms open on two sides. Ceiling slats were dangling.

It was obvious that Cade and his family had taken whatever possessions were salvageable and fled the place. The mud on the floors had dried into inches-deep, silty dust, but the stench still lingered. The work ahead of us would be anything but pleasant.

As we stood in the tiny front yard, Spencer Meloy gathered the group around him. "Folks, you can see the situation for yourselves." Our eyes followed the sweep of his hand to the clutter around us: rusting cans, shattered glass, pieces of splintered wood, old tires.

"We're not here to talk, but to work, so I'll make this brief. We're out to turn this damaged house into a thing of beauty for the people of this community. We hope to beg or borrow the fixtures we need to put in a bathroom. The kitchen is too tiny, so we're going to add about four feet to it. We've decided to knock out the partitions between the two front rooms to make a decent-size meeting room; we'll do the same to the two bedrooms upstairs.

"Now let's divide up into two work crews. Julie, you and Margo will lead the girls inside to do cleanup, Neal Brinton and I will form a wrecking crew to get the partitions down. Once the wrecking is finished, we'll become a carpentry crew. Let's get going."

When our female contingent had gathered, Neal Brinton warned us not to touch any electrical outlets until he had checked them. "Test every s-step for loose flooring. Beware of those dangling boards overhead; watch out for rusty nails."

Four of us took on the upstairs rooms to prepare them for painting. Most walls and ceilings were flyspecked and splotched with stains; the floors were caked with tracked-in mud. While scraping and sweeping out the debris, I began to realize the magnitude of the project we had taken on.

When I leaned out the front window in midmorning to get a breath of fresh air, I saw that the men had already raked up a mountain of trash and were shoveling it into burlap sacks to be carted off to the town dump. And there was a newcomer dressed in neat khaki, his blond-red hair looking redder than usual in the sunlight. Randolph Wilkinson! What was he doing here? I looked down at my filthy hands and mud-stained worksuit and moaned, "Not again!"

It seemed an eternity before a man's voice bellowed from the yard, "Lunchtime! All assemble in the front yard."

Neal had brought enamel wash basins, cakes of soap, and towels. Four wash-up lines formed, with several men emptying the basins and refilling them from huge cans so that each of us could have fresh water.

"Hello there, Julie." There was no mistaking the English accent; I turned to look into warm and smiling eyes. "Would you like to eat together?"

"Sure—" My hair was tousled, probably stringy, my face flecked with soot, my blouse sweat-streaked, my hands the color of mud. I smiled back weakly, angry at myself for feeling so self-conscious.

After we washed I felt better. Rand's exuberance was like a tonic. "Julie, you work your way to the head of the queue for two drinks, and I'll stake out a spot inside the house. Hold on a moment." He pulled from his pocket a white linen monogrammed handkerchief and, with a deft movement of his hand, flicked off a piece of soot from between my eyes.

When I returned with the drinks, plus the paper sack containing my egg salad sandwich, Rand had an oilcloth spread out in a corner of the front room and was emptying onto it the contents of a picnic hamper, obviously from the Hunting and Fishing Club's kitchen. Pieces of crispy fried chicken, dainty sandwiches of pimento cheese on whole-wheat bread, a salmon mixture with very thin slices of cucumber, tender ham with watercress.

"May I join you?" I looked up into the quizzical eyes of Spencer Meloy.

"Of course." Quickly Rand made a place for Spencer.

Then Margo and Bryan McKeever placed an oilcloth next to ours and we were a fivesome, but not a very jolly one. There was an awkward silence as we tore into our food.

"The ham is delicious," I enthused.

"Tinned Westphalian." At my questioning look, Rand added, "Imported from Germany."

It was so incongruous that giggles erupted spontaneously. Rand never lost his aplomb. Soon he was handing out delicacies to everyone in sight. Spencer declined them all and munched on peanut butter sandwiches. As the Englishman began asking questions about the project, I let Spencer do all the talking, while I compared the two men.

Though I had seen him carrying heavy, muddy pieces of timber, Rand's clothes were still fresh and clean. Spencer, however, was mud-soaked; even his shock of black hair was matted with dirt.

Rand's questions were polite, showing interest. He obviously did not understand why such menial work was not being done by the Lowlands residents themselves.

Spencer's answers had a surprising intensity, as if the young pastor were presenting his position to his trustees. "If church people aren't willing to do this kind of work for their suffering neighbors, then the Church has no meaning for today," he stated.

"I thought the purpose of the Church was to save souls," Rand responded as he bit into a cookie.

"I don't think you can meet the spiritual needs of people until you've met their physical needs."

"I see. Do you plan to use this house as a center to feed and clothe the people here?"

"That's our goal. We also want to give them a place to meet."

Bryan McKeever had been listening to this conversation with surprising interest. "I understand that my father turned this house over to you rent-free to fix up. Why don't you ask him to send some men down here to do all this work at no cost to you or the people who live here?''

Spencer shook his head. ''He might do that. But we think it's important to do the work with our own hands; then it becomes an offering of love to these people. That's a much better gift somehow.''

''How many residents of the Lowlands are members of Baker Memorial?'' Rand asked.

''Not very many. Margo here, for one. Neal Brinton. The church officers have been, well, somewhat resistant to people from the Lowlands joining the church.''

''I see. Alderton's version of the British caste system.'' Rand was thoughtful for a moment. ''Someone is always trying to obstruct the progress of social change.'' His gray-blue eyes suddenly swung to me. ''So, what do you think about this, Julie?''

I found myself coming alive. ''I don't think the class system belongs in the Church. We should not only accept these Lowlands people into membership, we should seek them out. I don't want to be a part of the Church if it isn't open to everybody.''

Bryan laughed. ''You'd have a hard time selling that to my father.''

Spencer Meloy seemed reluctant to close the discussion. Finally, when he arose to give directions for the cleanup of food leftovers, Margo and Bryan followed him. Rand turned to me.

''There's fire in you, Julie. I can see you out there in the street, carrying a banner for all the underprivileged people of the world.''

''I'm not a crusader, Rand.''

''That wasn't meant to be disparaging.'' His eyes turned to Spencer. ''Where's your pastor's wife?''

The question caught me off guard. ''Spencer's not married.''

Rand's smile crinkled around his eyes. ''I see.''

By midafternoon the house was beginning to take shape. The partitions were down and the missing sides of the building had been boarded up. Carpentry work had begun to extend the kitchen and build the bathroom. The upstairs rooms had been cleaned out and scrubbed and were ready for repairs. Graham Gillin arrived and, to my surprise, brought half the ball team with him.

I saw Rand drive away. Just then another car pulled up and a small man in a natty brown suit got out. Vincent Piley.

Mr. Piley strode over to where Meloy was standing, not bothering with pleasantries. "How much money is the church spending for this project?" he asked bluntly.

I saw Spencer's face tighten. "Oh, somewhere between $125 and $150," he answered.

Seeing that several in the yard had stopped work to stare at him, Mr. Piley lowered his voice. "And who authorized the spending of this money for the church?"

"The project was cleared with Tom McKeever. Since this house belongs to the Yoder Steel Company, he agreed to let it be used for a Community Center if we would repair the flood damage."

Vincent Piley looked somewhat discomfited. "The Board of Trustees should have been consulted."

"Let me explain, Vincent." Spencer's voice was controlled. "The church has allotted me $200 for use in local mission work this year and I chose to use the money this way."

Mr. Piley shook his head. "There's much more involved here than a little mission work, Spencer. This establishes a precedent, and frankly, it bothers me. I think we should call a special meeting of the trustees to thrash this out."

Meloy's voice suddenly tensed. "You have every right to call a trustee meeting, Vincent. But as pastor of this church, I have an obligation to lead our congregation in spiritual matters. If I had to wait to get the approval of the businessmen of our church to do this kind of Christian work, nothing would get done. Furthermore, since the building being repaired is not church property, I don't believe it comes under the jurisdiction of the trustees.''

"I don't agree with you." Mr. Piley turned on his heel, climbed into his car and drove off.

22

SUNDAY morning the Editor was too ill to go to church. "Your father just needs a day of rest," Mother reported at breakfast.

After getting ready for church, I looked in on Dad. He appeared so wan, lying in bed propped up by several pillows, that I wanted to cry. What had caused this setback? The encounter with Old Man McKeever in the *Vulcania?*

The rest of us walked to Baker Memorial and heard Spencer Meloy give an enthusiastic report of the work party held the day before. He used as a text the passage in Luke 10:1-16 where Jesus commissions and sends out the seventy for service and compared our group of work om to the early disciples.

A look at the faces of Mr. Piley and the McKeevers, huddling in the back of the sanctuary after the service, told me that they were not happy with the sermon. Spencer had obviously received a mixed response from his congregation.

When I arrived at the *Sentinel* office Monday afternoon, I was surprised to discover that the Editor still had not appeared. He had come down to breakfast, and though he was somewhat pale and shaky, I had assumed he was going to work. Obviously not.

Dean Fleming was sitting on the floor by the Goss press, its parts spread all around him. Emily Cruley had taken the day off to visit a sick aunt. I went to my desk, hoping to create some verse for the Poetry Corner now that Miss Cruley was not around to look over my shoulder. But Dean wanted to talk.

"I heard Spencer preach yesterday," he began.

"You did? I didn't see you there."

"Came late. Sat in the back row. Left during the final hymn so I could pick up Hazel at our church."

I waited, knowing Dean had something on his mind.

"Spencer's going to have a big problem with his congregation if he's not careful."

"Why, Dean?"

"Because he's pushing the Lowlands people on them."

"What's wrong with that? I believe the church should be open to everyone."

"So do I." Dean wiped the sweat off his bald head and moved his bad leg into a better position so that he could bolt two of the press parts together. "Trouble is, Spencer is pushing too hard."

I sighed, somehow nettled with Dean, yet aware that I had felt the same way after the service.

"Why don't you tell him that, Dean?"

"I would if I felt it would do any good. Spencer and I have talked some already. We go somewhat different directions when it comes to theology."

That surprised me and I must have shown it, for Dean began chuckling. "Don't read me wrong, Julie. I'm all for Spencer. He's sincere, idealistic, and a good preacher. I just don't believe that social action is the main business of the Church."

"Then what is?"

"Salvation."

I was sickened. "What do you think we should do? Go around the Lowlands asking people, 'Are you saved?' "

Dean put in the final bolt on the flatbed cylinder and used a chair to pull himself to his feet. "There's a right way and a wrong way to preach salvation. Big John knew how to do it."

"I heard some of those 'sin and damnation' preachers back in Timmeton. They're out to scare people."

"You wouldn't have felt that way about Big John."

"Perhaps not. But I prefer Spencer's approach."

"Then you're the one who should warn him. He'll pay attention to you."

"Why do you say that?"

"It's obvious. He likes young people. Better remind him that most of the people in his church are over thirty. If you don't, he'll end up in the same pickle your father was in at Timmeton."

"I sure hope not," a voice said behind us.

Dean and I whirled around to see the Editor standing there, listening. He had come in so quietly we hadn't even heard him.

"I didn't hear Meloy's sermon yesterday," my father continued. "But it's hard to believe that a church here in western Pennsylvania could be as prejudiced as the one in Timmeton."

Dean shrugged. "People are much the same wherever you go. They don't like to worship with people who're different." Then, changing the subject, "You'll be glad to know, Ken, that the press has been tuned up for this week's run."

My father nodded, intent on getting caught up with his work. Dean began tinkering with the job press and I returned to my desk. The three of us must have worked an hour or more, the only interruption being several telephone calls, which the Editor took in his office. I finished my proofs, then began daydreaming . . .

Rand and Spencer were so different. I could still see them sitting side by side: Rand so casual, Spencer so intense, Rand with all that fancy food, Spencer with his two peanut butter sandwiches, Rand's clothes so neat, Spencer dirt-covered from the top of his hair to the soles of his heavy work shoes.

Why had the Englishman come? He did not seem interested in our church project. And he, like Bryan, did not understand why we would not go out and hire laborers to fix up the house. "Plenty of people out of work," he had commented. I loved Spencer's answer—that we were down there as a gift of love to these people.

But how do you love people who are so different? By what you do to help them? Perhaps that was it. I had not known how to love that poor Lowlands woman, Sonja Balaz; we lived in different worlds. But if I could help fix up a place where she could come and sew and talk with other Lowlands wives, then I was showing her love.

Again I asked myself, why had Rand come? To be with me? That was a nice thought, but he could pick a dozen more interesting places to see me, if that were his desire. Then I sighed and admitted the reason for my dissatisfaction. Rand had come off as a bit of a snob. Westphalian ham! That food from the Club was just too much.

Dean had gone into the Editor's office to talk while I sat at Miss Cruley's desk to answer the telephone. When I returned to my own desk, I did not pay attention to their voices at first, until Dad's rose. "I tell you, Dean, that statement I made to the McKeevers in the *Vulcania* literally made me sick."

"Why, Ken?"

"Because it was so wishy-washy. I had a chance to take a stand against them and I caved in. My weak-kneed reply makes me cringe: 'I believe that you're sincere. I accept your sincerity.' My God, Attila the Hun was probably sincere. So was that megalomaniac Napoleon. So what!"

"So you've gotten real down on yourself again, Ken. What will that accomplish?"

"I don't know, but I'm discouraged. I felt in good shape before that *Vulcania* visit. Ready to tackle anything. Now I'm unsure of myself again, wondering how I'll cope with the future. All I see ahead are confrontations between me and powerful forces. Pressure to bow to their desires. Temptations to go against what I think is right.''

There was a long moment of silence. ''Ken, we've talked before about the Scripture that can help you here. It says that our Father in heaven won't let life deal us more than He'll give us the ability to handle.''

''I know that, Dean. But when I look back over my life, I I see a string of bucklings under pressure, a tendency to hunt escape routes for myself instead of standing and fighting. I don't trust myself not to fold the next time too.''

''You *will* fold if you're just trusting yourself,'' Dean observed. ''To be blunt, Ken, I don't think you trust God for anything.''

There was silence. Anger at Dean rose in me, then concern for my father. After a long silence, Dad finally replied softly, ''The truth is that God isn't that real to me. So how *can* I trust Him?''

''Which leads to the next question,'' Dean pushed on. ''Why did you enter the ministry in the first place?''

My father's answer went back to the time when he was seven and his father died, then to what it was like to be reared in an all-female household, including a possessive mother and two ambitious older sisters, and he admitted that he chose Haverford College in eastern Pennsylvania to get away from them.

While reading George Fox's writings in one of his courses, my father had come across this earthshaking fact: that God will break through to any given person who approaches Him with an open, hungry heart. This thought planted a powerful seed in Dad.

''I decided right then that I meant business about living the Christian life.'' The Editor chuckled. ''So I began a course of self-improvement. I moved away from my close friends into a single dormitory room in a tower up under the belfry. I stopped drinking and smoking, went regularly to church, studied the Bible, prayed each morning and night, and read religious books.''

"I can guess what happened," Dean said.

"From my solitary room in the tower, I would look down with contempt on my friends strolling the quadrangle," the Editor resumed. "There they were, going to the dogs while I was cleaning up my life; they dissipated while I was on the way to being a model person. But the harder I tried, the more impossible I found it to live up to even the simplest ethic of the Sermon on the Mount. I was a self-righteous, obnoxious failure."

Dean exploded with laughter. "Go on, Ken."

"I don't know what crazy thing I would have done next if some Christian missionaries from the China Inland Mission hadn't visited our campus. They had been through the raids and persecution by guerrilla bands that ravaged China after the Boxer Rebellion of 1900. They excited me with their verve and sparkle, which seemed all the more incredible after the harrowing experiences they had lived through. They talked in a personal way about their Lord. Their love for one another stabbed me. They described an 'inner light' as that still, small Voice within, which time after time warned them of imminent danger, and which gave them directions, guidance, and supply. That Saturday night, I asked God for what these men had.

"The next day all the world looked new. Sunlight sparkled on the ivy leaves. Each blade of grass shimmered with a vibrant life of its own—as though I were seeing the world on the first morning after the dawn of creation. Not only that, I felt a new vitality inside me. It was then I decided that the ministry was for me."

"And your mother and sisters—were they happy about this?"

"Not at all. They thought my decision immature and foolish, that I was being carried away on a tide of emotionalism. Mother always had ambitions for me in the business field," Dad recalled. "Yet the more they resisted my going into the ministry, the more determined I became. Of course, that resistance only proved that I was still fleeing their domination. So staring me in the face now is the question, was my call to the ministry authentic?''

"What about seminary?" Dean asked. "What happened there?"

"Another disaster. I ran into a highly charged intellectual atmosphere for which I was not prepared."

"How come?" Dean interjected. "From what I know of Haverford College, it's very intellectual. It should have prepared you for seminary."

"Perhaps so, but applying intellectualism to history or literature or economics is different from applying it to a man's faith. The seminary professors taught a liberal, neo-orthodox doctrine which viewed all miracles as myth and explained away any supernatural element in the Bible. Jesus' resurrection was solely a spiritual one. We were taught to accept only what can be explained factually or psychologically."

"Isn't that what you get in most seminaries, Ken?"

"I guess so. I should say that, by and large, those professors were some of the finest men imaginable—kind, likable, wanting to serve their fellow men—and most were intellectually brilliant. But I ended up in a state of confusion and terrible conflict."

"When did you marry Louise?"

"Just before my last year in seminary. Louise never had the conflicts I did. She's the strong one. And practical. Spends most of her time propping me up. It all came to a head one day shortly before my graduation. I remember burying my head in my arms on the kitchen table, and with sobs wrenching me, crying out, 'God, I don't know what I believe about You any more.' "

The two men were silent for a while, as I struggled with a new set of emotions concerning my father.

"Louise and I worked through it," Dad continued. "We became followers of Harry Emerson Fosdick and decided that we would do the best we could to bring comfort and help to the people we served. This worked rather well during the five years we spent at the Bucyrus, Ohio, church. And also during the early years at Timmeton. The problem was that I'd arrived at a philosophy of 'Don't rock the boat.' I felt that a steady but gentle influence was the most effective way of changing men's hearts. Wasn't that the way Jesus did it? Gentle, turning the other cheek—all that?''

"On the contrary," Dean said, "Jesus had biting words for church officials like the Pharisees. He was anything but an ecclesiastical politician."

I heard the Editor sigh. "Well, trying to be a politician did *me* no good at all. It didn't leave me feeling like a man. Any time I'd start to take an unpopular stand about anything, a gorge of fear would rise up inside me."

"Fear of what, Ken?"

"Fear of rejection. Losing face with the congregation. Losing my job."

"And Louise picked that up?"

"Yes. She couldn't understand what I was feeling. I guess she thought she'd married a strong man. But I was weak inside. So the tension between us built and built. And my philosophy could not deal with the issues in the Timmeton church. Then I just came apart."

"And now you're being put back together," answered Dean. He paused and I heard him move about in his chair. "There comes a right moment in the life of each person. Scripture has a beautiful phrase for it—'the fullness of time.' The fullness of time has arrived for you, Ken. Right now. You've spent years trying to be a strong man on your own efforts. It hasn't worked. Now you're ready for the better way."

That night while lying in bed, unable to sleep, I struggled with a new set of thoughts. Pouring out his heart to Dean Fleming was good for my father. Already I could see more strength in him. And those long hours spent with Dean and his friends had been good for him too. One conclusion was inescapable: those two words burned on the handle of the ax in Dean's cabin, "The Preparers," were the key to my father's recovery.

I just had to find out more about them.

23

Hᴵɢʜ school graduation day turned out to be an unforgettable experience—but not for the reason I expected.

On Saturday morning, June 22, the sixty-five graduates of our class gathered in the high school gymnasium to receive our diplomas. Since girls had to wear white dresses, Mother and I had found just what I wanted—a simple white crepe, expensive at $11 but something I could wear all summer.

The high moment for me came when our principal arose to give a special citation to "two members of the graduating class for leadership in community affairs." He read off two names: Margo Palmer and Julie Wallace! An exciting moment! And a complete surprise.

When we all arrived back home, there was a small white florist's box in front of the door. It was addressed to me. With fast-beating heart I tore it open. Inside was one red rose. On the card Rand had written: "I have a special graduation present for you, Julie. Will give it to you in a week or so."

The formal graduation dance that night was to be held at Haslam House in downtown Alderton. Bryan McKeever had said he would call for me at nine o'clock. I did not look forward to it.

My one formal dress was a size too small and frayed on both shoulder straps. The blue color was faded in spots, and during the last washing a lipstick smudge on the white ruffle covering my left shoulder had not come out. The truth was, I had never liked the dress from the time Mother bought it for the sophomore prom I had gone to in Timmeton. To me, it was a little girl's dress.

If I had pressed him, Dad would have bought me a new gown for this dance. In fact, he had asked me if I needed one. For a few seconds I had been terribly torn. Then I realized that there was nothing in the family budget for a $35 formal to be worn once or twice a year.

"The old one will do fine," I told him. The relieved look on his face was palpable.

Lacking a suitable dress was one of the reasons I had turned down two invitations to the dance. If Graham Gillin had asked me, I would have accepted. We were good friends now; I liked him best of the high school boys. He had invited Margo, a surprise since he and Margo had seldom dated.

Accepting Bryan's "deal" had been a spur-of-the-moment thing which I regretted afterward. Getting him to the work party had helped Spencer with Bryan's father at first, but Bryan had not fitted in with the other workers and, I suspect, ended up being critical of both the project and Spencer Meloy.

However, having committed myself to Bryan, I would see it through. I just hoped that he would stay sober. Both Mother and Dad were so concerned about the drinking and the possibility that the dance would last until dawn that I told them I would try to be home shortly after midnight.

Since Bryan was only slightly taller than I, it was necessary for me to wear low heels. When I put on my dress, I was in for a surprise: Mother had refurbished it completely. She had replaced the lipstick-smudged ruffle with lovely new material and added a sash of deeper blue. When I appeared before my father, he stared at me open-mouthed.

"Julie—you look stunning!"

I was thrilled. If only I didn't have to spend the evening with Bryan McKeever!

Yet Bryan surprised me too. He arrived looking handsome in his tuxedo. The cynical turned-down mouth was still evident, but he was very polite to my parents and complimentary of my appearance as he pinned a corsage of pink sweetheart roses on my dress. Then we climbed into the big black Packard his father had loaned him for the evening.

Searching for a topic of conversation, I asked Bryan about his interest in nature study. His head jerked toward me in surprise. "Who told you?"

"Is it some kind of secret?"

"Not really. I get kidded about it some." That's all he would say.

We parked on a downtown street and walked a block to Haslam House. In the lobby we joined a milling group of classmates waiting for the elevator to take us to the third-floor ballroom. When Bryan and I stepped onto the dance floor, I gasped with surprise. The decorations were a montage of enlarged photographs of school events interspersed with a series of long mirrors that gave an in-depth effect to the room. The dancers seemed to be multiplied five times. A spinning multicolor light from the ceiling produced a soft, changing focus from blue to red to white.

Tony Tomango and his Tomcats were playing, a local band who had gained statewide recognition for swingable music. A voice was warbling, "You push the first valve down, and the music goes down and round . . ." as Bryan led me onto the dance floor. I was soon caught up in the excitement as boy after boy cut in on Bryan to dance with me.

The talk was superficial, disjointed and always interrupted, but my feeling of exhilaration grew. These young people had become my friends in just nine months. How beautiful they all looked! And such nice smells, the girls with their soft perfume and corsages, the boys with cologne and the piney scent of aftershave lotion.

A large punch bowl soon became the focal point of activity between dances. I was thirsty and downed two glasses, noting that the mixture tasted a trifle sour.

The band had moved into "Stormy Weather" when Graham Gillin cut in. "You look beautiful tonight, Julie," he began, holding me close.

"Thank you."

"I didn't expect you to come to this dance. You once said you didn't go for this sort of thing."

"I love to dance.".

"If I'd known that, I would have asked you. Margo and I are good friends, but that's all."

Someone else cut in then, but the glow from Graham's words lingered. What a wonderful time I was having! But why was I feeling dizzy?

A bit later, I realized I had not danced with Bryan for almost an hour. Seeing him at the punch bowl, I finally got his eye. When we were dancing together again, my heart sank. He was wobbly on his feet.

"Are you feeling all right, Bryan?"

"I feel great . . . super," he said thickly. "I reserved a room upstairs. Want to come up and see it?"

I shook my head, wondering how best to handle that kind of situation. Then I quickly discovered why Bryan was so eager to get to the punch bowl. "The punch is spiked," he whispered.

"Spiked!"

"Yes. With gin."

I was stunned. No wonder I felt dizzy!

"Bryan, would you take me home when the dance is over?"

"Why?"

"Because the drinking really takes over then and I just don't, well, belong," I ended lamely.

"Then why did you come?"

"Because we made a deal."

"Then live up to it, Julie. We're going to drive up Seven Mile Mountain afterward."

Graham cut in. I was surprised at how much I enjoyed dancing with him. He held me close, kissing me lightly on the forehead, moving us far away from the stag line. I clung to him, my fears draining away as the band softly swung into "Good Night, Sweetheart." I knew I was dizzy, giddy and even a bit silly as I thought back to the time when I clung to his hand in the movie.

Then the music ended. For a long moment Graham held me close. Then he kissed me lightly on the lips. I kissed him back.

We located Bryan in the hall with Margo. Bryan's eyes were like dark agates, but he walked fairly steadily. "How about you and Julie coming with us?" Graham suggested.

"Let's do, Bryan," I said hopefully.

Bryan shook his head. "We'll go in my car."

How to get out of this mess? I couldn't just leave Bryan and go with Margo and Graham. There seemed to be no other course than to follow Bryan. As we walked through the hotel lobby I noticed a lot of changes in my classmates. Corsages had wilted, formal clothes were rumpled, carefully groomed hair was all awry, and too many had that glazed look that came from fatigue, too much to drink, or both.

Somehow ten honking cars managed to line up outside the hotel to begin the trek up Seven Mile Mountain toward Lookout Point. Fortunately Graham had asserted himself and taken the lead position from Bryan, who, in second place, terrified me with his erratic stops and starts. With so many horseshoe curves, our ride up the mountain had to be slow.

At the top, the procession pulled onto the paved parking area where our family had stopped the first time we had driven into Alderton nearly ten months before. Bryan turned on his car radio to Chicago station WGN, which aired band music. Soon other car radios picked up the same music and we all spilled out onto the outdoor dance floor, whooping and singing.

As the strains of "Smoke Gets in Your Eyes" wafted through the night air, the pavement was filled with dancers, scuffing across the sandy asphalt. The night air was warm and sweet. It could have been romantic if I had been with Graham, but Bryan was too unsteady to focus on dance steps. Soon he left me and my bruised feet and headed for the car. I wondered where he had hidden his bottle.

Graham and Margo tried to keep the group together and dancing. It was hopeless. When the music went off the air at two-thirty, Margo suggested that we go to the Stemwinder for an early breakfast.

"Bryan, I would like to drive home. May I?" I asked as we stood outside his Packard.

He brushed me off disdainfully. "Don't worry 'bout a t'ing."

"Then I want to ride with Graham and Margo." As I turned toward their car, Bryan grabbed my arm and jerked me into the front seat, slamming the door.

To my horror, Bryan started out in the lead before Graham could get turned around. The first two turns were handled safely, though I could see that Bryan needed the whole road to navigate.

Desperately, I looked behind. The cars were moving out of the parking area very slowly. Bryan was far in the lead.

"Slow down, Bryan, and let the others catch up," I pleaded.

He stared straight ahead, shoulders hunched forward.

"Please, please slow down," I shouted.

Then I saw the lights of a car coming our way. "Bryan, pull over!" I yelled.

He paid no attention.

I screamed the warning a second time, grabbing his shoulder and looking into his face. *His eyes were closed!*

He had passed out at the wheel! We were heading straight for the approaching car!

I'll never understand what happened next. I remember shouting, "Oh God, help!" Then I grabbed the wheel. I tried to jam my foot on the brake, but the gearshift was in the way. And then, all at once, there was a strength in my hands that did not seem mine, and I jerked the wheel hard. The tires screeched as our car veered to the right side of the road where there was a steep dropoff down the side of the mountain. The oncoming car whizzed past.

I don't remember stomping on the brake, but I must have. The next thing I knew, the car had skidded to a stop perpendicular to the road, with the back wheels only a few feet from the dropoff point. Numbly, I began to cry.

A blond crewcut head appeared at the car window. It was Graham. "Are you all right, Julie?" he asked.

"I guess so."

"How on earth did you miss that car?"

"I don't know, Graham."

The other cars had pulled to a stop behind us. As I climbed out, Bryan groaned, then retched on the front seat.

Graham took charge. "Help me get Bryan into the back seat," he shouted to a friend. "Julie, you go in my car; tell Margo to drive."

It was a shaken group that pulled up in front of the Stemwinder around four o'clock. There had been two other narrow misses and one car had banged hard into the rear of another and broken a headlight.

For an hour, Margo and I and two other girls, who were now sober from shock, tried to pour coffee down the others. Three had passed out, five had been sick; the smell of vomit made it hard to eat anything.

Bryan was still unconscious in the back seat of his car. When efforts to rouse him failed, Graham drove the black Packard to the front of the McKeever house, while Margo and I trailed behind. There he turned off the engine, leaving Bryan and the keys inside. Then he walked back to where we were waiting.

"I feel sorry for Bryan when his father gets in that car tomorrow," Graham muttered. "I cleaned it up some, but that car is gonna stink for a month."

It was five A.M. when Graham, his eyes rimmed with fatigue, left Margo in the car and walked me to the front door of our home.

"I'm sorry it had to end in such a messy way," he said.

I squeezed his hand. "There were some high moments tonight, Graham, thanks to you."

I let myself in as silently as I could. Mother was standing in the hallway, her patrician features drawn in taut worry lines.

"Wasn't that Graham Gillin who brought you home?" she asked, curiosity mixed with her concern.

"Yes, Mother, Bryan became sick."

"What happened?"

"Can I tell you tomorrow? And please let me sleep till noon."

"Of course, Julie."

With a sigh of relief, I went to my room, wanting nothing but the feel of clean sheets.

24

Monday morning was so beautiful that I put on my robe and slippers and eased quietly out the back door, clutching a pen and my journal. Leaning against the locust tree, I thought for a while, then began writing:

My performance at the dance Saturday night was that of a moonstruck teenager! Dumb too. Dumb not to know that someone could spike the punch. Dumb to ride with Bryan when he was so drunk.

The main trouble is that I'm in love with love. Randolph Wilkinson is romantic and remote. Spencer Meloy excites my mind, the only preacher ever to do so. And now, Graham Gillin. He was, well, sweet. And strong! I loved the way he took charge of the situation after Bryan passed out.

Free of school responsibilities, I was available now to work all day at *The Sentinel*. The Editor seemed uncertain how to handle it. "We can sure use you full-time here, Julie. When finances are better, I'll put you on the payroll."

"Don't worry about it, Dad."

"Well, set your own schedule."

I did and quickly got the assignment to cover what was happening with Spencer Meloy's project in the Lowlands. To almost everyone's surprise, the Community Center there had captured the enthusiasm of Alderton. In

the midst of a depression, when most people had been fo-
cusing on their own needs, suddenly a new spirit was let
loose in town. All at once people wanted to give—time,
things, whatever money they could spare. And with this
outpouring, some of Alderton's drabness lifted.

Alderton merchants, themselves still hurting from the
flood and the depressed economy, donated a variety
of needed items: Jordan's Hardware gave ten gallons
of paint; Strock Plumbers, some bathroom fixtures;
Lundstrom's sawmill provided tongue-and-groove lumber for the interior walls. Electrician Herb Pavilla offered
to do the wiring free, provided he could work on it even-
ings.

From all over town women came, bringing items of
furniture from their attics. What could not be used at the
Center was donated to needy families. Margo brought
pots and pans begged from her father at the Stemwinder.
The ladies of the Eastern Star voted not only to supply the
fabric but to make curtains for the windows. Not to be
outdone, the Garden Club undertook to plant some flower borders and supply hanging baskets for the porch. One
by one, the items appeared—a lamp here, a rug there,
some pictures, a mirror. To my surprise, even Miss Cruley proudly presented some pieces of china and glass-
ware.

From the Hunting and Fishing Club came a swing and
several wicker chairs for the front porch, folding chairs
for the meeting rooms and two institutional-type pots for
the kitchen. I could not help wondering how many rules
Rand had bent to send these gifts.

The Editor helped all this along with enthusiastic editorials in *The Sentinel* and by printing item-by-item
descriptions of what had been donated, prominently fea-
turing the names of the donors.

From Margo I gathered that the folks in the Lowlands
viewed all this with astonishment. Up to now, their section had been the town's stepchild. Why suddenly this
loving attention? Was there some ulterior motive in it?

One by one, they would look in, ask a few probing questions, then usually end up by telling a little about themselves, timidly sharing an edge of the heart.

One of those spreading the news was Sonja Balaze, the young Czechoslovakian wife, who had taken part in the work party. She came bringing her next-door neighbor, Janey Dobrejcok.

I remembered that Janey was the one whose seven-month-old baby girl had died in the flood. She was only a few years older than nineteen-year-old Sonja. Distressingly thin, her hair fine-spun and flaxen, her brown eyes large and haunted, she trailed the plump, pink-cheeked Sonja but had little to say except a shy *"Ach! Vita jce u nos,"* in her native Czech.

The two of them went wonderingly through the house, staring at the delicate apple green of the freshly painted walls or timidly fingering the curtain fabrics. This was for *them* to enjoy? They actually could bring other friends and children here? When were the first classes to begin? Finally they went off, smiling, letting us know how gladly they would be spreading the word.

But sometimes I wondered if, in our enthusiasm, we were not overdoing the care and beautification being lavished on this one house. Would not the result be too obvious and painful a contrast to the pathetic homes all around it?

I posed this question to Spencer Meloy when he brought in his bulletin copy to the *Sentinel* office that Thursday.

"The contrast is going to be startling all right," he admitted. "But if our church is to be a part of raising standards in the Lowlands, this has to come about by demonstration. One way to start is by training the people themselves in how to improve their homes. That's where the classes will come in."

"But, Spencer, they have so little to work with. You're the one who pointed out that many of them can barely keep food on their tables or clothes on their backs.

How are they going to get money for beautification—for lumber and paint and shrubbery?''

Meloy sighed. ''Julie, I don't know the answer to that. All I know is that our job as Christians is to offer hope to the hopeless, raise the sights of the discouraged, and thereby show them that church people care enough to give of their time, talent, and possessions.''

I looked quickly around the office to see if our conversation was being overheard. The only other person there was Emily Cruley and she was on the telephone. I lowered my voice.

''Spencer, are your church trustees bucking you on this project?''

He seemed startled. ''Why do you ask? Because of Mr. Piley's remarks at the work party?''

''Partly that. Partly what Dean Fleming said after he heard your sermon the day after. He was afraid you would get in trouble with your congregation if you pushed it too hard.''

''If you were in my place, Julie, would you push it?''

''I guess so. I want to see church people do something instead of talk and argue and get mad at each other.''

''Well, to answer your question, the trustees are not happy with the Community Center. Or with me. They think I've become a crusader, that I'm neglecting other church matters. But, thanks to Ken's newspaper copy and the way people have responded to the Center, I don't think they'll give me any trouble.''

As a prophet, he was far off the mark.

Spencer Meloy scheduled a dedication service with an open house afterward for Sunday afternoon, July 7, at three o'clock. Invitations would go to all workers and contributors; announcement posters were to be displayed on every street in the Lowlands.

My parents gladly offered our home of an evening to prepare this promotion and publicity. I invited Margo, who took a night off from her waitress job at the Stemwinder. And Graham, of course. He was now working in his father's store and the two of us had begun dating once a week. A chastened Bryan McKeever had called me to apologize for his graduation night behavior, so I invited him. Even Tim and Anne-Marie pitched in.

Soon we had spread out all over the floor stacks of old magazines, scissors, pots of paste, poster paint and brushes, all of which mingled with lounging bodies and gangling legs. Boy, now a rambunctious puppy of not quite four months, was in the midst of everything. After he had left his paw marks on several of our posters, he was banished to the yard, notwithstanding Anne-Marie's protests.

Mother and Dad joined us before we had finished, and so they were there when Bryan stunned us with his remarks. He had been sitting quietly most of the evening, lettering posters with surprising skill. Then out came a typical Bryan statement.

"I think we're wasting our time fixing up that old house in the Lowlands."

"Why, Bryan?"

"Because it will be washed away in the next flood."

Dad, who had been polishing his reading glasses, turned sharply toward Bryan. "Why so negative?"

Bryan shrugged. "That's the way my father reacts. He won't face the facts either."

"What facts?"

"That the mining companies, the steel company and the Hunting and Fishing Club have so messed up this area that we'll have nothing but floods from now on, each one worse than the last."

All of us were staring at Bryan in amazement. "How did you come to that conclusion?" Dad finally asked.

"I've studied the terrain, its history. The Indians knew best: they believed that nature served man if left alone. Both Brady Creek and Sequanoto River used to be four times as wide. What happened? Yoder's been dumping hot slag from the steel mill along the banks. Slag hardens like rock, so the river channels just become smaller and smaller. So we have worse and worse floods.''

My father's face was alive with interest. ''Bryan, have you ever said these things to your father—and grandfather?''

''Sure. Dad listens some. Grandfather just gets mad at me. Especially when I said his dam was going to break one of these days.''

''You told him that!''

Bryan suddenly became a little uneasy. ''I guess I shouldn't be so outspoken.''

Dad was leaning forward in his chair, as intense as I had ever seen him. ''Why do you think the dam will break, Bryan?''

The pimply-faced high school boy shuffled his feet nervously. ''This is just my opinion, you understand. But I don't think the spillways are properly constructed, especially when they built in those iron gratings to keep the fish from escaping over the dam. This puts too much extra pressure on the dam. I also think the road they built over the dam has weakened it.''

''Have you said anything about this to your father?''

''Yes. He's concerned too. But he can't sell Grandpa on anything today. They argue all the time.''

I looked at the others to see if they were as startled by Bryan's statements as I was. Outside of Dad and myself, they were not. Bryan was such a known troublemaker that no one took him seriously.

But I did.

After the Sunday morning service at Baker Memorial, Spencer Meloy was more ebullient than usual while greeting his members as they filed out. To me he whispered, ''The crowd at the dedication may be bigger than we expected. We'll have it outside.''

Our whole family arrived at the Center an hour early, bringing cookies and lemonade. The inside of the small structure was jammed with people. Outside, under bright

sunshine, Spencer was setting up a portable speaker's
stand at the top of the front steps.

We had expected an audience of mostly women and
children because even on Sundays so many men were at
work. Yoder, like all steel mills, had to run seven days a
week; thus every other weekend each worker had to take
"the long turn." As a result, many men missed both
church and family events on any given Sabbath.

To our surprise, men began to show up with their families. Fifteen minutes before the starting time, the yard
and street were jammed with people. Margo grabbed my
arm, panic in her voice, "There's not enough refreshments."

"It's too late to get more."

"Not if we go now—to the Stemwinder."

I found Dad, got the keys to the Willys, signaled Graham Gillin, and the three of us raced off. When we returned, I had to park the car blocks away because of the
crowd. Hundreds were packed together in front of the
Center. As we circled around the crowd with sacks of
cookies and extra drinks, I heard Spencer's voice:

> "In Thee, O Lord, do I put my trust; let me never
> be ashamed: deliver me in Thy righteousness.
> Bow down Thine ear to me; deliver me speedily:
> be Thou my strong rock, for an house of defense to
> save me.
> For Thou art my rock and my fortress . . ."

The words of the psalm reminded me of that scary
drive with Bryan down Seven Mile Mountain. But I wondered how many of those listening understood English
well enough to receive the message. Yet looking at the
hushed intentness of the upturned faces, I knew that
something was getting through.

By the time Margo, Graham and I had deposited our
sacks of food in the kitchen, Meloy had started on his
message:

Dear friends, we have a God who loves all His children in every nation and no matter what their station in life. This is the God to whom we are dedicating this little Community Center today. Whatever your native tongue is, whether you worship Him with the help of a rosary or a Prayer Book or an old family Bible handed down from Lutheran or Catholic, Presbyterian or Methodist or Baptist parents, is not the important thing. What's important is that you *do* worship Him.

This building is to be *His* building, meant for every one of you . . .

Before the closing prayer of dedication, Spencer did something quite spontaneous. Perhaps feeling alone up there in this unusual setting, he asked my father, who was standing on the edge of the crowd, and Neal Brinton to come and stand shoulder to shoulder with him, supporting and praying silently together. I'm sure he would have wanted one of his church officers to be a part of this too, but not one of them seemed to be present.

Without another word being said, the two men took positions beside Spencer, shoulders touching, a physical token of solidarity and support.

With his "Let us pray," the rustle of voices ceased, and the people stood reverently silent.

And now, Father in heaven, we dedicate this building to You and to Your purpose for it. First cleanse our hearts of any unworthy motives in relation to it. Then we ask You to cleanse the building itself as we set it aside from all common use for Your purposes.

Let this become *Your* house of worship, of teaching, of ministering to human hearts, of meeting needs, of caring for little children. Let joy reign here and good fellowship.

Let this place be as a light on a lampstand, a beacon on a hill, shining out for all to see. In Thy name we pray. Amen.

With both his arms upraised, Spencer Meloy's voice rang out, "God bless each of you. We invite you now to see the Center for yourselves and to have some punch and cookies."

The crowd swarmed forward. Our church project was no longer an idea and a dream, but a reality.

25

After the triumphant opening of the Community Center, the question was: would the Lowlands people consider the building as truly their own place?

On Monday night my father and I returned to the Center to retrieve some serving dishes and help out as needed. Neal Brinton was already there. He and several local women had been given keys to open and close the house whenever it was used.

Suddenly Neal's brother, Cade Brinton, strode into the house. More accurately I should say "blew in" because there was an air of determined gustiness about him. Dressed in denim overalls over a gray flannel sweatshirt, he also had on a black cap with a long visor, which he did not remove. For a long moment he stood there in the center of the front room staring intently at us.

My father stepped forward. "Can we do something for you, Cade?" he asked.

"Just wanted to see for m'self what you've done to my house."

"By all means, look around," Dad said. "We hoped you'd come."

"This house wasn't worth fixin'."

"We don't feel that way," was the Editor's reply. "People all over town helped restore this place."

Before Cade could reply, Neal appeared from the upstairs. "Cade! You here—?"

"Yeah, Neal. Gotta know what's goin' on around

here." He sounded defensive. "And I need to talk to Wallace here about Yoder's pretty little booklet."

Neal looked embarrassed. "Cade," he said softly, "I'm not s-sure this is the time or place . . ."

"Look, Neal, I'll pick my own time and place."

"Before we talk, would you like to see the rest of the house?" Dad suggested.

Cade shrugged and followed him, while I went to the kitchen to fix punch and cookies. Five minutes later I heard Cade's voice trailing Dad back down the stairs. "I hear tell you've already run off two printings of the ERP booklet."

The Editor's voice was patient. "That's right, Cade, and I think there are some good things about the plan. I like the idea of employees electing their own representatives to talk to management about grievances. Isn't that a step in the right direction?"

"Ain't what it seems. I knew you was fooled."

"Would you like some refreshments, Mr. Brinton?" I interrupted.

The intense man looked at me suspiciously, but sat down at the table and accepted the glass and plate of cookies I handed him. Then he turned back to the Editor. "So y'think that pretty little booklet reads nice, do you?" he continued. "I know just how it reads," he went on caustically. " 'It's for your good, men. You are to become Yoder *Industrians.*' " Then he quoted several passages. With his inflection the phrases sounded insincere, almost sinister.

Coming on the heels of his workingman's English, the big words rolling so sonorously off Cade's tongue took me by surprise. Then it hit me: this man had as sharp a mind as Neal did, but his prejudices limited its use. Cade's voice rolled on, " 'You Industrians will have a large voice in shaping the policy of this company. See it, men! The basic idea of ERP is to apply to industry the mechanism of republican government in political life.' Oh, *yeah?!*"

As Cade paused for some punch, Neal seized the opportunity. "S-sarcasm isn't the way to handle this, Cade. If you've got anything to s-say, tell it s-straight and cut out the double-talk."

Cade glared at his brother. "Okay, okay. What's wrong is, ERP's nothin' but a front to keep real unions out."

"How can you be sure of that, Cade?" Dad asked.

"Sure? Because Yoder and all the big-shot industrialists see nothin' but the devil and the Bolsheviks in what they call 'outside unions.' ERP is their last-ditch stand against us. Beginning with Carnegie, Charlie Schwab, J. P. Morgan, coming right on down to the McKeevers, they'd move heaven and earth and the government too to keep us men from organizing to put a decent roof over our heads and a little more bread on our tables."

The Editor remained unconvinced. "Cade, I'm no authority on ERP. But it does call for an election by secret ballot. Workers can choose their own representation to an assembly. That way, good talkers like you can be elected to present the workers' case to management. Isn't that a lot better than long strikes, with men out of work earning nothing?"

"Yeah, Cade," Neal cut in again. "And when you think of how many workers can't even s-speak English at Yoder, anything that gets us talking has got to be a s-step in the right direction."

Cade pushed his chair back and faced his brother. "Yeah, talkin's okay. But it's gonna take more'n *talk* to get a nine-hour day and a wage one can live on. Yoder steelworkers make about $600 a year. They need twice that to pay their bills."

Then he looked at my father. "Go home and read Section Eight of that pretty little booklet. They buried that part. Hoped nobody'd notice. There's a sentence there that says that the Board of Directors of the company can 'veto or annul'—yeah, they use those two very words—anything the assembly decides on. There's where the whole thing's phony. Read Section Eight for yerself, Wallace.''

Dad looked at Cade thoughtfully. ''I'll read it again, Cade. If you're right about that clause, then it should be rethought. But as for me, I'm acting only as the printer. I have no voice in Yoder Steel policies. Why appeal to me?''

''Because you're a publisher, and your paper prints stuff for people to read, don't it? Newspapers can start people thinkin', stir 'em up, can't they? Ain't that what newspapers are for?''

Dad nodded. ''Yes—that, and to print the news.''

''Well, there's plenty of news today about how companies are shafting the workers. People are behind us now. Congress just passed a labor bill that gives us workers the right to organize. You can forget ERP. We're gonna have an independent union at Yoder within a year.''

Cade was referring to the Wagner Act (or National Labor Relations Act) signed the past week (July 5) by President Roosevelt. As Dad and I drove home that night, he explained that this new law not only barred unfair labor practices but affirmed the right of employees to ''form, join or assist labor organizations to bargain collectively through representatives of their own choosing.''

''Then Cade's right. The ERP plan's a dead issue,'' I said.

''Not necessarily. Labor has no real leadership yet. Companies will push ERP harder than ever now to try and stop the unions.''

My sympathy was all with the worker. That night I resolved to do some research of my own about the union movement.

In the local library on the table farthest away from the main desk, I assembled my materials. One book traced the ERP concept to a 1913 episode between owners and miners in Colorado. In the place of Yoder Steel and the

McKeevers, as I pictured it, this earlier scenario substituted the Colorado Fuel and Iron Company and the Rockefellers.

It seemed that Colorado miners, like Yoder steelworkers, had high-rent company housing in a place called Mine City, situated in a winding canyon often knee-deep in mud. For the twelve-hour work span of steelworkers handling dangerous molten metal in a suffocating shed, one could substitute a dark, chilly underground so laden with coal dust that black-lung disease was all but inevitable.

I discovered that some miners worked in "low-coal" canals less than four feet wide, two to three feet high, where the men had to wield their picks while kneeling or lying prone. The misuse of explosives to loosen coal, plus improperly constructed mine roofs with resultant cave-ins, resulted in one of the highest industrial accident-and-death rates in the country.

On other counts the miners in 1913 had it worse than the steelworkers: they never saw cash, since the Colorado Fuel and Iron Company would pay them only in scrip. This despite the fact that Colorado law had abolished the scrip system, thus giving the families of miners the right to shop outside of what the workers called the "pluck-me" company stores.

On the Colorado statute books were other major laws which the company had steadily refused to put into effect. Though the eight-hour day had been law since 1905, it had so many loopholes that the coal companies could ignore it. Another law had given the miners the right to belong to a union and to be paid semi-monthly instead of monthly. The company paid no attention to it.

With each fact gleaned in my research, my sympathy for the miners increased. The coal diggers were paid only for the amount of marketable coal they brought out. Thus much of each day's labor was what miners called "dead work." I could scarcely believe all that "dead work" had included: laying the track, drilling holes for the explosives, clearing away the debris after the explosion and removing rocks to make way for the mine cars, even removing the slate and rock from the coal that had been dug.

Given so much backbreaking "dead work," the weighing of the coal, which would decide each man's paycheck, became an emotional issue indeed. Though workers, by state law, could have their own man on hand to check the weighing of each load of coal, they estimated they were robbed of 700 to 1,400 pounds of coal per carload because of "inaccurate" scales. But any miner who protested was told, "Down the canyon for you," meaning that he was fired.

In April 1912, the Colorado Bureau of Labor Statistics put the coal miner's average take-home pay at $1.98 per day!

When the company refused to change their policies or talk with the miners about these grievances, a strike was called for Tuesday, September 23, 1913. By September 22, 95 percent of the miners had quit work.

Eviction notices, effective September 23, were sent to all miners on strike. The union's answer was to provide a tent city some miles away at Ludlow, Colorado, for 9,000 miners, their wives and children.

As I pored over this piece of American history, I could picture that cold, rainy September day as the miners vacated their homes. There were not enough mule-drawn wagons, nor even pushcarts. Mounds of furniture, clothes, pots and pans, had to be moved out of the houses and dumped in the street, now deep in mud. Women and children could only wait, perched on soggy mattresses in the rain, until their turn came for a wagon.

Then began the slow mass exodus out of the winding canyon through the mud. The miners were in for a further shock when they arrived at the tent city: tents ordered from West Virginia had failed to arrive on time. The men and their families huddled together under wagons or makeshift cover as the rain turned to snow. When the tents finally arrived four days later, this inadequate shelter was all they had throughout that bitter winter of 1913–14.

Then the Colorado Fuel and Iron Company hired professional strikebreakers who had proved brutally effective in breaking up a West Virginia coal strike. So many shootings and deaths followed that the Colorado state militia was called out. But the militia could not handle the situation either.

Without warning on the morning of April 20, 1914, the massacre of Ludlow began. Machine guns and high-powered rifles, set up on the surrounding hills the night before by the strikebreakers, opened fire. The tents were riddled. As unarmed men futilely tried to protect their families, screaming women and children crawled into pits under the tent floors, lowered themselves into wells or fled toward the hills.

That evening a strikebreaker crawled to the edge of the tent city, poured kerosene on nearby tents, then with an oil-soaked torch set them afire. The flames swept through the city, killing sixty-six, leaving some forty-eight severely burned.

News of Ludlow appalled the nation. Pictures, cartoons, detailed reports, were distributed coast to coast. President Woodrow Wilson sent federal troops and mediators to the rescue. Incredibly, even with all the adverse national publicity, company management refused to meet with the government mediators.

Early in December, facing a second winter with nowhere to live, their endurance and all their resources gone, the miners gave in and called off the strike. The company had won.

Because it was such a hollow victory—for workingmen without hope, all spirit gone, make poor employees —company management hired Mackenzie King (who later became prime minister of Canada) to come up with a program to restore miners' morale. It was his study of the situation that formed the nucleus of the Employee Relations Plan (ERP).

John D. Rockefeller, Jr., over the protests of his father, ordered King's plan be tried in the mines and in their steel plant in Pueblo. I wondered if young Rockefeller was in somewhat the same position with his father as Tom McKeever, Jr., was with his, with both younger men having more vision and flexibility.

As my research on the labor-management problem grew, I was appalled at the abuses of human rights. Cheap labor was endlessly exploited. Terrible slums became an accepted part of America's cities. At the same time, huge profits were amassed. Cornelius Vanderbilt, the Rockefellers, Andrew Carnegie and others acquired large personal fortunes.

My father had said that America could never have become the richest and most powerful nation on earth without the ambitious drive and the financial wizardry of these business tycoons. I was forced to agree, but one question still haunted me: why did this have to be at the expense of so many people?

I typed my research, documenting it carefully—then, eager for his reaction, placed it on the Editor's desk. Glancing in from time to time, I could see that he was reading it carefully. Finally Dad called me into his office.

"Good job, Julie. I'm amazed you would do this on your own. But it makes dreadful reading, doesn't it?"

"Horrible. It was hard for me to believe that this Ludlow thing could have happened in America."

"We've come a long way in the twenty-one years since 1914."

"But have we really, Dad? I see the same mentality at work toward the steelworkers. Old Man McKeever doesn't see them as people, but as figures on his profit-and-loss statements. He won't even listen to his son or grandson."

The Editor raised his hand to stop me. "But there *are* progressive people in management today. And now with the Wagner Act, there will be even more. Of course they would prefer not to have unions, but they know they're facing the inevitable. Unions are coming because of just such horrors as the Ludlow Massacre."

"They why don't we support the union idea in *The Sentinel?*" I almost shouted.

My father's shoulders sagged and his eyes closed. Instantly I regretted the vehemence of my words and ached for him. I knew what he must be thinking: "Am I living through just another version of Timmeton? Always between opposing forces? Must it always be so difficult?"

26

R<small>AND</small>'s telephone call came later that week.

"Remember that graduation gift I promised you?" he asked.

"You gave me a rose and I loved it."

"That's not what I had in mind. There's a place I want to show you near Pittsburgh. Are you free on Saturday, July twentieth?"

"Yes, I believe so."

"Good. You may know of my uncle, Munro Farnsworth. The Farnsworths are inviting both of us to spend that Saturday night in their home in Pittsburgh. Auntie will write to you. Oh, yes. I've already checked it out with your parents. They approve."

This was a bit too much. "I *am* over eighteen, Rand."

The voice on the phone chuckled. "So you are. I just wanted to do what was proper."

"What clothes should I bring?"

"Pertinent question. We'll motor to a nice place for dinner that night. On Sunday, chances are we'll go to church."

With a thumping heart I stared at the receiver as I replaced it. This was a new stage in my relationship with Randolph Wilkinson. And such good timing too, with Graham Gillin gone with his family on a two-week trip to California. I raced to find Mother. "Rand just called. Wants to take me out a week from Saturday, then overnight with his relatives in Pittsburgh."

"I know, Julie. He asked our permission. Your father and I liked that."

"That part makes me feel like a fourteen-year-old. This isn't exactly my first date, Mother."

"Randolph wanted to do it properly, especially since you'll be gone overnight. That shouldn't bother you."

She was right. I was overreacting. "Mother, what will I wear?"

"I thought that would be next. Don't worry. We'll figure something out."

Saturday finally came—a sparkling day, sunny, delightful. I awakened with an upset stomach. Suspecting that it came from excitement, I did not mention it for fear of merciless family teasing. Well aware of the gap of eight years between Rand and me, it was important that I not act the part of the shy, overeager and inexperienced girl.

Rand arrived after lunch, looked approvingly at my white dress and took my arm as we left the house. Proudly he introduced me to his new Studebaker sports coupe, including a rumble seat and "floating power." With a fine flourish he stowed my "mackintosh," as he called it, and overnight case in the "boot" of his auto. Then, in a courtly manner, he opened the door of his car for me.

At the outskirts of Alderton, Rand turned to me with a grin. "By the way, we're not heading toward Pittsburgh."

"I see."

"No. Pittsburgh's due west, perhaps a tad northwest. We're heading almost north of Pittsburgh."

"I suppose you cleared this also with my parents."

"To be honest, no."

"Good. I don't like my whole future being planned by others."

"Are you unhappy with me for checking things out with your parents?"

"No-o. I guess it was the proper thing to do."

"And you are a proper girl."

"At least until I'm twenty-one."

"Twenty-one, eh? Then what will happen?"

"I'm not sure yet. I might go to New York City, live in Greenwich Village among the artists."

"To do what?"

"Write books."

"You could at that."

"Do you think I could, Rand? I mean, become the author of a great novel?" Even at the thought, excitement rose in me.

"If that's your heart's desire, I believe you could do it."

"Thank you, Rand." I sighed and leaned all the way back in the seat. "But for now, I may have to settle for writing articles and poetry for *The Alderton Sentinel.*"

"I haven't seen your poetry."

"I did a few for the Poetry Corner."

Rand turned, looked at me in surprise. "I recall some of those poems. They were rather good. But I don't remember seeing your name under them."

"You didn't and you won't. I'm the mystery poet of western Pennsylvania."

"You're twitting me, Julie."

"I'm dead serious. Miss Cruley found several of my poems, unsigned, in the filler file; she liked them and decided to establish the Poetry Corner as a regular feature. She's very proud of it. I don't dare let her know I wrote them. She doesn't like me."

"Don't mind her; she's just an old biddy."

I laughed. "But she's very impressed with you, Rand. Likes your correct English. It would surprise her enormously to know that you and I are off on a weekend together—and not in the direction of Pittsburgh at that. By the way, where are you taking me?" I hoped my nervousness wasn't showing.

That mischievous look was back in his eyes. "I suppose you're wondering how a proper Englishman could tell your parents we're going to Pittsburgh when in reality we're headed for my secret cabin in Catsutawney.''

"Where?"

"You've never heard of Catsutawney?"

"I've heard of Punxsutawney."

"Catsutawney is much more remote. It's also one of the loveliest spots in western Pennsylvania."

I looked at the passing scenery, at the road markers, then at the map, all the time wondering how to handle this. "Rand, I never would have suspected you of kidnapping."

He laughed, then reached over and touched my hand. "Seriously, I think you'll be impressed with the place I'm taking you."

I felt relieved, but didn't want him to notice.

An hour later we entered the outskirts of a tree-shaded town and drew up in front of a sprawling white clapboard building with dark red shutters and window boxes overflowing with red and white petunias. A swinging tavern-type sign read *The Caledonian Inn*.

A young man approached the car. "May I park it for you, sir?"

"You certainly may." Rand bounded around to my side of the Studebaker and helped me out.

"You'll probably want to freshen up," he said as he took my elbow and steered me to the front door of the Inn. "I'll show you the cloakroom, then wait for you in the lobby."

"Cloakroom?" I said in amusement. "But I left my raincoat in the car."

"Oh, sorry! I should have said 'ladies room' or that other term—oh, yes, 'powder room.' My anglicisms do keep cropping up."

The large sunny lobby was furnished with American antiques—mellow wood interspersed with painted Pennsylvania Dutch pieces. Beautifully framed old prints and maps graced the walls. Bouquets of fresh garden flowers were everywhere in copper or delft vases.

When I returned to the lobby, Rand took my arm. "Come, I want to show you the garden."

A spacious, wide verandah running the full width of the building across the back was furnished with cushioned white wicker chairs. Hanging fuchsias, ferns on stands, and canaries in ornate white Victorian-looking cages added to the charm.

Before us was a gently rolling landscape with the mountains on every side as a backdrop. The plantings and gardens fitted into the contours of the land itself. Graveled walkways wound through stretches of smooth emerald-green turf; in the center was a natural pond with graceful willows overhanging its banks. Here and there were beds of roses, old-fashioned floribundas, and the most colorful perennial borders I had ever seen.

As Rand led the way past head-high delphiniums, he grew more and more animated. "P'haps you can guess why I'm so fond of this place. So many features of it remind me of home. Ever hear of a man named Capability Brown?"

I shook my head. "What a name to live up to!"

Rand laughed. "You're right. Ridiculous. Anyway, that really was his name! He was an English landscape designer—eighteenth century. This place is done in the best Capability Brown tradition."

"I don't understand."

"Well, y'see, Capability Brown's talent was for planning around what nature had already put there. His emphasis was on form and shape, with the greens of grass and trees predominating. Today you meet his landscape work all over England."

"And how did you find this place?"

"Through the manager. I knew his sister back in England." He headed for the lobby. "Now there's something waiting for us in front of the Inn."

Outside stood a shiny one-seater horse-drawn buggy with large wheels and a yellow top. In it, dressed in

heavy twill pants held up by suspenders over a gray
pullover shirt, was a man with a black beard.

"Mr. Wilkinson?" he asked. He pronounced his "W"
like a "V."

"Yes. Thank you for being so punctual. Mr. Stoltzfur,
I want you to meet Miss Julie Wallace. Julie, Mr. Josiah
Stoltzfur has very kindly agreed to trust us with his buggy
and this high-stepping trotter for a couple of hours."

"Glad to lend you my 'courtin' carriage.' " Mr.
Stoltzfur climbed down from his seat, nodded pleasantly
to us, then sauntered off.

"Ever ridden in one?" Rand asked me.

"No, never." Then I couldn't resist. "Did I hear the
farmer call this a 'courting carriage'?"

"That's right. Mr. Stoltzfur is Amish, I believe.
That's the name they use for single-seated buggies." Despite Rand's studied nonchalance, an unmistakable trace
of red was creeping up his neck.

He helped me up onto the rugged black leather seat,
climbed up beside me, took the reins of the impatient
trotter—and we were off, rolling easily along the country
lanes, through pleasant patches of shade, past sturdy red
or white barns and neatly checkered, almost manicured
fields. From time to time we crossed little bridges of rattling boards over rushing streams. Everywhere there
were fat bumblebees and floating butterflies and bird
songs, as well as the pervasive fragrances of new-mown
hay and clover and honeysuckle, along with the good
honest smells of leather and of horseflesh.

The trotter was enjoying himself, and so were we. On
what appeared to be straight stretches, Rand would give
him his head. Then suddenly the buggy would roll
around a curve, causing me to be thrown against him. He
would put one arm around my waist to steady me, and I
would feel the lean hardness of his body.

It was turning into a magical afternoon with a timeless
quality, almost the feel of fairy dust scattered over everything. The rest of the world had been left behind. Rand

and I were alone, with the golden sunlight shimmering over the countryside and the benediction of its warm, slanting fingers on our heads.

Later, as Rand turned the trotter back toward the Inn, the sunlight deepened to twilight.

The surprises were not over. After freshening up for dinner, Rand and I were shown to a table in the dining room overlooking the garden. What I saw at my place made me gasp. There were five tiny vases in a semicircle around my plate, each filled with a different wildflower; the center vase held one of those rare Scottish harebells.

"Rand! How did you ever—I mean, how could you *possibly* have arranged this?"

"You're not supposed to know how I did it," he retorted, flashing me a pleased, boyish grin. "But I remembered your wildflower garden, Julie. The little vases are part of your graduation present. Mr. MacAlistair will see that they're properly packed for you after dinner."

"They're exquisite." What was dawning on me was not so much the charm of the gift itself, but rather how much thought and care had gone into the planning of every detail of this trip. I wondered, how could I, with my limited background, hope to impress such a man?

The dinner was an amazing meld of Pennsylvania Dutch dishes and British ones, like the sherry trifle for dessert. Each course was served unobtrusively without interrupting our conversation. Since there had been no presentation of a menu, I realized that Rand must have ordered the dinner ahead of time.

He leaned back in his chair, his eyes searching me out, contentment written on his face. "I should be honest, Julie, and tell you I had some qualms about bringing you here."

"Why, Rand?"

"Because of your strong feelings toward, well, upper-class wealth and all that."

"But I've always loved beauty and I often dream of

going to nice places. In my imagination I once pictured myself in a spot very much like this." I paused a moment to temper my enthusiasm. "I guess I would want to see the loveliness of a place like this made available to more people, not just the few."

Randolph nodded, still thoughtful. "Well expressed. I love this inn because for a few hours I'm back in my homeland. Which reminds me of a subject I promised to deliver on and never did."

"Yes, those strange-looking unicorns on your family crest."

He chuckled. "You did surprise me with your research on the Wilkinsons, Julie. Let's see now, where to start? As a little tyke I learned that the unicorn was a horselike creature with a single horn in its forehead. There's a bouncy nursery rhyme that goes like this:

> *The Lion and the Unicorn*
> *Were fighting for the Crown;*
> *The Lion chased the Unicorn*
> *All around the town.*
> *Some gave them white bread,*
> *Some gave them brown,*
> *Some gave them plum cake*
> *And drummed them out of town."*

"I like it. Does it have a tune?"

"Not that I know of. Years later I found that the nursery rhyme went back to the seventeenth century—about the same time the unicorns were put on our Wilkinson family crest."

"But why *three* of them?"

"A story's come down in our family about three Wilkinson brothers who undertook daring exploits for James the First on the continent of Europe, and so were awarded on their crest three unicorns." He grinned at me. "They're supposed to stand for valor, virtue and purity. I hope you're impressed."

"I am. But what's so pure about the unicorn?"

"Dashed if I know. Somehow it is connected with the Virgin Mary. Out of that came the legend that the invincible unicorn could be captured in only one way." Rand looked over at me with that roguish glint in his eyes. "Guess?"

"I can't imagine. By a valiant knight, perhaps?"

"Wrong. A virgin must be led into the forest and left alone there. Eventually a unicorn would find her and docilely lay his head in the virgin's lap. Then he could be captured." He smiled at me. "In the end, masculine strength will always docilely lay its head in the lap of beauty and virtue—contented, indeed delighted, to be captured."

"I love it."

"All women do."

As we lingered over after-dinner coffee, with Rand in no hurry at all, finally I asked, "How far are we from the Farnsworths'?"

He shrugged. "Not too far. May be close to midnight before we get there. Doesn't matter a bit. I've a key to the house and they consider it my home too. They will have retired long before we arrive. You'll find your bed neatly turned down with a note of welcome on your pillow."

Outside it was a starlit night with a little breeze springing up. Then we were in Rand's coupe, ready to start. All at once he leaned over and kissed me lightly, very tenderly. When he started to draw away, scarcely realizing what I was doing, I reached up with my arms and drew him back. His lips sought mine fiercely this time. For several giddy moments, my senses spun and whirled and pinwheeled. Then slowly we pulled apart, shaken.

Rand placed the key in the ignition, but did not immediately start the engine. "That wasn't in the plan, Julie."

"Why not?"

Even in the darkness I could see his look of surprise. Then he grinned. "Why not? Indeed, why not?"

This time he turned the key, the engine roared to life, and we drove on through the night to Pittsburgh.

27

Soon after dawn I stirred sleepily. In the fog of my half-waking state, it took me a few moments to adjust to the strange bedroom.

Then I remembered. *The Caledonian Inn . . . the drive with Rand . . . the Farnsworths.* There would be no more sleep for me this morning. I was too excited, too much in love. Rand and I! Again I could feel the security of his arms around me, his lips on mine.

I lay there in the big four-poster canopied bed, enjoying the sheets, silky-soft on my skin, and knowing that there was no hurry about getting up.

That kiss in front of the Caledonian Inn changed everything, I mused. *The difference in age was wiped out. All day long, two minds and two hearts had been reaching for each other. At that kiss, they merged.*

During the drive to the Farnsworths', Rand had pulled me close to him and had kept reaching for my hand. When we pulled up under the Farnsworths' porte-cochère, it started all over. Tender kisses leading to the same wild, giddy heights.

Then we had walked up the porch stairs and on through the front door, which Rand opened with his key. I had a vague recollection of an entrance hall with floors of black-and-white marble squares and, shining through the dim light, an incongruous-looking suit of medieval knight's armor, tall pikestaff in gauntleted hand. To my surprise, the curving stairs up which Rand led me were also marble. On the landing was a note giving directions to the rooms we were to occupy and advising us to sleep as late as we wished.

Rand had brought in my overnight case from the car, and after placing the bag on a chair, he kissed me once more, this time lightly on the forehead, and headed for his room.

I was in bed, light turned off, when there was a light tap on the door. Then it opened and Rand stepped in quietly, moving to the side of my bed.

"Everything all right?" he whispered.

I nodded, too tense to trust my voice.

Rand stood there uncertainly for a moment, then sat down on the side of the bed and began to stroke my hair. Faint rays of moonlight drifted across his face. I could not see his eyes and this bothered me.

He leaned down and gently kissed my forehead, then each eye, then the tip of my nose; finally his mouth pressed hard against mine. A series of conflicting emotions surged through my body.

"Rand, I'm scared."

It came out as a gasp, louder than I intended. Rand straightened up, got to his feet, then reached for my hand, which he kissed lightly. "Good night, Julie," he whispered and departed.

I was a long time getting to sleep. Lingering with me was the warmth of Rand's breath, the faint scent of cologne, and the softness of his mouth; in my mind I kept fingering them over and over like beads of a rosary.

Rand had held off saying the words, but his love had enveloped me all day long through his tenderness, thoughtful gifts and finally the ardor in his eyes. If he had slipped into my bed, I honestly don't know what would have happened, for I loved him as I had never thought I could love anyone.

Now that the morning light was bringing the room's details into sharper focus, I interrupted my reverie to look around. The high white ceiling above me was set off by a gracefully molded cornice; there were three tall windows with filmy curtains and draperies of the same heavy blue and white silk damask as on the four-poster bed with its massive pineapple posts. All of the furniture was dark and heavily carved.

Having satisfied my curiosity about the room, once again I let myself luxuriate in the thought: *how suddenly one's life can enter a completely new phase*. Before yesterday there had been my girlhood—years of learning, growing, searching for an identity. The dates with high school boys and the embarrassment of their clumsy, groping hands seemed back in another era. Rand's maturity was a true separation of man from boy.

Yesterday, with the flowering of my love for Rand, I felt as though I had entered a gate marked ''Womanhood.''

I stopped my happy, sensuous musings to face a fact. Marriage. A solemn thought indeed! Was I ready to face marriage at eighteen? A new procession of questions whirled through my head. College? That sounded impossible, considering our family finances. Career? Yes, but not the most important thing. Then what *was* all-important? My love for Rand. It was total, reached to the depth and height of me. Any kind of worldly success I could possibly achieve in any field faded into insignificance beside this.

I did not know whether Rand loved me in the same way, but this I did know: if he asked me, I would marry him right away.

My parents. Would they object? They would consider me too young, but Rand could persuade them. Since there was no money for college, what alternative could they press upon me?

Hearing voices outside, I slipped out of bed and peeked through the curtains. An elderly gentleman, *must be Mr. Farnsworth,* and Rand, looking a bit disheveled, were walking through the garden. A frowning Mr. Farnsworth was doing most of the talking. When Rand's arm suddenly pointed to my room, I pulled away from the window. With a sinking feeling, I gathered they were talking about me—and it did not seem to be happy talk.

Yet shortly after that, when I put on my Sunday dress and slipped downstairs, the Farnsworths welcomed me warmly. Munro Farnsworth was a grandfatherly type with a mane of white hair, sideburns and glacial blue eyes.

His wife, Cynthia Wilkinson Farnsworth, was quiet and motherly with curly blond hair and a warm smile. It would be easy to call her "Auntie" as Rand did. She led the way to a breakfast room. "Randolph will be here in a minute," she purred.

My heart quickened when Rand walked into the room. *What would I see in his eyes?* His quick, warm smile reassured me. Now I could face the Farnsworths with some measure of confidence.

During the breakfast conversation I learned that Munro Farnsworth was one of many steel barons who had constructed mansions on this high bluff known as Sewickley Heights. As I asked questions about their Pittsburgh life, the old gentleman was studying me.

After breakfast Rand started to lead me out into the garden when his uncle intercepted us. "You'll be with Julie for the rest of the day, Rand. Why don't you talk to your Auntie for a while and give this young lass and me a chance to get to know each other?"

As Munro Farnsworth led me to his den, I had the whimsical though not reassuring thought that there were unicorns, *not lions,* on the Wilkinson crest. The aging steel mogul ambled on ahead of me into a dark room paneled with mahogany. He nodded toward an overstuffed chair near the marble fireplace as he walked to a large paper-strewn desk and retrieved a black pipe resting on a sheaf of papers. Then he sat down in the chair opposite me.

As he carefully tamped tobacco into his pipe and then lit it, I noted the painting over the mantel, an immense

English landscape with a wide gilt frame. To the left of the fireplace was a marble bust on a pedestal. *A Roman god with a broken nose?*

Mr. Farnsworth saw me looking at the bust. "Picked that up in Naples. A.D. 13, the experts think. Very valuable."

He waved his pipe toward the landscape painting. "A genuine John Constable."

"Lovely," I murmured.

Pulling slowly on his pipe, he asked suddenly. "How old are you, my dear?"

"Eighteen."

"I see. Just out of high school?"

"Yes, sir."

"Planning on going to college, I suppose."

"I want to. At the moment, I don't see how we can afford it. Also I'm needed at the newspaper."

"Of course. You're a proofreader, are you not?"

"Yes. And I do research, write some poetry and— other things." The line of questioning was making me increasingly uneasy.

"Your father's taken on *The Sentinel* at a bad time. Small newspapers are struggling everywhere."

"My father loves the challenge. Every member of our family is helping out."

"Do you think your father was properly prepared to run that newspaper, being so new to Alderton?"

"He's learned a great deal in a short time."

"I understand he was a clergyman before he came here. Do you think that qualifies him to make judgments about business and political matters in Alderton?"

"I think he is qualified for this. Yes."

Mr. Farnsworth relit his pipe while I tried to keep from squirming. "Randolph says you have a special interest in the problems of workers, that he joined you on some sort of cleanup venture for flood victims."

"That's right, Mr. Farnsworth. The people in the Lowlands are suffering from poor housing and undernourishment. They're the victims of—'' I stopped, realizing I was heading into deep water. "These working people need help and Alderton citizens have been just great in their response.''

"Randolph is a very warmhearted person,'' the industrialist continued. "He likes people, which makes him good at his job. But sometimes he's too softhearted. People then misread him and think he means something that he doesn't.''

My mouth suddenly went dry and I did not answer.

"You see, my child, Randolph has a mission in life that in some ways prevents him from being in control of his own destiny.''

"What kind of mission, Mr. Farnsworth?''

"It has to do with one word. Ancestry. The Wilkinsons have a long and important family history, as I see you've discovered, going back hundreds of years. Randolph is a very important link in that history for the future. That's why he's here. To learn. To meet the right people. Then to marry the right woman.''

"And who are these 'right people'?'' I asked, feeling the rebuff deep in the pit of my stomach.

Mr. Farnsworth fixed a steady, metallic gaze on me. The words that came out were cool, carefully thought out, numbing. "The Wilkinsons, my dear, are a class-conscious family. They consider that proper marriages are absolutely essential to the preservation of a strong family line. There is perhaps only one condition where the pure blood of the line might be diluted somewhat—''

"And that would be?''

"If the other family has wealth.''

I stared at the tall industrialist—first in amazement, then in a slow-burning anger. Forgotten now was my resolve to be softspoken, careful, and even a bit demure. His arrogance touched a fuse inside me. "That's the most awful description of ancestry I've ever heard, Mr. Farnsworth.''

His head jerked up in amazement. "How's that?''

"You are saying, aren't you, that inner values like integrity and courage mean nothing to you? What's important is that your family members make money and marry people of social prominence."

Now he was glaring at me. "Young lady, you're putting words into my mouth that I never said."

I was trembling so hard I could barely speak. "I'm sorry, sir, but your meaning was clear. And it certainly doesn't sound like America, with its freedom of opportunity where a poor boy can grow up to be President."

His cold eyes bored into me for a long moment. There was a certain hesitancy in the words that followed. "You are right about America being a land of opportunity. Our free enterprise system is basic to our way of life."

I fought down a frantic desire to flee the man and battled the tears now just under the surface. I forced myself to rise to my feet slowly and look directly into those flinty blue eyes. "I don't know why I'm such a threat to you, Mr. Farnsworth. Randolph and I have never talked about marriage, but if we had, I would certainly stand all the Wallace ancestors right up against all the Wilkinsons and Farnsworths and feel not one bit inferior."

Taken aback, Mr. Farnsworth stood and glowered at me. Then he dropped his eyes and spoke more softly. "What I said is no reflection on your family. Perhaps I was too blunt." He plowed on. "But that's the way I'm accustomed to handling things. Sentimentality is a poor way to run a business—or to build a family line."

When we rejoined Randolph and Mrs. Farnsworth on the patio, I hoped that someone would suggest we go to church. Something deep inside me yearned to share this experience with Rand. It was not to be. Conversation was so strained for the rest of the morning that I did not relax until Rand and I were alone in his roadster on the way back to Alderton. He was making a valiant effort to be lighthearted, but underneath I could sense that his spirit was as heavy as mine.

"I can tell, Julie, that your talk with Uncle Munro was not very pleasant."

"I'm afraid not."

He sighed deeply. "He's as hard as whinstone. Something of a snob as well. In that respect he's not very different from generations of Pittsburgh steel millionaires. The trouble with most of them is that they pretend to be what they are not."

"How do you mean?"

"Some were crude characters, straight off the raw American frontier. So when they made money fast—astronomical fortunes—they pretended they had culture and knowledge that simply weren't there. So they were forever pulling bloopers."

"Such as?" I prodded.

"Such as, when one steel man was building his mansion, the architect asked him if he wanted a porte-cochère. His reply was 'Hell, yeah! Better put in six of 'em. And see to it that the flush don't sound loud, will ya?' "

We laughed together, relieved to ease the tension. "And I suppose they were picking their teeth with gold toothpicks?"

"You have the idea," came Rand's answer. "Only you can't imagine the lengths to which some of these new millionaires go. One tycoon built an Ivanhoe stronghold with turrets, moat and drawbridge. Few know anything about art, yet they've bought Renoirs and Gainsboroughs and Turners, even the Renaissance masters, by the truckload. They sport private cars on rails with liveried butlers, keep $500,000 yachts. Or they try to buy up Balkan princelings or English dukes and earls for their daughters."

Rand's contempt for his uncle's philosophy soothed me somewhat. As if reading my thoughts, he said more seriously, "But for Auntie's levelheadedness, my uncle would have been as bad as some of the rest. With her help, somehow they've at least managed to stay on the fringes of that kind of nonsense. But deep down my uncle is a snob.''

''He grilled me mighty hard,'' I admitted.

''About what?''

I stared out the window at the passing scenery and wondered how honest I should be. ''About my goals in life.''

''What did you tell him?''

''That I wanted to join the Bolsheviks and destroy capitalism in America.''

Rand laughed so uproariously that for a moment I thought he was going to swerve off the road. ''How I should like to have seen the expression on his face!''

''Well, I might just as well have said that. He thinks I'm some kind of flaming radical. What did you tell him about me, anyway?''

''Too much, probably. Uncle Munro is very conservative about women. I think he's still living back in the last century.''

''It isn't funny, really. Your uncle is on the boards of both Yoder Steel and the Hunting and Fishing Club. While talking to him, I realized that he knew a lot about my family—our concern about the dam, our support of the Community Center in the Lowlands—and for some reason, all of this makes me his enemy.''

Rand pondered this a moment. ''Well, you and your father have probably been overzealous about the dam.''

''You think it's safe then?''

''Yes, I do. There are probably thousands of earthen dams throughout the world that are not as strong as this one.''

''What about that missing engineer's report?''

''What report?''

''The one done by an engineer just before the railroad sold it to your Club. It was supposed to have been attached to the sales contract. It just disappeared. No one seems to know anything about it.''

Rand was silent for a long moment. ''I don't know

anything about it. Engineers' reports can be strikingly different, I've heard. I'm sure no two engineers would agree on this dam.''

Something inside me was ebbing away as we became silent for what seemed like a long time.

''I'm afraid I've put you through a difficult weekend, Julie. I'm sorry,'' he finally said.

My eyes suddenly filled with tears. ''Rand, don't say that. This has been a great weekend. Yesterday was the, well, a most wonderful day. Nothing can ever top it.''

He squeezed my hand but said nothing more until he pulled up in front of my house.

28

My report to my parents about the weekend concentrated on the enchantment of Saturday with a detailed description of the Caledonian Inn and the ride in the buggy. I made no mention of the grilling I received from Munro Farnsworth, talking instead about the Farnsworth estate and delightful "Auntie."

The Editor listened to all this approvingly, making only sparing comments, but I could see that I was not deceiving Mother. Throughout my recital, she was staring at me with that knowing look mothers have when they suspect that their daughters are holding something back. Still, she did not question me.

It was with relief that I escaped into my room where I could set aside the unsettling experiences of the weekend and finger over and over the tapestry of bright memories Rand had woven. What a flair he had for the unusual! I had reveled in the delicate meeting of mind to mind, of spirit to spirit . . . the discovery of all the little things two people have in common . . . the physical excitement of being together.

In truth, I felt like dancing and twirling and skipping and singing. Was this what it was like to be in love? I grabbed a sheet of paper and now the poem I'd labored over a week or so ago flowed out of me.

My Love is come,
And stars are bright,

Melody flows
From out the night.

The Little Bear shouts,
The Dipper drips wine,
All of this Beauty
Is mine, is mine.

Let dawning be red,
As fair as that day
When my Love will come
To stay, to stay.

The trees are dancing
In rhythmical sway,
And this is the tune
They play, they play:

Her Love is come
And stars are bright,
Melody flows
From out the night.

Above what I had just written, I scrawled the title "Rhapsody." This one could never make the Poetry Corner. I would not dare, for Rand knew now that I was *The Sentinel*'s anonymous contributor. I tucked the sheet of paper in my journal. The poem should be safe there from any prying eyes at home or at the office.

On Tuesday morning I opened the *Sentinel* office since the Editor had been delayed with telephone calls at home. Miss Cruley was attending her sister's funeral out of town.

Rand telephoned to say that he was having to fill in for the Club's maître d' in the dining room all week. "The poor bloke cracked a bone in his right foot."

Minutes later the Editor arrived, concern on his face.

"Julie, has Margo or Neal mentioned anything about a meeting of steelworkers at the new Community Center in the Lowlands?"

"No."

Dad pulled up a chair and straddled it. "Spencer told me that last Saturday night Cade Brinton used the Center for a meeting of these men."

"What's so alarming about that?"

"It wasn't Spencer who was alarmed, but Tom McKeever. He telephoned Meloy, mad as hops. Said that Cade is an anti-American traitor stirring up trouble, that church trustees will not have the Center used to promote the union movement. Claimed there was damage done to the house."

"But, Dad, the new labor law encourages workers to get together and form unions."

"I know. But McKeever doesn't like it. He's called a meeting of church trustees for tonight. Asked Spencer if he would 'like to come.' "

"So is Spencer going?"

"Of course he's going. But he wants to talk to us first. He feels the trustees may try to force his resignation unless he knuckles under."

"Knuckles under to what?"

"McKeever will probably demand that Baker Memorial sever all connections with the Center. Since Yoder owns the house, McKeever holds the trump card."

"And what did Spencer say to that?"

"He told Tom that this would make Yoder Steel seem like 'an Indian giver' to the Alderton community."

"That's right."

"Julie." Dad's eyes examined me. "Would you drop whatever you're doing, go down to the Lowlands and find out what went on at that Saturday night meeting? Check out any property damage. I'll tell Spencer to hold off coming here until you get back."

"On my way," I said, shoving aside my papers. "You're in this with Spencer, aren't you?"

My father's eyes were thoughtful. "Yes, Julie, I guess I am."

Before hiking to the Lowlands on foot, I paused a moment to reflect. Who would give me the information I needed? Neal Brinton? He was at work. Then I thought of Dean Fleming. Since he had joined the machinists union years ago, could he have attended that meeting?

I got Dean on the telephone. "Yes, Julie," he responded, "I was there."

"Could you tell me what happened? I mean, was it raucous or wild?" Then I explained the assignment Dad had given me.

"I can't describe it over the phone. This is a party line." There was a pause. "Tell you what, I'll come to the office a little early and fill you in on what happened."

Dean estimated that about fifteen men had attended the meeting, all eager to talk about their grievances. The men were angered by the fact that during recent slack times, those involved in union activity were being either fired or laid off two to three days a week, while "company" men were still getting full-time work.

Another resentment was that Yoder had forced them to sign cards stating that the company could deduct from their wages anytime it chose the cash value of the food boxes handed out in 1932 when families had literally been going hungry.

Dean's estimate of Cade Brinton struck me as thoughtful and fair. "He gets too emotional. Like his speech about the food boxes: 'Mark my words, men, when the company gets ready to take that money out of your paychecks, they'll do it. And you won't be able to do nothin' about it unless you've got a union to squawk.'

"Cade's got a lot of bitterness in him," Dean went on. "That's partly because he knows too many horror stories, like Ludlow and the killings in the 1892 Homestead strike. But he knows his facts and he's got some

good ideas. As for his being an anarchist or a Bolshevik,
that's a lot of tripe.''

Neal, he said, had presented a plan for the men to consider, involving ERP. Suggested they elect pro-union men
as company delegates to attend regular meetings of an ERP
assembly, then persuade men in other plants to do the
same. Next they would have to figure out a way for these
men from different companies to get together. That way,
maybe they could take over ERP and give it some clout.

Even Cade had looked impressed, Dean told me. Finally, there was a general give-and-take about the lousy
toilets, the heat, the long hours, and yes, the bowling
tournament.

The meeting had ended with an amazing scene. The
lights had been turned off. A candle stuck in a bottle was
placed on a table with a crucifix standing beside it. One
by one, the men had come forward, solemnly kissed the
cross, and vowed that they would work for their rights as
free Americans to belong to a union, vowed that they
would never turn scab.

''Dean, what does that mean—'scab'?'' I asked.

''Means turning against fellow workers by accepting
employment from the company that's being struck.''

''Dad heard there was some damage to the property.''

Dean looked puzzled for a moment, then he smiled.
''After the meeting, several men did a little arm-
wrestling and broke a table. They promised to fix it. But
if they don't, I will, Julie. No problem a-tall.''

''So you wouldn't say there was anything sinister or
wrong about the whole affair, Dean?''

''Not a thing. Actually, kind of touching. Companies
will do all they can to stop the union movement despite
the new law, so there's bound to be trouble. Too bad they
don't do the right thing with their employees.''

Spencer Meloy dropped by the *Sentinel* office that afternoon and nodded vigorously when I described what had
happened at the meeting of the steelworkers.

"I knew it. I just knew there wasn't rowdyism or real property damage. Now, let me get all these facts down on paper so I can report them to the trustees tonight."

Early the next morning, a grim-faced Spencer was back at the *Sentinel* with an account of the meeting. Baker Memorial had seven trustees who formed the Council as the governing body of the church. The men, led by Tom McKeever, Jr., as chairman, had met around the conference table in the church library.

McKeever opened it by listing the duties of the trustees in connection with all property owned or used by the church. An account of the meeting at the Center followed, painting a picture of rowdy, shouting radicals who had damaged property and voiced threats toward Yoder Steel.

When given a chance to speak, Spencer had countered with his facts: that the damage to one table was easily repaired; that the mood of the meeting was moderate with the main discussion focused on how to improve the company ERP plan. He stressed how desperately these workingmen needed *some* spot to meet and talk through their problems, give vent to their feelings.

"By law, these men have the right of free assembly," he had reminded his trustees. "Even to promote the union idea. To deny them this right could indeed edge them closer to communism."

When he received a stony-faced response, Spencer admitted that he had lost some of his equanimity. "May I remind you, gentlemen, of this: our church constitution also states that the authority of the Council is *always* subject to the will of the congregation, making this church, I am proud to say, a true democracy."

Vincent Piley had then spoken. "Our pastor is quite correct. It would appear to me that the proper procedure at this point is to present the matters mentioned here tonight to a full meeting of the congregation, with the purpose of deciding whether to dismiss or retain Mr. Meloy as our pastor. Therefore, I make a motion that we call a congregational meeting for Monday, the twelfth day of August, and that, in accordance with church law, public notice of this meeting and its purpose be duly given from the pulpit for the next two successive Sundays, on July twenty-eighth and August fourth.''

There had been no discussion. When the vote was taken, it was unanimous: seven "ayes." Spencer knew then that he had walked directly into their trap.

From the look on his face, the Editor must have been reliving some bad memories. "The congregation has the final word, Spencer," he finally said. "How do you think they will vote?"

"I don't know. If we had more young people, I would win. But the Community Center project isn't the only issue, maybe not even the most important. There is real resistance to almost all of the changes I've initiated.''

In Alderton, news traveled fast. There were few vacant places in the pews at Baker Memorial for the eleven o'clock service the following Sunday.

The atmosphere was tense and expectant when, simply as one of the announcements, Pastor Meloy read the formal notice about the congregational meeting for August 12. He seemed calm and matter-of-fact, stating as the main purpose of the meeting "to decide whether to dismiss or retain the pastor.''

There was a deep silence in the sanctuary. I looked at young Tom McKeever's back three pews in front of us, watched the proud, square shoulders draped in impeccably tailored worsted fabric fidget uneasily. I wondered if his father was here, then realized I hadn't seen the Old Man in church for months.

Sitting there, I noticed how well dressed all the members of this congregation looked despite the depression. Of the Lowlands people, only Neal and Margo seemed to be present. When it came time for Meloy's sermon, there was a hush of expectancy.

The Head of our church is Jesus Christ. He told us that the church is His body on earth—literally His voice, His hands, His feet—and that He Himself is the Head of that body.

What kind of instructions has Jesus given us? By His own words He announced that His Father had sent Him to earth to bring the gospel to the poor, to heal the brokenhearted and those with broken bodies, to preach deliverance to the captives, and to set at liberty those who are bruised. About ninety percent of His ministry was to the flotsam and jetsam of society—the poor, the blind, the crippled, the outcasts, the lepers.

But Jesus' never-ending ministry to the less privileged not only annoyed but offended the church officials. So they challenged Jesus on this. Why did He insist, they demanded to know, on spending His time with the scum of the earth—publicans, sinners, people outside decent society, even *eating* with them? Why would any prophet of quality so lower himself, they wanted to know?

His reply was simple: "These are the ones who need me."

No sinner had sunk too low for Him to reach out, lift up, forgive, restore. From no diseased body would He turn away. He did not hesitate to reach out and touch the loathsome leper before He healed him—something nobody else would have done. The woman of the street who anointed His feet with perfume, the adulteress about to be stoned—He alone would not judge, would not reject. He alone knew how to point the way to the new beginning of a clean, fresh life.

No wonder we are told that "the common people heard Him gladly."

I looked at my father and saw that he was staring at Spencer, mesmerized. I had never heard Spencer so intense or so inspired.

But, you are asking, how does all of this apply to Baker Memorial Church? If this church is to be part of Christ's body on earth, a real church, and not just become the Alderton Sunday Morning Club, then we have to get on with *being* Christ's voice and hands and feet.

My friends, we have made a good start with our Community Center in the Lowlands. I am very proud of the way some of you leapt to this challenge. But there are others here who feel we should not be involved in relating to the needy or those less fortunate, those who are so different from us. The question of whether I am to be dismissed or retained centers on those issues.

It is my conviction that, having made a great beginning, for us now to pull out and say that this church will have nothing more to do with the Center would be disastrous to human relationships in this town and would dishonor Jesus Christ. He tells us, "Inasmuch as ye did it not to one of the least of them, ye did it not to *Me.*"

So dear friends, the decisions are before us. The choice is yours.

The words of the closing hymn, written by James Russell Lowell, came starkly alive for me. As we sang I wondered how much effect these words had on others:

> *Once to every man and nation*
> *Comes the moment to decide,*
> *In the strife of truth and falsehood*
> *For the good or evil side.*
> *Some great cause, God's new messiah,*
> *Offering each the bloom or blight,*
> *And the choice goes by forever*
> *'Twixt that darkness and that light.*

Though the cause of evil prosper,
Yet 'tis truth alone is strong.
Truth forever on the scaffold;
Wrong forever on the throne.
Yet the scaffold sways the future,
And behind the dim unknown,
Standeth God within the shadow,
Keeping watch above His own.

As our family reached the vestibule, we encountered Tom McKeever, Jr. He greeted us politely, his always-interesting gray eyes hooded. To my surprise, I overheard him say to Meloy, "Spencer, you gave us much to think about." And he walked out the door.

Our family discussed the service as we walked home together. "If ever I heard a sermon with fighting words, that was it," I said. "Yet McKeever didn't seem to be angry. Why?"

"I see Tom as a man driven by his father and the circumstances into which he's been thrust," Dad said thoughtfully. "He's also a man torn on the inside. Bryan as much as said this to us."

"Well, he's sure out to get Spencer or we wouldn't be having a congregational meeting in two weeks," said Mother.

"I believe he was being forced into that position," continued Dad.

"Do you think Spencer hurt himself or helped himself this morning?" I asked.

My father did not answer for almost half a block. "It was a most courageous sermon. Probably an uncompromising one."

He would say no more.

29

ON Monday morning I tried to write in my journal, but the words would not come. Even to myself, I did not want to admit how upset I was at Rand.

The afternoon before, he had called with his usual cheery voice, but I detected an artificial note in it. He told me that he was still having to fill in for the maître d' until the man's foot was better. *Don't be selfish*, I admonished myself. *Here's a chance to show Rand that you're old enough to take disappointments gracefully.* Deep in my spirit, however, I sensed that something was wrong. For some reason, Rand did not want to see me.

Disconsolate, I took my journal with me when I walked to the *Sentinel* office that morning. Since the work flow always built up as the week progressed, Monday was often the day I had the most free time to write. I wanted to try to sort out my feelings for Rand and could always think better on the pages of my journal.

The day turned out to be anything but quiet. When I arrived the telephone was ringing; there was mail to open. Laying my journal down on Miss Cruley's desk for a moment, I divided the letters into separate piles, unaware that a sheet of paper had slipped out of my journal onto her desk.

Most of the letters were from Alderton citizens regarding local matters. One hand-delivered letter was dated ''Sunday afternoon.'' I held it out to show the Editor.

Having been a member of Baker Memorial Church for thirty years, I was distressed today over the action taken by the trustees of our church against Spencer Meloy.

It is a big mistake, in my opinion, to divide our church with a congregational meeting to vote whether we keep or fire Reverend Meloy. Our pastor is a young man, inexperienced and, perhaps, overzealous regarding social concerns, but he is the best preacher Baker Memorial has ever had. It would be a big loss to the community and to our church if he were removed from his pastorate.

From just this one letter, it was easy to deduce that the Meloy controversy would be more than just another church squabble. The pastor had made many friends in Alderton. I wondered if my father was now strong enough to team up with Spencer in an effort to win the church battle coming up in two weeks.

Then came a more sobering thought: if Rand was pulling away from me, it could be because he was being hemmed in on three sides—first the dam issue, then the union controversy, and now what looked like a church power struggle, with men like the McKeevers and Munro Farnsworth taking opposite sides from the Wallace family.

That evening, Spencer Meloy called Dad and asked if he could come by and talk. He made a special point of requesting that Mother and I be in on the discussions.

When he spread his lanky frame sideways on our loveseat to avoid the pointed ends of two springs, Spencer did not seem to be depressed. Instead, his greeting was hearty, his face wreathed in a warm smile, his eyes alive with expectation. Could he actually be looking forward to the struggles ahead?

The Editor must have been surprised too by Spencer's lightheartedness. He began firing questions at the young pastor.

"Do I understand, Spencer, that all it takes is a majority vote from the congregation to dismiss you?"

"That's right."

"How do you feel the vote would go if held tonight?"

"I honestly don't know, Ken. I haven't tried to figure out the 'fors' and 'againsts.' "

"I gather you do not intend to resign, but to resist this ouster attempt."

"With all the strength I possess."

"What specific charges are they bringing against you?"

"So far, no formal charges."

"They couldn't get away with that in the main denominational churches. There, it takes formal charges involving heresy or dishonesty or immorality to bring action against a pastor. Have you been accused of any of those?"

"Of course not."

"Then if there are no formal charges, what are the over-the-back-fence ones? What don't they like about you?"

Spencer reached into his pocket and pulled out a sheet of paper. "Thought you might ask, so I made a little list. On paper, some of the items sound ludicrous . . .

"First, I am accused of resisting authority and of having a rebellious attitude."

"Give us some examples."

"There was Vincent Piley's appearance at the work party."

"I gather he questioned you about the use of church money for renovating the Community Center. That's rebellion?"

"In their eyes, yes. One Sunday I allowed a Bookmobile to park on the church grounds so that Sunday School teachers could buy materials for their classes. I hadn't asked the Council's permission."

The Editor nodded. "Were they right?"

"Technically, yes. But such a small thing."

"What else?"

"I'm bringing in too many outsiders. There are seventeen applications for membership from Lowlands people. These have been tabled for now. We're too crowded, some protest; the older members can't always sit in their accustomed pews. One trustee has stated, 'It's been a nice quiet little church and we want to keep it that way.' "

"At a time when many churches are almost empty, they should be jumping for joy that you're packing them in."

"You'd think so."

"Any more charges?"

"Oh, sure. Things like, my sermons run too long and that delays Sunday dinner. And that I didn't show up at the last church bazaar. That miffed some of the ladies. Oh, and that I'm really too young and immature for their church—"

"Wait a minute, Spencer. Let's go back to your missing the church bazaar." Dad pursed his lips. "Seems a petty complaint, but to most churchwomen you'd need an awfully good excuse for not being there at all."

"I realize that now. The women had worked on it for months, and I had no excuse. Truth is, I drove to Pittsburgh to see a baseball game."

"Call that a learning experience, then. Anything else?"

Spencer's voice took on a rueful note. "They say I preach too much about justice for the poor and about other negatives in our society. They want to be reminded that everybody knows that Alderton is a nice community with friendly, fair-minded citizens."

My father was nodding his head. "I get the picture. One more question—*do* you have resentment in your heart against these men, Spencer?"

Spencer's voice was very soft. "I do have some resentment. I'm ashamed to say that one Sunday when a trustee rebuked me because the service had gone overtime to nine minutes past twelve, I lost my temper. I stood on the top church step and said, 'You can go to hell.' "

Dad chuckled while shaking his head. "That's one vote you'll never get."

"I apologized to him later, but you're right. He's a hundred percent against me."

"Which won't help. But the crucial question is, are you willing to let God take resentment from you?"

"Yes, of course. Now let me ask *you* something, Ken." Spencer agilely moved around the bumps in the loveseat so that he was facing my father directly. "If you were I, what would you do?"

The Editor's forehead creased and he jammed a clenched fist into the palm of his other hand. "My situation in Timmeton was different, of course. I feel now that I handled it all wrong."

Mother and I stared at Dad as he continued. "I suppose there are times when it's right to resign, *but not if there's a principle at stake*. When I quit the Timmeton situation, it made me feel less than a man. I wish I could do it all over again. If so, I would have made them kick me out."

"So you think it's right for me to fight?" Spencer leaned forward intently.

"Yes, because there's a principle at stake. Forget all the other stuff—they simply don't want you opening the church to outsiders. But Jesus' message here is clear: preach the Word to the whole world.

"You've made mistakes, Spencer. You've been somewhat highhanded, insensitive to the women, and frankly, your theology could use a little more balance. But you're a dedicated, all-out servant of the Lord, courageously blazing a new trail here in Alderton. I'm with you all the way."

The two men stood up and embraced. Mother and I both had tears in our eyes, not so much for Spencer as for my father.

* * *

Spencer Meloy was in no hurry to leave. Mother served us some lemonade, which we drank, then Meloy pulled some papers from his coat pocket.

"Julie, can you and I find a quiet spot where we can go over this week's bulletin?"

Mother and Dad both got up. "We're going to bed. Why not stay right here?" the Editor suggested.

As my parents said their good-byes to Spencer, I found myself studying the young pastor in a new way. His angular, somewhat ungainly body had little magnetic quality, but it spun off waves of vitality. That lantern jaw was the key to Spencer's character: strength, courage, tenacity. The boyish look that appeared so often on his face was the clue to his immaturity.

We sat down side by side at the dining-room table and went over the bulletin in a perfunctory way. Finally, Spencer pushed the papers aside. "I don't want to talk about the bulletin any more. I want to talk about us."

"What about us?"

"We make a good team. We have the same likes and dislikes. We think alike. I could almost tell this the first time I looked out over the congregation and saw your face. It was almost as if the Lord said to me, 'That's the one for you.' "

Spencer's eyes were so intense that I dropped mine. "You *are* impulsive, aren't you?"

"Perhaps so. I've been an activist all my life. I believe in the axiom 'Faint heart ne'er won fair lady.' "

"Why would you be interested in me? I'm so much younger. I still want to go to college—if not this year, then next."

"None of that bothers me, Julie. I can wait. But you're the oldest eighteen-year-old I've ever met. When we talk together, I feel we're intellectual equals."

I could not hold back a grin. "Better not let your trustees hear you say that."

He smiled too, then turned serious. "Don't you feel a oneness in spirit every time we're together?"

"Yes, I do."

"That's what's important. I know you're the right girl for me. I love you and want to marry you."

How can this be happening? I thought. *I'm not in love with Spencer Meloy. I'm in love with Rand. So what do I say now?*

I reached for his hand. "Spencer, I don't know how to answer you. Marriage is something far off in my thinking. I like you, I enjoy your company, I'll be rooting for you in the church battle, but that's all I can say right now."

Only a flicker of disappointment crossed his face. "Then that'll have to do for now. But remember this. I'm a very determined person. I don't give up easily."

He stood up and I walked him to the front door. There he hesitated, leaned down and kissed me lightly on the forehead. Then he opened the door and walked out without another word.

30

TUESDAY morning I awoke with a raging headache. When I tried to get up, the room began to spin. Weakly, I called Mother and sank back into bed.

Mother thought it best to ask our family doctor to come by and have a look at me. A rotund, bouncy, friendly man, he sat by my bed, chatting and questioning me. Finding that I had a fever, he said, "Stay in bed today and drink plenty of fluids. If you still have a fever tomorrow, let me know."

After the doctor left, I lay there thinking, *No wonder he can't find the right medical tag for this. It's all in my head—or heart. The cause: romantic complications. Does Mother suspect?*

I yearned for a call from Rand. Did he know? Did he care? If Spencer heard I was ill, I sensed, he would be here in minutes. Graham too, if he were in town. I thought of asking Mother to telephone them, then decided against it.

The next day, I felt better. On Friday the Editor let me drive the Willys down to the office, a rare concession. We were now using the car only when we went to the Fleming farm or for trips outside Alderton.

That day I had the unique experience of seeing the paper with the eyes of any Alderton subscriber. Taking up a copy with the smell of printer's ink still fresh on it, I looked over it, interested in seeing how well Emily Cruley had done my job that week.

Everything looked fine. But then, as my eyes fell on the Poetry Corner, I clapped one hand over my mouth and almost dropped the paper. There, printed in full but unsigned, was the poem "Rhapsody" I had hidden so carefully in my journal.

How did Emily get her hands on it?

When Miss Cruley walked by, I asked her who had submitted "Rhapsody" to the Poetry Corner.

"I really don't know. It was in Monday's mail. Came unsolicited, I guess. There wasn't even an envelope."

"How strange!" Then, seeing Emily begin to stiffen, I patted her on the shoulder. "You did a fine job with this issue."

"Thank you, Julie," she chirped. "I'm glad to have you back at work. You have become quite useful to us here at the paper."

I beamed at her. From Emily Cruley, this was a fine compliment indeed!

After dinner that night when the Editor was alone at his desk, I could contain myself no longer. "Dad, about that poem 'Rhapsody' in the paper today. Did you read it?"

"Yes. Thought it pretty good."

"Where did it come from?"

He looked at me sharply. "Emily said it came from a reader."

"That's true—if you call me a reader. I wrote it, Dad. Somehow it slipped out of my journal and into the mail I opened last Monday. That was one poem I didn't want printed."

"Too revealing of your private thoughts, Julie?"

"Possibly. It could turn out to be really embarrassing."

The Editor swung around and reached for my hand, his eyes warm and admiring. "My girl has grown into quite a beautiful woman. I'm not at all surprised that romance has begun to confuse your life."

"That's the right word for it."

"Care to give me the details?"

"Not for a while. But on the other matter, I *am* a little tired of being the anonymous poet of *The Alderton Sentinel.*"

The Editor laughed. "I understand perfectly. The time has come to reveal our mystery poet to Emily Cruley."

"I don't want to be there when that happens," I said, trying to visualize the look it would bring to Miss Cruley's face.

Rand telephoned Friday night. His voice was still hearty, but somehow I was not reassured. If I would be free, he would like to drop by early the next afternoon. We could decide then whether or not to take a spin in his roadster.

It had been exactly two weeks since our big weekend. Scarcely an hour had gone by that my thoughts had not darted to this dashing, reddish-blond-haired Englishman. Had I been foolish to allow myself to fall in love with him? Much of the rapture and the joy were gone now, replaced by an aching uncertainty. All my feminine instincts told me that in two weeks he could have found a way to see me, had he really wanted to.

Sitting in the Editor's swivel chair in front of his old rolltop desk, I waited for Rand. Nervously I brushed some lint off my yellow blouse, the brightest thing I had to wear. When his sporty roadster pulled into our driveway, I stood at a window, hidden behind its curtain, studying him as he walked across the yard and up the front steps. Usually Rand moved rapidly. Today there was a trace of reluctance in his gait.

I made a quick decision: no point in riding with him in search of a pleasant rendezvous spot. Better to talk right here.

When I opened the front door and looked into Rand's eyes, my fears were confirmed. He greeted me lightly, smilingly, but then dropped his eyes.

As he walked through the doorway, he reached for my

hand. I let him take it, but then pulled it back. For a moment he stood there uncertainly.

"Let's talk here in the living room, Rand. I've been under the weather this past week and should probably stay home."

"Ill?"

"Nothing, really. Slight temperature. In and out of bed for two days. But I'm fine now."

"Oh-h." He looked solicitous, concerned, and yet awkward.

"The rest of the family has driven over to the Flemings' farm," I explained to him. "So we're alone here. Would you like something to drink?"

"That would be fine." He looked relieved as he followed me into the kitchen, where he gave me a detailed account of his experience as the acting maître d' in the Club dining room.

I put ice into two glasses and poured out the soft drink he had chosen, then smiled up at him. "I've missed you, Rand. It's been a long two weeks."

"For me as well." He hesitated. "Let's stroll about in your back yard, Julie."

Some warmth was returning to my blood. I looked at him steadily, quizzically. "You're not afraid of being alone here with me, are you?"

He chuckled. "Never. But I'm an outdoorsman, Julie. Especially this time of year."

We took our drinks and headed out the back door past the cherry tree and on under the old locusts to the rock ledges. For a long moment Rand stood there, absorbing the beauty of the view while he appeared to be struggling with something on the inside. He took a final gulp of his drink, deliberately set the glass down on a rock, then reached for my hand.

"You do look a bit peaked, Julie, but good to my eyes. How can I tell you how much I treasured that time with you two weeks ago!"

"It was beautiful," I murmured softly.

"I'm sorry that Uncle Munro mucked it up for us."

"Why do you say that?"

"Because it's true. We were living in a make-believe world and he jolted us out of it."

"What is the real world in your eyes, Rand?"

He let my hand go and walked over to pick two Scottish harebells which he then carefully placed in my hair. I wanted to hug him, but I didn't dare. He looked at the flowers and at me—tilting his head first to one side, then to the other, his eyes almost devouring me. "You and those harebells are young and fresh and untouched beauty. I don't want either to change—ever."

"But that doesn't answer my question."

"It does, if you stop to think about it."

I sighed. "Are you saying that I am too young for you?"

He did not answer for a moment. "Yes—and no."

"What does that mean?"

"It means, yes, you're too young—no, of course you're not too young."

In frustration, I stared at him, then shook my head.

"Julie, let me try to explain something. You came into my life unexpectedly; you caught my attention from that very first mud bath. Then I became intrigued by your passion for causes, by the insatiable curiosity of your mind. I don't know any other girls like you. I found myself just wanting to bathe in the freshness of your spirit and your zest for life."

He looked off into the distance, then reached again for my hand. "I went into the Pittsburgh weekend with that same desire: to have more of that refreshment which comes from you. And it went just as I planned it—an enchanting day. And then something happened that I hadn't planned. You changed from the bubbling young princess into a very real woman."

"And that upset you?"

"Yes—and no." He laughed. "There I go again. I'm a chump, really. I intended to give you a tender, broth-

'erly kiss and then take you to the Farnsworths. But there was a fire in you I hadn't realized.''

My eyes held his as I spoke. "Rand, you romanced me in the way every girl dreams about. You *were* the fairy prince. Through the details you planned so carefully, you made the world seem like an enchanted place. Yes, there was fire in me. Yes, I wanted you to know how I felt. Was that wrong?"

"Julie, it's cheeky of me to ask this. Do you kiss others the way you did me that night?"

"No, I do not."

"I'm glad . . ." Then he stopped, obviously embarrassed. "Not that I'm against your kissing other young blokes, it's just that you are such a, well, warm person," he finished lamely.

"That's nonsense," I said, annoyed. "What you're telling me is that you had this lovely fantasy going about my being some kind of wide-eyed young sister to you and then I proceeded to spoil it."

Rand looked uncomfortable for a moment, then laughed. "There you go, pinning me to the wall again."

"You should be pinned to the wall for all that talk about kissing. The truth is, you played your role so well that the princess really did fall in love with the prince. Silly, maybe, but true. I don't know much about kissing and I don't like trying to analyze it. I just wanted you to know how I felt about you."

"Well, it shook up my world."

"Why, why did it change things between us?"

"Because I was suddenly obliged to look at you differently. The fantasy world was wiped out. All at once you were a very alive woman in my arms. I loved it, but I wasn't ready to handle it. I'm . . . I am not in a position to fall in love."

I shook my head. "You make it sound so . . . so heavy. Being in love doesn't mean that you put on a ball and chain. I'd never want that."

Rand looked intently into my eyes. "I don't think you

are a mite casual about love. You're an all-out person. I've never known anyone like you for singleminded intensity. Your poems show that.''

"Oh, you read that poem. It wasn't supposed to be in *The Sentinel.*"

"What poem?"

"Then you didn't see it in yesterday's paper?"

"No, should I?"

"Please don't," I said, wanting to bite my tongue. Then, realizing that Rand had to have an explanation, I told him how "Rhapsody" had escaped my journal and gotten into print.

"I should enjoy enormously reading your journal sometime."

"No, you wouldn't. It might confirm your opinion of me as a love-starved woman."

He grinned for a moment, then turned serious again. "Julie, the problem lies with me, not you. You have every right to condemn me roundly. But I think you're a delightful, wonderful person—"

"Who is in love with love," I interrupted.

"Who does not need the handicap of someone from another country, reared in a different culture and with a different goal in life."

"How are our goals different?"

"Well, you are—or will soon be—a journalist with a passion to help the poor, to expose wrongdoing, and to bring justice to the underprivileged. I'm not against any of those goals, but I have been reared and trained in business management, to make money, to manage our landholdings."

"Rand, I don't think our goals are incompatible. I have no passion to be a career woman, nor does it seem possible at the moment for me even to go to college."

"Which is too bad. You are college material if ever I have seen it."

"That can come later. Since I have such a passion for

reading and learning, some type of schooling will be going on all my life.''

Rand took both my hands and looked at me intensely. ''I won't play games with you any more, Julie. I care about you too much to take advantage of your love in any casual relationship. You are an all-out person and I can't fill the role you would have for me.''

Despite all my efforts at control, the tears began sliding down my cheeks. I pulled myself away, turned my back on Rand, and flicked at them angrily with one wrist.

''Please don't.'' Rand's hands patted my shoulders, then his arms slipped around my waist. I leaned my head back against his shoulder. Slowly he turned me around and kissed my forehead, then each eye, then my mouth.

The magic was back. A thunderbolt shot down my spine, and sobbing, I clung to him. When the fierceness of the kiss abated, he stroked my hair and brushed his lips tenderly over my forehead. ''I love you, Julie . . . I love you . . . I love you.''

His words kindled the fires again until Rand pulled away and led me to one of the big rocks where we sat side by side. ''You see what happens.''

''Yes, I see.''

''When we are together, it's frighteningly inevitable. So do you think we can have a casual relationship?''

''No.''

There was pain in his eyes and something new stirred inside me. How to describe it? A chipping off of that big mass of selfishness inside me. For I not only loved Rand, but I cared about him in a new way. Compassion? No, stronger than that. I could begin to feel what he was feeling, even though it was not what I wanted him to feel. He had a problem with me—he couldn't marry me, or did not want to marry me, or wasn't ready to marry me. But he loved me. I could live on that for a while.

Rand noticed the change in me at once as we walked, hand in hand, back to the house. ''You're not upset with me?''

"No."

"And you understand what I was trying to say?"

"Yes, I do. That you are not in a position to be serious just now, that you do not feel it's even right to see me."

He was silent for a while. "Have I hurt you?"

"Yes. But your love was healing."

"I had no intention of saying that, but I cannot take those words back." He smiled at me and squeezed my hand.

On the front porch, he still held my hand. He was struggling inside again. I brought his hand up to my lips and kissed it gently. "You helped me to grow up a little today, Rand. I understand the real world better than you think. You're caught in it and I will pray for you every day. Count on that, even though I don't know how good my prayers are."

Rand grinned at me. "They'll be good enough."

He was reluctant to leave even then, but forced himself to do so. As he climbed into his roadster and drove off, I wondered when I would see him again.

31

On the big wall calendar above Dad's desk at the *Sentinel* he had circled August 12 with red crayon and written: "Meloy's moment of truth."

Everywhere I went, people were talking about the upcoming vote. In a large town the size of Alderton, church disputes would ordinarily create little attention, but there was something unfamiliar, indeed novel, in the conflict now swirling around Spencer Meloy. For one thing, he was an attractive, personable man, who had demonstrated a genuine desire to lighten the plight of society's underdogs.

For another, folks generally sensed the courage in the man: he was not intimidated by the wealthy or powerful, else why had he bucked them and not quietly resigned and left town?

Finally, the church's method of handling the situation was different. In most denominational churches, a crisis involving the pastor would never come to a congregational vote. An ecclesiastical higher-up in a distant city would make the decision. Baker Memorial, being independent, had its own constitution, and the procedure necessary to oust its pastor offered the potential for real drama.

The Church Council had drawn up this set of ground rules for the meeting, then had them circulated to all members:

1. Only communicant members of Baker Memorial Church in good and regular standing will be eligible to vote.

2. Each side will be allowed to have three persons speak publicly at the meeting prior to the voting.

3. Voting will be by secret ballot.

4. No visitors or nonmembers of Baker Memorial will be allowed in the meeting.

The night before the church meeting there was a brief but tense scene between my parents. Mother had been silent during dinner, then went to the kitchen. Dad had followed her.

"Why are you so upset, Louise?" I heard my father ask.

"I don't think you should get involved in this Meloy fight."

"How you've changed! In Timmeton you said I didn't fight hard enough."

"That was different. That was *your* battle. This one isn't. This one could cost you *The Sentinel.*"

"Meloy has asked for my help. I can't turn my back on him."

"Will you pray hard about this before you act?"

"Of course I'll pray."

On the night of the congregational meeting, my father, mother, and I walked to the church while Tim and Anne-Marie remained at home with a neighbor. It was a beautiful starlit evening, redolent with honeysuckle. My father held Mother's arm to support her over the rough places where tree roots had upheaved the bricks in the sidewalk.

"Ken, are you speaking tonight?" I heard Mother ask.

"Yes, Louise."

The subject was then dropped, as if by mutual consent.

Ahead of us, the church was in darkness, while the Sunday School building behind the sanctuary was lighted, the door standing open; people were streaming in.

As we walked up to the door, we were stopped by a trustee, Sheldon Wissinger, president of one of Alderton's banks.

"Sorry to detain you," he said affably enough, "but I've been given the job of checking everyone against this membership list."

He glanced down at the sheaf of papers in his hands. "Let's see now, 'Wallace.' Ah yes, here you are." He reached into a box on a small table beside him and handed a printed ballot to each of us. "You may go on in," he said.

Finding it hard to believe that a banker could be taking such a routine job so seriously, I searched the man's face for any hint of a smile or dry humor. None—none at all.

It was only ten past seven, but the assembly room, which seated two hundred people, was already more than two-thirds full.

After finding seats, my first move was to look closely at the ballot Mr. Wissinger had handed me. It was a slip of paper somewhat larger than most tickets or ballots, perforated down the middle. On one side were the block letters: FOR RETENTION; on the other side: FOR DISMISSAL. I sat staring at the slip. The wording was so stark. There was an increasing air of unreality about this entire drama.

Dressed in a blue business suit, Spencer was sitting on one end of the front row of chairs. His long legs crossed, one arm across the back of the chair beside him, he smiled or nodded in greeting to his parishioners as they entered the room.

In contrast to Spencer, the church trustees were in perpetual motion, checking lists, moving chairs and tables. Their constant whispering to each other lent a note of conspiracy to the proceedings.

Neal Brinton and Margo walked in together and took seats near us. Both McKeever men arrived, along with the seldom-seen young Mrs. McKeever, who wore dark glasses because, the rumors went, she had a drinking problem. When Bryan followed them, he caught my eye and waved.

Then I froze. Strolling in behind the McKeevers and taking a seat directly behind them was Randolph Wilkinson! My mind almost exploded. Rand had never said he was a member of Baker Memorial. I had never seen him at a service. Yet he was obviously on the approved list.

While adjusting to this startling development, my eyes caught a movement at one of the windows. I saw faces crowded there, peering in.

"Mother, look!" I nudged her.

Every window was filled with faces. Apparently, curious nonmembers and those who had been turned away by Wissinger's checklist were determined to see the meeting anyway and to hear as much as they could. Some probably included the seventeen applicants for membership, on which the Council had postponed action until after tonight's vote.

To one side of the small speaker's stand, a folding chair was now placed. Then a white-haired man with a huge stomach ambled up and deposited himself in the chair with a grunt. Following that, someone lugged in an oversized wooden box and carefully deposited it on the fat man's lap. On the floor beside him sat a large wastebasket.

"What's that box?" I asked the lady sitting to my right.

She smiled. "That is the town ballot box from Mills Ford, used there in all local elections. Someone has borrowed it, I imagine."

I could only stare at the man, whose stomach protruded over the edge of the ancient contraption. The box had a stained oak finish, brass handles, a hole in the top in which to deposit the ballots, and a large crank at one end.

Donald Whipkey, comptroller of Trentler Wireworks

and chairman of the Church Council, rose behind the speaker's stand and called the meeting to order. Since extra folding chairs had been set up, I guessed there were about 250 people jammed into the hall. "Reverend Meloy, would you open the meeting with prayer?" he asked.

At least one gracious gesture, I thought.

A resonant voice filled the room. "Lord, whenever and wherever we are gathered together in Your name, You have promised to be in our midst. This is *Your* church, not ours, Lord. We ask You to guide all that happens here tonight in this room. We ask only that what we say and do here will further Your kingdom on earth and be to Your glory. Amen."

"Thank you," Mr. Whipkey said smoothly. "According to the bylaws adopted by our congregation, all procedures are to be handled under Robert's Rules of Order. Therefore, under this authority, I hereby declare this meeting an executive session."

He paused. "First, then, we need to appoint three tellers to count the votes. The Council has nominated the following men. Will they please rise as I read their names?"

Mr. Piley was one of the three named.

"Are there any objections?" Mr. Whipkey challenged.

Barely pausing, he continued, "Then these three are hereby asked to serve."

A man near the back rose and was recognized by the chairman. "I understand that there were thirty signatures requesting this meeting on the original petition submitted to the trustees. I would like to ask that those thirty names be read out loud, here and now."

Mr. Whipkey paused, then answered crisply, "Request denied. I must refuse to read those names because friendships and business relationships in Alderton are involved."

The man in the back persisted, "Who validated those signatures, then?"

"I did, together with the secretary of the Board."

Another man raised his hand and was acknowledged. "Are those names being withheld at the request of the signers?"

"Yes, they are," the chairman answered. "So now let us get on with the business of the evening." He then explained that the six speakers, three for and three against Pastor Meloy, would alternate as agreed upon previously.

The first was a white-haired older man, a former corporation executive. He explained how running a church depended on close cooperation between the pastor and members of the Church Council, that the pastor had bypassed the Council or gone over their heads.

"Perhaps this is due to Mr. Meloy's youth and lack of experience," he said. "I'm sure he's sincere enough. But the question has arisen, is Mr. Meloy too immature to handle a church like this one? Regretfully, I conclude that he is. I think our church cannot move forward with Spencer Meloy at the helm."

A doctor, one of Alderton's general practitioners, was the first to speak for Meloy.

"I would like to make two points," he began. "Baker Memorial Church has a responsibility to this entire community. Our pastor, by establishing the Community Center in the Lowlands, is helping to fulfill that kind of responsibility to Alderton. That should be cause for gratitude, not persecution, which is what we are doing here by this courtroom type of meeting.

"Second, I am a professional man. So is our pastor. What's happening here tonight is no way to deal with a professional man. I find even the wording printed on the ballots offensive. Mr. Meloy can stand severance from this church, but can this church stand severance from Meloy?"

He took a piece of paper out of his pocket and unfolded

it. "I have here a letter from one of the seventeen people who were denied permission to join this church last Sunday. May I read it?"

Several loud "no's" were shouted at him.

Mr. Whipkey raised his gavel and pounded. "We must keep order here. I'm sorry, but if the writer of this letter is not yet a member of Baker Memorial, then reading a written statement would be as much out of order as a statement delivered in person."

With a look of disgust, the doctor returned to his seat.

The second speaker, an undertaker, attacked Meloy on a spiritual basis, claiming that the church was in great danger from Socialist preachers who put their emphasis on doling out bread, when Jesus had made it clear that "man does not live by bread alone."

Following that, a middle-aged woman, the mother of three teenagers, said that Meloy's preaching had made God real to her, and that his friendship with her teenagers was helping them to find themselves.

The wife of one of the trustees then spoke against the pastor, stressing his insensitivity to older people, an articulate argument that impressed me. The clock on the wall read 8:45.

Then Mr. Whipkey said, "Our last speaker before we cast our vote is Mr. Kenneth Wallace, publisher of *The Alderton Sentinel.*"

As Dad made his way to the front, I darted a quick look at Mother's tense face. Was she still opposed to his taking sides in the issue?

"I have felt great emotion here tonight," Dad began, his voice deep and clear. "This bothers me because, regardless how each of us feels, we need to make this decision on the basis of facts, not emotions.

"My family and I are relative newcomers to Alderton. Since our arrival, I have learned about the areas of need in this community. The depressed state of our economy has brought some agony to all of us, but especially to people in the Lowlands. They're a part of our community. Therefore I was delighted when I learned of the thoughtful generosity of Tom McKeever and his father on behalf of Yoder Steel in making a building owned by them available as a Community Center. What a wonderful gesture by a business enterprise!''

The room was very quiet. The authority in his voice had captured everyone's attention. I glanced at the McKeevers. Their eyes were riveted on the Editor's face. So were Rand's.

''During the recent flood Pastor Meloy called this church 'a caring place.' I liked that phrase and felt it was true. When a church ceases to care, then you may be certain that it has become too insulated. And in such insulation we can become so wrapped up in high-flown spirituality that we convince ourselves it's the Church's business to care for men's souls—*and nothing else*.

''At that point the Church becomes so heavenly it's no earthly good.''

A laugh rippled across the room, the touch of humor a relief in the charged atmosphere.

''Sticking to facts again, the reason that the Church is a caring place is because it belongs to Jesus Christ. Our church charter says so. And Jesus commands us to love and to help our neighbors. Not just the neighbors we feel at home with socially, but our neighbor, whether we like him or not. Whether he likes us or not.

''Our pastor's first duty is to obey Jesus Christ. This comes before his duty to the Council. Facts again, my friends. You can go back and read the ordination vows our pastor took, if you question this.

''So, with the work on the Community Center, Spencer Meloy was not leading us to a vague do-gooder venture in the Lowlands; he was following both the dictates of his conscience and his vows to Jesus Christ.''

As the Editor paused to look at the faces before him for a moment, the room was very quiet. Then for the first time, Dad's voice grew emotional.

''Let me say here that I have learned something in this

regard from Spencer Meloy. In every man's life there come those lonely decision times when he has to face his conscience. The test of his manhood—and often the direction his life takes from that moment on—depends upon the choices he makes. Often the right decision in God's eyes means rejection by his fellow men, sometimes even by his Christian brothers. I honor our pastor for his courage in following the guidance of his conscience."

There was a pause as the Editor struggled for self-control. "What I feel we need here tonight, friends, is a new spirit. Appreciation for the generosity of the McKeevers and for the other leaders of this church who have worked hard and sacrificed time and money. Appreciation of Spencer Meloy's caring heart for the underprivileged and his eagerness to serve his Lord.

"There are fine people in this church," he continued with a sweep of his hands and a broad smile. "You all know that a little lack of communication is no cause for panic. Many of you tackle worse problems every day.

"So let's allow God's spirit into this meeting now. There is not a thing wrong with Baker Memorial or with my friend, Spencer Meloy, or with you men on the Council, who also are my friends, that a loving Father in Heaven cannot solve. Give Him that chance, please."

As Dad began making his way back to his seat, spontaneous applause broke out, but I noticed that only two or three of the men in the front row joined in. The expression on Spencer Meloy's face was something to see. Such gratitude written there!

Mr. Whipkey hurried to the speaker's stand. "Thank you, Mr. Wallace," he said firmly. "This concludes discussion on the issues before us. Now we vote on the dismissal or retention of our pastor, Spencer Meloy."

Bryan McKeever voted ahead of me. Instead of throwing the unused half of his ballot in the wastebasket, he walked up to me and placed it in my hand. It read "For

Dismissal." Bryan had cast his vote for Meloy! His father caught this action and frowned at his son.

Rand voted quickly. He still had not met my eyes.

Finally, the voting completed, we waited impatiently for the three tellers to start counting. I looked at Spencer. What was going on in his mind with his future so at stake?

Then the tellers were back. It reminded me of a jury filing back into a courtroom and the judge asking, "Gentlemen of the jury, have you reached a verdict?"

A sheet of paper was handed to Mr. Whipkey. He studied it for a moment, looked up, cleared his throat. "The results of the balloting are—126 votes for dismissal." He paused. There was almost a collective holding of breaths in the room. "And 115 votes for retention."

Spencer Meloy had lost by eleven votes.

There was a stunned silence. A flicker of shocked disbelief on Spencer's face, then hurt. Dad shook his head slowly. Mother wiped her eyes. Margo was sobbing.

I glared toward the McKeevers. Bryan, I noticed, had separated himself from his parents and was approaching Spencer. Rand was walking toward the door.

Then Rand stopped and turned toward me. His eyes were sad. He gave me a brief wave and walked out the door.

32

THE drama of the church vote dominated my thoughts for days—the strength of my father's speech . . . the margin of only eleven votes . . . the sight of Spencer shaking hands with each member of the Council afterward . . . the presence there of Randolph Wilkinson.

Rand came as a part of the McKeever camp and so must have voted against Meloy. That was hard for me to take. Once again I reviewed our conversation the previous Saturday afternoon on The Rocks. Rand had ended our relationship. But why? Pressure from Uncle Munro? That could be part of the reason, but surely not all. Conflict of interest with his job? Possibly, but not the whole reason either. Did he really feel I was too young for him? That seemed more likely. Yet when we were together, the age difference had not seemed to be important.

I sat bolt upright in bed as a new thought struck me. There was another woman! Why had I not thought of that before? But where? In England?

Then I recalled something his Uncle Munro had said: that proper marriages for the Wilkinson clan were "absolutely essential." *Randolph Wilkinson had come to America to find a proper wife!* Perhaps he had already found the woman in Pittsburgh. *That was more like it.*

I lay back on the pillow and tears slowly began to trickle down my cheeks.

The next morning a poem poured out of my despairing heart.

To watch, while underneath the things he said,
This I might endure—just to feel his breath
Of sudden hatred on my yielded head,
My fragile love was flung to final death.
But this is more than I can bear: to know
That underneath his fervent words of love
The current of his life will always flow
Still undisturbed by word of mine—above
All raging tempests of the heart—To guess
That I must be to him—one more—one less.

To make certain that this cry of the heart would never escape from the pages of my journal, I pasted it firmly on the last page.

Tuesday morning, Spencer Meloy came striding into the *Sentinel* office, stood in front of my desk and fairly beamed at me.

"Julie, if I hadn't just lost my job, I think I would propose to you right now."

"What's so romantic about a newspaper office on a Tuesday morning?" I asked, scrambling to match his mood.

"It's not this setting. It's you. Each time I see you, I'm more convinced than ever that we're right for each other." Spencer's eyes never left my face.

"If Miss Cruley heard you say that, she'd think you had lost your senses. She considers me too young and frivolous for a newspaper office, much less matrimony."

"Miss Cruley may be a valuable employee; but if she were graded on her knowledge of romance, I'm afraid it would be an F."

"And what grade would you get, Spencer?"

"Touché, Julie. I've neglected this subject too much in recent years. Something very important happened yesterday morning, though. I decided to put my books aside and learn more about people."

"Let's see now, you've already been at it a day, so I must be about Number Seven."

Spencer chuckled. "No, yesterday it was all males. Today you're Lesson Number One—Female Division."

"I can't believe this mood of yours, Spencer. If I hadn't heard the vote count myself last Sunday night, I would think you had won a smashing victory."

"In a way it *was* a victory, Julie. It freed me from a situation that was all wrong from the beginning. Baker Memorial and I were incompatible. In fact, losing that vote could have been the best thing that ever happened to me."

"How can you say that?"

"Because I'm already beginning to do the kind of work I love most. I've met with Neal Brinton—yes, and Cade too—to see how we can bring some justice to those people in the Lowlands. They need a pastor. Someone who will help them spiritually and physically. They seem to want me—and I feel drawn to them."

The Editor had come up behind Spencer as he was talking. "How will you make a living down there?" he asked.

Meloy turned around in his chair. "I don't know yet, Ken. I'll seek support from other Alderton churches. From businessmen, too. My family will help some, I think. Any suggestions?"

"Yes, I have." Dad pursed his lips. "I'll do something in *The Sentinel*. We should be able to rally some support."

"One thing you need to understand, Ken, before you commit yourself too quickly," Spencer interrupted. "I'll be helping workers push the union movement. I've studied the ERP booklet and I agree with Cade. Management still holds all the cards."

The Editor paused but a split second. "That doesn't scare me, Spencer. I, too, have come to feel that the system is wrong. Management has to give a lot more than it does in ERP."

I stared at my father in surprise. This was new thinking on his part. Excitement stirred in me. The lines of a new battle were being drawn.

The telephone call came early Thursday morning, before the Editor had arrived. Miss Cruley answered and I didn't pay much attention until I heard my name mentioned.

"Let me be sure I understand you," Emily said. "You are Mr. Sloan of *The New York Times* and you want to speak to Miss Julie Wallace."

I bolted to my feet. "I'll take the call in here," I shouted, rushing for the corner office.

With trembling hands, I picked up the receiver. "This is Julie Wallace."

The connection was fairly clear, but I kept asking the man at the other end of the line to repeat his statements, incredulous that I was hearing him correctly.

"The article I sent you about Yoder Steel. Yes, I wrote it."

"The New York Times would like to use a part of your article in a series we are doing on the union-management issue," the voice said.

"I guess that would be all right. I mean, sure. It's okay."

"We'll pay you one hundred dollars for the use of about a thousand words."

"A thousand words, did you say?"

"Yes."

"Will I receive a byline?"

"No, but we'll give you credit by name for the material we quote. Now, I need some facts about you, Miss Wallace. Are you a reporter for *The Alderton Sentinel?"*

"Yes."

"For how long?"

"Oh, about a year."

"Do you mind telling me your age?"

"I'm nearly nineteen. Use nineteen, please."

"We researched your facts, Miss Wallace. They checked out okay. Your father is publisher of *The Alderton Sentinel*. Does he support the union cause?"

"Well, I guess you'd have to say he's neutral."

"I see. You two must have some lively discussions."

"Yes, sir. We do."

"I guess those are all the questions I have. Do you want your check sent to *The Alderton Sentinel?*"

"That would be fine. And could you send us a copy of the article you're doing?"

"Yes, of course, we'll do that." Pause. "Thank you for thinking of *The New York Times* with your article, Miss Wallace."

I hung up and walked out of Dad's office in a daze. The Editor had come in and was standing by Miss Cruley's desk.

"What did *The New York Times* want, Julie?" he asked.

"You know that article on Yoder I wrote which you didn't like? I sent it to *The New York Times*. They want to use one thousand words of it. They're paying me one hundred dollars."

Both Emily Cruley and the Editor stared at me in utter disbelief.

That week a heat wave suddenly descended upon Alderton. Dean discovered an old fan on the third floor and this was used to keep the press cool. The rest of us worked in pools of perspiration which spotted our typed copy, smeared the proofs and even besmirched some of the sheets that came off the press.

When I proudly demonstrated to the Editor that I had learned to set linotype—though at far from the speed and efficiency of Miss Cruley—Emily announced that she was taking a two-week vacation. While she was gone I would be responsible for all local news and features, set everything in type and proofread the whole paper, which was now a standard eight pages.

Meanwhile our whole family was involved in helping Spencer Meloy set up his new ministry to the Lowlands. Spencer's enthusiasm and charm were infectious. The local Methodist church agreed to sponsor him and provide forty dollars a month for expenses. Another twenty-five dollars a month was promised by the Presbyterian church.

With these commitments as a base, Meloy rented, for twenty dollars a month, a small three-room, two-story house, which he planned to turn into a combination office and living quarters. When Mother and I went to help him move in, we were dismayed at the condition of the building.

The outside clapboard had once been painted white, but weather and flood damage had left it a dingy gray. There were several broken boards on one side, six or more missing shingles on the roof. The downstairs had a tiny kitchen, including a sink and a two-burner gas stove. A broken ice chest sat on the back stoop.

A twenty-foot-square living room was the only livable spot in the house. Spencer had already moved in his desk and chair from the church manse. A sofa, some folding chairs, small tables and a few lamps were needed to complete the furnishings.

The upstairs bedroom was a joke for a tall man like Spencer. The ceiling was barely six feet high in its highest spot, then tapered down in the back until it was only four and a half feet from the wooden flooring. Spencer said he needed a stubby-legged single bed. The fact that he would never be able to stand straight in his bedroom didn't seem to bother him. "I'll only be there to sleep," he said cheerfully.

There was no bathroom in the house, nor did there seem to be an outhouse in the back until we saw one two houses away. This sturdy, dark green, square structure, which had four separate two-hole units, was obviously a communal toilet for as many as eight houses in the area.

Before his pastorate with Baker Memorial was terminated, Spencer worked out with the Council a new procedure for use of the Community Center. Baker Memorial would sever all connection with the Center; the church would not help either the Center or Meloy's new ministry there financially. The McKeevers agreed to allow the Lowlands people to use the Center rent free, but only for teaching clinics and the like. No political gatherings or men's meetings would be permitted. Those using the Center would be responsible for repairs, maintenance, and supplies.

Meloy was distressed with Baker Memorial's complete disassociation with the Lowlands work and with the terms Yoder decreed for the use of the Center. The men's meetings would henceforth have to be held at his house.

On Wednesday, a copy of Monday's *New York Times* arrived in our office, addressed to me. Eagerly, I tore off the wrapping, then with trembling fingers turned the pages until I saw it—the lead article in the second section: "Passage of Wagner Act Means the Union Movement Is Here to Stay—First in a Series."

I read through two columns about how this historic act had legitimized collective bargaining and given the union movement new respectability. Then the article began to tick off what was happening in various companies. The paragraph with my name began:

Yoder Steel of Alderton, Pennsylvania, is another company with a heavy paternalistic approach to its employees. As a result, strong union sentiment is developing. Miss Julie Wallace, a reporter for *The Alderton Sentinel*, has done in-depth research on what she calls "deplorable working conditions" in the plant and "severe hardships" suffered by steelworkers in a company village dubbed "The Lowlands."

Miss Wallace reports that in 1934, five steelworkers died from plant accidents and fifty-five were injured, some seriously. Already this year, four deaths have occurred.

The article then went on to quote ten paragraphs of my report, mostly material I had gained from Neal and the publicity man at Yoder, about conditions in the Lowlands. The facts were stark, as I read through them again. The McKeevers and other executives at Yoder weren't going to like having this information spread about widely.

The windup paragraph of my part of the *Times* article shook me.

Julie Wallace, age nineteen, is not a radical trade unionist, but the attractive blonde daughter of the *Sentinel*'s publisher, Kenneth Wallace. Father and daughter frequently disagree over issues like the union movement, Miss Wallace stated to the *Times*. Intensely involved in trying to help the families of steelworkers through a church program, Miss Wallace stated unequivocally, "It is time for companies like Yoder Steel to emerge from the dark ages and treat their workers like human beings. If changes don't come, then workers are going to form independent unions, and this nation will have years of labor-management warfare."

I handed the *Times* article to the Editor with a rueful look. "Gee, Dad, I didn't think they would make me out as such a reformer. And I'm a blonde, too!"

My father read through the whole article slowly and calmly, though I saw him wince a bit toward the end. He looked at me with a smile. "This is mild compared to the article you gave me to read on Yoder."

"That's the one I sent the *Times*."

"Well, they have been selective and very fair in what they used."

"Do you think anyone in Alderton reads *The New York Times?*"

"A few do. Mr. Piley, for one. This article will make the rounds of all the executives at Yoder, you can bet on that."

"They won't like it."

"Probably not. And they will hope that no one else in Alderton reads it or hears about it."

"I sure don't want it to cause any trouble for you, Dad."

The Editor gave me a long, searching look. "Julie, there has hardly been a week over the past ten months when we haven't been in some kind of hot water. This will stir up some things that probably need stirring. I'm proud of you, daughter, for your initiative. If they throw stones at us here, we'll just throw 'em back."

33

THURSDAY afternoon the Editor dropped his weekly editorial on my table. "We can't let the *Times* scoop us entirely," he said with a wry grin. The title jolted me upright: "Unions—Their Time Has Come."

After raising the question of whether American industries were being fair to their employees, the Editor moved on to *The New York Times* series on labor-management problems:

> Investigations by *The New York Times* show that most companies throughout the nation use unfair hiring and firing practices and pay starvation wages. Companies which do provide housing for workers generally provide poor maintenance, wink at inadequate safety standards, and charge high prices in company stores.

> The *Times* has quoted from an article on the Yoder Steel Company written by *Sentinel* reporter Julie Wallace as follows:

> Rents in the company village called "The Lowlands" are so high that in order to exist, sometimes three families have to crowd into one of the undersized three-room houses.

The Editor then went on to quote two more paragraphs I had written on the bad conditions in the Lowlands. Then he attempted to give some balance to his editorial:

Yoder Steel is actually more progressive than most companies which operate employee housing, since it provides accident benefits for injured workers, modern safety equipment in the plant, and has presented a new Employee Relations Program (ERP). The ERP is a first step toward giving laborers a chance to air grievances and seek better working conditions.

Much needs to be done to improve conditions in the Lowlands. One step was taken this week by the Rev. Spencer Meloy who agreed to become a chaplain to the Lowlands community. He has set up an office there and will be sponsored by the Brooks Street Methodist and Fairview Presbyterian churches of Alderton. Spencer Meloy was formerly pastor of Baker Memorial Church (see separate news story).

The Editor urged support for Meloy, stating that one of Spencer's objectives would be to work toward the improvements of working conditions either through ERP or *a separate, independent union.*

As publisher of *The Sentinel,* I have studied the ERP booklet carefully and applaud this first effort by President Tom McKeever, Jr. While the Yoder plan has some fresh ideas in the area of settling grievances and creating machinery for joint labor-management discussions of problems, the company reserves the right to discontinue the plan if and when it so chooses.

This really is the heart of it. To the worker, company control means that he will always get a bad deal. That is why the independent union movement is growing so fast.

The greatness of America is that we can worship where and how we please. We can stand in a public square and preach any political philosophy we choose. We are free to go where we want to go.

Yet most workers in America do not have enough say about their conditions of employment. I believe this to be wrong. I think it hurts the employer as much as the employee because it takes contented workers to turn out good products.

It is the conviction of this newspaper that the future health of our citizens—all our citizens—depends on the willingness of Alderton industry to hear the voices of workers, who not only want to better their working conditions, but also to have a say in how this is done.

The editorial thrilled me. The Editor had handled the issue calmly but so forthrightly. *Most businessmen will not like it*, I thought, *particularly Yoder*. But the whole nation is now beginning to face up to a wrong situation that needs correction.

Graham Gillin was back from his California trip and asked me to go to the movies with him that Friday night. The film was *Spitfire* with Katharine Hepburn. Afterward, as we walked leisurely toward Exley's and sat side by side sipping ice cream sodas, we talked about the future.

"Getting your article in *The New York Times* must give you some big ideas about a career in publishing," he said.

"Actually, my thoughts are in a different area tonight," came my reply. "I'm envying your going to Penn State this fall."

"It's not too late for you to enroll there."

I shook my head. "Not this year. Maybe next."

"I'll miss you, Julie. We could have some good times together at college."

The idea was appealing and my eyes must have showed it.

Outside, we walked toward his car hand in hand.

"Would you like to drive up Seven Mile Mountain Road?" he asked with a grin.

"And do what?"

"I know a quiet spot where we could park and neck."

He laughed and I joined him.

"Graham, I like you too much to go out and just neck with you."

"What do you have against necking?"

"Nothing at all. Except most girls tell me in confidence that necking is not very satisfying."

"Have you ever tried it?"

"Not really. I think I'd rather talk, like we're doing here."

Graham shook his head. "You're pretty impossible, you know. A guy is totally on the defensive with you."

"I don't want that. Honest. I like our relationship now because it's so natural and easygoing."

Graham was silent as he drove me home. He walked me up to the front porch and stood there awkwardly. I reached for his hand and moved close to him. "Would you kiss me goodnight, Graham?"

He did so—quite vigorously. When he saw that I liked it, he did it a second time. And a third.

During the next week, eighteen letters arrived at *The Sentinel*, sixteen opposed to my father's editorial on unions. Most were from businessmen who declared that Bolsheviks were running the union movement—was *The Sentinel* for that? Three canceled subscriptions. The two favorable letters came from workers.

The Editor was philosophical. "Working people don't generally write letters," he said. "I expected the written reaction to be much worse."

There were some positive results. The Oak Street Congregational Church promised twenty-five dollars a month for Meloy's work. A total of seventy-five dollars in checks and cash was contributed by mail. Most of the telephone responses were positive.

Young Tom McKeever's call to the Editor came Wednesday. All I heard was my father's side of the conversation, as he calmly fielded some obviously hot statements from the other end.

"I'm sorry, Tom, but I don't think the booklet goes far enough, and I had to say so."

He was silent, listening.

"Meloy is hardly out to overthrow the government. He has a passion to help the people in the Lowlands. That seems quite Christian to me."

Another pause.

"Get the series from the *Times,* Tom. You need to know more about the Wagner Act and what's happening with labor in this country. I say you should be ahead of the union movement by recognizing the real grievances of workers."

The Editor's patient voice continued.

"What you feel you must do in running your business, you must do. That's the same principle I use in publishing this newspaper."

When Dad finished the conversation, I walked quickly into his office. He was agitated, his face was flushed, but his hands were surprisingly steady.

"Tom didn't like the editorial," he said.

"So I gathered. Did he threaten to cancel Yoder's ads?"

"No—and that surprised me. He was upset. He spoke the usual phrases about union agitators. He lashed out at Meloy. He said *The Sentinel* wasn't building good community spirit with editorials like that. But he didn't threaten a thing."

"It's the Old Man who does the threatening."

The Editor was thoughtful. "There's a strange chemistry between father and son. I sensed that Tom was trying to spank me almost by rote. Somehow I don't think his heart was in it."

* * *

When Dean Fleming arrived that afternoon, he stopped by my desk with a bemused expression on his face. "You sure started something with that article you sent to *The New York Times,*" he said.

"As a union man, I thought you'd approve."

"I'm not a union man the way Cade is—or even Neal," Dean said carefully.

"That surprises me. Are you opposed to Dad's editorial?"

"No, I felt that it had good balance, though he will receive strong opposition. The union movement is necessary because company owners are too greedy. And sooner or later we'll have union leaders who will be just as greedy and arrogant as management leaders."

I stared at Dean in astonishment. "If union men heard you speak like that, they'd, well, they'd kick you out of the union."

Dean grinned. "Are you going to expose me, Julie?"

"Of course not. But why are you telling me this?"

"Because I hate to see you and your father get involved over your heads."

As had happened several times before, I was confused and frustrated by Dean Fleming. Then he leaned forward and patted my hand. "Don't be angry. Someday I'll try and explain to you what I believe in more detail."

The Editor, hearing our voices, opened the door of his office and beckoned Dean inside. They talked quietly for a while and then departed, destination not announced, leaving me alone in the office.

As I bounced from answering the telephone on Miss Cruley's desk to the subscription files, to the linotype machine, then to my proofs, a wave of self-pity engulfed me. What had I gotten myself into with my eagerness to learn every aspect of newspaper publishing? With Emily Cruley on vacation, I would have to work six days a week, plus some nights, to get the next two issues out.

A deep yearning to be going off to college in September almost overwhelmed me. The challenge of college courses, the making of new friends and, yes, having a boyfriend like Graham seemed utterly attractive. Graham was unpredictable, sometimes even a bit wild, but underneath all that egotism and racy talk was a person I had come to like very much.

Something else bothered me. There was scarcely time now for quiet periods with my journal early in the morning. Too much of my writing was focused on mundane activities, editing the reports of correspondents and doing an occasional news item like the church dismissal of Spencer Meloy. It had not been easy to make that a straight news story.

Spencer's ability to rebound from defeat and so quickly begin a new ministry in the Lowlands amazed me. It made no sense until you talked to Spencer and felt in him the depth of his compassion for the poor.

While I too railed against the injustice of the Lowlands and could write about it with passion, moving into a workers' village, as Spencer had done, was something else. I was not sure I could do it—and that disturbed me. This was an admission of a lack of love for these people. I had made some progress in being a more outgoing person the past year, but deep down there were things about myself I did not like. Nor even wanted to look at.

It was after five when Rand called. He must have been surprised that I answered the phone because he hesitated a long moment, then finally blurted out, "I didn't expect to get you, Julie."

"Sorry, Rand. I'm all there is at the moment."

"I need to talk to your father."

"He's out now. Want him to call you back?"

"No. Tell him I'll reach him at your home tonight." He paused. "I liked his editorial on unions."

"He'll be glad to hear that. There's been a lot of criticism, but it doesn't seem to bother him all that much."

"What do you make of that?"

"I don't know. Something's changed him. He used to get sick and go to bed if anything went wrong."

"Your father said some things at that church meeting which, well, impressed me."

"I didn't know you were a member of Baker Memorial, Rand."

"I joined recently. Haven't been very regular in my attendance though."

"I've never seen you there."

"I did come to the Lowlands work party."

"I remember."

There was an awkward silence.

"Julie, do you consider yourself a religious person?"

To my dismay, I found myself stumbling in my answer. "Well, in some ways. I . . . I believe in God. I go to church when I can hear someone preach like Spencer Meloy. He truly cares about all types of people. Why do you ask?"

"I'm not a religious person. I guess I've believed in some kind of universal force—but since your father's talk that night I've been doing a lot of thinking. I need to see him."

When we ended the conversation a few minutes later, I felt deeply dissatisfied with my answer to his question.

34

EARLY Friday morning the Editor left suddenly for Pittsburgh in the Willys. He returned home about seven P.M., looking preoccupied, and thanked us for delaying dinner. During the meal he evaded our questions as to what the trip was all about.

After Tim and Anne-Marie had gone to bed, I was sitting in the old Morris chair in the study reading through a stack of weekly newspapers we received on an exchange basis, clipping short items for possible use in *The Sentinel*. Mother had her mending basket in her lap; Dad was looking over the latest issue of *The Saturday Evening Post*. Suddenly he lowered the magazine. "Can I trust both of you to keep something *strictly* confidential?"

Quickly we reassured him.

"Randolph Wilkinson came by the office yesterday afternoon after you left, Julie," he continued. "Handed me a copy of that engineer's report on the Lake Kissawha Dam."

"The one that was missing!"

"Right."

I almost jumped out of my chair. "Where did he get it?"

"From the state files in Harrisburg."

"How?"

"He went there last Tuesday, identified himself, then asked if they had a copy of the report. They did. Then he explained that the Club copy had disappeared and asked if he could obtain one to take back to the Club. The state official made a copy for him right there. No questions. Rand didn't even have to lie.''

"But why would Rand do this?"

"It seems that my little speech for Spencer pricked his conscience. I talked with him on the phone a long time Wednesday night after he tried to reach me at the office. When he brought the engineer's report to me yesterday afternoon, he said he was tired of being a part of a network of deception.''

"He said that!"

"That he did.''

"Have you read through the report?''

"Yes. It contains some rather startling items. The big one is that if the dam breaks, the new waterway below it could not begin to divert all of Lake Kissawha to Laurel Run. In fact, Alderton could have more water dumped on it in half an hour than all of the past floods combined.''

"That's hard to believe,'' Mother interjected.

"But wasn't the new waterway built for the purpose of diverting any overflow from Lake Kissawha into Somerset Valley?'' I asked.

"Yes. But according to this report, it will handle only minor overflows or breaks.''

We all sat there stunned, trying to digest this bombshell.

"So that's why you went to Pittsburgh today,'' Mother said.

"Yes. I asked Cy Stearns if he wanted to see the missing report. He said he did. We spent half the day going over it.''

"You implied there were several upsetting things in the report, Dad. What else is there?'' I asked.

"You both can read it if you like; it's quite technical, though. The engineer who did the report, by the way, was a man named Hershel Thomas. He died in 1929.''

Dad pulled out a notepad from his pocket. "Mr. Thomas found three engineering defects in the dam.

First, at the time of the sale to the Club, repairs needed to be made to the original core.''

"What kind of repairs?" I asked.

"I don't know. Only a good engineer could tell us that. At the very least they should have used a sturdy cyclopean—"

"A what?"

"According to Stearns a cyclopean is a wall of rubble," the Editor replied. "This probably should have replaced the defective clay core."

"You said *three* major defects, Ken," Mother prompted.

"The second is that they covered over the five sluice pipes with a double thickness of hemlock planking, thus making them useless for drawing off water in times of heavy rain."

I could see that Mother was struggling, as I was, to assimilate that information.

"Third, in order to replace the narrow ten-foot-wide road that runs across the top of the dam with a two-lane one for the convenience of the guests, the height of the dam wall was lowered two feet. By the time the engineer had inspected the dam, the wall had settled even more in the center. So now, in the middle portion the dam's only four and a half feet higher than the bottom of the spillway."

"Bryan was worried about that, remember? But why is this bad?"

"Because, during spring and fall rains or any high water, the spillways can't do the job they're meant to do. That makes it easy for a high lake to flow over the top of the dam wall. And the continuous pressure of this kind of steady flow will break down most anything."

"What about the iron gratings that keep fish from escaping the lake?" I asked. "Bryan felt they were a problem."

"Bryan may be right. The Club installed them after the report was done and the sale had been completed."

"Surely, Dad, when an engineer handed in a report like this, someone must have paid attention to it. What does Stearns think happened?"

"He believes that when the railroad presented McKeever, Sr., with the engineering report, McKeever promised to correct the dam's defects as a condition of the sale. But there were no teeth in the sales contract to guarantee that repairs would be made."

"Did this surprise Stearns?"

"No. He says there are no laws requiring this." Dad studied his notes for a minute. "I also learned that neither the federal nor the state government has any jurisdiction over privately owned dams except when they are on navigable water routes."

"Like rivers."

"Yes."

"Did the report make any recommendations?" I asked.

"Yes. The engineer urged that a thorough overhauling be done of the present lining of the upper slope, that the five sluice pipes be uncovered, that there be construction of additional discharge pipes, plus the reconstruction of the spillways to discharge excess water safely."

The Editor sighed, then pocketed his notes. "I debated all last night and today whether to tell you about this. I hesitated for fear of scaring you. Then I thought, this is silly. We've struggled through some desperate times together as a family. I'm not going to hold anything back now."

"I'm so glad you didn't, dear," Mother said. "I want to know the worst that can happen. And you've told us. Now, can you explain why the elder McKeever doesn't see how important the dam's safety is to his special interests at both the Club and Yoder Steel?"

"I asked that question of Stearns. He just shrugged and said, 'Money?' It seems to be well known in business circles that McKeever is in deep financial trouble."

Mother was shaking her head. "It makes no sense that

such big companies as Yoder and the Pennsylvania Railroad would let a dam be a danger to their property. Dear, are you sure that somewhere between the time of the sale and now, these basic structural weaknesses in that dam haven't been repaired?''

"If so, why the secrecy? Why no statements from McKeever to this effect? All he says is, 'The dam is safe.' ''

"Kenneth, I hope you're not thinking of tackling this in *The Sentinel.*''

"I don't know yet, Louise. What if the people of our town—the whole valley—are really in danger?''

"Then there's got to be some other way. You can't be a one-man crusade. The editorial on unions is enough for this year.''

My father was unconvinced. "The engineer's report is a substantial piece of evidence against McKeever's position on the dam. There's another factor too that I can't dismiss. Bryan McKeever's statements about the dam keep floating back into my mind. If he told the truth—and why should he lie?—then the dam may be the one weak link in the McKeever empire.''

The Editor and I were both at *The Sentinel* early the next morning. He agreed to take the calls while I completed the week's tally of subscriptions to see if the editorial on unions had been damaging. To my surprise, I discovered that there had been only five cancellations. On the plus side: twenty-five new ones.

When I brought the good news to my father, he was pleased. Then he waved me into his office.

"Rand just called. Last night a portion of the road across the dam caved in. New leaks have sprung up on its face.''

"What does he suggest we do?''

"Run a story in *The Sentinel.* He's really worried now.''

"Are you ready to do that?''

"I'm sure thinking about it.''

"Then you'll need some pictures."

The Editor looked at me sharply. "What are you suggesting?"

"That I'm the one to get them—if Rand will help me."

"Hmm . . ." Dad studied me. "If you were to act like a teenage sightseer, you might get away with it."

I winced at the teenage reference. "Will Rand agree to this?"

"I think so. But I'll call him to check it out."

The telephone conversation was brief. Then the Editor turned to me again. "Rand seemed a little hesitant at first about getting you involved. But we finally agreed that it would work provided you act very casual, disguise yourself a little, and do not take notes or pictures when anyone else is around. You are to drive the Willys into the Club parking lot tomorrow afternoon at two. Rand will join you there and give you instructions. Fortunately, Old Man McKeever is out of town."

When I pulled into the Club grounds the following afternoon, I saw that they were as beautiful as ever. The old hotel, Victorian gingerbread work and all, was a dazzling white; the lawns, a lush manicured green; the flower beds, a riot of vivid color—yellow and red cannas, sage, borders of begonias and pansies. The waters of Lake Kissawha were a placid blue mirror, sparkling in the sunlight, as nonthreatening a body of water as one could imagine. Four sailboats were out, though they were almost becalmed.

It was almost exactly two o'clock when I stopped the Willys in the parking lot. With no breeze and the sun beating down, I felt perspiration begin to gather on my forehead. *Hurry up, Rand.*

While ten minutes passed, there was a constant flow of traffic in and out of the parking area as the resident members and their families milled about. *This is not a good place to meet*, I sat there thinking, *too many people.* Twenty more minutes went by.

It was two-forty before Rand appeared. He stared at me a moment before he climbed in beside me. "Good disguise. At first I didn't recognize you." He seemed very tense.

"Mother helped me put up my hair last night. This is one of her old picnic hats. I bought the dark glasses."

"Julie, I can stay here only briefly. Let's talk quickly."

"Is something the matter?"

He hesitated. "I'm not sure. Just learned that the *Vulcania* is back. The Old Man could appear at any moment."

"So what would I do then?"

"Do you think he would recognize you?"

"I don't think so. We've never talked. Only place I've seen him is at church."

"I've heard him mention you by name," Rand persisted.

"What would he do if he did recognize me?"

"Nothing probably, except tell you to leave. Unless he saw you taking pictures."

"Rand, I don't think he'll notice me. Let's don't call it off unless he appears right now."

"So be it, then. I suggest you act like a village lass visiting a friend on the grounds. When I leave, wait a few minutes, then stroll very casually toward the dam. The watchman is off on an errand. By the way, I fired James, but for some reason the Old Man hired him back and told me he was untouchable, whatever that means."

My face must have reflected my inner fears.

"Don't worry, he'll be gone for two hours, at least. I suggest that you take several pictures, not only of the lake and the dam, but of the Club as well. When you're finished, hustle away. Can you manage all that?" he asked anxiously.

"Yes."

"I'll leave you, then."

"Rand, I think what you did—getting that report—took a lot of courage."

"I don't know what's gotten into me. I'm doing things that don't make any sense from a career point of view."

"My father was deeply touched."

I had so many things to ask him, but he was getting out of the car and seemed quite tense again. "Remember, now," he concluded, "you're here visiting a friend."

I waited a few moments, then slipped out of the car, pencil and notepad in my purse and the strap of my camera case slung over one shoulder. It was simple to amble around and stare at the lake, the trees, the Club grounds—all the while pretending to snap pictures. Eventually I got caught up in the spirit of it and found it an exhilarating game.

By indirection my course took me to the dam. Where was the new damage? Other people were also wandering about, so I tried to blend in with them.

The road across the breast of the dam had never been paved. As I walked out on it I saw that even on this calm, sunshiny day, the water on the lake side was no more than six or seven feet below me. From that side, Lake Kissawha stretched so far into the distance that I could scarcely see the misty wooded ridge at the other end.

When I turned around and looked in the other direction, there was a sharp drop of some thirty feet to a rocky, tumultuous creek bed. The stream was redirected to the left by a man-made ridge of earth and concrete. After a few hundred feet, it was lost to sight in a series of bends and twists.

I walked down to the base of the dam, not far from the spot where Margo and I had eaten our picnic lunch nearly a year ago. Once again I caught my breath at the stark appearance of the front of the dam. What had seemed like a mound of dark rubble last fall—with a strange resemblance to a squat, hairy animal—was now covered with green bushes, tall weeds and grasses, brambles, saplings, and quite a number of half-grown trees. Looking closely,

I saw why the vegetation was growing so luxuriantly: constant seepage.

Backing up some, I took pictures of the leakage from all angles. Then I climbed back up to the top of the dam, keeping watch for other people. No one was in sight. I noted that part of the road had caved in at the far end of the dam, away from the main building. There was a hole about two feet deep and perhaps five yards long. I knelt at the edge to peer in and saw mostly small pieces of loose shale.

There would be no great difficulty in mending the road. It was what I saw next that startled me—deep transverse cracks zigzagging from opposite corners of the hole. At one place where the crack was about an inch wide, I poked a stick in, but it did not hit bottom; there was no way of telling how deep the crevasse went.

Observing once again that no one was around, I shot pictures from all angles, wondering what the best technique was for photographing a dark hole. As supplementary material, I took especially careful notes and measurements.

All that done, I started back toward the parking lot. Halfway there, I was startled to see a man approaching me from the edge of the lake. He was walking fast. I froze. It was Tom McKeever, Sr.—the Old Man!

Had he recognized me? My heart began to pound.

"You there. Young lady. Stop, please!"

I turned toward him in mock surprise. "Me, sir?"

He strode up, puffing slightly, frowning, staring hard at me. "Are you a member of this Club?"

"No, I came to visit a friend."

"And who is that?"

"A waitress who, I've just learned, no longer works here. This is such a beautiful Club and the lake and grounds are so lovely and well cared for. I just couldn't resist walking about. Are you the watchman?"

Old Man McKeever looked slightly nonplussed as I

continued to simper and ramble on, trying to take the role of the mindless teenager as best I could.

"What's your name?"

For that question I was not prepared. What to do? I did not want to lie, yet I dared not tell the truth.

"Julie Paige."

"I see." He scowled at me for a few moments. "Why did you walk so far away from the Club?"

I put on the most innocent look I could muster, trying to show my uncertainty. "I—I didn't realize I had walked so far. It's so-o-o beautiful. My parents will love the pictures I took of the lake."

Again the Old Man looked uncertain.

"If you'll excuse me now, sir, I'll go back to town." With that I turned and headed for the parking lot. I felt his eyes riveted on my back as I forced myself to walk at a leisurely pace.

When I reached the old Willys, I rejoiced that the engine started up at once. Quickly I wheeled out of the parking lot and headed down to Alderton.

35

*THERE was no mistaking the setting—the Caledonian
Inn. I was searching for Rand, but he was nowhere in
sight. I pushed open the door at the back of the Inn and
walked out into the glorious garden. While I was savoring all this beauty, a rotund man lurched around the corner of the building and made for me.*

*I began running and could hear close behind me his
heavy breath. Ducking behind the perennial border, I
tried to head toward the meadow, only to find that my feet
were sticking to the ground. I could barely move.*

*My pursuer was closer now. The fingers of his sweaty
hand were about to clutch my upper arm.*

I screamed . . .

And woke up—with a pounding heart.

The identity of my pursuer was clear: Old Man Mc-
Keever. He was an alien in this lovely spot. But where
was Rand? Was the dream a warning? Could *The Sentinel*
be in danger? Its editor? Even our family?

I tried to push away my fears with the thought that it
was only a bad dream. Then, jerking myself back to real
life, I wondered what might have happened there at the
Club if I had told Mr. McKeever my last name. Would he
have confiscated my camera and the pictures of the dam?
Had me arrested for trespassing? Despite my little disguise, had he guessed who I was anyway?

When I had reported on my scouting assignment to

Dad, I had made light of the encounter with the Old Man. I had caught a flicker of admiration in the Editor's eyes at my on-the-spot inspiration to use the name "Paige." Even so, Dad was apprehensive, I could see it in his eyes.

"Tomorrow I begin work on the editorial," he had said. "But"—and here his anxiety showed—"after I've gotten something on paper, I'd like to talk to you and your mother about it."

The three-way conference, held the following night, was reminiscent of that earlier one that took place soon after we had come to Alderton. In the intervening months, all we had been through had bound us closer together as a family. Despite all obstacles, even the flood, we had built *The Sentinel* into a paper that commanded respect.

As we gathered in Dad's study, I could tell that Mother was upset. The Editor had not consulted her ahead of time about his eloquent plea on Spencer's behalf at the congregational meeting. She had been proud of her husband that night, even to the shedding of a few tears, but I sensed that she had felt left out. Sitting in the Morris chair, sorting a basket of towels, there was a trapped look in her gray-blue eyes. Can you tell your mother you love her with a look? I tried to when she glanced my way.

Dad began by leaning back in his chair, his hands locked behind his head. "Let me try to summarize where we stand," he began. "Then I'll read you the rough draft of my editorial."

Mother's brow creased. "So you've already decided to run it, Kenneth?"

"I decided to write the editorial, pray about it, talk it through with you and Julie. Fair enough, Louise?"

"Yes, dear. Fair enough."

"First, there are some sharp differences of opinion as to whether or not the Kissawha dam presents any threat to Alderton or any of the townships closer to the dam.

"McKeevers Junior and Senior steadily maintain that

the dam is safe. Others of us, now including Bryan Mc-Keever and Randolph Wilkinson, feel that it is a threat to people in this whole area. Our concern is based on the engineer's report obtained by Rand last Tuesday, plus what seems to be the deteriorating situation of the dam itself.

"Not only has the road above the dam partially caved in, but deep transverse cracks show clearly in the pictures you took, Julie. They could go right on down to the dam's core. By the way, considering everything, your pictures came out rather well.

"So now, let me read you a rough draft of my editorial.

There continues to be much discussion in our community about the Kissawha lake and dam owned by the prestigious Allegheny Hunting and Fishing Club. Is it safe? Could the dam be breached? If the dam did give way, would Yancyville, Mills Ford and Alderton be in real danger?

Several months ago, *The Sentinel* ran a feature story on this Club. The article detailed something of its history and lauded the resort as an asset to western Pennsylvania. A brief summary was included of the dam and its collapse some eighty years ago, and its repair and sale by the Pennsylvania Railroad to the Hunting and Fishing Club back in 1926.

The Sentinel received criticism for this story from some of the Club's top executives. They assured us that the dam was inspected regularly and is completely safe. They also pointed out that even should the dam ever give way, Alderton would not suffer. First, the rerouting of the Kissawha stream into Somerset Valley should handle 90% of any overflow or breaching. Second, our town is 6 miles from Lake Kissawha, connected by a valley varying in width from 300 to 2,500 feet, through which the water would have to spread. "So what if downtown Alderton did get another two feet of water? We've lived through worse in many a spring flooding," they said.

Their arguments were persuasive and *The Sentinel* had no reason to pursue the matter further until last week. Then, an engineer's report made at the time of the sale of the dam to the Hunting and Fishing Club came into our possession. Prepared by Hershel Thomas (who died in 1929) for the Pennsylvania Railroad, the report faults the dam's inadequate spillways and states there is a high-hazard risk of structural weakness which could result in a major breach at the center of the dam. The engineer also warns that, were the dam somehow to be breached, the new waterway would not prevent some 500 million tons of water from pouring down on Yancyville, Mills Ford and Alderton.

The report indicated that, in the eventuality of a major collapse of the dam wall, the damage to these three towns below could be devastating in terms of property damage and loss of life.

The purpose of this editorial is to urge the Hunting and Fishing Club to act *now* to undertake and complete the major repairs to the dam recommended in the engineer's report. A copy of this report is available in our files if the Club has lost its copy. We also address this editorial to the Pennsylvania Railroad and the Yoder Steel Company in the hope that these large corporations will use their persuasion with the Club for remedial action in handling these safety problems.

The Editor laid the sheets of paper on his desk, then looked at Mother and me expectantly. "Well—what do you think?"

For a long moment we were silent. Then Mother asked, "Kenneth, if you print this editorial, won't Randolph lose his job?"

"That's possible. The Club Board of Directors will certainly want to know how we got the report."

"Is that fair to Randolph?"

"He faced that possibility when he got the report for us, and he has agreed that *The Sentinel* should do something to alert people."

"Dad, don't you think you should include a paragraph about the road cave-in and the leakage, if you plan to use my pictures?"

"Yes, I can slip it in just before the windup statement."

"Kenneth, how significant will the report of a dead engineer be today? Can't the McKeevers trot out other so-called experts to insist that the dam is safe?"

"Of course they can—and probably will."

"And their line would be that you're just trying to frighten people."

"Yes. They would say that too."

"Then what good would it do to print this? Public opinion would be divided. And the dam could last another hundred years."

"I've considered all that, Louise. Why should we get involved in something that offers so little gain and so much possible loss? I asked the same question a month ago. At that time I concluded that there was no logical, sensible reason for me to be involved. Then I did something quite risky, now that I look back on it. I prayed a dangerous prayer. It was that if God wanted me to say anything more about the dam in *The Sentinel*, He would bring to me in a surprising way some new evidence. Well, He did. Bryan McKeever may not be a credible witness to most, but his statements about family differences over the dam impressed me. But it was Rand bringing us the missing dam report that really did it."

There was a long silence in the room. Then Mother said, "Kenneth, I respect that prayer. But aren't you moving too quickly? Shouldn't you check out the report more carefully?"

"The validity of the Thomas report cannot be questioned," my father replied patiently. "The problem is, Louise, that this is just one engineer's opinion. I could spend months, years, fooling around with it. But I feel a time pressure. I feel responsible as a publisher to the people of this community."

"Are you sure you're not being overdramatic, Kenneth? I think you're still angry because you gave in to the Timmeton men and so are determined to prove something here in Alderton. If it will salve your conscience or whatever, you go ahead and print this editorial," Mother said with sudden emotion.

"I'll not do it unless we're in agreement," my father said calmly.

"What do you think will happen, Dad, if you go ahead?" I asked.

"Plenty. I think the McKeevers will move against our family and *The Sentinel* with every means at their disposal. This, on top of the editorial on unions, will make them furious."

"So we could lose the newspaper?" Mother asked.

"Yes, Louise, we could. Our decision must be made never forgetting that possibility."

"Then let's think even beyond that. You've already left the ministry, Kenneth. We've already sunk all my inheritance into *The Sentinel*. So if we lose that too, then what?"

"I don't know what. Except"—and here emotion welled up in him—"if I do not believe that when I do what's right, as God enables me to see the right, He will take care of our future needs, then I would be a man without any belief or faith. I would be a man with no base to stand on. Adrift. In limbo."

Mother and I both stared at him. "Something's happened to you that I'm not sure I understand, Kenneth," Mother said helplessly.

Dad gave her a loving look. "Shall I take that as a compliment or a criticism?"

"Certainly no criticism. I rejoice over your new conviction, even if I don't understand its base. But aren't you going to give Mr. McKeever one more chance to agree to dam repair before you run the editorial?"

"Would that be your recommendation?"

"Definitely," came the reply. "That's both fair and wise."

Dad turned to me. "You haven't said much, Julie. Do you agree with your mother's suggestion?"

"Sure. Nothing to be lost, everything to be gained by that move. You could mail the editorial to Mr. McKeever."

My father nodded. "Yes, with a covering letter telling him that I won't run it if he will agree in writing to do the work recommended in the engineer's report."

Mother's eyes flared. "But Kenneth, isn't that blackmail? 'Agree to what I propose or I'll expose you through the newspaper'?"

"It's bringing pressure to bear, all right. What's the alternative?"

"I'm for postponing a decision on sending the letter. There's got to be some other way."

"What are you afraid of, Louise?"

"Financial ruin, obviously. Friends—everyone—taking sides. Discord everywhere, even in our family."

"Discord in our family is the last thing I want. That's why we must be agreed on this."

Mother just shook her head, looking more trapped than ever.

"Louise," Dad's voice was gentle, "for most of our married life, you have criticized me for not standing firm in the face of threats and obstacles. Why would you now give me the opposite advice?"

A sad little smile played around the corners of Mother's mouth. "I guess my materialism is showing. This week, for the first time, I could see the possibility of our making a decent living from *The Sentinel*." There was silence in the room for a moment. Then she added,

"You're right, Kenneth. We can't be afraid of where truth and rightness will lead. Yet I *am* afraid—"

As she admitted this weakness, my heart went out to Mother. I could feel the misery inside her. And I understood why she could not yet fully trust my father.

"I have no choice but to agree with you, Kenneth." Mother's voice sank almost to a whisper. "Go ahead with the letter to McKeever."

The Editor looked at me, question marks in his eyes.

"Yes, Dad. I'm with you all the way."

Three days later, the draft of the proposed editorial, together with a covering letter and one picture of the dam, was mailed to Mr. Thomas McKeever, Sr.

Two days dragged by, seemingly interminable, with all of us wondering how Mr. McKeever would react to the letter.

The following morning, the old gentleman telephoned the Editor: could he see Dad aboard the *Vulcania* Saturday afternoon at three o'clock?

36

I SHOULD go with him! The thought came to me the night before Dad's second command invitation to visit the *Vulcania*.

At first the prospect of another face-to-face meeting with Old Man McKeever was terrifying, especially coming after that nightmare. But I would be with my father, I assured myself. *And Dad ought not go alone to the* Vulcania *this time*.

I presented the idea to the Editor Saturday morning as we drove together in the Willys to *The Sentinel*. At first he dismissed it. "I'll not crumble before the McKeevers," he assured me.

"That's not the point. They want you alone up there. You don't know what tricks they may try. Knockout drops, for example."

The Editor guffawed. "What an imagination, Julie! The meeting is for three p.m., so there'll be no food, no drinks, no polite conversation. Just blunt talk."

"I think my being there will distract them."

"They'll be very annoyed if I bring you, that's true."

"Won't that be good? Might make them change their strategy."

Dad was silent for a while. I sensed he was seriously considering it for the first time. "I'll have to telephone in advance, telling the McKeevers I'm bringing you."

"Why do that? Let it be a surprise."

Dad parked the Willys and grinned at me as we walked into the *Sentinel* office. "I'll see what Dean thinks."

I was out on an interview late that Saturday morning when Dean Fleming arrived. When I returned, I could tell the two men had been talking. Dad waved me over.

"Dean likes your idea. He wants to come along too and wait in the car for us."

"That'll be great. Strength in numbers."

At 2:45, the three of us climbed into the Willys and headed up Seven Mile Mountain. When Dad turned down the road leading to McKeever's Bluff, I remembered the spot where Graham Gillin had parked last fall. Ten months ago. It seemed like ten years.

The road, cut through a thick forest and heavy underbrush, was so pocked that the Editor had to drive with extreme care. Finally we broke through the canopy of green into a clearing. In the middle of the bluff, set back about twenty feet from the cliff, was the *Vulcania*. But it was not quite as Dad had described it to me.

The railroad car was smaller than I expected, mud-speckled on the side, and the "c" was missing from "Vulcania" in the lettering. The brass was not polished, nor was the uniformed footman there to greet us. The car sat on tracks which cut back into the forest and connected with the main railroad line less than a mile away.

After Dad parked, I stopped for a moment, captivated by the view of the valley below. The drop-off from the bluff was sharp for about thirty feet, then more gradual. I could see Seven Mile Mountain Road winding like a white ribbon below us into Alderton.

McKeever's servant, Karel, was waiting to let us in. He stared at me in surprise, and though I tried to gaze pleasantly into his scarred face, my eyes dropped. When the Editor explained that our driver would wait in the car for us, Karel merely nodded.

McKeever was sitting at his desk in the far corner of the car. He was alone. When we walked toward him, his eyes bore into me, recognition colored his face. I was suddenly very glad that Dean Fleming was waiting for us outside.

"I didn't invite you to bring your daughter," he said, glaring at my father. He had not risen from his chair, nor did he invite us to sit down.

"That's true. But I decided I wanted her with me."

"I see. Well, ask her to go outside and wait while we talk."

"No, Mr. McKeever. If you can't talk to both of us, then my daughter and I will leave now and go home."

There was heavy silence for a long minute as the two men locked eyes. Then McKeever shrugged. "Have it your way. I'll say what I have to say in *my* own way, though. If it offends you daughter, don't say you weren't warned."

He turned to me. "You, Miss Wallace, alias Julie Paige, are a trespasser, a liar, and a sneak." He pointed to a picture of the dam on his desk. "You took this photo, I suppose."

I looked at the picture and fought down a surge of panic. "Yes. And for your information, my name is Julie Paige Wallace."

McKeever's eyes were slits. "I know more about you than you think, thanks to reports from Randolph Wilkinson, whom I paid to check on your whole family." After letting that devastating thrust sink in, he turned to the Editor. "You both might as well be seated," he said.

My father drew up two chairs and we sat down. I recalled what Dad had said about McKeever's desk being on a higher level, so that he could look down upon people he talked to. Now there was an additional handicap. The afternoon sun was directly in our eyes. Was this planned, too? We moved our chairs out of the sunlight.

"I can't see you over there," the Old Man snapped.

"Then please pull down the shade behind you," the Editor returned pleasantly. "The light is in our eyes."

McKeever made no move to swivel his chair or to

lower the shade. Instead he just sat there, staring fixedly at us for a moment. Then a still longer moment.

We waited, wondering how long the eyeball-to-eyeball contact would continue.

"You don't like this town, do you?" the Old Man began.

"I'm liking it more every day."

"Then why did you write this trash?" A pudgy finger thumped the pages on the desk.

"Because I feel there's a legitimate question about the safety of the Kissawha dam."

A single four-letter word cut through the air like a bullet. We sat immovable, said nothing.

McKeever's face was flushed, his chin jutting out. "Wallace, you print this article and *The Sentinel* will be finished in this town."

"What does that mean?"

"It means that I will personally see to it that you and *The Sentinel* go out of business."

I stole a look at my father. He stared at McKeever calmly, almost compassionately. "Threats will accomplish nothing," he said. "If you want to talk this thing through sensibly, we'll stay. Otherwise, we'll say good-bye now." With that, he started to rise from his chair.

Immediately McKeever shifted tactics. He began a long harangue about how much time and money he had spent on the Club and the dam; how misinformation had been spread by people who were jealous of the Club and wanted to hurt it; about how many good inspection reports he had received about the dam in recent years.

The Editor listened patiently, then slowly shook his head. "Only a reputable engineer's report carries any weight on something like this. Not someone in the Pennsylvania Railroad's freight department."

"If you're referring to Roger Benshoff, he's the head of the department, a knowledgeable man on dams."

"But not an engineer with the qualifications of Hershel Thomas."

McKeever's rage, just under the surface, erupted again. "How did you get a copy of that engineer's report?"

"From the state office at Harrisburg."

"Who gave it to you?"

"I decline to answer that."

"Someone stole it. That's a crime, you know."

My father shrugged. "A certain state official was cooperative. It was not stolen."

"We'll see about that." Then came another long diatribe about dishonest reporting and libelous stories.

The Editor stood up and I prepared to join him.

"Wait a minute!" It was a shout, almost a frenzied command.

My father paused.

"You said you would not print the story if repairs were made."

"That's right."

"Let's talk about that."

"Let's do." The Editor sat down again and waited.

The Old Man scowled down at the papers for a moment before speaking. "I've already spent over $10,000 this year on repairs."

"Those are temporary, makeshift repairs. In no way do they get to the heart of the problem that the engineer's report pinpoints."

"Do you realize how much it would cost to do what that engineer suggests?"

"No, but I believe that the Pennsylvania Railroad and Yoder Steel might help finance the repairs. They both would have much to lose if the dam broke."

McKeever snorted. "They would offer nickels and dimes."

He stared at the Editor for another long moment, his eyes less hostile. "I'll make a deal with you, Wallace. You kill that story and I'll get my boys at the Club to set up a long-range plan for strengthening the dam."

"What does that mean?"

"It means you have my word that we'll do something more than what you call 'makeshift repairs.' "

The Editor shrugged. "Mr. McKeever, you are going about this the wrong way. Don't make a deal with me. Deal with the people of Alderton. My only part will be to represent the people through the pages of *The Sentinel.*"

"What *do* you want, then?" the Old Man rapped out.

"I want a letter from you to the people of Alderton and the surrounding communities, stating that an engineer's report indicates that major repairs are needed on the Kissawha dam. Then, in that letter, you, as president of the Hunting and Fishing Club, will commit yourself to a specific program to get major repairs done as soon as possible. I'll print your letter on the front page of the paper in place of the editorial you have before you."

The color had risen again in McKeever's face as the Editor finished his statement. A series of obscenities exploded from the Old Man's mouth. "Hell will freeze solid before you get a letter like that from me," he spat out.

"That means you have no intention of doing anything except cosmetic work on the dam," the Editor concluded mildly.

"It would take everything I have, and more, to do what you think should be done to that dam," the Old Man growled.

"I can't believe your partners at the Club and at Yoder Steel would not share in the expense when they are shown the devastation that 500 million tons of water would cause if loosed on our community."

"Wallace, you are a naïve, birdbrained preacher who should have stayed tucked away in the Church because you don't know a blasted thing about dams and what makes them safe or unsafe. No one believes for a moment that the Kissawha dam is going to break. There are a hundred dams in this country in worse shape. Who cares? The government doesn't. Nearby cities don't. Nobody but wooly-minded radicals like you, who run around crying and wringing their hands about danger to the people. Go ahead, Wallace. Print your [obscenity] story, and I'll see that you become the laughingstock of this town—yes, and of the whole state. And I'll also see that you get your butt busted and lose everything you have to boot. I'm a mean S.O.B. when aroused, Wallace, and you've aroused me.''

The confrontation was over—almost. Without a word, my father and I rose and headed for the door.

The Old Man's voice shot out behind us. ''One more thing, Wallace. Print that story and you may lose more than the paper and your money.''

Dad wheeled to face McKeever. ''What does that mean?''

''You heard me. Just think about it.''

For a final moment, the two men stared at each other. Then, my father and I walked out through the door of the *Vulcania*.

As my father drove the Willys slowly and silently through the thickly wooded area toward Seven Mile Mountain Road, I was trying to grasp the whole significance of McKeever's statement about Rand. Meanwhile, Dean waited patiently for our report.

''I believe the old codger's mostly bluster and bluff. Sorry that Julie had to hear his vile language,'' the Editor finally said. ''Watching him there in that ridiculously ornate private railroad car, enthroned behind his desk, that angry-bulldog look on his face, I felt a pang of sympathy for the old boy. His days are ebbing out and he's clutching at power he may no longer have.''

''Don't underestimate the McKeever power, Ken.'' There was a troubled look on Dean's face. ''Did he threaten you if you print the editorial?''

''He sure did,'' I answered. ''He said he would put us out of business—and more.''

''More what?''

''No specifics,'' Dad answered. ''That's where I think it was pure bluff and bluster.''

"You may be right," Dean said slowly. "But if you don't mind, I'd like to bring a cot to the *Sentinel* office and sleep there until the next issue is off the press."

"Are you serious?"

"Very much so, Ken. If you go ahead with that editorial, I intend to sleep there—with my shotgun under the cot."

The Editor had already departed the office and Dean was limping toward the door when I stopped him.

"Please, I need to talk to you, Dean."

He looked at me searchingly. "Now?"

"No, sometime when we have an hour or so and won't be interrupted."

"For that I think we should drive to my farm late some afternoon."

"Then let's wait until after the next *Sentinel* comes out. It'll be wild here for the next week."

"Fine. Want to give me some idea what's on your mind?"

I hesitated, unsure how to focus my churning thoughts. "Dean, my father stood toe-to-toe with McKeever today and I didn't see him flinch once. I want to know what has changed him, and you know what it is."

"You should ask him, not me."

"I already have. He wouldn't give me an answer. But I'll try him again."

Dean placed a hand on my arm. "I'll give you one suggestion, Julie. Read the Acts of the Apostles in the New Testament before we get together."

Then he squeezed my arm and left.

37

SUNDAY morning I awoke at dawn, propped myself up in bed, and poured out my heartache about Rand into the pages of my journal. How could he have been so deceptive? As I pondered my silly girlish idealism and love for Rand, I began to sob.

Then, almost angrily, I shook off my tears. Rand had gotten us the engineer's report. That was not the act of a McKeever informer.

Putting aside the journal, I picked up my Bible, turned to the book of Acts, and began reading:

> The former treatise have I made, O Theophilus, of all that Jesus began to do and to teach, until the day in which he was taken up, after that he through the Holy Ghost had given commandments unto the apostles whom he had chosen.

I stopped, disheartened. Why was the Bible so hard to understand? The print was small, the sentences long and involved, and the meaning so often obscure. Thumbing through Acts, I saw that there were twenty-eight chapters, running to almost forty pages. Finding the clue to the change in my father was going to be long, tedious work.

However, the text became easier and more interesting as I read slowly on. Almost two hours later I had finished the twenty-eight chapters. I put the Bible aside and stared out the window at the brightness of a new summer day, thinking . . . thinking some more.

I turned back to the first chapter and underlined the first fourteen words of verse eight: *But ye shall receive power, after that the Holy Ghost is come upon you.*

Rereading the passages that followed, it appeared that the Holy Ghost had "fallen" on the disciples in the Upper Room—whatever that meant—*and then they did indeed experience some kind of inner transformation.*

In all my church and Sunday School experience, no one had ever explained these verses. The only teaching I remembered was that the miracles which had happened in Acts were for those early days only; such things did not happen today, I had been told.

At the breakfast table, Dad told us to be ready to leave for church by ten-thirty.

"It's so beautiful outside," I suggested, "let's take a drive and have a picnic instead." With Spencer gone, Baker Memorial no longer interested me.

My father shook his head. "We're still members of Baker Memorial. We'll go to church there and then perhaps have a picnic."

Because of the lovely weather, the acrimony over Meloy's dismissal, and the fact that a retired preacher from Pittsburgh was filling the pulpit, attendance that morning was pathetically small. I watched my father walk over to Mr. Pilcy and young Tom McKeever afterward with a pleasant word of greeting. Before we left the church, I think he had spoken to everyone there.

Later, after we had eaten a picnic lunch by The Rock, I cornered my father in the study as he was reclining in the Morris chair, reading the Sunday paper. Sitting on the floor at his feet, I carefully framed my question.

"Dad, what has happened to you in recent months? You're not only healthy again, you're—different."

He smiled, reached over to stroke my head. "The

simplest way to answer your question is to say that God has healed me."

"Healed you of what, and how did He do it?"

"He touched my spirit."

I shook my head in frustration. "Touching your spirit healed you of malaria? I don't understand."

The Editor was silent for a long moment, his hand still on my head. "I did have a touch of malaria, but that wasn't my real sickness. The Timmeton church battles were too much for me. My mind snapped. I broke down. You may remember I was gone for a month. It wasn't on a preaching mission; I went to a hospital in Louisiana. When I came home I wasn't well. That's why I had so many relapses. It's time you knew the truth about all this, Julie."

Another missing piece to the Timmeton puzzle! The focus on malaria had been a subterfuge to cover up Dad's breakdown. My mind was whirling.

"How can you tell that you're well?" I asked.

"I don't know for sure that I am. But the change you notice comes from deep inside. I'm less fearful. Less self-centered too, I think. People here have helped me a lot."

"Are these the men you and Dean get together with?"

"Yes. You've met some of them at *The Sentinel.*"

"Are they The Preparers?"

"Yes."

"Why is there so much secrecy about them?"

"It's not so much secrecy. To function properly, we must operate quietly, not drawing attention to ourselves."

"I asked Dean about the change in you. He said that I could find a clue to this by reading the book of Acts."

"So you've been talking to Dean, then?"

"Just briefly. We're getting together again sometime."

"I see. Then I'll let him explain to you more about The Preparers." He paused. "I don't want you to think I'm trying to hide anything from you and the family. Your mother has questioned me too. Someday I'll be able to talk more fully about it.''

''One more question. You heard McKeever say he paid Rand to spy on us.'' My voice was trembling. ''Do you think it's true?''

''Rand is paid by McKeever to manage the Club. It would be in the Old Man's character to ask Rand to check on us.''

''Don't you feel, well, betrayed?''

My father reached down to stroke my head again. ''I know how it must strike you, Julie. I'd feel betrayed too, if Rand had not presented us with the Thomas report.''

''Is there any chance that Rand is still playing McKee ver's tune and that for some unknown reason the Old Man wants you to have the engineer's report?''

Dad shook his head. ''Rand and I have talked several times. He may be the one who has really changed.''

When I arrived at the newspaper office Monday morning, Emily Cruley was back at her desk. I told her how glad I was to see her.

''Thank you, Julie,'' she replied coolly. ''I've gone over the two issues put out while I was gone. Made notes of the mistakes.''

My enthusiasm began to subside. ''I hope there weren't too many.''

''Quite a few, actually.''

''Subscriptions are really up,'' I countered.

''Hmmph. That surprises me, considering the way your father's bringing politics into the paper.''

As I started back to my work area, she put a warning finger over her mouth. ''Mr. McKeever's back there with Mr. Wallace.''

''The Old Man is *here*?'' I shot back in dismay.

''No, no—it's young Mr. McKeever.''

Somewhat relieved, I went back to my desk. The voices of the two men filtered through the cardboard-thin wall.

"It's a time of crisis for all us, Ken," Tom McKeever was saying. "Not just in Alderton, all across the nation. Guess you heard this morning's news about the textile strike. Yoder has been forced to lay off more workers. Alderton is still trying to recover from last spring's flood. As for *The Sentinel*—well, Ken, it's never made a profit. Everyone knows that."

"We're doing better than most people think."

"I'm glad to hear that. But I can guarantee you one thing: you hurt yourself when you print editorials like that one about unions. This one on the dam would finish *The Sentinel* for a lot of us in town. If we don't work together, none of us is going to make it."

"I agree with that principle. But, Tom, as a publisher, I *do* have a responsibility to the people the newspaper serves."

"Ken, on the level now, what do you know about dams?"

"Not a lot."

"You've come up with one engineer's report. My father can match it with another engineer's verdict that pronounces the dam as safe as your bathtub at home. Who's to judge?"

"One man is objective, one is not."

"That's your opinion."

There was a moment of silence. Then Tom McKeever said, "Let me sum it up this way. My father and I don't agree about a lot of things. But we *are* in agreement about this editorial you say you're about to publish in *The Sentinel*. That would be a costly mistake. It will cause trouble for us. It will hurt you and *The Sentinel* because you'll lose a lot of advertising. Also, my father, when crossed, can be nasty. He swears he's got something on you that would finish you in Alderton. Ken, I urge you to kill the story for the good of all of us."

"Tom, you're a reasonable man and I respect you. I wish it were possible for me to do what you're asking. I'd like to because I value you as a person and want to be your friend. But there's a lot at stake here for all of us, and I *have* made a decision. I'm convinced it's a right decision. Therefore I dare not change it.''

There was silence, then a scraping of chairs. The door opened and Tom McKeever walked out, grim-faced, my father behind him.

"Well, Ken, if you change your mind, let me know.'' Then, McKeever wheeled to face the Editor and shake his hand. His face was enigmatic, yet I thought I detected in his good-bye a grudging note of admiration.

Late that afternoon, I ran to answer a thumping on the back door.

"Margo!''

With a cry of anguish, I pulled her inside. Her hair and clothes were disheveled, her blouse torn. There were dark smudges on her face and a red blotch marred one side of her neck.

As I was gently helping her into a chair, the Editor appeared from his office. "Margo, what happened?''

My friend took several deep breaths before she tried to reply. "Dad beat me up. He was drunk and said some things about you, Mr. Wallace, that scared me.''

The Editor looked at me. "Julie, help her clean up and then we'll hear the full story.''

I grabbed Margo's hand and led her up the stairs to the ladies' room on the second floor. There Margo scrubbed her face, neck and hands. I tried to repair her blouse with a safety pin.

My mind was churning. What new threat faced my father? I felt icy tentacles of fear stirring my insides.

When Margo and I arrived back downstairs, the Editor led us into his office and closed the door. "Would you tell us the whole story now, Margo?'' he said quietly.

Margo reported that her father had spent the morning closeted in the Stemwinder office with some men. She had been in the dining room and bar area, preparing the place for the usual midday opening.

"The meeting in Dad's office broke up about eleven-thirty," she continued. "Dad seemed okay then, but he began drinking heavily when we opened for business at noon. By midafternoon he could hardly stand up. He was embarrassing everyone. I finally led him to his office. He lay down on the couch, babbling away as he often does. I didn't pay much attention until he raised up and said, 'We're gonna fix that meddling friend of yours at the newspaper. And his paper too.'

"I should have left him alone, but I got scared for you, Mr. Wallace. So I pressed Dad for more information. Suddenly he jumped up and began hitting me. He told me he'd kill me if I said anything. When he passed out on the couch, I decided to come here."

The Editor took her hand and held it gently. "Margo, do you know the names of those men who came to see your father this morning?"

Margo shook her head. "Only faces. They come to the Stemwinder all the time. One is that watchman Julie and I ran into at the dam."

"The one who fired the shot over your heads?"

"That's the one."

My father then asked Margo if she would be willing to stay at our house for a few days.

Alarm spread all over Margo's face. "I can't do that, Mr. Wallace. If my father thinks I ran down here to blab on him, I'll never be able to go back. He must not know I came here."

An hour later, we let Margo go back to the Stemwinder, but most reluctantly. Dad then called Spencer Meloy to ask him to watch out for Margo. Spencer's assent was prompt.

"Margo has already been helping me with the Lowlands work," he said. "She'll make a fine assistant and if I can find some money to pay her, she won't have to work in the Stemwinder any more."

* * *

Dean Fleming and three of his cohorts arrived at the *Sentinel* office at six p.m. with sandwiches and coffee. I studied them more carefully than I had done in the past One, I knew, worked as a switchman at the railroad, another at Trentler Wireworks. The third was employed at the lumberyard. Three things about them impressed me. They used no coarse language. They laughed a lot. They obviously cared for each other.

I heard the next morning that they had stayed until three a.m. Then one by one they slipped out and went home, until at six only Dean was left. He had dozed off on his cot next to the Goss press when he was awakened suddenly by a crackling noise outside the back door.

Fire!

The back entrance was ablaze!

Quickly he rang the fire department, then began to beat at the flames with his blanket. Within minutes the fire truck was there and the flames were extinguished, but the back door was blackened by the fire.

At seven a.m., Dean called the Editor, who knocked on my door to give me a brief report before he left for the office.

When I arrived there at eight, onlookers were crowding into the back alley to stare at the damage. As I entered the front door, I could hear Miss Cruley's shrill voice asking people to leave.

Graham Gillin was there, shaking his head. "Someone set that fire," he muttered. "Poured kerosene on the back door. You can still smell it. Why would they want to do that, Julie?"

"That someone doesn't want us to publish *The Sentinel* this week," I answered.

"Why? What are you printing?"

I hesitated. "Graham, only the Editor can answer that one."

He nodded, then headed for the back of the building,

his muscular body wedging through people like a knife cutting cheese.

Later the owner of the building, George Cummings, appeared and glumly reviewed the damage with my father and Dean Fleming. Cummings wanted *The Sentinel* to cease publication while repairs to the back entrance were made. The Editor and Dean convinced him that the newspaper work inside the building could continue while the work was done. Canvas could be hung over the door to protect the equipment from the elements. Dean and his good Samaritans would continue to guard the premises at night.

Although the pungent smell of smoke hung over the office, we got in a half-day's work that Tuesday. Emily set the editorial in type and both the Editor and I proofread it. Meanwhile, Dean had increased the watch from four to eight men for an all-night vigil. At no time would there be fewer than four men on guard.

When the Editor and I arrived at the office Wednesday morning, Dean greeted us with a sleepy wave. "One more night's watch and we can touch home base," he said. It had been decided to print the paper on Thursday morning and distribute it that afternoon, thus eliminating the need for protection Thursday night.

Dean and his friends had gone home to sleep when Graham Gillin appeared, a baseball bat in one hand and a sports magazine in the other. "You can relax now, Julie," he said with his sly grin. "I'm your protection until Dean gets back this afternoon." He swung his bat with a menacing flourish.

At about one-thirty in the afternoon, the Editor was out for lunch and Graham was in Dad's office, using the telephone. Emily was at her desk in front. I was reading proofs when there was a sharp ripping sound. Looking up, I saw the piece of canvas covering the burnt-out back entrance being torn away. Four masked men carrying clubs and sledgehammers plunged through the opening. I jumped to my feet.

"Get that big press," shouted one.

"I'll take care of the girl," snapped another. One of the men bore down on me. I knew him despite the mask—James, the watchman.

"Graham!" I screamed.

The watchman dropped his club and grabbed me in his arms with a bear hug, ripping my blouse off one shoulder. From the corner of my eye, I saw a crew-cut form hurtle out of Dad's office and tear into my assailant like a projectile. All three of us landed on the floor.

Dazed, I rolled away and watched Graham bang the watchman's head onto the wooden floor until he was unconscious. Another man then jumped on Graham and the two went rolling across the floor, grunting and pummeling each other.

Then I saw Emily enter the fray, swinging her black subscription case at one of the men. When he flung her aside like a rag doll, she scrambled to her feet and ran out the front door, bleating like a wounded lamb: "Help! Police! Someone please help!"

Crash . . . crunch. The sounds were of metal beating upon metal.

"No!" I cried, jumping to my feet. Two men were now trying to subdue Graham. Another was unconscious and the fourth was hammering at the Goss press. I flew at him.

"Get away," he snarled at me as I beat my fists on his back. Then I grabbed one of his arms.

"Get her off me," he shouted.

A man's hand jerked me back, and I tumbled to the floor again, where one of the men pinned me down.

The hammer blows at the press continued while, sobbing, I lay pressed down on the floor.

"Let's get out of here," one man shouted.

The pressure on me lifted. As I sat up, the three men sped out the back entrance. I heard a car start in the alley and drive off.

The watchman still lay on the floor, unconscious. Graham had also been knocked senseless, but he was beginning to stir.

I looked at the press and wept. It was a mass of twisted metal. Then I ran to Graham.

38

THE *Sentinel* office looked as though a small tornado had ripped through it. Metal off the Goss press was scattered all over the floor. Two tables had been overturned. A tray of type had been spilled, with hundreds of letters strewn about the floor. The unconscious watchman lay under a broken chair, his blood intermingled with black splotches from a shattered inkwell.

I was sitting on the floor, holding a wet cloth on Graham's forehead, when he slowly opened his eyes. He raised up, grimaced and clutched his left shoulder. Painfully he climbed to his feet as he stared at the twitching form of the watchman. Then he recovered his baseball bat from Dad's office—in the heat of the battle he had not thought to use it—grabbed one of the fallen chairs, and settled into it beside the inert assailant on the floor.

"I'll cover this skunk, Julie. You call the cops."

"I'm sure they're on the way," I said numbly.

Within minutes people began streaming into the office, led by an agitated Emily Cooley. Two policemen arrived. Then an ambulance, siren shrieking. Clutching his shoulder, Graham Gillin climbed unassisted into the ambulance. The still-unconscious watchman was then wheeled out on a stretcher.

The Editor arrived from lunch, panting, just as the ambulance drove off, siren once again wailing. When he saw that I was unhurt, relief filled his eyes. Then I broke down.

* * *

Later that afternoon, a crestfallen Dean Fleming, a white-faced Editor and I, still very shaky, gathered in Dad's office to assess the situation. A hysterical Emily Cruley had been sent home. My father had urged me to take the day off, but I had refused.

"I underestimated them," Dean muttered. "They knew we were well prepared for a night attack, so they came in daylight. Waited until you went to lunch, Ken."

"Stupid of me to leave," my father growled.

"Stupid of me not to plan better for the daytime," Dean interrupted. "A bold move on their part—almost successful."

The Editor turned to him quickly. "Is the press repairable?"

"I think so. It'll take time. Two or three weeks. The gears are only bent and the flatbed can be fixed. I can't tell yet about the impression cylinder. That may have to be replaced. Give them another ten minutes and the whole press would have been junk."

"You can thank Graham for that," I said. "He took care of three of them. Just one man did the real damage."

"If only I had been here," Dad grumbled again.

"Glad you weren't, Ken. You could have been badly hurt. Julie, can you tell us again what happened? Slowly this time."

Once more I went over the attack. When I admitted to jumping at the man with the sledgehammer, Dad stared at me in amazement. At the end, he was shaking his head.

"Maybe it was wrong to buck the Old Man. We can't cope with his goons. And I shouldn't endanger my family any more. Don't you agree, Dean?"

Dean took a long time replying. "Up to now I wasn't sure the dam was a real issue. Thought you were trying to prove something with that editorial, Ken. And that Julie had read too many adventure books. This attack has changed my thinking. We're up against evil. Raw evil. It has to be dealt with. Since you started something here, I'm afraid you have to finish it. With our help.''

"What are you suggesting, Dean?''

Dean lowered his voice. "That you get on the phone and find another Goss press near here. We'll let the word spread that *The Sentinel* is out of business. This'll get McKeever off our backs. Meanwhile, finish setting up this issue, lock up the forms, and truck 'em to whatever press you find.''

The light returned to the Editor's eyes. "Good plan, Dean. Catch 'em by surprise.'' Then his eyes clouded again. "I don't see how I can put my family through any more of this.''

"I'm all for Dean's idea,'' I said, fighting off the waves of fear that had been engulfing me all afternoon.

The Editor grinned at me. "Somehow I expected you to say that. But I won't buck your mother if she's against it.''

"You'd better deal with Emily Cruley first,'' Dean suggested. "She's a wreck. Suggest she take off three or four days. Don't tell her that we're looking for another press.''

Dad nodded. "Emily surprises me sometimes, though. Just when I think she's impossible, she'll settle down and be a little bastion of strength.''

All the women surprised my father.

When dinner was over, we detailed to Mother what had happened at *The Sentinel.* Her reaction was anger. "How dare he do that! And in broad daylight too! The man is a Hun. He must be stopped.''

Both of us were taken aback and, yes, elated by Mother's vehemence.

Dad later called Miss Cruley and suggested that she take a few days off to recover from the shock of the episode. There was a long silence, and then I could hear Emily's voice crackling over the phone.

"Well, all right, Emily, if that's the way you feel

about it,'' he said and hung up. Then he looked at Mother and me with a wry grin. ''She said she had already taken two weeks off, that of course she will be in the office tomorrow.''

But the third woman, his daughter, wasn't able to keep up her good act. I fell apart.

When I went to bed that night, waves of fear engulfed me. The memory of the watchman's hands wrapped around my chest, pressing against my breasts, was hard to shake off. In desperation, I got up, went to the bathroom, and filled the tub with hot water. For a long time I soaked in it, scrubbing myself over and over.

Back in bed with the light turned off, I sought sleep once again. Though it eventually came, the dreams that went with it were frightening. In one, I was being pursued by leering, evil men who chased me up Main Street toward home. But the street was filled with water and my legs were numb from the cold. Boy was beside me, yipping and splashing to keep up. Then suddenly he disappeared under the water.

I began to sob as the men drew closer. Just as they prepared to grab me, I fell head first into the water. Then I woke up.

My face was wet with tears, my pajamas soaked from perspiration, my body shaking with chills. I turned on the light by my bed and looked at the clock: 3:00 a.m.

Trembling, I climbed out of bed, changed my pajamas and slipped back between the sheets. Sleep was a long time coming.

I awoke Thursday morning to find my father standing by my bed. ''You've had a rough night, haven't you?'' he asked.

I nodded and smiled back weakly.

Our doctor came by several hours later, took my temperature and gave me some pills. ''Two days in bed, at least,'' he ordered.

I groaned. *Why do I have to fold up this way whenever exciting things happen?* I wondered.

A late-morning sleep made me feel so much better that I quickly drained a glass of orange juice Mother had left by my bed. When I heard my father arrive home for dinner, I could barely contain my eagerness for the news of the day. I was about to disobey his orders and invade the first floor when I heard his footsteps on the stairs. He entered my room and sat on my bed, his eyes rimmed with fatigue.

"First, tell me how Graham is," I asked.

"His shoulder is not broken, only dislocated. Doctors say he'll be okay in a few weeks. He was at the office today, arm in a sling, inquiring about you."

I sighed in relief, then asked about *The Sentinel*. The Editor reported that a Goss press was available at the *Cloudsville Times*, ninety miles north. The printing could be done Saturday, with distribution on Monday. "If" —he paused—"if we want to go ahead."

"But Dad, I thought we were all in agreement."

"I admit to having second thoughts about it. Too many people are being hurt."

A pang ripped through me. "You're not including me in that, are you?"

"Yes, I am." Tears suddenly welled up in his eyes. "Nothing is worth having you go through what you went through yesterday. I love you too much for that, Julie."

I couldn't check the tears either, and for a moment the two of us clung to each other. Then I found my voice. "There's nothing the matter with me that a little rest won't cure. We all agreed to go ahead with the editorial. Please don't back down now."

My father stood up and walked to the window, staring out at the early evening shadows on the yard. "There are times when I think we're all crazy. The dam could last another hundred years, even if McKeever never does a thing to strengthen it. Who am I to try and buck the whole McKeever clan?"

"We've gone through this before, Dad. You're doing what you believe is right. We're all in agreement."

"Not Emily. She told me bluntly today that I was a fool."

"Is she leaving?"

"She didn't say she was. By the way, she expressed real concern for you today, Julie."

The thought of Miss Cruley worrying on my behalf silenced me for a moment.

My father sat down on my bed and reached for my hand. "Dean Fleming called my attention today to a passage of Scripture in the book of James. Let me read it to you."

He arose and picked up my Bible from the desk and riffled through the pages. "Here it is—James 5:14.

Is any sick among you? Let him call for the elders of the church; and let them pray over him, anointing him with oil in the name of the Lord. And the prayer of faith shall save the sick, and the Lord shall raise him up; and if he hath committed sins, they shall be forgiven him.

"I had to confess to Dean that, during all the years I was a pastor, the carrying out of this passage had never been done in my church," Dad said. He probed me with his brown eyes. "Are you willing to be prayed for in this way?"

There was a trace of embarrassment in my father's eyes, for as a family, we had mostly prayed separately and in secret, according to another passage in Scripture. I urged him to go ahead.

"Good. Then I'll ask Dean and Spencer Meloy to join me. They're downstairs."

"But Dad, you didn't tell me there were others involved. I look awful for company," I cried.

"They're not company," he replied gently. "They're

elders of the Church who've come here to pray for the sick.''

''At least let me comb my hair first,'' I moaned.

A few minutes later, the three men had posted themselves by my bed, looking very formal. Dad pulled a small vial of oil from his pocket, placed a few drops on his fingers, and then touched them to my forehead. Spencer read the passage from James again. My father spoke a short prayer of faith that I ''would be healed of all infection causing the chills and fever.''

Dean prayed more vehemently, ''expelling all dark forces'' from my room in the name of Jesus and asking the Lord to erase the memory of the attacker's physical assault upon my person.

Spencer's prayer was more of a benediction, that I be able ''to go forth, renewed in spirit, healed in mind and body.''

Then—a bit self-consciously—each of the three men kissed me gently on the forehead and left the room. Their words, their tenderness, their love, stayed with me a long, long time.

I remained in bed all day Friday, sleeping, reading, and writing in my journal. Once more I read through the book of Acts. The fear thoughts were gone. Wondering if prayer had somehow chased them away, I kept praying, in case they tried to return.

Before he left for work, the Editor had stopped in my room to ask me if I still felt he should go ahead with the editorial. When I said he should, Dad patted my hand and left. After he arrived home for a late dinner that evening, my father reported that the forms had been all locked up and Dean was ready to drive them to Cloudsville early the next morning. The two men had decided not to disclose this plan to anyone, even Emily. The Editor simply told her they wanted to have the forms ready when Dean had the press repaired in two or three weeks.

* * *

On Saturday I got up and dressed, still feeling shaky but determined to hide it as much as possible.

Margo was my first visitor. She was depressed that despite her warning, the *Sentinel* presses had been smashed up. She surmised that the success of the raid had kept her from being further roughed up by her father. On a happier note, Margo talked about how much she enjoyed her work with Spencer Meloy. It consumed so much of her time and energy that she hoped to quit her job soon at the Stemwinder.

Spencer Meloy arrived next, dressed in old baggy pants and a sports shirt. "Excuse my appearance," he began, "but I'm invited to lunch with the Balazes. We're painting their house this afternoon. I was planning to invite you to join us, until you decided to have that wrestling match with those thugs last Wednesday. So I invited Anne-Marie instead."

Before leaving, he took my hand and held it. "I feel very close to you, Julie," he said softly. "You are in my thoughts every day. And remember this, I'm a persistent man."

Graham Gillin, his arm still in a sling under his orange and blue football jacket, dropped by after lunch with disturbing news. The watchman, James Sanduski, had escaped from the hospital that morning. "A policeman was supposed to be sitting outside his room," he said. "Someone slipped up—or was bribed."

I stared at Graham in dismay. "Are we in danger from him?"

"Naw. He'll keep out of sight. But it means that the police have no case. They had hoped to get a confession out of James."

I was relieved to hear that Graham's injury would not keep him home from college, but was distressed that the doctor had said he could not play football for another month. "My scholarship may be withdrawn," he conceded. "And freshman football is important at Penn

State. That's where they peg you for a future spot on the varsity."

"It's not fair, Graham. The Penn State football coach needs to know what a hero you were."

Graham laughed. "You tell 'em then. You're the writer."

"I will."

"There's something else, Julie. I love you. But then you know that."

"You've never said it before."

"I don't like to say things like that to a girl unless the feeling is mutual. And I didn't intend to say it now, especially since I've only got one arm."

"Well, I've got two," I said, And I put them both around his neck and kissed him. "As long as I live, Graham, I'll never forget the sight of you tearing into that watchman."

Later that afternoon I was upstairs dozing when Mother appeared in my room. "Randolph Wilkinson is downstairs. Are you well enough to see him?"

"Yes, Mother." With sudden nervousness, I scrambled to my feet and reached for my lipstick to brighten my pale face.

Rand here. What can he want? I smiled wanly. *Must be a courtesy call on the sick.*

When I walked into the living room, Rand, in white slacks and dark blue blazer, was standing at the window. He turned and smiled, his eyes warm and uncertain. We stood for a moment, awkwardly, facing each other.

"Horrible experience for you, Julie. And for *The Sentinel*. I'm terribly sorry. How are you feeling?"

"Better, thanks." When I motioned for him to sit down, he chose the loveseat. I sat in a chair facing him.

"And to think it was James who led the attack. This time, I can assure you, he has been sacked from the Club. A bit late, of course. The Old Man himself said he had to go." Rand shifted around on the loveseat.

Will we ever replace that uncomfortable monstrosity of a sofa? I wondered, struggling to find words for Rand.

"The Club is in a bit of a turmoil," Rand continued. "Mr. McKeever's angry about one thing or another." He grinned wryly. "Mostly about the appearance of that engineer's report on the dam."

"Does he suspect you?"

"I don't think so. If he did, I'd be in deep trouble."

"What do you think would have happened to you if *The Sentinel* had come out yesterday with Dad's editorial?"

Rand moved again on the loveseat. "Difficult to tell. McKeever's moods are so unpredictable. It would be hard for him to fire me because of Uncle Munro. McKeever's a dangerous man to have as an enemy though."

"That's what my father discovered. McKeever's fortunate that James escaped today from the hospital." Then, I stopped. "Rand, can we be honest with each other?"

"I hope so."

"McKeever hired those four goons who smashed up our office, right?"

"Probably. But I doubt if anyone can prove it now that James has escaped."

"Why is McKeever so determined to stop the editorial?"

"If he is forced to make those repairs on the dam recommended in that engineer's report, it will bankrupt him."

For a moment I stared at him in amazement. "But he's so rich. And there are other wealthy men on the board of the Club. Why can't the expense be shared?"

Rand hesitated. "Julie, I'm not sure I should be telling you things that are Club business. And I don't have all the answers myself." He paused again. "I'll just say that McKeever owns such a large percentage of the Club and the surrounding property that the other board members haven't the power to overrule him."

"That explains why he does as he pleases at the Club. Does he own most of Yoder, too?"

"The McKeever family does."

"When my father and I went to see him on the *Vulcania*, he said something to me that has bothered me ever since. He said, 'I pay Randolph Wilkinson to check on you, Miss Wallace.' What did he mean by that?"

There was a lengthy silence. Rand was embarrassed.

"You asked me to be honest with you and I've tried. This one is a heavyweight, though." He sighed. "McKeever asked me months ago if I would get close to both you and your father. It was his idea that you print our menus. Also the ERP booklet. He wanted your father under his control."

There it was in his own words. Rand had not sought me out because of personal interest, but as an assignment from his boss. The words hurt so much that I fought off waves of nausea.

"Then, the date . . . the date we had at the Caledonian Inn, was a suggestion from that . . . that repulsive old man?" I quavered.

Rand squirmed again. "His idea, my execution. I'm sorry. You asked for truth and I could have given you a neat little lie here. I didn't expect to enjoy that day with you as much as I did. What started out an assignment became an enchantment."

My battered feelings were only slightly restored. As I stared at him sitting there so uncomfortable on that lumpy loveseat, I was glad, for the first time, that we had not replaced that old piece of furniture.

"I've heard that every girl, at some point in her life, has silly, romantic illusions over an older man," I began again, fighting to control myself. "You've been that for me. I hope I've grown up enough to appreciate your honesty, Rand. I'm not sure I have, though. If only you hadn't treated me so much like a princess."

The engaging grin was back. "You *are* a princess."

"But not fit for an English nobleman."

"Too good for him."

"Are you engaged to be married, Rand?"

The shift in direction surprised him. I saw him weighing his response: truth or falsehood. Truth won again.

"There is a woman in Pittsburgh. We are not officially engaged."

"Do you love her or is this something your family wants?"

"Despite what Uncle Munro may have told you, I would never marry for social reasons. Only for love." Rand's voice was still gentle.

Relieved by this answer, I changed direction again. "Why did you go to all that trouble to get that engineer's report?"

Rand's face turned serious. "The speech your father gave for Meloy thumped me hard. Especially his words about the testing of our manhood. Right then, I didn't like myself, nor all the deception I was a part of."

"But why the dam?"

"Because I was troubled by the way McKeever avoided making repairs on it. I felt someone needed to force the issue. You and your father are the only ones I know who are concerned about it."

"Then you don't think the dam is safe?"

Again a pause. "No, I don't. Yet I wouldn't place a wager that it would break soon. That's why it's so hard for people to go against McKeever. They just don't know."

Rand did not try to kiss me good-bye. Our relationship was suddenly different. I expected to go upstairs and have a good cry, but no tears came. The hurt was too deep.

39

THE Editor and I were in the office early Monday to help with the delivery of *The Sentinel*. Seven thousand copies of this special edition had been printed in Cloudsville on Saturday. Dean had returned to his farm that night and kept the whole run concealed in his truck over Sunday. He had already unloaded his cargo in the *Sentinel* office by eight o'clock Monday morning.

Eagerly I snatched up a copy. Page one featured the twin assaults on *The Sentinel*: the fire and the smashing of the Goss press. The final paragraph read:

> When asked if he had any explanation for the two attacks, publisher Kenneth Wallace would only say that local police were questioning James Sanduski, one of the assailants, who had been captured on the scene. The police are expected to issue a statement this week.

With the watchman's escape, the police would have no statement to make. I wondered how vigorously they would seek to recapture James. Would they track him to the Stemwinder? Or did McKeever's power reach so far into the police department that they would do nothing?

At the bottom of the front page, spread across four columns, was the feature editorial, entitled "New Questions Arise: Is the Kissawha Dam Safe?" Dad had trimmed his copy some, and sharpened the lead paragraphs, but the tone of the editorial was moderate.

I heard a throat being cleared and looked up to see Emily Cruley standing in front of my desk. "How do you feel, Julie?" she asked.

"Much better, thank you."

She cleared her throat again. "I'm glad to hear that. Let's see, you've been here almost a year now. A good training period for you."

Emily started to walk away, then turned back. "If you write any more verses of poetry, Julie, I'd like to consider them for the Poetry Corner. And from now on, we would want to use your name as author." There was a formal little nod and she returned to her desk.

I was stunned. For Emily Cruley, a momentous gesture of recognition.

Distribution of *The Sentinel* began quietly late Monday morning. Mother made one of her infrequent appearances to help out. Anne-Marie and Tim were joined by two of Dean's friends to make direct deliveries to subscribing businesses and homes. Dean and the Editor drove the bulk of the run to the post office. Five hundred extra copies were given free to places like Haslam House, the local hospital, all churches and nonsubscribing businesses.

Since word had spread that *The Sentinel* was out of business, the delivery caught the whole town by surprise. Tension in the office grew all day Monday. Would we get angry cancellations? Calls of support? How would people react?

The only telephone calls that came were for extra copies of the paper. Tim was on the run the rest of the day.

There was little conversation at home that night. We were almost too tired to eat. Even Anne-Marie and Tim didn't object to Dad's "early-to-bed" orders.

Tuesday was surprisingly quiet. By midafternoon, the Editor wondered aloud to Dean and me if McKeever would make any move.

"Bound to," said Dean. "He's been challenged."

Both men had left the office and I was on the verge of walking home to dinner when the call came from Rand. He wanted to talk to my father or Dean. I was his third choice. He hesitated, then out came the news.

"I've been sacked."

"By McKeever?"

"Yes. He ordered me to the *Vulcania* this afternoon. *The Sentinel* was on his desk. He asked me if I was responsible for unearthing the dam report. I told him I was. Thought for a moment he was going to attack me physically. Never saw him so angry."

"Oh, Rand! How terrible for you! Did you have to admit it?"

Rand seemed to be considering the question. "I thought about it, believe me. For weeks now, I've prepared for this session, knowing that sooner or later your father would publish something involving the report. I figured I had to tell the truth sometime. So why not right off? Cleaner this way." He paused. "Please relay this news to your father." Then he hung up.

The telephone began ringing Wednesday morning, starting with a terse call from the advertising department of Yoder Steel, canceling all their ads. Local businessmen followed. Most were embarrassed. "Things are tight now, Ken. Check back next month. Changing my ad program for a month or so. Perhaps later this year."

Ever since the shirt ad episode, Sam Guither had been close to Dad. He came to see the Editor, and I heard their conversation. "Tom McKeever runs this town, Ken, and he's out to get you. He's told us not to run ads in *The Sentinel* if we want to stay in business."

"Sam, how can you businessmen let him get away with this? If he knows he can tell you what to do, he'll become a dictator, determining your every move."

"I don't like it, but I can't buck him all by myself."

"Talk to the others. If you're united, he'll back down."

"I'll talk to them. That's all I can promise."

By dinnertime, the bad news was complete. Every advertiser had canceled. The last call before we left the office was a crusher. George Cummings, owner of the building, said he was serving notice on *The Sentinel* that as of this date, August 28, we would have three months to vacate the premises. "Check your lease, clause ten, if you question my legal right to do this," he said and hung up.

For the rest of the week, there was an almost funereal atmosphere in the office as we prepared to print the next edition Friday in Cloudsville, for a Saturday distribution in Alderton. Subscription cancellations were now coming in by telephone, accompanied by verbal tongue-lashings. Emily Cruley took the brunt of this onslaught.

Meanwhile, Dean Fleming had the pieces of the Goss press spread all over the floor. His grim report: $300 for new parts. Repair time: two to three weeks. Having four issues printed in Cloudsville would run another $150. "Figure five hundred for everything," Dean told the Editor.

"I don't have it," he replied. "I guess it's to the bank again."

"McKeever's a director at your bank. Did you know that?"

"No, I didn't."

"How much do you owe the bank, Ken?"

The Editor thought a moment. "Still about six hundred."

"Was it a demand note?"

"Afraid so."

"That could be more trouble."

Dad sat down, white-faced. "I've only five hundred in the bank to handle all our needs. Where do we go from here?"

"Don't panic, Ken. We're not beat yet."

"I'll fight to the last, but I can't let my family starve." Dad paused a moment, his face tight. "I rent my home, Dean. Do you suppose McKeever can get us pitched out of there, too?"

"Well, if he does, you'll just move in with us."

Dad grinned boyishly. "You're a savior, Dean."

"Please don't call me that, good friend. There's only one of those."

As Dean had predicted, the bank foreclosed Dad's note. "I've only one week to repay the six hundred," he told us Friday morning.

"And if you don't?"

"They take over the newspaper."

"You'll have the money next week," Dean stated.

"I can't let you do it."

"This paper will survive," Dean continued. "It has to if the integrity of this town is to survive. You'll have the money next week to keep *The Sentinel* going."

Late that morning as Dean was packing the locked-up forms for this week's *Sentinel* into the back of his truck, I asked to go with him to Cloudsville. Dean was agreeable. So was the Editor. Around noon I climbed in beside Dean with a brown paper bag containing sandwiches and two soft drinks.

As Dean drove out of Alderton, I studied him. In a faded green T-shirt, casual tan jacket, brown corduroy slacks and thick workman's shoes, he appeared to be the typical hired hand. How misleading looks could be! Dean Fleming not only was a near genius with machinery, he also seemed to be the epitome of spiritual man, cloaked in veils of mystery. I hoped to unwind some of those veils in the four hours it would take to drive to Cloudsville and back.

"Dean," I began, "the past few days my father has taken blows that would have put him to bed last spring. What changed him?"

"Did you read the book of Acts?"

"Yes, several times."

"What clue did you find there?"

"It seemed to me that the disciples were mostly weak men before Jesus' death. Then the Holy Spirit gave them some kind of power. This isn't supposed to happen today."

"It does, though. Not often in churches, except Pentecostal."

"I don't know any Pentecostals and if there are people today who have this power, why haven't we seen them?"

"You probably have seen them, only they don't wear lunchboards saying 'I'm filled with the Holy Ghost.' "

I laughed. "But I've been to a lot of churches with my parents, heard many sermons, but never anything about the Holy Ghost. It sounds so spooky."

"You and ninety-nine percent of all Americans feel the same way. It's a sixteenth-century term, not a word for today. But your father's included in that other one percent."

It took a while for that to sink in. "You mean Dad has received this power, like Peter and John and all those disciples?"

"That's right. Only he'll say nothing about it because people won't understand. Not even to you, unless you push him. And maybe not then."

I thought back to what I'd read in Acts and remembered that the disciples had been ridiculed by many people. "My father hasn't acted like the disciples did. He talks the same; he even says he's still uncertain about things."

"But you said he was different. That's the way the Holy Spirit works in people."

"I'm sorry, Dean, but I still don't understand."

"If I had my Bible with me, I'd stop and read you some Scripture that would explain it better."

I shook my head. "That's what I thought you'd do if I came to see you at your farm. Preachers are always reading the Bible to explain something instead of telling it in plain, simple English.''

Dean roared with laughter. ''So you've picked this time to grill me, when my hands are busy and I can't read Scripture to you. Julie, the Bible has answers to all problems. It says things much better than I can.''

''Sorry, but I don't agree. I've a reasonably good mind, but the Bible confuses me. Like the Holy Ghost. Try to sell that to people today and they will laugh at you.''

Dean Fleming was silent for a moment. ''That's why Big John Hammond said we had to move quietly, even secretly.''

''Does all this have anything to do with The Preparers?''

''Yes, it does.''

''What are they?''

''The Preparers isn't a story for *The Sentinel*, Julie. If I tell you something about them, you have to promise to keep it quiet.''

I digested that for a moment. ''I promise.''

Dean's eyes were now very serious. ''I guess it all began with John the Baptist, an outdoor man, who prepared the people of his time for the coming of Jesus Christ. Check Scripture on this, Julie. 'Prepare the way for the Lord,' John kept saying. After Jesus died on the cross and then was resurrected, another outdoor man, Peter, picked up this mantel and began preparations for the Saviour's return.''

Then Dean described in detail how small, often secret groups of men carried on this idea down through the centuries. There were such orders as The Shepherds of Bethlehem, The Fishermen of Galilee and later The Woodsmen of the World. Few details are known because the men kept their actions secret.

''John Hammond became so fascinated with what these men did,'' Dean continued, ''that he researched all the medieval guilds, then even studied the Odd Fellows—

who were mostly day laborers and mechanics at the beginning, but who helped the poor, widows and orphans. He concluded that good works done in secret somehow generated a certain extra power. Big John, a few loggers and I banded together to form The Preparers. We were really an extension of many other little-known small groups of courageous, selfless working people down through the ages. The one thing these groups seemed to have in common was a commitment to serving Christ.''

He paused to reflect. ''The Preparers has never been an official organization. Nothing has been put on paper. We meet regularly at my cabin and decide what projects to take on. We pray together a lot. Study the Bible too.''

''Why is the ax your symbol?''

''Because the ax was the logger's tool. Every group picks its own symbol. A fish for The Fishermen of Galilee, a hammer for carpenters, and so on.''

''Why are only men involved?''

''No particular reason except that the work they do is so dirty and physically demanding,'' Dean replied. ''I guess men have always started secret societies to be together as men. Some of these groups unfortunately are not as constructive as The Preparers. Our purpose is to be servants to all, as Jesus was, and to prepare people for the return of the Lord.''

''But why do you include men like my father who have jobs where they do not work with their hands?''

''That doesn't matter. As Preparers, they learn to work this way. We believe that a man finds the essence of his spirituality by the physical work he does, without compensation, for others.''

''I don't understand your very intense interest in my father, Dean.''

''Ken has been hurt by fellow Christians. Therefore fellow Christians should be the ones to help him get back on his feet.''

''Why the secrecy?''

Dean smiled. ''There's a passage in Scripture that

says, 'Tell no man.' I know that seems a contradiction to the Scripture that says we Christians are to go into the world and proclaim the good news of the gospel. That's for those called to evangelize. We are called to do our work in secret.''

Then as we drove the last few miles into Cloudsville, Dean gave me a theological explanation of the Holy Spirit as being the Third Person of the Trinity, along with God the Father and Christ the Son.

When we started the drive back home, the freshly printed issues of *The Sentinel* packed carefully in the back of the truck, I was eager to resume our discussion.

"Have you talked much with Randolph Wilkinson?" I asked.

"Very little. He's your father's project. I gather he's struggling with the basics, just as you are."

"He's also trying to become a more honest person. It cost him his job."

"Good thing, too. He needs to get away from McKeever. Rand surprised me. I never expected him to buck the Old Man. That took guts. I know he hurt you, Julie, but he's not all froth and good looks."

"How did you know he hurt me?"

"He told me."

The thought of Rand talking to others about me this way was suddenly disconcerting. I pulled my mind into a new direction. "Dean, is Spencer Meloy one of The Preparers?"

"No. His theology is mostly focused on helping people with their physical needs. All that's important, of course, but he'll hit a dry spell someday and need something more than social causes to keep him going."

"I guess you're describing the kind of religion I have, Dean."

"For now, yes. But if you're serious about writing on the deeper life, you simply cannot ignore the centrality of Jesus and the Holy Spirit. Big John made a prophecy about God's plan for this century. He said that ninety-nine percent of the world will largely be in spiritual darkness for the first fifty years. Then the last fifty years will see a tremendous surge of spiritual vitality and an equal onslaught of Satanic forces, followed soon after by the Second Coming of Jesus. You'll probably be here to see it. I won't.''

"I'm not sure I want to be in God's plan after seeing what happened to my father in Timmeton.''

"Painful, I'm sure. But so is what he's going through now." He paused for reflection. "A watershed time for your whole family.''

"You mean a testing time.''

"More than that. Change through growth. Don't be afraid, Julie. You are very special to the Lord.''

Awed, somewhat numbed by Dean's words, I was silent for a long moment. "How do you know these things, Dean? I mean, you are so flat-footed in your statements that one could call you a fanatic.''

"I *am* a fanatic, Julie. I try to keep it under wraps with most people. The Lord has indicated that my time on this earth is limited, but I still have important work to do with certain people. You are one of those.''

I shook my head. "You talk as if you have some kind of direct pipeline to God, that you speak to Him regularly. They put people like you in mental institutions, Dean.''

Again he chuckled. "God has a way of communicating to people who truly seek Him out. Not exactly as He did with Old Testament figures like Noah and Abraham and Moses, but I believe He does it today in His own way. Have you never experienced Him this way?''

After a pause, "Yes, just once.''

"Tell me about it.''

With some reluctance, I told for the first time the full story of the night Bryan McKeever had passed out at the wheel of his car and I had called for and received God's help.

Dean was thoughtful. "That confirms what I've felt

about you, Julie. God has special plans for you. Just don't be in such a big hurry to grow up."

With that, we were both silent until we entered Alderton.

When I walked into the house at about seven-thirty, I found the family already at the dinner table. They greeted me with silent nods, except for Tim, who was crying, head down. Anne-Marie looked at me with tears in her eyes.

"Boy's dead!"

"What happened?"

Tim lifted up angry eyes. "Someone poisoned him, that's what."

"When?"

"This afternoon."

"How do you know it was poison?"

"We took Boy to the vet," Dad said sadly. "He's pretty sure it was poison because of a certain smell in Boy's mouth."

"What a hateful, cowardly thing to do!"

I tried to brighten the meal with a description of my trip. But there was such heaviness in everyone's spirit that I suspected there was still more bad news.

Mother confirmed it as I was helping her with the dishes. "We are being evicted from our home," she said.

"What!"

"The owner called your father this afternoon at his office. There's some clause in our rental agreement that allows him to do this. We have to move out by the first of October."

Another numbing blow! I shook my head in dismay. "Well, I guess we'll have to move in with Dean and Hazel. They invited us, you know, if something like this happened."

Mother just stared at me.

After the dishes were done, I found my father in the

study, sitting at his rolltop desk. When I lashed out at our landlord, he looked at me numbly. "That's not the worst of it." Then he handed me a letter to read. "Vincent Piley circulated this letter to just about everyone in town."

Written on Yoder Steel stationery, it vigorously refuted *The Sentinel* editorial, calling it irresponsible journalism, and assured Alderton citizens that in the most unlikely case of dam leakage or flooding, the new waterway would direct any overflow into Somerset Valley. Then came this final bombshell:

> Another reason *The Sentinel* is not to be trusted involves Kenneth Wallace himself. He is new and inexperienced in publishing, having been a clergyman in Timmeton, Alabama, until he came to Alderton a year ago. An officer of his church told me that because Mr. Wallace had suffered a nervous collapse several years ago and had been hospitalized for almost a month, there was reason to believe he was mentally unstable. I and others here in Alderton believe that Mr. Wallace has still not recovered from that illness, which makes his credibility and that of *The Sentinel* questionable, to say the least.

I was shaken by the letter, only too aware how most people felt about mental disorders. "How are you going to answer this?" I asked the Editor.

He shook his head. "I'm not."

Boy was buried Saturday morning out by The Rocks. Tim requested all members of the family to be on hand for an 8:00 a.m. funeral. At 7:55 we gathered in the kitchen for a "proper march" to the grave site.

My father was dressed in his formal preaching gown; Mother, the children, and I in our Sunday clothes. If I was tempted to smile at the strange sight of a backyard funeral for a dog, one look at Tim's face stopped me. His eyes were puffy and red; his face stricken by the death.

Slowly we marched from the kitchen to the grave site. A surprisingly deep hole had been dug at the farthest corner of the yard. Beside it lay Boy's body, wrapped in a small brown blanket. My father asked Mother to give an opening prayer. She thanked God for Boy and his happy spirit and for giving our family so much fun. "Take Boy into Your heavenly animal kingdom," she concluded.

Dad opened his Bible and read several verses of Scripture. Then he turned solemnly to Tim. "Do you want to say a few words of good-bye to your friend?"

Tim nodded vigorously, the tears streaming down his face. "So long, Boy. I miss you so much. But I know we'll see you again, because God won't let such a happy dog just . . . just . . . just go away forever. Be a good dog in that new place you're in. Don't forget, Boy, I love you."

That little talk left us all dissolved in tears. Anne-Marie just shook her head when Dad asked her to say a few words.

Then it was my turn to read a special poem for the departed. It was a hurried, maudlin effort about our "aching loneliness," with Boy to be placed "in cold and furrowed earth" and other such phrases.

My father and Tim then lifted up Boy's body and placed it gently in the grave. Dad picked up the shovel to fill the hole with dirt, but stopped, thinking perhaps, that this might be too hard for the children to take. Standing very erect, he asked us to close our eyes as he pronounced the benediction.

Mother, Anne-Marie, and I filed back into the house while Dad and Tim stayed to fill up the grave. Into the ground over the body a wooden stake was driven with the word BOY printed on it crudely, and the date of death, *September 6, 1935*, underneath.

Then we changed into work clothes and headed for the *Sentinel* office to distribute the current issue.

* * *

When we gathered for breakfast Sunday morning, I wondered if my parents intended to go to church. How could they face the people at Baker Memorial after the circulation of Mr. Piley's letter?

The question never came up. Dad was already dressed for church. Mother had been weeping, I could tell, but she did not say a word that gave away her true feelings.

We walked to church as a family, nodding to everyone we saw. At the entrance to Baker Memorial, we all shook hands with the usher; my father asked him to seat us in the front row.

After a boring sermon by the substitute preacher, the Editor led the way out of church, shaking hands and smiling at everyone he encountered. Most people seemed embarrassed; some hostile looks were cast our way. The Piley family had been sitting near the rear of the sanctuary. They were gone by the time we got to the front door. None of the McKeevers were in church.

After we had greeted everyone in sight, we walked back to Bank Place again as a family.

Never had I been prouder of my father.

40

I<small>N</small> this issue of *The Sentinel* the Editor had continued the story of the four-man attack, playing up Graham as "the high school football star who, heedless of injury to himself, tore into three of the masked invaders." A picture of Graham in his football uniform was featured.

I clipped the story and picture and sent them with a short note to the Penn State football coach, imploring him not to discontinue Graham's scholarship because of an injury suffered in a heroic effort.

The story also recounted the escape of James Sanduski and quoted a statement from the police chief that efforts were being made to recapture him. No further mention was made of the Kissawha dam nor of the response to the editorial about it.

So far, twenty-five letters had been received, all but three criticizing *The Sentinel*. Several referred to the Piley letter.

Monday's mail was so heavy that the Editor took the whole stack to his office to open. After the blows of the past week, I could tell he was braced for more bad news. He turned over all this week's writing assignments to Emily and me, with the exception of the editorial, which he promised to have done by Wednesday.

With all the advertising elminated. Emily and I would have to scramble to fill the extra space. On a sudden impulse I did a short story of Boy's funeral, the words flowing out from my deep emotion. The focus was on Tim's

369

bereavement, and it was titled "Why Would Anyone Poison a Happy Dog?" I wondered if the Editor would okay it.

Next I called Spencer Meloy to get an updating of his work in the Lowlands. Spencer had so much news that he came to the office and talked for an hour about the way the Community Center was bringing the Lowlands people together. I spent the rest of the morning writing it up as a feature story.

The movie *It Happened One Night* was back for a rerun at the Palace after winning the Academy Award as best picture of 1934. The film technique of its director, Frank Capra, had received such worldwide recognition that it made an interesting feature story for *The Sentinel*. Graham took me to see it again Monday night, our last date before he would leave for college.

Afterward, we sipped sodas at Exley's Drug Store and reminisced over our first date at this same film almost a year before. Graham was embarrassed that his father had discontinued the ads for his auto supply store in *The Sentinel*. "We had quite a family row over it, Julie. McKeever's gone too far this time. Tell your father to keep up the fight."

We were silent for a while as a question formed in my mind. "Graham, do you go to church?"

"Not very often."

"Why not?"

"Church bores me, I guess." He thought a minute. "I'd go more often if Spencer was the preacher."

I laughed. "We're both the same. We like action. Spencer does something about a problem."

Graham took a long drink from his glass. "I believe in God, but He seems pretty far away from what goes on in this world."

"I used to think that way too, Graham. Now I'm not so sure."

Later that evening Graham suggested we drive up to Lookout Point. I didn't object one bit.

* * *

At breakfast the next morning I told Dad about Graham's encouraging words. He smiled grimly. "I hope he's right. The mail is amost entirely against us."

On Wednesday I was saying good-bye to Graham when Dean Fleming arrived and presented my father with a check for $750, enough for the $600 loan payment plus some extra. "We will survive," were his words, which Dad reported to us at dinner that night with misty eyes. After the bank note was paid on Thursday, the Editor mailed off a check to the *Cloudsville Times* to cover the first two printings they had done for us. There was barely enough money left to pay Emily her weekly salary.

My father had approved all our copy on Wednesday and set up the front page himself. To my surprise, he featured my story on Boy's death in a box on page one. Dean Fleming drove the forms to Cloudsville on Friday and once more we distributed *The Sentinel* on Saturday. When I read through the paper again that afternoon, it looked strange without the ads, but it had a lot of reader interest. A biased opinion, perhaps, since I had written most of the paper myself.

Spencer Meloy called our home shortly after seven on Sunday morning. I answered. "We're burned out," he said in a voice that shook with anger.

"What are you saying?"

"The Community Center burned down. Fire started about five a.m. The fire truck was here about ten minutes later. Not in time to save the building, but in time to keep the flames from destroying the rest of the block."

"What caused it?"

"No one knows. One fireman said defective wiring. I don't believe him."

I told Spencer that Dad and I would come right down.

The Editor and I dressed, gulped down some cereal, jumped into the Willys and drove to the Lowlands. Smoke was still rising from the ashes when we arrived. A crowd had gathered, sad-faced men and women who stared at the charred debris with such mournful faces that I felt almost sick with anger at Old Man McKeever. Who else would be behind this?

Margo and Spencer were there, picking through the smoldering ruins. Margo had in her hands a half-burned basket from the front hall; Spencer was holding a large blackened pot. As all of us stood there, feeling utterly helpless, Spencer looked up, his eyes suddenly alive.

"We're going to build a new center here in the Lowlands that will be twice as big and four times better," he promised.

As the Editor and I walked to work Monday morning, his spirit was heavy, his face drawn. "I just don't see how much longer we can go on this way," he murmured. "I can't expect Dean to keep lending us money. His resources must be limited."

"He considers it his fight, too," I said.

"I know, but there has to be some kind of positive response from the people here in Alderton that they want *The Sentinel*. If they're as opposed to it as the mail indicates, I won't want to continue publishing, no matter how much money Dean has."

I had to agree with him. Without support from local citizens, there would be no point in continuing.

"The people have to speak out now," Dean said later. "Especially after that fire in the Lowlands. Ken, let's get our group together at the cabin." It was late that night when the Editor got home.

Tuesday morning I saw the stacks of letters piled up on my father's desk. On a sudden impulse, I asked if I could read them. The Editor readily agreed. On my desk I set up two piles: eighty-six against the editorial, ten for it.

It was simple to catalogue the ten positive letters. All but one were handwritten on personal stationery. The one typed letter came from a retired businessman.

Putting the eighty-six "anti" letters in categories was

harder. The first discovery was that sixty-five of them were typed. This disproportion at first seemed to indicate that most of those letters were from professional people. But as I skimmed through the typed letters, I discovered that all but five were on plain bond typing paper. Only five professional or business people had used company stationery.

Quickly I read through the twenty-one handwritten letters. Only two were on business or professional stationery. *This has to be significant*, I thought. *But what does it mean?*

When I had studied the typed letters, I realized that they were all about the same length. The same words and phrases kept reappearing.

Then I noticed something else: in one piece of correspondence, the bottom of the lower-case letter "t" was broken. Then I almost jumped out of my chair. The same broken "t" was in a second letter. And a third!

Quickly I searched through all sixty-five typed letters and found that twenty-one of them had the broken letter "t." The same typewriter had been used for twenty-one letters!

Then if one person had written twenty-one letters, would further analysis show that other letters had been mass-produced? It did.

Grouping together those letters that used the same phrases, it was easy to conclude that probably only four people had written all sixty-five typed letters.

Next I turned to the names of the people who had signed the letters. Hard as I tried to find similarities, I had to conclude that each signature was genuine. Then came another thought. I checked our subscriber list and discovered that only nine of these eighty-six critical letter-writers were subscribers.

When I took these findings to the Editor, he pounded his fist on this desk in excitement. "The best news I've had in days. Someone engineered most of these negative letters! They're phoney! Julie, that's great work!"

* * *

Wednesday morning the Editor asked Emily to do a similar analysis of our subscription list to see how many we had lost. She worked on it to midafternoon, then came back to us wide-eyed. "I just can't believe it," she said. "Our subscribers are increasing, not decreasing." The Editor, Dean and I crowded around her report.

On October 1, 1934, total subscribers were 4,340. On January 1, 1935, the number had fallen to 4,183. Then the rise began. By August subscriptions had risen to 5,016. On September 1 they were 5,162.

During the first ten days of September, when the flood of negative mail and calls had poured in, subscriptions had not fallen but *risen by another 138*.

The Editor was incredulous. "But, Emily, I thought we were getting a lot of cancellations."

"Mr. Wallace, I confess to you that I was thoroughly deceived by these people," Emily said with flushed face. "They used abusive language to me on the phone and then demanded to have their subscription canceled. I told them this had to be done in writing and assumed this was happening."

"Another McKeever intimidation trick," Dean growled.

"These letters have been mailed by real people," I said, quickly checking names in the phone book. "There are several not listed here who probably don't have telephones."

The Editor nodded suddenly in understanding. "McKeever ordered his staff to use two types of intimidation. One verbal, one written. The verbal can't be checked, so real names were not used. Since letters would be answered, real people had to be involved—employees, friends, relatives. Four persons wrote all the letters, which were distributed for valid signatures before being mailed out."

"The people of Alderton are for us," I said passionately. "The tide has turned. You just watch."

My father grinned, then slapped Dean on the shoulder. "What can we do to start a tide of dollars coming our way?"

"I don't know, Ken. My problem is that blasted press. Sometimes I feel like throwing the whole mess in Lake Kissawha."

"Don't do that. The dam is shaky enough as it is."

Miss Cruley had been placing in my work basket indignant letters of another kind. Readers' response to my article on Boy's death astonished me: "I'm livid with anger to think that someone in our community would do such a despicable thing . . ." "Alderton has reached a new low with the poisoning of your dog."

And then one with teeth as well as feeling: "All I can do to show my fury at those who are trying to destroy *The Sentinel* is to enclose this check for ten dollars. Please send subscriptions to the list of names and addresses below. You have the most interesting newspaper in the whole state of Pennsylvania."

The Thursday morning mail brought eight letters addressed to "Kenneth Wallace, Publisher," all marked "Confidential." A few minutes later I heard a shout, then my father appeared with a look of jubilation. "You won't believe what I have here in my hands! You just won't believe it!"

Emily and I sped to his side. In one hand were eight checks. They ranged in amounts from $14.40 to $40.00. The total was $236.80.

"These are from eight of our advertisers. They're paying for the ads we're not running. It's their way of— well, read the letters." Dad was shaking with excitement.

The first was from Graham Gillin's father, who normally took an eighth of a page at $24.00.

Dear Ken:

I am very distressed at the treatment you have been receiving from certain elements in our community. Although I am not yet ready to resume my ads in *The Sentinel*, I'll be sending you the equivalent of my ad each week to help you meet your expenses. Enclosed is my check for $24.00

Do not be discouraged by the hostility you have met. Most of us like you and respect you. Carry on the good fight!

Ted Gillin

P.S. Please keep this matter confidential.

"Emily and Julie, we must protect these men. You two and Dean have to know about their actions because we're all involved with the paper's finances. But please, don't reveal this to anyone else." And the Editor fairly pranced back into his office.

Another four advertisers came personally to make their payments in cash and to pledge the Editor to secrecy. This additional $102.40 meant that we were assured $339.20 each week for the indefinite future.

Sam Gaither spent ten minutes in my father's office. "I'm not for unions, Ken," I overheard him say, "but I believe working men are getting a lousy deal. Your editorial on that issue was needed. As for the dam, I personally don't think there's any real danger, but McKeever's efforts to put you out of business disturb us deeply. That's why we got together . . ."

By the end of the week a new phenomenon was occuring—a sharp, dramatic increase in special job printings. Both Thursday and Friday Dean had to bring in two helpers to turn out the orders. His repairs on the Goss press had to be done at night.

After the Friday mail had been tabulated, we were all dazed by the turnaround that had taken place. The figures read like this:

Contributions by twelve businesses $339.20
Other cash contributions   57.00
New subscriptions this week: 250.

Cash received for new subscriptions (this week and past weeks) @$1.50	468.00
New ads: 5 ($14.40 each)	72.00
Job prints	104.00
	$1,040.20

It was the biggest week of cash receipts in *The Sentinel*'s history!

The following Monday, we had the largest influx of mail ever on any single day: over two hundred new subscriptions, plus thirty-five emotional letters addressed to me about Boy's death. Seeing them piled up on my desk, the Editor shook his head in amazement. "You just never know what will touch people's hearts."

Mail continued to flow in the rest of the week. Wednesday afternoon Neal Brinton dropped by, stuttering worse than ever with excitement. "S-s-something real big. Yoder management met yesterday on the union issue. It got hotter-n Furnace Fifty-Nine. Young Tom McKeever resigned in a s-s-showdown with his father."

The Editor, Dean Fleming and I stared at Neal in amazement. "I could sure see it coming," Dad finally said.

"S-s-starting today, I've decided to join Cade full-time in his union organizing," Neal continued. "Burning down the Community Center was the final s-straw. Yoder claims it was an accident. *No one* believes that. I think this was why young Tom resigned."

Thursday morning I looked up from my work to see Bryan McKeever bearing down on me. He had an envelope in his hand, an enigmatic grin on his face.

"I suppose you've heard the news," he began.

"That your father resigned?"

"It's true. He and Grandpa have been shouting at each other for weeks. Guess what most of it was about?"

"*The Sentinel?*"

"That and your family. Grandpa has it in for you."

"I hope your father doesn't feel that way."

"He doesn't, and this letter to your father covers that." He paused. "That story you wrote about your dog really got to my dad."

"Do you think the Old Man poisoned our dog?"

"No. But he probably arranged it."

Bryan spent a few minutes with the Editor, then left, waving at me over his shoulder.

I peeked into my father's office. He was so choked up, he just pointed to the letter and check on his desk.

The handwritten letter had one sentence: "I'm so very sorry about all that has happened." Then there was a P.S. "Somehow, some way, we'll get another place as a Community Center for the Lowlands."

The check was for $300. The Editor immediately endorsed it and mailed it to Spencer Meloy.

The Goss press was repaired in time to print the current week's *Sentinel*, a huge saving of time and money. The run was the largest ever: 7,500 copies.

When we tallied up the week's receipts on Saturday, we were stunned by the total: $1,346.45, a new high.

"Now we can pay off all our debts," the Editor said in announcing the totals. "And here's a check for what we owe you, my good friend. How can we ever thank you?"

Dean limped forward to accept the check, an almost embarrassed look on his face. "You always overplay my role here, Ken."

When we arrived home for dinner, Mother greeted us stonily, her face a thundercloud and her eyes afire. "I just can't take any more," she sputtered.

"What happened, dear?" my father said, taken aback.

"Can't you smell it?" she exploded.

"I smell something," Dad conceded.

"A jar of that wine blew up, that's what. That red

wine the children brought home is splattered all over the basement. Which now smells like a brewery."

My father grimaced, then took her in his arms. "We have reason to celebrate." And he told her of the week's record income. "Tomorrow night I'm taking the whole family out to dinner. Don't worry about the wine, dear. We'll clean it up later."

He paused, then continued. "There's more good news. I had a call from our landlord today. He told me that we won't have to move out of our house next month. I believe he's going to find some way of postponing the eviction month by month."

The tide was turning our way all right, as Dean had predicted. But another statement from our remarkable friend stuck in my mind: "We're still a long way from winning this battle."

That weekend was quiet and peaceful. For a change, the Editor and I did not go to *The Sentinel*; instead, with Tim's ankles showing beneath his pants cuffs and Anne-Marie desperately needing a dress, the whole family went shopping. That evening the Editor took us all out for dinner at Haslam House. Looking about the dining room as we ate, I marveled at the dignity and efficiency of the service. In the midst of all the recent turmoil of our lives, Haslam House seemed the epitome of solidity and durability.

That night the news on the radio featured a labor leader named John L. Lewis. Members of his United Mine Workers had posted signs everywhere, reading: *President Roosevelt wants you to join the union*. The commentator then gave details of the new Social Security Act, passed August 14, which he predicted would someday make retirement much easier for Americans. We paid little attention to a bulletin about the hurricane which had struck the Texas coast. The storm had moved inland after causing moderate damage, with heavy rains forecast by midweek for western Pennsylvania.

* * *

The volume of mail was down Monday, but new subscriptions were still coming in. The residents of Alderton and surrounding areas seemed aware of *The Sentinel* as never before.

That afternoon an official from the Pennsylvania Railroad appeared at the office and asked to see the engineer's report on the Kissawha dam. He read it through carefully, then waited while Miss Cruley walked down to City Hall to make a copy for him. He left *The Sentinel*, on his way to the Hunting and Fishing Club.

Wednesday afternoon a telephone call came to my father from a law firm in Pittsburgh. A few minutes later the Editor opened his office and motioned for Dean and me to join him there. He gave us the news in a low voice.

"McKeever is suing *The Sentinel* for two million dollars. He claims that irresponsible and erroneous reporting on the dam has damaged his credibility and caused him physical and mental suffering . . . and so forth and so forth. The lawyer read the full statement to me, said we would have it in writing by tomorrow and advised me to retain legal counsel."

"He has no grounds to sue," I said hotly.

"He doesn't need grounds," replied Dean. "He's been hurt and this is his way of lashing back. A last-ditch effort to get back at you financially, Ken."

"The legal costs could sink me," the Editor admitted.

"My suggestion is to get a good lawyer and battle back. If you win, McKeever has to pay all the costs."

"My Pittsburgh friend, Cy Stearns, can help me here," Dad said slowly. But the tension lines were back on his face.

Later that night the Editor was at his desk, bending over what I assumed were accounts. He was so fatigued he could hardly keep his eyes open. Not the right time to ask him questions, I decided.

But he saw me and looked up. The love for me in his

eyes made me choke up for a moment. Impulsively I went over and kissed him. "I love you, Dad," I said softly.

He took my hand and held it to his cheek. "What a difference a year has made in you."

"How have I changed?"

My father smiled. "You've grown up so much, I scarcely know you."

"You've changed too, Dad."

A look of protest crossed his face, then he relaxed. "I guess I have—some. For years I lived in inner terror that I was, at heart, a weak and indecisive man. I think it was this fear that made me sick. Dean showed me how foolish all this was. 'Face the truth, Ken,' he told me. 'You *are* weak. All of us are. Come to terms with it.'

"But then he pointed out I didn't have to stay this way, that God was certainly not weak. Dean has helped me understand that if I have the Spirit of God within me, then His strength would replace my weakness. I've been trying to live that for the past six months."

That night I wrote for a long time in my journal. Something was happening inside me, too, that I did not understand. The article on Boy, for example. It seemed that once again I was getting help from something outside myself.

41

SATURDAY, September 21, 1935, began in such a normal way.

There had been heavy rain across western Pennsylvania on Friday as predicted. It rained especially hard north of Alderton between midnight and six a.m.

When we gathered for breakfast, Mother outlined for Tim some chores she wanted done that morning. The twelve-year-old objected so vigorously that Dad had to silence him. "You will do what your mother says," he ordered.

"Troy Gillin and I were going hiking today," Tim protested.

"Call Troy and tell him you can't go until after lunch. It's too wet this morning anyway."

Muttering to himself, Tim turned to his breakfast as his sister entered her plea. "They're expecting me at the Fleming farm this morning. Queenie's about to have her puppies."

My father sighed. This was harder to handle. "Call Hazel and ask her if you can come out after lunch. If not, then I guess you can do your chores this afternoon."

Dad then stated that this was the day he had chosen to clean up the basement mess caused by the bursting wine bottle.

Anne-Marie was soon back to report that Hazel needed her this morning. Dad capitulated and agreed to drive her to the farm in the Willys. As Anne-Marie skipped out the front door, she stuck out her tongue at Tim, who scowled back at her.

Life and death for everyone in Alderton that day hung on such small decisions as to where they would be in the early afternoon.

I carried my lunch to *The Sentinel*, planning to work through the afternoon. When I arrived, Emily Cruley was already there, poring over the subscription list, her black leather case open on her desk with the ledger planted in front of her. She announced self-righteously that it would take her all day to bring it up to date.

Dean Fleming was due in the office after lunch to work on the Goss press.

When Emily asked me if I would take all telephone calls, I moved into Dad's office. At eleven-thirty Rand phoned, very agitated. "Julie, I need to see you. Are you free this afternoon?"

"I'm here at *The Sentinel* all day."

"I'll be there shortly after one."

"Is something wrong?"

"Yes. Things here are in a fright. After he sacked me, the Old Man told me to stay until the Club was closed up. But since that official from the railroad stopped by to see him yesterday, he has been in a towering ill humor. This morning he called and told me to clear out by noon today. All my things are in the boot of my car."

"Did you know he is suing *The Sentinel* for two million dollars?"

There was silence, and then a whistle at the other end of the line. "He's lashing out at everyone in sight."

"The Old Man's not there now, I gather, or you wouldn't be talking so freely."

"He's at the *Vulcania*. But you never know when he'll show up. Can't wait to get out of here. I'll see you in about two hours."

At twelve-thirty Rand called again. "Julie, I'm not sure when I can make it. The rain last night was so heavy that the lake is rising very rapidly. We've opened the spillways, but it looks as if there'll be an overflow. I'll ring you up later.''

Rand telephoned a third time while I was eating my sandwich. His voice was tense. ''I'm leaving right now to see you.''

''Is the dam all right?'' I asked.

''I can't tell. A lot of men are there working on it.''

When he hung up, I had an eerie feeling that I should call him back and ask him to meet me at our home instead. *How silly!*

When Rand arrived, he walked swiftly back to the Editor's office. As he closed the door and turned to me, I was astonished at his appearance. His hair was a tousled mess, his face was flushed, his shirt rumpled. I had never seen him so wrought up.

''Dean just called,'' I said. ''Worried about the dam. He's coming down to grease the press. Thinks we ought to clear out.''

Rand nodded, flicked a shock of red hair out of his eyes and grinned at me. ''May I kiss you?'' he asked.

The look in his eyes made me tremble. ''Why so sudden?''

He pulled me to my feet. ''No reason. I've been wanting to kiss you for two weeks now—no, three—no, it's closer to four.''

I started to resist, but his lips closed over mine. His intensity so overwhelmed me I could scarcely breathe. When we broke apart and I caught a breath, his lips found mine again. Moments later I pulled away and sat down numbly in Dad's chair.

''Rand, please.''

He shook his head, sat down beside me, and began to stroke my hair. Then he drew my face toward him and kissed each eye and the tip of my nose before he reached my mouth again. It was hypnotic.

The telephone rang. I was so weak I could barely lift the receiver. ''Hello.''

A strangled voice spoke, one of Dean's friends. "Get out quickly! The dam broke! A wall of water is heading for Alderton."

Rand saw the fear on my face and grabbed my hand as we ran out of the office toward the front door. "The dam broke!" I shouted at Emily.

As we reached the door, two people from the street had pushed it open from the outside. "Too late!" one shouted. "You can hear the water coming. To the top floor!"

We all turned and scrambled frantically up the stairs.

42

THERE is no way I can describe the mammoth tragedy of Saturday, September 21, 1935, except to put together chronologically the graphic details given me over a period of months and even years afterward by my family and friends, as well as other survivors.

The heavy rain of Friday night covered all of western Pennsylvania. In the mountain area just north of the Kissawha dam there was a torrential downpour that totaled nearly 15 inches in a three-hour period. The runoff into the lake from the two feeder streams, Bear Creek and Smather's Run, began about 6:00 Saturday morning.

One viewer described these streams at 9:00 a.m. as "going berserk." Smàther's Run, seldom more than 10 feet wide and 2 feet deep, was nearly 50 feet wide and stripping branches off trees 5 feet off the ground.

At 10:00 a.m. a resident of the Hunting and Fishing Club climbed into his small outboard and chugged around the side of the lake. "The meadowland was under water in spots almost 300 feet from the edge of the lake," he reported. "Debris everywhere, mostly logs washed down from a sawmill miles away. The lake was a mass of junk."

All available heavy-duty manpower had been gathered by 11:00 that morning as the lake rose quickly and threatened to spill over the dam. The sluice guards and spillways were opened wide. Then one group of men began to pry away the drift guards and tear up the road to get at the heavy iron gratings in the spillway which kept fish from escaping down Brady Creek.

To ease the growing pressure on the earthen dam, several men grabbed pickaxes and shovels and began digging a ditch about 25 feet from the dam's breast to act as a makeshift spillway. Another group had gone to the far end of the dam to dig a new waste-weir. After twenty minutes of work they hit hard rock and had to give up.

By 12:00 the water had reached the top of the dam and began to spill over into the creek below. The earthen channels and cement buttresses directed the overflow to Laurel Run, which had changed in a few hours from a gentle stream to a small river of surging brown water overflowing its banks as it coursed down into Somerset Valley.

The panting, gasping workers tearing up the road to dislodge the gratings encountered iron grids rusted and wedged in by years of overgrowth. The heaviest crowbars wielded by the strongest men could not budge them.

By 1:00 p.m. logs, tree branches and other flotsam flowing into the lake from the two feeder streams had reached the dam, adding to the pressure on it. Suddenly workers were horrified to see several large concrete blocks loosen, then tumble thunderously into the stream below. A geyser of water shot 30 feet into the air.

At this point the workers made a final effort to slow the overflow by pouring wheelbarrows full of rocks across the road atop the dam. The heavy rocks were washed off like pebbles.

At 1:30 dam erosion had created a V shaped notch about 6 feet wide and 2 feet deep in the breast of the dam. As it continued to widen and deepen, the workers knew the dam was lost and began a retreat toward the Club. Suddenly a big chunk of the roadway over the dam collapsed and was washed away.

Within minutes the opening was so large a yacht could have cruised through it. A sheet of water nearly 60 feet wide was now pouring over and through the opening. So far the concrete buttresses had easily diverted the heavy overflow away from the Sequanoto River into Laurel Run. Onlookers then witnessed an awesome sight. The main part of the earthen dam and the road above it did not burst or crumble, it just moved away. The water, treetop high, exploded over the dam like a living force, sweeping everything before it: trees, other vegetation, rocks, concrete, and all man-made objects.

The onslaught of water hit the new waterway area with the roar of an express train. Twenty-foot-high mounds of earth supported by cement retaining walls crumbled, then dissolved into hundreds of missilelike objects and became a part of the roaring torrent that joined the Sequanoto River as it thundered toward Yancyville.

It was 2:10 p.m.

It took only 27 minutes for Lake Kissawha to empty over 500 million tons of water into the valleys below. Engineers later estimated that 118 tons of water per second pounding away at the dam wall had pushed away 90,000 cubic yards of earth and stone, which went tumbling downstream.

The workers watched, incredulous at the sheer velocity and brute force roaring into the valley. The water snapped century-old four-foot-thick trees as if they were twigs, sometimes uprooting them altogether, and propelled them forward like matchsticks in the debris-filled, swirling torrent. The growing mass of water tore huge boulders from the stream banks and rolled them over and over as if they were marbles.

What remained of the lake bottom was now 800 acres of brown ooze, separated here and there by a few small streams flowing quietly in the direction of the dam. Black bass, pike and trout were flopping about in the mud at the bottom of the reservoir basin.

The course of the flood waters was strangely selective, though it mostly followed the Sequanoto River bed, which flowed through Yancyville, Mills Ford, and then into Alderton. Yancyville was the first hit.

Anne-Marie, who had stayed through lunch and was to be picked up later by Margo, was in the kitchen of the farmhouse with Hazel Fleming when she observed Queenie behaving strangely. The usually placid dog, now pregnant, was dashing about the yard whining and whimpering. Suddenly the collie sped toward the small cabin as if in great pain. Anne-Marie, who could not stand to see any animal hurting, hurried after Queenie to see what was wrong.

From her position on the hillside beside the cabin, Anne-Marie heard the flood coming before she saw it. "It was like the roar of a fast freight rain," she said later. The noise was obviously painful to Queenie's sensitive ears. Whimpering even more, the dog crept close to Anne-Marie's legs for protection.

Now the booming freight-train sound was closer, just around the bend in the river. Anne-Marie stood rooted by the cabin, craning her neck to see. Her first impression was that a dark mist was rolling in. The she saw a 50-foot-high wave of debris hurtling forward. She watched in horror as the wall of junk slammed into the right side of the farmhouse. Above the sound of splintering wood and crashing glass, her own screams seemed disembodied.

The roof of the farmhouse tilted sideways. The trunk of a large tree then tore through the second-story window above the porch, leaving half of the tree hanging grotesquely outside, swaying in the air. The whole building dissolved and was sucked up into the dark mass.

Behind the mountain of trash came the water: huge, churning waves over 75 feet high, carrying along on their swirling surface cows, horses, pigs, trees, sections of fences, boulders.

And yes, human bodies. A woman's long hair floated on the water. *Could that be Hazel?* Then the heaving waves thrust a man's body halfway out of the water, only to suck him under again.

Sobbing, Anne-Marie turned her head away. A thunderous crash drew her gaze back. A second wave of water, equally high and spread over a wider front, had crushed the two walls of the big red Fleming barn. The ripping, tearing sound of wood, plus the terrified squeals of the animals, sickened her. Just a half-hour before, she and Hazel had gone to feed the two Guernsey cows, the riding horses, and the beloved old swayback Shorty. All were now a part of the rushing, tumbling torrent.

The flow of water continued for about 20 minutes, then stopped. Because the log cabin had been built on higher ground, the raging water had just missed it. In fact, the cabin was standing there serenely intact, as though viewing with equanimity the total annihilation of the farmhouse, its mistress, and the barn.

Dazed, blinded by her tears, Anne-Marie made her way back down the hill. What had been a gracious dwelling minutes before was litter-strewn ground: a piece of brass, fragments of glass, a kitchen knife, a dented pot, several broken springs, fragments of wood and metal. That mighty body of water had swept away everything else.

Half of Yancyville was demolished by the flood, half was spared. Those farms, houses and stores on the west side of Seven Mile Mountain Road were swept away. Buildings on the east side were on higher ground and suffered only minor damage.

Just below Yancyville the steel bridge over the Sequanoto River took the full brunt of the waters. Said one observer: "The bridge squirted into the air in a crazy L-shape, then exploded into pieces and was gone."

Mills Ford was the next target.

At 2:11 the Allegheny Local, an eight-car passenger train which serviced some twenty stops between Altoona and Pittsburgh, stopped at Mills Ford to discharge and take on passengers, mail, and freight. The exchange usually took 5 minutes.

At 2:13 the railroad clerk received a frantic call from the Yancyville station. He listened for less than 10 seconds, then raced outside, shouting at the conductor. ''Get the train out of here! The dam broke and the water is heading this way!''

A whistle blew, the loading of freight was stopped, and the train pulled out of the station, one minute ahead of the water, slowly building up momentum. A mile south of Mills Ford the tracks turned from the riverbed and climbed to higher ground. Would the train reach this spot in time?

With a grade crossing 300 yards ahead, the engineer pulled the cord of his locomotive whistle. He never let it go for the next 2 1/2 minutes.

The first wall of water hit Mills Ford at 2:16. Warned by the train whistle and shouting word-of-mouth, over half the population had scampered to higher ground. The station clerk, who fled with the others, later described the approaching mass as ''a brown hill a hundred feet high rolling over and over.'' A flour mill, five stores, eight houses and the railroad station were obliterated by the first onslaught of water. Pieces of railroad track were spinning and flying about ''like someone had rained down a shower of steel spikes from above.''

The second wave of water collected three more houses, a wooden church and a warehouse. As the roof of one of the houses disappeared down the valley, a naked man was seen on top of it, holding frantically to what remained of the chimney.

Ahead of the water the engineer of the Alleghony Local had pushed his throttle as wide open as he could. But before the lifesaving high ground could be reached, the track bed ahead made a sharp turn around a bend in the river.

A truck driver on Seven Mile Mountain Road several hundred feet above the railroad tracks saw the train's race against death. The water, a tumbling, foaming, debris-clogged mass, closed the gap quickly as the train made its circuitous turn around the bend in the river.

A hundred yards was the difference. The engine had

reached high ground, but the roiling water thundered into the last five cars and sucked them up like pieces of kindling, sending them tumbling and bouncing about until they broke apart. The engine and three other cars were yanked sideways and flipped over.

In the seconds that passed before the second wave of water struck, seven people scrambled from the first three cars of the train and reached high ground. Then the second force surged into the helpless and prostrate train and lifted up its parts as an ocean wave picks up flotsam along a beach.

The last view the truck driver had was of engine and cars cartwheeling down the floor of the riverbed like a toy train bouncing down a flight of stairs. Death had won the race.

As the first body of water approached Alderton the weight of its accumulated debris—trees, buildings, automobiles, trucks, railroad cars—slowed it down. At times it appeared to be an almost gelatinous mass, giving out logs, hunks of metal, bodies and boulders along the way. The second body of water caught up to the first about a quarter of a mile north of the turnoff road to McKeever's Bluff.

When the second mound of water hit the first, there was a thunderous roar, as though a bomb had gone off. The whole mass seemed to explode into a thousand multicolored pieces. The rays of the afternoon sun revealed one section of the mass as emerald green, another jet black, still another an oily brown, while pieces of metal caught the sunlight in a weird pinwheel effect. Then for no discernible reason, the watery ball veered to the right and ripped a gaping swath through the wooded area behind McKeever's Bluff.

Several viewers lived to describe what then happened. "Like a scene in a movie spectacular," said one. "As though the god of water picked up the *Vulcania* like a small toy and threw it over the cliff."

Another said, "It looked from a distance as though the

water just nudged the *Vulcania* over the cliff. The *Vulcania* seemed to struggle for a moment as if clawing for its life, then it fell.''

The car twisted completely around before tumbling the first hundred feet, where it hit a clump of trees. For a few seconds the *Vulcania* hesitated, then spun, pirouetted and plunged forward end over end.

''It crashed, bounced, slammed into the ground, bounced again as if it had been a pogo stick,'' reported one witness. ''I think it did that four or five times.''

At the last crashing impact, a burst of flame shot out one end of the car. Then the *Vulcania* began a slow, rolling, bouncing fall the last few hundred yards up to the outskirts of Alderton. It was a flaming torch when it finally came to rest at the bottom of the hill. A wall of water rolled over the *Vulcania*, dissolving it and the two human beings inside into a thousand fragments.

When the dam waters hit Alderton, they were about 30 feet high, 500 feet wide and 2 miles long.

The time was 2:19.

43

I<small>T</small> takes a moment to react to crisis. When the cry came, "To the top floor," I darted about looking for my sweater. Rand's shout brought me to my senses. He grabbed my hand and fairly propelled me up the stairs.

Emily Cruley had been reluctant to leave her desk. The panic in the faces of the two women pushing through the front door ignited her. Out of the corner of my eye, I saw Emily scrambling toward the stairs, subscription case held tightly to her bosom.

At the top of the stairs I heard a shout, turned, and observed Dean Fleming coming through the front door. He gave a quick look about the office and scurried jerkily after us up the stairs, the bad leg hardly slowing him down at all. In addition to the six of us who raced upstairs from the *Sentinel* office, five others had scampered up the staircase from the side entrance.

The view out of the north window of the second floor was frightening. Panicky people were running and scurrying about on the sidewalk in a state of confusion, some heading one direction, some another. The din was growing: dogs barking, women screaming, men shouting, whistles blowing, church bells ringing.

Two comparable scenes flashed through my mind. The first was a picture I remembered in an old religious book of confused people running about on the Day of Judgment. The second was a sight that had turned my stomach as a little girl in Timmeton: a hen flopping around, this way and that, after Dad had chopped her head off.

Suddenly we saw the reason for the pandemonium below. A dark, misty wall of water was bearing down upon us, one block away. The sound that preceded it was like rolling thunder.

"Upstairs!" The order came from Dean Fleming.

My last glance at the dark mass revealed all sorts of objects swirling in it: an automobile, a bicycle, a push-cart, street signs, the bodies of several men, plus a woman holding her child.

Rand held my hand as we rushed up the twisting stairs to the top floor; behind us came Dean and Emily, who still clutched her black case. The third floor contained trunks and boxes scattered about, old-fashioned clothes trees standing upright, sporting costumes and uniforms; clothes on hangers dangling from hooks in the rafters; still more elaborate costumes on department store dummies. One corner contained boxes of Christmas decorations.

Rand pulled me aside, placed his mouth close to my ear. "Whatever happens, Julie, I love you."

Grinding, buckling noises shook the floor; the entire building groaned. Rand and I fell on the floor as a huge tree crashed through one window. The bodies of a brown dog and a half-clothed man burst through the opening. Our screams were drowned by awesome noises all around us.

How can I find the words to describe the sounds and sensations of a building breaking up? Swirling waters were hurling assault after assault at the foundation. Timbers cracked, then splintered; mortar crumbled; entire walls heaved and buckled.

A rain of dirt and small particles showered us from the ceiling. When the building suddenly tilted, costumes and decorations flew in every direction. Rand and I were back on our feet, arms around each other. Dean was next to us, protecting Emily with his body. I heard these words:

> God is our refuge and strength . . . Therefore we
> will not fear . . . Though the waters, roar, though
> the mountains shake . . .

Abruptly the floor under us split in two. Next, the seams at the top of the gabled roof ruptured and we could see daylight just above us. Water began pouring in through the openings and the floor began to sink under us.

Numbly, I saw the opening above us as the only escape. Then I found myself thinking that clambering through that space would take no more agility than climbing the cherry tree in our back yard, as I had done dozens of times. I jumped on top of a nearby trunk, pointing to the daylight above. Rand leaped up beside me, grabbed me with his sinewy arms, strengthened by years of rowing, and propelled me toward the light above.

Desperately, I clutched the broken edge of the roof and pulled myself on top. Then I turned to give Rand a hand. He was gone.

The building seemed to explode underneath, throwing me halfway off my platform of safety. Pieces of timber fell about me. The mass of water catapulted my perch forward as I clawed to keep my handhold. It was tipped at a crazy angle and spun around several times, banging into logs, bales of wire and metal junk. Dazed, I coughed up brown fluid and clung to my section of roofing.

Twice my raft almost spun over as I found myself on the crest of a river of debris, cruising through downtown Alderton, watching building after building crumble, then disintegrate. The rushing floodwaters had been slowed by Alderton's stone, brick, and wooden structures. I guessed we were moving no faster now than 15 miles per hour.

I sensed I would not survive if I remained on such a

wobbly raft. The roof of a small house swirled by. In desperation, I leaped toward it. My feet went into the water, but miraculously I was able to pull myself on top of it. Then that rooftop was struck by another wall of water and began to buck and lurch like a wild bronco. On hands and knees, scrambling and clawing, frantically I clung to it.

I had just a moment to wonder about Rand, Dean, and Emily when the branches of a tree swung by and knocked me off my rocking rooftop. Down I plunged into the murky depths. "This is death," I told myself with surprising calm as blackness settled over me.

But then I was catapulted up to the surface beside a large piece of wreckage. I reached out and grabbed a sodden canvas awning dangling off a piece of house siding. I tried to pull myself up but could not. All my strength seemed to have drained from my arms and hands. There was no way I could hang on for long.

The words Dean Fleming had muttered came back to me: "God is our refuge and strength . . ."

"Lord, if You have anything for me to do in this life, please save me," I pleaded.

For years afterward I would have the same dream: I was hanging, dangling, gripping that canvas with my fingernails, spitting out putrid water, flinging heavenward my stumbling prayer, knowing that soon my grip would loosen and I would sink down, down . . .

I felt something brush by. A large tree, torn out by the roots, nuzzled me. With a sudden infusion of strength I pulled myself into the branches and then onto the large tree trunk. *Wonderful, protective trees! How I have always loved you!*"

As I lay there on my stomach, I was able to stare out at scenes all around me—an immense steel girder poking up through the muck; a woman's body clutching a baby and turning over and over in the water; one of the store dummies, floating by serenely, hardly distinguishable from other bodies; an entire family—father, mother, and two little children—kneeling on the siding of a house. As the current quickened, speeding by me went one dead cow, the bodies of two riding horses, the back of a hay wagon, and a school of rats swimming smoothly behind a staircase that could have come from our office building.

One hefty woman covered with tar was riding astride a barrel which kept rolling from side to side while she screamed in terror. A man rode past me, standing on a large garage door. It was Salvatore Mazzini, the Italian shoe repair man, all alone and totally naked; he raised one hand toward Heaven in supplication. Aware that I was shivering, I looked down and made a shocking discovery—all my clothing had been torn off. I, too, was stripped bare. "Please, let this be a bad dream," I heard myself saying.

But it was not a bad dream. I was astride a large tree, bruised, naked, terrified, as the flood debris verged into one body of water moving along the riverbed. My tree had slowed down so that instead of holding on to the branches with all my strength, I could sit up a bit and look forward. What I saw was not reassuring. Dead ahead, about 300 yards, was Railroad Bridge, that stone relic from the past century. People had called it ugly, too small for modern traffic, and a transit hazard for all except the smallest boats. It was built to last centuries.

One anguished look now told me why. Much of the flood had rushed over, under, or by either side of the bridge, which had resisted an immense tonnage of water power. It had remained firm when assailed by logs, trees and pieces of housing. Trucks, railroad cars and whole houses had not budged it. When a locomotive smashed against two stone pilings, bystanders later reported that the bridge trembled, but held.

All these big objects blocked up the passageways underneath the bridge, creating a pileup that had quickly reached the top of the bridge and was backed up hundreds of yards in an area as wide and long as three city blocks. Then came the most terrifying sight of all.

Fire suddenly shot out of a small house that had

crunched up against the far left section of the bridge. As I watched, the flames leapt high, obviously fed by oil or gasoline. With a brisk breeze now blowing, the entire mass backed up behind the bridge could soon turn into a fiery torch.

What escape was there? The water had slowed down enough that for a desperate moment I considered swimming for the bank. But it was too far off and the water was churning with debris.

Could I steer the tree away from the fire? Several kicks in the water quickly showed me the futility of that approach.

Despairingly I looked behind me for help. Dirt-colored water extended as far back as I could see, floating the wildest collection of objects, living and dead, swimming and drifting, all heading for Railroad Bridge. *And all set to pile up on top of me*, I thought with horror. I wanted to scream, shout, cry, but to whom? Everyone around me was either dead, seriously hurt, or struggling to survive. At least I was astride something unsinkable.

There was nothing I could do, except . . . Then I remembered feeling this same terror once before—during that wild ride down Seven Mile Mountain in Bryan's car.

I prayed again, "Lord, are You there?" It was a pathetic plea, a bare whisper, as though I were ashamed to call attention to myself in my nakedness. *How ridiculous! I'm about to die and yet still concerned about how I look. Have I always been this vain?* Then I laughed. The whole thing was ludicrous. I was stripped down to nothing. I came into the world with nothing on; I was going out the same way. Why was I ashamed of being the way the Lord made me?

The thought freed me. I straightened up, realizing that in my hunched-over state, I had assumed an almost fetal position. I was certainly not ashamed of my body—in fact, I had admired it in the privacy of my room. I looked around me again. Then I stood up to see better.

The sun had gone. The sky was overcast and drops of

rain pelted down. I liked the feeling of the rain on my body. I looked up and let it wet my face. Tears came, I don't know why. They poured from my eyes and mixed on my face with the rain.

A new, tingling sensation flooded me. It seemed to start in my feet and work upward. How to describe something I had never felt before? Exhilaration. Joy. Elation. Warmth. A combination of all. But something more, too. Caring. No, stronger than that. *Love.* That was it!

I was being suffused with love. Washed in it. It penetrated every cell in my body. I was being totally, completely loved. By whom? By Someone I did not know, but wanted to know very much.

I stood as straight as I could and reached for the invisible sun.

44

Nineteen minutes had passed from the time the dam was breached until the wall of floodwater smashed into the outskirts of Alderton. North Bridge took the full impact. Three cars were crossing the bridge at the time; the cars pinwheeled and somersaulted into the air like toys, then were swallowed up. The asphalt surface on the bridge simply disappeared, leaving the bridge skeleton tilting at a grotesque angle.

The wave of water then seemed to separate. One mass roared southwest into downtown Alderton. The other veered to the east side of the Sequanoto River and bore down on the Lowlands.

The first building hit in Alderton was the one-story brick dwelling and office of dentist Harry Froehling. It was smothered by the 30-foot-high mass of watery debris. Only the foundation was left. Harry had dashed to safety only minutes before.

Next struck was a vacant two-story wooden structure that had once been used as a stable. It exploded in a shower of kindling.

Jordan's Hardware was obliterated before the mass bored into the three-story *Sentinel* building. Observers seemed to agree that this structure put up a fight. The dark, broiling wall broke around the building, causing it to shudder violently. As the follow-up waters continued to cascade into it, *The Sentinel's* home began to totter and tilt. The roof split with a shriek, a part of it torn away.

People were seen spurting out of the top, spinning, whirling, scrambling, clutching at anything for support.

Then, slowly, the whole building broke apart, floor by floor, and was swept away. Dean Fleming held on to Emily Cruley as they were propelled through an opening in the roof. He managed to get Emily up on a piece of roofing before a tumbling beam knocked him unconscious and he was sucked down into the torrent. Emily was later pulled from the waters, still alive and still clutching her black leather subscription case to her bosom.

Rand was catapulted into the turgid waters and, being a good swimmer, tried to keep himself afloat. Bruised and buffeted, he grabbed a heavy beam as it sped by and hung on to it grimly until his legs were smashed by the pileup at Railroad Bridge. It took rescuers several hours to pry him loose from the debris; by then he was near death from loss of blood.

Of the seven others who scrambled to the top floor of the *Sentinel* building with us, only one survived—a woman who was rescued from the mess at Railroad Bridge.

After conquering the *Sentinel* building, the floodwaters roared into the heart of Alderton, looking for bigger challenges. Salvatore Mazzini's shoe repair shop was no obstacle. It was swept up like a piece of flotsam as the old man leapt onto a garage door that was spinning by. Mazzini's body was recovered later, burned almost beyond recognition by the fire.

Onlookers thought that surely the six-story Haslam House, a solid brick structure, would withstand the roiling waters. At first it seemed to. As the first wave crashed into the brick building, it trembled, but held. It resisted the following assaults too, until a tumbling locomotive gashed a deep hole on the west side of the building, at about the second-floor level. The wound was serious. Waters rushed into it, causing the hole to widen. Screams poured out from the guests as the top floors began to settle. The relentless, flowing mass of debris bubbled into the hotel like poison, smashing doors, splitting seams, breaking furniture. The ballroom, scene of our graduation dance, contained the instruments and music stands of a band that had been practicing only moments before. Warned of the approaching waters, members of the band had scrambled to the top floors of the hotel. Soon their left-behind trombones, saxophones, trumpets and a bass drum were sucked into the mass of flood debris. When the third and fourth floors of the west side of the hotel collapsed, the whole building shuddered, bobbled, groaned and then broke apart.

Eighty-eight people were in Haslam House when the floodwaters arrived, including Vincent Piley, Tom McKeever, Jr., and two executives of the Pennsylvania Railroad, who were meeting in Tom's sixth-floor suite. When the hotel was swept away, only twenty-four survived. One of the survivors was young Tom McKeever. The others in his suite drowned.

The flood was almost capricious in what it devoured and what it spared in Alderton. All buildings on the eastern end of Main Street for a depth of four blocks were destroyed. Stores on the western end were damaged, but not seriously—not even as badly as in the April miniflood. Gillin Auto Supply and Gaither's Clothing Store were two that were spared.

Separated by North Bridge into two masses, the floodwaters pouring into downtown Alderton divided once again, one section wiping out that four-block section east of Main Street and continuing to Railroad Bridge; the other veering west and destroying a dozen residences. The unpredictable floodwaters demolished Baker Memorial Church but left almost intact the church education building, scene of Spencer Meloy's dismissal, and came within a block of Bank Place before dissipating.

The mass of water and debris that veered east of North Bridge created more havoc than her twin sister. First to receive the onslaught was the Trentler Wireworks warehouse. Waters thundered into this tin structure, ripping it apart as if it were a cracker box. Pieces of tin siding were soon whirling and twisting in the vortex. Far worse, hundreds of bales of wire were spewed up and out of the building, glinting in the waters like an explosion of fine, silvery hairs. Thousands of feet of wire soon entangled everything in the debris-filled waters, creating a new horror for those swimmers who were still struggling for their lives. A dozen deaths were later attributed to the strangling effects of these silvery tentacles, which wrapped around trees, railroad cars, automobiles, houses, animals—and human beings.

The flood mass licked at the edges of Yoder Steel and then barreled into the railroad yards south of the steel plant. One roundhouse seemed to melt under the onslaught; the other was badly damaged. A dozen engines were lifted up and tossed aside like wood chips on an ocean wave. Several went cartwheeling with the main body of debris that later hurled itself against Railroad Bridge. A tank car of gasoline rose ten feet off the ground, spun, crashed into an engine and split in two, spraying gasoline over everything within a 100-foot radius.

Twenty-five freight cars and eighteen passenger cars either broke apart or simply floated away. Five engine tenders were later discovered half-buried in the sand. One boxcar tore throught a small Roman Catholic church nearby, scattering pews, statues and religious artifacts. Some were later recovered miles from the site. The waters tore up the railroad yards, with hundreds of broken tracks cascading throughout the area, ripping through houses, impaling people and animals.

Spencer Meloy received a frantic call at 2:15 that the dam had broken. "You've got fifteen minutes, maybe twenty, before the water hits Alderton," he was told. "Clear out those in the Lowlands."

That Spencer was at home when the call came probably saved three hundred lives. Margo and four wives of steelworkers were meeting with him. The six of them ran from the house through the streets, screaming warnings. Hardly anyone even bothered to open doors or look out their windows. Next they banged on front doors, shouting, cajoling, begging people to run for their lives. A few caught on and began to pile belongings onto carts, bicycles, even toy wagons.

"You haven't time to save anything but yourselves!" Spencer would shout.

Margo began to grab babies and children, pulling, prodding and pushing them toward the sloping wooded area a few hundred yards away.

Gradually a slumbering, heavy-spirited community came to life. Night-shift workers appeared, roused from sleep. The trickle of people moving toward the eastern ridge grew into a throng. But many kept returning to their homes to pick up more belongings.

As the flow of people to the area of safety and back seemed almost equal, Spencer grew frantic. He looked at his watch. "We have only minutes!" he screamed. "Everyone to higher ground!"

Then he saw Margo running back into the housing area. "No more time, Margo," he shouted.

"There's another baby," she sobbed, and kept running.

"Too late. Come back," Spencer yelled.

Margo shook her head and kept going. Spencer started to run after her, then stopped. He had to keep people moving to safety.

A minute later, the first rumble was heard from the north. "Here it comes!" someone shouted.

All listlessness disappeared. Panic took over. People began swarming from the houses now, stumbling, scrambling toward higher ground, dropping heavy household items as they ran.

Then they saw it—a brown wave 30 feet or more high, devouring everything in its path. It was a hundred yards away when Spencer saw Margo dash out of one of the houses with a baby in her arms. A sob in his throat, he began to run toward her.

"Pastor, don't!" someone shouted.

Spencer was moving against such a frenzied tide of people that he soon realized the futility of his effort and stopped.

The wall of dirty brown debris ripped into the Lowlands exactly 15 minutes after the warning. Some Yoder houses were lifted off their foundations like tea leaves and swept intact toward Railroad Bridge; others dissolved into hundreds of pieces. One row of six houses was upended to a vertical position for an agonizing moment. A bed with a man in it shot out one end. Two other bodies spilled out of windows. Then the houses collapsed inside each other like a deflated accordion.

Margo was not the only person running for her life. A bearded steelworker was sprinting beside her, holding a bottle of whiskey in one hand and a small radio in the other. Three heavyset women were 20 feet ahead of them, but losing ground fast. All were running east while the floodwaters bore down on them from the north.

The baby Margo was carrying was small, but heavy enough to slow her down. As the steelworker ran by her, she shouted something at him. He paused, turned, dropped the whiskey bottle and grabbed the baby from Margo, barely shifting his stride.

Six people in a race against death. The steelworker picked up speed and with the baby, clambered up the bank to safety. Margo passed the three women who, seconds later, were swept off by the water to their death.

As Margo clawed her way up the bank, the lip of the flood caught her, spun her backward. "Spencer," she wailed, her eyes imploring.

Meloy lunged toward her, his eyeglasses flying off as he tried to dive into the water. Two men grabbed him and pinned him to the ground. Margo's body was sucked into the swirling waters and she was gone. Death had claimed four of the six.

The wall of muck surged through the Lowlands, leveling nearly every house; over one hundred people there were drowned. Some five hundred reached the safety of the eastern slope, thanks to the heroic efforts of Spencer, Margo and the four housewives.

Next the waters slammed into the Stemwinder. The two-story building shook violently, groaned, then split apart with a loud explosion. A mass of broken liquor bottles, kitchen utensils, silverware, tables and chairs, plus another six bodies, joined the turgid, debris-jammed water as it streamed south.

Sam Palmer's body was found the next day a mile from the Stemwinder. James, the watchman, had been in his home in the Lowlands when the flood struck. His body was never found.

After destroying most of the Lowlands and the Stemwinder, this section of the flood surged back into the Sequanoto riverbed, joining the torrents that had coursed through Alderton. This mass now aimed its fury at Railroad Bridge, which so far had resisted every punch thrown at it.

Dazed rescuers on and about Railroad Bridge were involved in a frantic attempt to pull out survivors trapped in the mass of junk piling up on the north side of the bridge. When the fire broke out, the screams of burning victims seared forever the minds of those who watched.

Part of the water sideswiped Railroad Bridge to the east and went roaring down the Sequanoto riverbed. A man driving north on Route 143, which paralleled the river, described the water coming toward him as "a brown mist, about ten feet high." He stopped his car and scrambled up the bank on his right. The last he saw of his car, it was tumbling end over end down the road he had just traveled.

The floodwater coursed 10 miles down the Sequanoto riverbed before dissipating into dozens of small streams and rivulets. Debris was scattered over a 100-square-mile area south of Alderton.

Tim and Troy Gillin started out from Troy's house at 1:30 p.m., telling Mrs. Gillin they planned to hike across Railroad Bridge, then continue either east through the forest paths that led to Somerset Valley or south alongside the Sequanoto River.

They turned south.

45

I HAVE two vivid memories from the moments just before plunging into the mess in front of Railroad Bridge. One is of the roaring fire about twenty feet to my left and the hideous screams coming from it. The other is of the huge black horse on my right. He kept popping up out of the water, then disappearing into the muck only to reappear once again like a monstrous rocking horse. I knew he was dead because his hindquarters had been severed.

As we jolted to a stop I burrowed into the tree branches. Then it seemed as if a whole mountain landed on top of me.

Some time later the shouts of rescuers revived me. "There's one under that dead horse!"

Grunts. Curses. "One big heave. Now!"

The weight lifted. Two men pulled me up. A blanket was thrown around me. Someone brought a makeshift stretcher and I was placed on it. The fire was so near I could feel its heat.

Through pain and shock I dimly remember being carried off the bridge. There I was placed beside the road with other wounded, many of whom seemed to be in serious condition. When I tried to test my body, a spasm of pain shot through my back. I decided to lie still until a doctor could examine me.

Meanwhile the ambulance shuttled back and forth, taking the seriously injured and burned to the hospital. It was getting dark now and all about me was turmoil and confusion, groans of pain and sobbing, frantic people searching for relatives. I wondered where my parents were. Tim and Anne-Marie? Rand? Dean? Shudders of fear shot through me.

The ambulance was back again. A man stood over me, saw my eyes were open. "How bad you hurt?" he asked.

I just shook my head. He called another man and they lifted me into the ambulance. At the hospital I was carried inside and placed on a mattress on the floor of a hallway already lined with injured who awaited attention. An hour must have passed.

"Julie!"

I looked up to see my father. His face was contorted with a mixture of anguish and joy. Then he was kneeling beside me, clutching my hand, his eyes brimming with tears.

"I think I'm all right, Dad. I was knocked out. My back hurts, but I can move my legs okay." Sobs choked me.

My father sat down beside me, still holding my hand. "We'll have to wait our turn. Only a few doctors here. So many hurt and burned."

"How about Mother, Tim and Anne-Marie?" I asked.

"Your Mother and I were home when the flood came. It missed our house. Anne-Marie was at the Fleming farm. Tim and Troy went hiking down the river road . . ." He stopped, his eyes full of pain. "You're the first one we've found."

My head fell back and I closed my eyes to digest this news. Both my brother and sister caught in the path of the waters!

"What about Rand? He saved my life when the building collapsed."

"He's here in the hospital."

Fear assaulted me. "He's badly hurt, isn't he?"

Dad nodded. "Left leg seriously crushed."

I propped myself up on one elbow. "What about Dean? Miss Cruley?"

"Emily's all right. Dean's—" Dad's voice broke. "Dean drowned, Julie."

"No, no." Tears filled my eyes. *If only Rand and Dean hadn't come to* The Sentinel, *I thought silently. If only I'd followed through on that inner nudge to have Rand meet me at home.*

A harried doctor began checking over the patients on the hall floor. He tested my reflexes, then had me wheeled to the X-ray room. Not until the X-rays proved to be negative was I given a hospital gown and allowed to get on my feet. "Slight concussion, bad bruises and twisting of the lower lumbar region," was the diagnosis. "Keep her here overnight."

It was Spencer Meloy who, in the midst of the Lowlands chaos, suddenly remembered that Anne-Marie was at the Fleming farmhouse at the very center of the flood onslaught. And Margo was supposed to pick her up in the early afternoon.

Despite his agony over Margo's death and the continued need for rescue work, Spencer had a sudden compulsion to go to Anne-Marie. Though many roads were washed out, he borrowed a car and headed for Yancyville. Two hours later, after traversing a series of back roads, he got his vehicle within a mile of Dean's farm. When he found her, Anne-Marie was still dazed and incoherent. Spencer carried her to his car, with Queenie trailing behind.

An hour later the ten-year-old, clutching her beloved Queenie, was delivered to Mother's welcoming arms. Never before had Spencer driven a car without his glasses. He said he never missed them. Later he could not believe he had carried my sister almost a mile.

I learned of Anne-Marie's rescue when Dad returned to the hospital later that night. Meanwhile there was turmoil all about me. Makeshift wards were set up in every available space; I was moved into the nurses' off-duty room, along with seven other women. Mattresses were lined up on the floor for us to sleep on.

When I questioned medical personnel about Rand, they just shook their heads. There had been no time yet to chart patients by name. Was he still alive? Was this all a bad dream?

No, the moans of the wounded, the sounds of weeping and the hurrying figures in white all about me made it only too real. It was a miracle that I was alive. How had I survived?

Then I remembered. Those last moments before I hit the bridge, something important had happened. I had called out to God and He had responded. Not by voice, but by His presence. The memory stirred me and my lips began to move.

"Please, Lord, Help Tim the way you did me! And Rand!"

Tears began to roll down my cheeks. So many people drowned. Who else besides Dean? I closed my eyes and sleep came.

Early next morning my father reappeared. I stared at his face, looking for a sign. It was sober.

"Rand is still in critical condition. He lost a lot of blood, but the doctor thinks he'll make it." Dad hesitated, a flicker of a smile on his face. "They decided they didn't have to amputate his left leg."

"Thank God!"

I stayed at the hospital until eleven a.m., hoping to have a glimpse of Rand. I learned that he was moved from the operating room to the recovery room, but was kept there because no other beds were available. Visitors were not allowed. Dad checked me out of the hospital, drove me home and then left to look for Tim.

Mother took me in her arms and we both wept. "Anne-Marie will be all right," she finally said. "She's sleeping now. Queenie stays by her bed and I haven't the heart to separate them. I won't until Queenie's puppies come." She stopped and tears again filled her eyes.

"There's still no sign of Tim. They found Troy's body by the riverbed about two miles south of Railroad Bridge."

Stricken, I sat down suddenly on the sofa. Mother and I stared at each other wordlessly. *My little brother gone. If Troy's body had been found, soon they would . . .* I didn't want to finish the thought. Neither Mother nor I could console each other.

It was long after midnight when my father returned home. They still had not found Tim. Somehow I got to sleep, but I awoke at dawn, aching in so many places I could barely get out of bed. Anne-Marie was still so dazed that Mother told her not to get up. At breakfast we gathered around the table listlessly, red-eyed from weeping and lack of sleep. Dad's face seemed carved in stone.

"Any news of Tim?" I asked.

My father shook his head. "Spencer and I are going out early this morning to search farther south."

"How many people have died, Ken?" Mother asked.

"Hundreds. Biggest flood disaster since the Johnstown flood in 1889. It'll be weeks before they get the mess cleared away in front of Railroad Bridge."

"Who are some of the victims?"

The Editor cleared his throat. "You know about Dean and Hazel." His voice broke. "And Troy. Old Man McKeever died in the *Vulcania*. Vincent Piley, Sam Palmer . . ." Dad turned stricken eyes toward me. "And Margo."

"Oh, no!" The words pierced my consciousness like a rifle shot. My best friend gone! The tears flowed again.

"Do you know how she died?"

"They say she went back to save a baby. Got the baby to safety, but didn't make it herself."

Somehow that helped. To me, Margo had always been heroic. Courageous. Honest. She had taught me what it meant to be a friend. And now she had died saving someone else.

The Editor told us of other heroes. Neal and Cade Brinton both had shown indefatigable strength in getting women and children of the Lowlands to safety. And Bryan McKeever. Sensing the dam was in peril, around noon he had taken the family car and driven to Lake Kissawha. After a quick glance at the frantic efforts going on to save the dam, Bryan had begun a Paul Revere–type warning excursion down Seven Mile Mountain Road, urging everyone in sight to seek higher ground. Only a half-mile from McKeever's Bluff, he had abandoned the car and barely reached safety before the mass of watery muck thundered past.

After breakfast Dad left to continue the search for Tim, warning us to stay away from Railroad Bridge and downtown Alderton. "Police have it all cordoned off," he said.

"We must do something to help," Mother declared.

"Then open up the house to homeless people. We could take in a dozen if they don't mind sleeping on the floor."

Dad turned to me. "Please stay home and rest, Julie."

I shook my head. "I'm all right now."

When I walked into Rand's hospital room later that morning, he was asleep. I stood by his bed silently, not wanting to wake him. The gray color of his face frightened me. He looked dreadful.

Rand turned slightly and his hand fell off his chest. Timidly I reached over and touched his fingers. Then I cradled his hand in mine; a tear rolled down my face and splashed on his hand. It moved ever so slightly.

I looked back into Rand's face. His eyes were open and his lips slowly spread into a smile.

"We made it, didn't we?" he said.

Around one o'clock Mother and I each nibbled at a sandwich and drank a glass of milk for lunch, waiting tensely for the Editor to return. Anne-Marie had gotten hungry earlier and Mother had taken her a tray of fruit, crackers and juice to have in bed.

We had just finished our snack when we heard the front door open. Both of us rushed to the hall.

My father stood there, a stricken look on his face.

"Not Tim!" Mother moaned and began to totter as Dad rushed forward to grab her. For a moment they clung together. Then Dad saw me and reached forth an arm. Quickly I moved forward and buried my head in his shoulder. Then a sobbing form sped down the stairs; Anne-Marie joined us.

But it was Mother who needed Dad the most. When she collapsed in his arms, he picked her up like a child and carried her upstairs to their bedroom while I tried to comfort Anne-Marie.

Though his heart was breaking over the loss of his son, I heard my father talking quietly to Mother hour after hour on through the day and into the night.

46

O<small>N</small> the night of October 10 Donald Whipkey slowly mounted the platform and moved his heavy frame uncertainly before the speaker's rostrum. About 150 members of Baker Memorial Church were gathered in the education building, which was serving as our church until a new sanctuary could be built.

"Friends," he began somberly, "this is a sad occasion for our church and community. Before we get to business matters, I would like to pay tribute to the thirty-two esteemed members of Baker Memorial who died in the flood."

In alphabetical order he began reading the names, pausing after each one for a moment of silence. Fifteen names were announced, then, "Thomas McKeever, Sr." There was a ripple of whispering in the hall. The spectacular death of the Old Man had been front-page news in most American papers. Less publicized was his bankruptcy, declared a week after his death.

The list continued. Then, "Margo Palmer." That one choked me up. How I missed my dearest friend!

"Vincent Piley.

"Timothy Wallace."

With swimming eyes I turned to my father on my right. His eyes were pain-filled. Mother, two seats away, had her handkerchief out. Anne-Marie, on the other side of mother was sobbing. Rand, on my left, moved his crutches about tensely.

Tim's funeral had been held right here in this same hall. Dad had asked Baker Memorial Church trustees to allow Spencer Meloy to conduct the service. Although multiple funerals were being held constantly in all Alderton churches, Tim's had caught the attention of many local people. The hall was nearly filled that morning; many came from the Lowlands. Those attending were a cross-section of all the Alderton populace.

"None of our efforts could have done more for church unity than what that boy's death did," the Editor had sadly remarked afterward.

Mr. Whipkey paused a long moment before reading the last name: "Florence Whipkey." His wife had drowned in the Haslam House collapse.

The meeting resumed. Church committees were restructured, and a new one was formed to plan the rebuilding of the sanctuary. Because of several deaths a new pulpit supply committee was established, with nominations for membership made from the audience.

"I propose Kenneth Wallace," came one voice.

Dad quickly rose from his seat. "Thank you most kindly, but I must decline."

I was disappointed. Dad could have been truly helpful here. Yet he was too involved, I knew, in reestablishing *The Sentinel.*

"And now we come to a very important announcement," Mr. Whipkey continued. "Baker Memorial needs an interim pastor to lead us in Sunday worship here in this auditorium until we are able to rebuild our church home. And, of course, until we find a new full-time pastor. Your trustees spent many long hours deliberating over this selection. The man we decided upon is eminently qualified through years of pastoral service. He is also a greatly respected and admired man in our community. It was not easy to persuade him to serve us, but he finally agreed. Our selection, ladies and gentlemen, is Kenneth Wallace. Will you come forward, Ken."

There were gasps of surprise from many of us. Spontaneous clapping. Then, as my father strode down the aisle and mounted the steps to the stage, everyone in the audiⁿorium stood up. The applause went on and on and on. Tears were streaming down my face.

This is for you, Dad. A tribute to your courage. You stood almost alone for what you felt was right.

My father was strongly moved by the demonstration. He stood there smiling awkwardly, eyes misty, until the clapping finally stopped.

"Your response touched me deeply for one basic reason," he began. "It tells me I'm no longer that newcomer from the South, but a fully accepted member of this courageous, suffering community. Almost everyone in this room shares in our grief."

As he paused to wipe his eyes, I was suddenly proud of my home town in a new way. The Alderton people were a special breed: generous, forthright—yes, indomitable, in the way they absorbed pain, loss of possessions and death of loved ones.

"I came here to serve as a newspaper publisher," the Editor said. "This will not change, as details have been worked out for us to resume publication of *The Sentinel* next week." (Loud applause.) "I have a new partner, who is here in the auditorium: Randolph Wilkinson. I know you can't stand up, Rand, but wave your crutch." (More applause as Rand, grinning broadly, held a crutch high in the air.) "We believe that in a few months Alderton will be ready for a daily newspaper." (More clapping.)

My father paused, a twinkle in his eye. "With all that work and activity lined up ahead, when Donald Whipkey first approached me to be interim pastor here, I declined. Donald persisted. I agreed to pray about it and give him an answer by six tonight. This afternoon after lunch I spent three hours walking about our community, praying. I was shocked all over again by the devastation to our homes and businesses. Once again the full impact of our dead grieved me. We not only have to rebuild buildings here in Alderton, but lives.

"And then the words were firmly planted in my mind. *'You are also My pastor.'* There was no question about this call from God upon me. We Wallaces generally make decisions as a family, but there was time only for me to get a confirmation from my wife before we arrived here tonight. Julie and Anne-Marie, I apologize to you that we couldn't all be in on this decision.

"I accept your appointment as interim pastor. I care about every one of you and will serve you to the best of my ability."

As my father stood straight and tall before his audience, I marveled at the sense of authority he conveyed. And as had happened so often recently, my mind drifted again to Dean Fleming and the intriguing small band of Preparers. How much we all owed these men who had so changed the direction of our lives. And sudden confirmation came to me about a step I needed to take.

We were gathered together in the living room after dinner several weeks later—Dad, Mother, Anne-Marie, Rand, Spencer and Graham, who was home for the weekend from Penn State. It was a subdued yet happy time.

Randolph had moved into a small apartment near the temporary new headquarters of *The Sentinel.* Launched into a learning period about newspaper publishing, his partnership financed by Munro Farnsworth, he had surprised and delighted the Editor with his ideas for increasing advertising and subscriptions. Rand was only slightly slowed down when he learned that several operations would be needed to repair the damage to his leg.

Spencer reported that he now had support from every church in Alderton for his project of developing a new community center for Yoder steelworkers and their families. A combination of government and business money was being lined up to finance the construction. With Tom McKeever, Jr., back as president of Yoder, Spencer said he expected that the company would recognize the steel-workers' union under Neal Brinton's leadership and would work out an employment contract within a year or two.

As Spencer talked, I noticed how Anne-Marie followed his every movement with worshipful eyes. She had been this way about him ever since he had rescued her and Queenie, who recently had presented us with six puppies.

Graham, saddened by the death of his younger brother, was quiet during dinner until I started asking questions about Penn State. Then he opened up. "It's a beautiful campus. I know because I've walked every inch of it. My shoulder is so much better that I've started working out with the football team."

Our three guests were about to leave when I cleared my throat a bit nervously and said I had an announcement to make. "We all terribly miss Dean Fleming and his sister, Hazel," I began. "I doubt if we will ever know all that Dean did for people. Yet I must admit that he was often a thorn in my side. He would correct me when I made mistakes and challenge me if he thought my thinking was fuzzy. I didn't like it much then, but I sure do value it now."

I was struggling now for the right words. "If Dean was sometimes a mystery, his group of Preparers were even more so. It annoyed me that these men could always just go off somewhere whenever they felt like it to do their lofty deeds. I asked him why only males were qualified for this. He just laughed at me and said that he guessed women should form their own religious groups, that I was always trying to reach too far, too fast. As usual, I didn't care too much for his correction."

I paused, fighting the emotion welling up inside. "A week before the flood, Dean drew me aside one day. He said he had established a trust in the Alderton National Bank in my name for five thousand dollars. It was available to me only for education. He said it should more than take care of my tuition and expenses for four years of college, that it would help prepare me to be what God wanted me to be.

"I didn't say anything about this at the time, not even to my parents, for I wanted to stay here and work on *The Sentinel.* The other night at Baker Memorial when Dad told why he agreed to be the interim pastor there, I knew what I was supposed to do. I've been on the phone with the enrollment office at Penn State. Since Mother and Dad have approved, I'm all set to begin my college education there on February first at the start of the second semester. I'll find a way to make up the first semester."

"Julie, that's great news!" I knew that Graham would have grabbed me in his arms if the others had not been present.

Spencer looked disappointed.

Rand's expression was one of dismay.

After an evening of animated talk about education and careers, and after saying good-bye to the three men who had become so close to me, I walked out the back door and stood there alone in the yard under a cloudless, moonless sky. The air was crisp, but I was not chilled. The vastness of the starry heavens stirred me. What a beautiful big world God had made!

As I strolled toward The Rocks, dead leaves rustled under my shoes. What was dying now in nature would revive in glorious new life six months from now, I mused. Just as Alderton would be reborn through men like my father and young Tom McKeever and Spencer Meloy and Neal Brinton and Rand and yes, even Bryan McKeever. What courageous people they were! How grateful I was to be a part of it all.

Suddenly I marveled at my sudden and new sense of freedom. Dean had been right. I had been too eager to grow up. It was great to be eighteen.

Since Then

Seven Mile Road had been widened and repaved many times since 1935, but it still was a winding two-lane passageway down the mountain. As I drove slowly, I noted the old familiar landmarks: the curve where Bryan McKeever had nearly plunged us to our death on high school graduation night, the spot where Dad had slid into the ditch during a cloudburst on the day we first approached Alderton.

So many memories, so much living bound up in this mountain and the valley below!

Then there was the turnoff to the Allegheny Community, renamed in 1938 from the Hunting and Fishing Club. Though the development was still private and exclusive, it was now owned and operated by a new breed of millionaires like Tom McKeever, Jr., and his son Bryan, who welcomed the press, were open to publicity and occasionally ran for public office. Lake Kissawha was a much smaller version of the one that had devastated Alderton forty-eight years before. A modern concrete dam dispersed spring floodwaters into three separate tributaries that wound down through a hundred-square-mile radius below.

Even now, so many years later, the terror of those twenty-seven minutes on September 21, 1935, remained fresh. *Oh Tim, how much we have missed you! And Dean . . . and Hazel and Margo . . .* so many gone so quickly.

After several miles I turned onto the dirt road that led to the Fleming cabin, which Dean had left to my father "for use by The Preparers." The rest of the land, where the barn and farmhouse had stood, had gone to Dean's children.

In 1973 Dad had retired from *The Sentinel* and bought the property nearest the cabin, where he and Mother built a home. Mother's death in 1978 at eighty-two had been a grievous loss to us. Her strength at our lowest moments had kept the family intact. Ever since the Alderton flood Mother and Dad had been extremely close, enjoying their proliferating family, which now included five grandchildren and fourteen great-grandchildren.

Dad, at eighty-eight, amazed me: clear mind, good eye sight, straight body. He loved to walk the mountain trails, still wrote a column for the newspaper and did much of his own cooking. Only his hearing was deteriorating.

With a sense of quickening excitement at the prospect of seeing my father, husband, son and grandson—four generations in the cabin at the same time—I parked my car in the parking area and walked briskly toward the front door.

"Grandmother!"

Startled, I turned toward the voice. Dean, our tall, blond, eighteen-year-old grandson, was running up the slope from the cabin. He hugged me, then drew back and looked at me solemnly.

"Good book you wrote. Only one problem," he said with a grin.

"What's that?"

"Not enough sex."

"You can get that anywhere today," I replied, giving him a playful poke in the ribs.

The cabin door opened and the three other most important men in my life came outside. My husband was the first to embrace me. Then he laughed.

"Julie Wilkinson, I saw you strike our grandson.

Aren't you a bit old at sixty-five to be giving out corporal punishment?''

"Never, Rand. Not as long as they need it. Right, Timmy?"

Our thirty-eight-year-old son chuckled, kissed me, then placed his hands around my waist, as though measuring it. He looked at Randolph. "Her waist isn't much bigger than in those pictures of her way back when she was an eighteen-year-old reporter for *The Sentinel.* You picked a trim one, Dad."

"I sure did." Then Rand placed a short-stemmed pink rose in my hair.

The Editor was standing on the steps, gazing over the family scene with a look of contentment. "Come on inside, all of you," he said as he kissed me tenderly.

The five of us sat down in a semicircle in front of the fireplace, catching each other up on recent family news. Randolph had flown in from London two days before. I had driven up from our home in Virginia, where I had holed up the past three months to finish my manuscript. Our son Timothy had been made publisher of *The Alderton Daily Sentinel* six months before, taking over from Randolph, who had then gone to England to supervise renovations on Harperley House. Our daughter Mary Louise, her husband and children would arrive tomorrow. Harperley House, the manor residence I had first heard about from Randolph in the *Sentinel* office, had become our home for part of each year. Yes, Scottish harebells still grew there in profusion, and the mahogany balustrades had survived several more generations of Wilkinson children sliding down them. And what fun to watch a child's delight in discovering Harperley's secret passageway from the house down to the River Wear, an escape route Rand's ancestors had used to elude Cromwell's advancing troops.

Anne-Marie, that irrepressible sister of mine, was due in tonight, along with her husband, Spencer Meloy. Their marriage back in 1945 had been a surprise to many, considering the eighteen years' difference in their ages. But not to me, who knew them both so well: Anne-Marie had been in love with Spencer throughout her teens. After rearing three children while Spencer pastored a church in a small coal-mining town in West Virginia, the Meloys had accepted a missionary assignment in Guatemala as a joint venture, even though Spencer was in his retirement years.

As I looked about the cabin at four generations of Wallace-Wilkinson family, a wave of gratitude overwhelmed me. How had we been so blessed! *The Daily Sentinel* had grown into a multimillion-dollar publishing business which now included two other Pennsylvania newspapers, a national home and garden magazine and an international book publishing house.

My mind drifted back to the agony of trying to choose among Rand, Graham and Spencer during my college years. After graduation from Penn State in 1940, I had come very close to marrying Graham Gillin. When World War II started we decided to wait; then Graham had joined the Navy pilot training program in 1941. During the battle for Midway in June 1942, Graham was killed when his dive-bomber was shot down after scoring a direct hit on a Japanese carrier. Graham was an authentic and publicized American hero.

In the year after Graham's death, I became very close to Spencer, but something stopped me from marrying him. Was it my sister's adoration of him? My inner confusion? Or because the fire between Rand and me had never died down?

Randolph had tried to enlist in both the British and the American military forces during the war, was rejected by both because of his leg injury, and then served in the British Home Guard for several years. When he returned to Alderton in 1944, our love was instantly rekindled. We were married in December 1944.

And tomorrow at the annual family picnic there would be a moment of silent memory and gratitude for Tim, whose boyhood exploits had grown over the years into almost legendary feats.

Dad interrupted my nostalgia. "Let's begin with an important announcement from Dean."

I turned to look at our grandson, whose main interests in life so far had been sports, cars and girls.

Dean was slightly embarrassed. "It's no big deal," he said. "I just spent a week at a conference of Christian athletes. They convinced me that the Lord wants men with a real spirit of adventure. So I decided it was time for me to get with it. I've always admired Dean Fleming and the way he lived and died for his faith. I've been proud to carry his name. And so I want to be one of The Preparers."

"I think that *is* a big deal, Dean," I said.

As we congratulated young Dean, I realized suddenly that this was the missing piece in my manuscript. Now there were four generations of our family in The Preparers. Once I had resented the men-only character of this small group. No longer. Over the years I came to accept and then support this exclusiveness as its main strength. The quiet impact of The Preparers in developing leadership in men had constantly amazed me. Dean's decision was the perfect ending to the story begun so long ago . . .

Not Quite the End

. . . At this point the Editor rose and picked up a hand-carved wooden box from the table. He stood before his family, body erect, eyes intent. At eighty-eight there was no diminution of tensile strength in his spirit. The man who arrived in Alderton weak and vacillating back in 1934 to face a watershed year of personal testing had been for almost half a century a bastion of strength.

"Let me begin this little speech by paying tribute to Dean Fleming." He paused. "I met him at the lowest point in my life. He challenged me, just as he had been challenged by Big John Hammond, and just as each of you here in this room has been captivated by a compelling philosophy of life.

"We've learned that we can overcome our frailties by giving ourselves to Someone bigger than we are, Who becomes our life, our strength, our purpose. Once I was ready to die for Jesus Christ, I could begin to live—with boldness and direction.

"As you know, Julie, that ax above the fireplace has been the symbol of The Preparers ever since Big John's time. The ax is not used so much today, but it still stands for hard work, personal involvement and the preparing of land for better living. This ax was first presented by Big John Hammond to Dean Fleming. At Dean's death, it was given to me. When I die, it will go to Rand, then to Timothy and after that, we hope, to young Dean.

"Julie, perhaps without realizing it, you have been a part of this work for years. You have used your special gifts as a writer to share your spiritual discoveries with millions of people. We decided it was time to give recognition to this. Therefore, we present you with this gift."

Inside the wooden box, lovingly carved by four generations of Wallaces, was a small but exact replica of the ax over the fireplace—in jade. A line of small diamonds, inlaid and spaced evenly from top to bottom, sparkled like the stars at night.

"Each of those nineteen diamonds represents a book you have written, including this one," the Editor continued. *"Each of your books, like diamonds, has shown the light of the Lord to people hungry for spiritual truth. In each one, Julie, you have been a true 'preparer' as you readied our hearts for the coming of the King."*

Leonard E. LeSourd
Boynton Beach, Florida
January 12, 1984

Catherine Marshall

is the author of a number of best-selling books, including *Christy*, *A Man Called Peter*, *To Live Again*, *Beyond Our Selves*, *Something More*, *The Helper*, and *Meeting God at Every Turn*. Her books have sold over sixteen million copies and these include several collections of sermons and prayers by her late husband, Peter Marshall, which have recently been put together in the volume *The Best of Peter Marshall* (Chosen Books).

In 1959 Catherine married Leonard LeSourd, who was editor of *Guideposts* Magazine for twenty-eight years. In 1974 the LeSourds joined John and Elizabeth Sherrill to form Chosen Books Publishing Company in Lincoln, Virginia. Her son, Peter John Marshall, an ordained Presbyterian clergyman, has a national speaking ministry and lives in Orleans, Massachusetts.